RUNNING *from* BLOOD

Dear Jamo,

Thank you so much for vibing with me! I hope you like the adventure and all the LgbtQIA+ representation.

your friend,

M. W. Upham

PAGE PUBLISHING, INC.
Conneaut Lake, PA

First originally published by Page Publishing 2020

ISBN 978-1-64701-377-6 (pbk)
ISBN 978-1-64701-378-3 (digital)

Printed in the United States of America

Chapter 1

KATHERINE

THE NEW WORLD

As he yanked her through the woods, Katherine cried, dragging her feet.

"Keep moving!" he shouted, roughly pulling at her arm.

Where are we going? Katherine thought to herself. She could hardly see, and being pulled so hard hurt her arm. As she was dragged from her usual cage through the dark woods, she couldn't help but wonder if this was going to be her end. Why didn't he just kill her? She had seen him kill countless other people, so why was he making the effort to get her tangled in these deep woods? She had a thousand questions she wanted to ask but was too scared to utter even one.

Finally, they stopped at an old house deep, deep into the woods. The white-haired man pulled open the door and shoved her inside. She fell to the floor with a loud thud. When she sat up, he had come inside and closed the door behind him.

"This is where you live now," he said. "The nearest town is just a mile west from here. Do you understand?"

She nodded quickly and looked down, mustering all the voice she could. "How will I eat? I have no money."

He looked down at her with disgust then tossed her a bag of deutsche marks. "This should last you at least three years, if you don't get greedy and waste it. The house is in decent condition. I saw to that before I brought you here. If you make a good living for yourself and manage to leave, I don't care. But listen to me when I say it is over between us." She nodded so fast she thought her head might fly off. She didn't know if she would have called their relationship a consensual "us," but she knew there was no point in arguing with him.

"But hear me." He spoke slowly. "If you ever speak of our partnership or intercourse to another being, if my family's name ever passes across your lips, I will come find you. And I will suck every last drop of blood from your body and leave your bones to the wolves."

When he spoke like that to her, she again felt like no more than a slave in the dungeons of a castle. She nodded and felt herself reply "Yes, master" as she had always been taught. Seemingly satisfied with this answer, the man turned and vanished without another word, leaving Katherine in the house, two months pregnant, alone.

She woke up the next morning on the floor in the corner of what she assumed was the living room. With last night's events now at her doorstep, she had to find a way to get by on her own. She took out the little purse he gave her. How much money did he think would last three years? She would be lucky if these deutsche marks lasted even six months! Did he have no idea how much things cost outside his castle? No doubt she would be out of money shortly after completing her pregnancy, and that was if she spent next to nothing a day. Plus, she couldn't work after, with a child relying on her. She had to get a job, and quickly. She was already two months pregnant, and soon she would start showing. No one would want to hire her after they found out she would need maternity leave soon! She had to land a job while she could still conceal it as a secret.

Katherine thought of the bigger problem at hand. She had never been to a town before. How was she supposed to act around so many other busy people? She had been born and spent her whole life in the confines of vampire slavery. She looked around her new living quarters with full light now. The windows were all in good condition, the door shut and locked. The floor was very dirty, the walls and table were very dusty, and by God, under the dirt and grime was the ugliest green-striped wallpaper she could imagine. If she focused on a little cleaning, she could solve those problems when she got to them. The only furniture in the house was a table, three chairs, a nightstand, and a bed frame. The kitchen still had some old cabinets that were covered in dust; maybe there was something inside she could use.

Getting up, she noticed for the first time how sandy the floor was. It was like someone had dumped at least two buckets of sand all over the wooden floor. Katherine needed to look for a broom or at least some food for breakfast. She opened the cabinets and found a bag of onions, which were trying to grow through the cloth, and a rotten bag of potatoes. And even deeper back was a small bag of semirotten carrots.

As she was trying to find food, her mind turned to her new home. How had he found this place? She didn't have much experience in the world outside, but she didn't think spare cabins were usually just lying around for free use. She gave Egon credit; he could be resourceful when he needed to be. But why hadn't he just killed her and been done with it? No doubt he wanted her gone, as a child would be fair proof of the acts he had forced upon her. Of course, it wouldn't be seen that way by his family. They would see it as her tempting him. But they would both receive punishment. She would no doubt be killed, her child too. Egon, however, well, he might be outcast from the castle, but he wouldn't be killed. He was too important to the family to kill; that was for sure. But he was too much of a coward to let that happen. He would never brave the unknown world outside.

Maybe he didn't want to kill her because he didn't want his child to die with her? But Katherine still didn't understand why he would care so much. He was cruel, mean, and enjoyed every act of killing and torture he bestowed upon others. But what if there was a side of him that he didn't show? If he wanted his child to live and saved both their lives in turn, perhaps there was a soft, gentle side to him. If that was true, it was no wonder he didn't show it around his family. It was always that way with vampires—pure animalistic desire. Never any feelings and never love. Any compassion or weakness was snuffed out before anyone had the chance to question it. So who could really say for certain what his motivations were? Maybe by sparing her, he just wouldn't have to dispose of her body.

Dumping the potatoes out into the forest, she noticed two of them were salvageable. It wasn't exactly a meal, but it would do. All she needed now was to find some meat, but that seemed unlikely since she didn't exactly know how to hunt.

I could go to town and buy some, she thought to herself, *but that would involve spending some of the limited funds I was given.*

She walked to the bathroom and opened the closet. Inside was a broom. Surely she could use this to tidy up later. As she was about to walk out, her reflection caught her eye in the mirror, and she saw how dirty she looked. Her black curly hair was completely disheveled. Her clothes were torn and full of sticks from the journey, and her face was caked in dirt. If she was going to go to the village later, she had to at least look presentable or else raise a lot of questions. It didn't seem smart to be spending so quick anyway. Maybe she should just stay here in the house. But then again, she couldn't live off potatoes and onions, couldn't she?

Katherine felt her stomach rumble and made the decision. *To town it is.*

She wrestled with the sticks in her dress. It looked like a slave dress, but with a safety pin she'd found on the bag of potatoes, she could at least make it look better. Ripping up the potato bag to use as rags, she gave herself the best cloth bath she could manage, wiping away most of the dirt from her face and legs. She didn't look half bad. In the mirror, she brushed her fingers through her curly black mess until it looked almost like a passable haircut. So what if she was a little messy? It would have to do.

After sweeping out the sand into the forest, Katherine walked down to the village. She couldn't help but remember last night's events, now that there was time to think. It all happened so fast. First, she was sleeping in her cell after visiting her sister; next she was being dragged through the forest by Egon. She couldn't help but think back to a few months ago. She hated living in the cells of the castle, but at least she knew how things were there. She knew what she was—she was food, livestock. That was it.

This whole mess started four months earlier. Egon decided he didn't crave the touch of vampire women like he used to.

Maybe I was just some sort of forbidden fruit, she thought to herself. Vampires weren't supposed to breed with their slaves. It was dirty, and they both knew that. *It's not like I wanted to be with him anyway*, she thought, looking up at the pale-blue sky. *But if I had to be visited by a vampire every night, at least he was the king of the castle, and at least he wasn't ugly.*

She remembered Egon, who had pale skin, sharp teeth, and pure white hair. But it wasn't those things that she remembered most. She remembered his eyes. Those bloodred eyes. They always looked angry, and even worse, they always looked hungry. But if she really looked, sometimes she thought she could see longing. Longing for something different. For a change that would never come. That, or a challenge.

It must get awfully boring, being the king of your whole world, getting everything you wanted when you wanted it. In a way, she did feel a little bad for him. But she also felt hatred for him. He had been responsible for the killings of several of her closest friends and family. Every time she started to feel even remotely bad for his boredom and longing for adventure, she remembered his cruelty, his mercilessness, and his greed. Why couldn't he just be happy with his vampire brothers and sisters? He had to rape her. He had to try the forbidden and unknown, at her expense. If he really hated his life so much, why didn't he just leave? Why didn't he just run away, change his appearance, start a new life? She would never understand that.

Down in the village, people were racing left and right, to and from every cart, shop, and store. It was so hectic Katherine barely knew where to look to find what she needed. Every stand was packed to the brim with different items. As she walked along the cold dirt road across the market, her eyes spotted a cart stocked with what looked like a variety of meats. She walked over and examined it further, then decided on buying some cheap "slightly off the date" pork. It was only a little shiny on the top. Surely it would do. It wouldn't taste amazing, and it would feel like suicide trying to eat it while pregnant. But it was the cheapest, and she really needed to be frugal right now. It would suffice.

As she inspected the town, Katherine tried to keep an eye out for any shops that might be hiring, but even more so, she was trying to see if she could spot her old home. She looked toward the forest.

It figures, she thought. *Of course, you can't see the castle from town.* She didn't know how, but they had managed to hide it from view. It seemed so impossible for such a big place to be so well hidden. The village had a small stream running through it and was surrounded by mountains. *It must be there*, Katherine thought, *hidden behind the mountains. Where else could it be?*

She wondered how many times the villagers had gone off looking for it, only to come up empty. They must have known it was there since every year people would just "disappear." That was always how it was. Every few years in the castle, they would bring new humans in from the town for feeding.

Keep the blood fresh, but the genes pure, Katherine thought.

Though she supposed it hardly mattered anymore, that part of her life was over. She knew that since she had already lived there, the castle wouldn't be taking her back in anytime soon. She had to focus on where she was now.

As she walked home, she thought about how she would make enough money for two mouths. In town, she saw lots of stores. Maybe she could get a job at one of them. She saw that a meat-packing company was looking to hire someone. They were probably looking to hire a strong man, but maybe they would hire her instead? She'd have to try at the very least.

When she got home, she chopped up the potatoes and onions, put them in a pot she found in the cupboard, and filled it with water. After lighting a fire outside, she put the pot onto the hot coals, hoping it would be hot enough to boil the water. Once that was done, she started chopping the pork. After draining the potatoes and onion in the sink, she put the pork in the same pot as the potatoes and put it on the fire. When the potatoes and onions cooled, she scooped them into a large bowl with her hands, then dumped the cooked pork on top of it.

"It's bland, and it doesn't smell great, but it would do for today. Tomorrow, I'll find a job. Then I'll be able to actually cook some real food for myself," she whispered as she fell asleep on the floor in the corner.

"Katherine?"

Hearing a voice, she looked around. She was back! Back in her old cell. It was strange to say, but she never thought she would miss the confines of a cage so desperately. It felt so familiar, which was such a comfort. She ran to her old bed, a small little straw mattress with a blanket on top. She missed her mattress. It was so comfortable compared to the cold cabin floor.

"Katherine?"

She turned around, seeing her father and sister. Her father and sister! They were alive! She ran to them, arms open for an embrace. But a large flash of light made her shield herself. Opening her eyes again, she saw her father's body lying lifeless on the floor of the cage, and her sister was staring at her, horrified. Egon had her sister, Eileen, by the neck from behind and was gently caressing her face. Eileen was shaking from head to toe, eyes shut with fear, trying not to focus on how her life was being held in the palm of a madman.

"You will keep our secret, won't you? Katherine?"

Katherine nodded quickly. "I will keep the secret! Just let my sister go!"

Egon smiled, flashing her with his sharp teeth, before speaking again. "Good, we wouldn't want something to happen, for any little…accidents to befall you and your dearly beloved sister. If you tell, mark my words, I will kill you both."

Katherine doubled over. Her head was spinning, and she felt she was going to be sick!

Waking with a terrible start, she ran to the bathroom and threw up all the food she ate the previous day. What a horrid dream! Maybe eating pork last night, even though it was cheap, wasn't the smartest plan. She should have known yesterday when she could barely get it down. Well, it certainly didn't taste any better coming back up. She took a moment to calm down.

"It was only a dream," she told herself, though she knew it wasn't really a dream. Her father was dead, and her sister would be too if she stepped one toe out of line. Egon didn't say it when he dropped her off, but she had no doubt it was true.

Going to town, Katherine asked every shop owner left and right for a job. The meat-packing company didn't want to hire her, as she expected. However, a small little general store was more than happy to have a new counter girl. The shop was very small, but it was stocked with lots of cute little jars of jelly and cans of meat and pickled foods. The walls were covered with this tacky white wallpaper with pictures of different fruits on them, but it wasn't too noticeable, because in front of almost every wall was a shelf stocked to the brim with the items for sale. Working the counter was a tall dark-skinned woman with poofy hair.

"My name is Katherine, and I'm looking for a job," Katherine said, trying not to think about how foolish she looked dressed in rags, asking for work.

The woman gave her a quick glance up and down, then a sweet smile. "Perfect! We were going to put up a hiring sign next week. Have you had a job before?"

Katherine shook her head. "But I can work really hard! And I'm a very fast learner. I'll do whatever job you need me to do," she said, trying to make up for her lack of experience.

"Well, you really came at the perfect time. The position's available if you want it. We need a counter girl desperately and someone to help me stock jars and cans. And as long as you can show up on time every day, I don't see any problems."

Katherine smiled happily. "Yes! Yes, I can show up on time. Yes. Oh, thank you! You don't know how much this means to me."

"It's not a problem at all. I'm sure you'll be a fine employee." She smiled. "Just be here every day by eight. Then you can leave at four. But you can have Sunday and Monday off since we're closed those days. Sound good?"

Katherine nodded enthusiastically. "Thank you for this. You have no idea how much I need this job, ma'am."

"It's no problem, and you can call me Gelda. We don't have to act formally here. Yes, it's a business, but I think friendship in business promotes loyalty." She nodded to herself to confirm her own ideals.

"Gelda then. Thank you so much."

"You can thank me by working hard. Here's your uniform. If you really need pants, you can have a pair of mine, though they might be a little long." She leaned down to hand her a shirt.

Gelda was right. She was very tall and very skinny. Her skin is so dark compared to Katherine's. Her hair was dark black and seemed to curl out of control even though it was in a pom-pom-like ponytail on the top of her head. Being so tall must make it easy to reach tall shelves, she supposed, thinking that it might come in handy when shelving and packing cans.

The shirt was a black slipover. She supposed that made sense. It wouldn't stain as easy and would always look at least a little clean, but it had no logo or mark showing the store name. She would have to buy her own pants at a resale store. That shouldn't be too hard. She could use some of the funds Egon provided for her. This hardly seemed like a uniform, Katherine thought, but when she looked down at her rags, she supposed the shirt was being provided so she wouldn't look like a homeless woman. It was nice of Gelda to give her these without flat out saying, "Your current clothes look like trash." She felt thankful for that, it was very considerate. Soon, she would have to pick up new clothes anyway. Then maybe she could own more than one outfit.

Gelda smiled. "You can start tomorrow, and starting today you're allowed to take any food that's past its date. I don't want any of my employees going hungry. We'd have to throw it out anyway, so why not give it to our loyal workers? I know we can't really afford to pay our employees as well as the shops around us. I hope this will make up for that," Gelda said, giving a small laugh.

"Thank you," Katherine said. So what if they didn't pay as well? she thought this new job would really work out! And what was better, free food was nothing to joke about in these dire times! That should cover my meals for a while! It was one less thing to have to worry about.

Knowing she would soon have a steady income coming into her life, she bought some bread and took some jam and canned ham from her new place of work.

It's so kind of Gelda to give me free food before I've even worked an hour, Katherine thought.

Gelda seemed like a really generous person. She gave her new clothes without even really knowing her! She certainly was trusting. She didn't know how hard of a worker she'd be, yet she gave her free food for the work she would do in the future. Gelda must have had a good family, and no reason to distrust others, Katherine thought.

After a quick stop at a clothing store, Katherine went home. She felt so relieved she didn't have to cook tonight. Being pregnant certainly had a way of taking the energy out of her. And the jam and bread certainly tasted better than whatever she wanted to call last night's meal. But after opening the ham, she quickly decided against eating it when the smell made her stomach lurch. She never had a problem eating meat before she had a baby in her. Katherine could only hope this new development of nausea wouldn't last too long.

On her first day, Katherine was relieved to discover how kind Gelda was. Katherine knew nothing about the world around her, yet her new boss was very patient and willing to teach her everything she needed to know. It made working no trouble at all! And more importantly, it gave her something to do and people to talk to.

Every day she showed up on time and looked for Gelda in the building. She had been working for two weeks, and now surely her new friend would be willing to give her some answers to the questions she had been asking herself. How much did the town really know about the horrible place she came from?

"Gelda, how much do you know about vampires?" Katherine asked cautiously.

"Ohhh! Vampires are horrid creatures. The rumor is, they're seven feet tall! And uglier than any beast! They'll suck your body so dry it'll turn straight to dust. Everyone knows they're around here somewhere. Maybe they're hiding among us. You aren't one of them, are you?"

"What? No, no!" Katherine said hastily. She couldn't believe the town had so much of it wrong. They weren't any taller than average, and she had never seen them turn someone to dust. They were beautiful, frighteningly beautiful. But not in any human way. They were gorgeous, only to tempt humans into their trap. After seducing them, however, they turned horribly ugly. Their eyes went red with bloodlust, and they showed you their true form before devouring you.

Gelda laughed. "I'm just messing with you. I don't really believe in that stuff, though I might be the only one in the town who doesn't. Why are you asking about these silly mythical creatures all of a sudden?" she questioned.

"It's just that I had heard some rumors about a vampire around this town. I was wondering what you knew."

"Oh well, there are lots of vampires around this town," Gelda replied sarcastically. "They're called politicians. They'll suck the blood and money right out of you if you let them." She let out another round of laughter from her own joke.

Katherine didn't laugh.

Gelda stopped laughing when she saw her friend's lack of amusement. "Oh, you're serious? Well, a few people vanish every year. Turned to dust, everyone thinks. And every year the whole town goes on a long hunt for the mythical vampire castle. But we never find it. It must be hidden in the mountains. At least that's what my dad says. But no one is brave enough to go up there and look. I can't say I blame them. I don't believe in the things, but it's cold and spooky up there regardless."

Katherine nodded. "But how do they know that they're vampires and not some other creature or thing?"

"Lots of people have said they've seen them. My dad said about three weeks ago that he saw one going through the woods, and he heard a girl screaming. When he spread the news to the town, everyone freaked out as they always do. Now they think she's surely dead. How sad is that? I swear this whole town's gone crazy."

Gelda's dad saw Egon and her? She didn't remember scream-ing in the woods, or Egon surely would have silenced her without another thought. Why was her dad in the woods?

"If everyone is so scared. Why don't they just leave?"

Shrugging, Gelda turned back to her task at hand. "People are stubborn, I guess. Plus, I think they picture some sort of great, big reward if they can successfully prove their story."

"What does your dad do for a living?" Katherine asked, chang-ing the subject a little.

"Oh, he's long retired. But ever since my mom went missing, he has been obsessed with finding the vampires. He's convinced that they stole her from him, just like they 'stole' my older sister. But if you ask me, I think she just left him, and supposedly my sister ran away. But old age has made my father crazy. Before Mom disap-peared, he didn't pay very much attention to her. It's no wonder he lost her. I'm an adult now, so I can accept that if she's happy, I'll be happy for her."

"You aren't even a little mad at her?"

"Maybe I was once, but it was a long time ago."

Katherine felt for her. She knew it was hard to lose a parent. She had lost both her parents to Egon and his family. She wondered what it would be like to lose a family member because of abandonment.

That's one good thing, I guess, Katherine thought, *Being in con-stant fear, it keeps us together.*

Focusing back on work, Katherine packed a can of strawberry jam on the shelf. She didn't mind packing cans if Gelda was with her, but she thought counter work was a little easier physically. As long as she could do basic math, then counting money and change was fairly easy. The hardest part was not getting frustrated with angry custom-ers, and standing on your feet all day long. Things were finally start-ing to look up! And when the first paycheck came, it was followed by a wave of self-security. All was well now that she had food and money. It was time to start looking at furniture.

Cleaning up the house was hard work. The floor was so dirty before she was able to get a mop to clean it. Katherine felt very for-tunate she didn't have any carpet. That would take even more tools to clean. After it was done and the dust was cleared off the walls, she could see the furniture she needed more clearly. She already had tables and chairs. Maybe she could get a couch! Yeah, a nice couch. She knew it was dorky, but she really hoped for floral print.

A trip to town led to the official buying of furniture. Just as she had hoped, there was a yellow couch, coated in red and blue flowers. She really thought pink would be a better base color, but she liked yellow too. It was the color of the sun! After paying a moving company to move her new furniture to her home, the place seemed much more suitable to raise a family.

Just as she had suspected, she and Gelda grew very close. Over the next few months, Gelda showed her all the newest ways to deal with curly black hair and what clothes to pick out to match Katherine's bright blue eyes. Gelda seemed to know a lot about what was current and what to wear, which was a big help for Katherine, who had no idea. Sometimes, Gelda even bought her things. Katherine always insisted she didn't need to, but Gelda had bought her a little golden band and a matching one for herself. Friendship bands, she'd called them. Katherine had never had a friendship band before and thought the whole notion of wearing something to prove your loyalty to them was somewhat odd.

She learned that Gelda loved desserts, which didn't show due to how skinny she was and her biggest complaint was always that clothes didn't fit right on her tall and skinny frame. But she always made do, and Katherine always thought she looked beautiful no matter what she was wearing. But Gelda never agreed, trying desperately to manage her thick curls or trying to put it up in a ponytail to and showcase her oval face along with whatever outfit she was wearing at the time. Katherine loved her hair; it always looked so soft. Out of the ponytail, it formed a huge afro around her head. She wanted to touch it so bad but thought it might be rude to ask. So she didn't.

Katherine was always trying to find dresses that looked good on her ever-growing body. *Why does pregnancy have to make me look so fat!* she thought. *I have been throwing up almost everything I eat, and yet I'm still gaining weight!* Looking through the clothes rack, she picked out a nice yellow dress and put it on. It fit her stomach, but her breasts were practically spilling out of the top. It felt much too tight.

Gelda looked over at her. "You're, what, five months pregnant now?" she asked.

Katherine groaned. "Four. Don't push my pregnancy along faster with your words."

Gelda only laughed as she handed her a pink dress with white lace edges. "I'm sorry, I'm sorry. It's just, have you prepared at all? We haven't even talked about maternity leave, and you look much further along than four months. Why won't you talk about it?"

"No, I haven't prepared. I just don't feel like talking, that's all," she said stubbornly. She didn't want to think about the baby yet. She just wanted it to go away. But it was getting harder and harder *not* to think about the baby, what with her constant morning sickness. It even started to kick! And whenever it did, it kicked her right in the bladder. She had almost peed her pants more times than she could count.

"Well, we should at least talk about maternity leave. I can grant you about four months if you really need it." Gelda said, giving her a playful nudge.

"Thank you. I appreciate it. But I would really rather come in and work as soon as I can."

"What? Why? I'm giving you paid time off. You should really just take it."

Katherine just held her stomach and stared at her feet. She didn't want to think about having to be alone with the child. She didn't know what it would be like or if she would be able to care for it. She certainly didn't want to spend months alone with nothing but her wretched baby for company.

"No, I think it's best I come back as soon as I can. You're my only friend, after all, and I really will need someone to talk to after I have it," she said, knowing it would both flatter her friend and quit her pestering.

Gelda smiled and gave a sigh. "All right. Well, I'll let you decide when you want to come back, okay? I think you'll change your mind. And I know I pester, I'm sorry, but I really just want to be there for you, you know? How about we go baby clothes shopping! And look for a crib! It'll be fun, I promise. Maybe it'll make you feel better about all this."

Katherine hesitated. She knew her friend was trying to be nice, but this just didn't sound like a fun time to her. "No, no. Thank you, Gelda, but not right now."

"All right, all right," Gelda said, backing off. "But when you do decide to go, I'll be around if you need help."

Katherine nodded, eager to end this conversation.

When they weren't shopping, they were down in the restaurants. Katherine discovered that her new favorite food was chocolate ice cream, but if that was too hard on her stomach, vanilla was good too. So Gelda took her out for the cold sugary sweet very often. Gelda's favorite food to eat was definitely cake. Katherine thought she was eating it all the time. She always brought some with her to work in a small box. She wouldn't dare bring it up, but she swore Gelda sneaked off at least five times a day to grab a quick bite of her little sweet snack. It was a wonder her friend was so skinny, what with all the sweets she consumed on a daily basis. Life seemed normal—well, at least as normal as it could ever be—and Katherine was happy for it.

Several months later, however, pregnancy was becoming a very urgent problem. She couldn't work if she had a child to take care of. Trying to avoid the problem completely, she barely thought about it. She liked her new life. She had Gelda as a friend and had enough to get by, and that made her happy. She was independent, but soon, she would be tied down once again by a child she didn't want.

"You're expecting soon, aren't you?" Gelda asked as she shoveled a spoon of strawberry ice cream into her mouth.

"Yeah, but I'm not sure I'm really prepared. I haven't been to the doctor for any checkups. I don't have any names picked out," she said, not feeling up to eating today. The stress of the impending date was too much, even though she knew she should at least attempt some food.

"Maybe you could ask the dad for help. You said he isn't around, but surely you could contact him. I mean, it is his baby too, and he should take responsibility! Eat your ice cream! It's not good to starve yourself."

Katherine stayed silent, forcing in a spoon of the icy dessert. She didn't want to talk about him. Gelda quickly caught on to her discomfort. She always dodged her questions and the topic of her baby's father, so it wasn't unusual behavior.

"Fine, don't tell me. But you should know that he needs to take responsibility. You act like he's some sort of monster! Whatever. Just know I'm here for you if you need support—which reminds me. I picked up this baby book for you," Gelda said, reaching into her bag and pulling out a bright-colored picture book.

Katherine took the book, looking at the happy mother and baby on the front cover. This could be her and her child, if she wanted a child in the first place. But even if she didn't want children, she was still grateful.

"I really appreciate this, Gelda."

Sometimes it was hard to believe Gelda was so kind. Katherine always avoided her questions, yet Gelda never relented in her undying support. However, Katherine wasn't sure if that would change should she find out the truth. She knew she would be outcast from town if anyone found out she was a slave from the disturbingly close vampire castle. Sometimes, despite her freedom, she felt like she had no one to talk to and no one to rely on.

A part of Katherine felt bad for keeping secrets from her best and only friend. Maybe she really would understand. Sometimes, she wondered if she already knew. But what if that was only her delusion and she wouldn't understand after all if she told her?

I can't afford to lose her, she thought to herself.

So despite her mixed feelings, she kept her secret. She was determined to keep the father of her baby, and where she came from, a secret until the day she died.

"Eileen…or maybe Lucius," she said as she forced herself to take another bite.

"What?"

"That's what I think I would name it, depending on if it is a boy or girl."

"Nice names. Do they hold any meaning to you?" Gelda looked at her eager to finally get some answers.

"Yeah, Eileen was my sister's name, and Lucius was my father's. I didn't plan for this baby, and I don't feel like I love it, even though it's been with me for several months now and I can feel it kicking," she said with sadness. "But I think I could love the kid if I could relate them to someone else I cared about."

"That's a good idea. My younger sister went through a similar thing. When she first had her daughter, she didn't feel attached to her until several weeks went by and got really depressed. Some mothers just take a bit more time, I think."

"Maybe," Katherine said. She hoped she would feel love for her child. She really did. However, a part of her feared she never would, since the child was not one made out of love but simply forced upon her through an unwanted act.

"You never talk about your family. Where do they live?" Gelda questioned, hungry for more details.

"Far away. They live very far away, in a different country. I moved here after my father died to try to meet a husband to start a new life," she lied. She had to admit, it was a good story for being made up right on the spot.

"Ahh, I see. It must have been hard to lose your father. Was he sick?"

"No, he was killed." That much was true. He was killed, but she would never say he was killed by being eaten alive. Or who ate him.

"Oh, I'm so sorry. I shouldn't pester you about these things. I just get concerned, you know?"

"I know, it's okay," she said. What else could she say? Gelda was clearly only trying to care for her. She was kind that way. Katherine knew she wasn't trying to be a bother. She was sure she would be more than thankful for Gelda's love and support once the baby was born. She only hoped that it didn't look like its father. That was all she could ask for at this point.

"So you've moved? What country did you used to live in, before you moved to Germany? I mean, you don't have an accent at all."

"England," Katherine lied. She wasn't even quite sure where England was, but she knew it was a country very nearby. "My parents moved there from Germany before I was born. But I wanted to come back, just to know what the country is like, you know?"

"Ahhhh, England. You know, I used to date a boy from a town over there. It didn't work out, but he had the most beautiful voice you've ever heard, and he was very charming. His name was Gabriel, and he always spoke of the delicious fish and chips from England and the beautiful ocean side. He promised to take me to see it, but he never did. Bastard left me for one of his 'proper English women' from home."

Katherine patted her shoulder in sympathy, but if she was being honest, she was only half listening. She was too busy thinking about the upcoming baby. She was only seven months pregnant, so she still had two months left. Such a short amount of time would surely fly by if she let it. She had to start preparing. Just because she didn't want this kid, didn't mean it was not going to come regardless. She hadn't even picked out a crib! Or a high chair. Or anything. But with the date coming on her shortly, she knew it was time to start getting ready.

Chapter 2

KATHERINE

THE MISERY OF CHILDREN

About a week later, Katherine woke with a startling pain. She felt her whole body seize up, and she could barely breathe for several seconds, which seemed an eternity. *Contractions*, she thought. *No, it's too early! Not yet. I don't have anything picked out. I still have a month at least! Maybe two!* She lifted the sheets and found that the entire mattress felt like it was covered with water. Had she peed herself? No. She had to call someone. She had to get ahold of Gelda! But she lived down in town. How was she going to get ahold of her! She had no phone!

No, no, she wasn't thinking straight. She couldn't get Gelda. What if her baby was born with white hair and sharp teeth! She had to do this alone. She stumbled to the bath. Water birth—she knew how to do this. She had seen her mother help other mothers in the dungeons this way. Why did it have to be this way? She wanted to scream. No, if she was going to have a baby, she had to just suck it up and do it.

You can do this, she thought. *You have to do this.*

"Just fill the tub, and get inside. Breathe slowly," she said to no one as the contractions got closer and closer together. *How long were the contractions supposed to last again? Oh god, I don't remember! There is no need to panic. This is no time to panic! I have to keep a level head,* she told herself as she tried to catch her breath. But she was just so scared. It was a nearly impossible task.

She stripped down and crawled into the bath. *Deep breaths. Easy breaths. Contraction. Repeat. How long is this going to go on for?* She was in so much pain. When was the right time for pushing? It seemed like these contractions were lasting forever! One hour turned into two, and by then, the bathwater seemed like it was freezing! Maybe she had acted too quickly. "If you're going to be born, just get born!" she wanted to shout. But at the same time, she wished they would stay inside her forever. At least then she wouldn't have to go through this terrifying experience.

Katherine would have given anything to be in a hospital. But she knew it wasn't a realistic thought. If she gave birth to vampires, who knew what the community would do to the two of them? Maybe they would condemn them from society or burn them at the stake.

No, she reminded herself. *You might be frightened of dying alone, but you're more likely to die in a hospital if you give birth to a vampire!*

As she was lost in the thought of her fears, suddenly her pelvis felt very heavy, and she had begun pushing without realizing it. "Finally." She sighed. She took a deep breath and put a towel between her teeth. "One. Two. Push!" She screamed and bit down as hard as she could. She had only started pushing, and already she felt ready to be done with this whole thing.

What she never expected was the headache that came with the pushing. She tried to prepare herself for the pain and tearing, but she never expected the throbbing in her head. And with every push, she felt her ears pop, and her head felt like it would burst! It was definitely the worst migraine she had ever experienced.

Katherine pushed and pushed for what felt like hours until finally a little baby sunk to the bottom of the tub. She scooped it up. "A boy," she said, talking to herself so as not to feel so alone, though she was right to do this by herself. He was small and fragile looking. He had a head full of snow-white hair and two small little fangs poking through his lips. All other teeth were missing, however.

Love him, she thought to herself. *Love him, if anything, to spite his father.*

She put little Lucius to her breast and winced as he bit down. She could tell he was only after milk and didn't mean to nip her with his teeth. Then suddenly, her body jolted.

"What?" she said aloud. And she felt more contractions and more pushing. "No, no, this can't be happening. I can't handle another!" But that hardly mattered. Her body forced her to push, and she reluctantly complied. This one came quicker, and she birthed a second baby. A girl!

Katherine pulled this one to her as well and huddled her next to Lucius. Two babies. How was she going to manage this? She wasn't even sure she could manage one baby. Just like her older brother, Eileen had snow-white hair and prickly little fangs. However, she was even smaller than Lucius and was not so eager to attach to her mother.

Maybe that's a good thing, Katherine thought. *Maybe she'll die, and I won't have anything to fear. In fact, they are both very skinny and small. Maybe they'll both die.* She mentally slapped herself. How could she think such a thing? They were just little babies, yet here she was, speaking of their death like it would be a blessing. Surely such a thought would send her straight down to hell. After several minutes, Katherine stood out of the bath on wobbly legs. She carried her babies as best she could to the couch. She wrapped them in cloth diapers and laid them down, then wrapped the rest of them in blankets for warmth. After she was done, they fell asleep. She was lucky in that aspect, she supposed. She decided to change the sheets. She couldn't imagine sleeping on the floor with how much pain she was in. And when she was done, she fell into bed. She closed her eyes. A small part of her was glad to not feel so alone anymore.

Maybe I can love them after all. At least I'm going to try, was her final thought as she fell asleep.

The next morning, she woke to the sound of a baby screaming bloody murder. She got to her feet and went to inspect the racket. It was Lucius, crying and kicking on the couch, face turning red from screaming so loudly. She picked him up and tried her best to calm him.

She rocked him gently to no avail. Then she tried feeding him. She stuck her nipple into his mouth, the way her mother had shown her how to do when nursing her younger sister, but he wouldn't latch on.

She checked his cloth diaper but found it completely clean. Why was he crying so much? What did he want? After what felt like hours of cradling, coddling, she just couldn't get him to stop. Why couldn't he just eat and shut up! It was like her own newborn was rejecting her with every fiber of his being, even going so far as to punch at her arms as she cradled him. Despite his small size, his little fists started leaving bruises and welts all over her arms. It was only when the racket woke Eileen that he finally stopped crying.

Katherine set him down, not caring how or why he was suddenly deciding to be quiet. As long as he wasn't crying, it was enough for her. Eileen hardly ever cried the first day, but after hours of silence, she started to make unhappy noises of discomfort. She never screamed like her brother, never tried to push her away, but when she was hungry, she would give little whines that almost sounded like a puppy getting kicked. Her coos of discomfort were so quiet that sometimes if Katherine wasn't careful, she would miss them completely. But if Eileen cooed too long, Lucius would start screaming in protest of his sister's unhappiness. They really were a pair.

"You gave birth by yourself! How awful!" Gelda exclaimed. It had been a few days since the birth when Katherine finally decided to visit her friend. "You could have come down. I should have been with you to help! Oh, what a bad friend I am. I'm so sorry! How are you feeling?" Gelda exclaimed, stocking another can of beans on the shelf.

"It's all right. It's not your fault. Besides, I wanted to do this alone. And I'm feeling fine now. I took some time to recover," Katherine said.

"You're crazy, you know that? Anyway, where is the little baby? You didn't bring it with you? You know I would have let you bring it with you to work. I could have entertained it with some toys! Speaking of, boy or girl?"

Katherine really didn't bring down the babies. She didn't dare— not just because of work but because of their features. She knew they would be recognized almost immediately, and then her secret would be out forever. No, no. The children must always stay at home. But of course, she couldn't say that.

"No, and he's at home," Katherine admitted sheepishly. It wasn't completely a lie, but saying she had twins would only raise more questions from her curious friend.

"So it's a boy! You know you shouldn't leave your baby alone. It's dangerous! Did you decide if your breastfeeding or not?"

"I am. I don't really feel like spending the money on formula. It's just too expensive. And he's not home alone," Katherine lied. "My sister came up yesterday. She's going to stay home with him and help me."

"Oh?" Gelda questioned. "Well, if you need an extra hand, don't be afraid to ask. And feel free to take a few weeks off work. Just come back when you can, all right? It's not going to be the same without you here."

Katherine smiled. "Thank you, Gelda." And she gave her a hug.

"But I need more information! Did you name him Lucius like you said you would?"

"I did, but I still don't feel attached," Katherine said hesitantly.

"That will come in time. Don't stress about it. Did the delivery go all right? Is he sleeping okay? I remember when my sister gave birth, her baby never slept."

"I guess your sister's baby and mine have that in common. He only ever seems to sleep when I'm not around, almost as if he doesn't trust me."

"Huh? I've never heard of that before. Maybe he just needs some time to get used to his new surroundings or something. He's just a baby after all."

"Yeah, just a baby," Katherine said, looking down at her hands. She thought about how she would miss her friend while she was away. But surely staying at home and becoming acquainted with her new children wouldn't be so bad.

Walking through the forest after picking up some food, she heard screaming far away from her house. She ran up the pathway and inside to find Lucius, screaming his little lungs out. Katherine dropped the groceries down on the floor and rushed to him. She bounced him softly, but he would not relent. She tried feeding him, but he refused.

What does he want? She thought to herself.

She cradled him for hours, and still, the screaming didn't stop. Finally, he stopped screaming, only to fall asleep. Eileen, however, stayed completely silent the whole time. It was now well dark as she laid them both on the couch once again. It turned out that being a single mother was harder than she ever could have imagined. As hard as she tried, she just couldn't understand why her son wouldn't stop crying! Why wouldn't he just be quiet and let her care for him? He was making it completely impossible! As she finally started to drift to sleep beside her children, Lucius started the racket once again.

It was hard to believe such a small baby could make such a loud noise. So again she tried to nurse him. He must have been hungry because he immediately grabbed her breast in his tiny fist and bit down onto her nipple and started suckling hungrily.

Katherine winced. She had always heard that breastfeeding was painful at first, but she didn't imagine it hurt this much. As he drank, she felt like the grip he had on her breast was growing only more and more painful. When he was finished, she put him on the couch again. Surely she would have to buy a crib soon. When she went to inspect the rawness of her breast, she saw two very distinct bite marks around her nipple and a huge bruise where he had grabbed her.

"Filthy vampire vermin!" she screamed.

He had sucked her blood! Surely he hadn't just inherited his father's looks. Why would she have thought that? It seemed a very foolish idea now. Clearly he was going to be a vampire with immense strength. She looked at him, and he stared back with her own bright-blue eyes. At least that much he inherited from her. She soaked up the blood from her nipple and stuck the bundled-up cloth in Eileen's mouth. Surely if Lucius needed blood to drink, Eileen did too. But even with the cloth in her mouth, her daughter stayed silent. She always stayed silent.

Several months went by, and Katherine wasn't about to put her life on hold for a couple of bouncing baby vampire brats. So every day she still went to work. What they did while she was gone she couldn't have cared less. And there was going to be no more of this drinking her blood nonsense. At least, not the blood she was using. Every month she gave them her pads and tampons to suck on between meals of human food. Lucius always grabbed at the blood-soaked cotton excitedly, starving for blood at the end of every month. But Eileen only ate when she wasn't looking. The extra blood from her uterus was the most they were ever going to get from her.

Why should I strain myself and put myself in harm's way for a couple of kids I didn't ask for? Katherine thought. But a part of her did feel bad. They were her kids. However, no matter how she tried, she couldn't manage to make herself feel any sort of attachment to them.

Every day she came home, Lucius was screaming. He would only stop when he could sit with both her and his sister at the same time, she discovered. *Such a needy kid*, Katherine thought. Every night she would wait for him to fall asleep in her arms, and then she'd put him on the couch before heading to bed to get some rest of her own. Eileen didn't die as she had secretly hoped and instead grew bigger just like her brother. She now could open her eyes and loved to look around. She would make soft crying noises whenever Lucius crawled too far from where she was sitting.

One afternoon after work, Katherine was on her usual walk home. She felt good about her day so far. Both the kids had been fast asleep when she left, so she didn't have to worry about feeding them till she got home. She supposed she could have fed them before she left the house, but she hardly got any sleep nowadays. She wanted them to rest so she wouldn't have to leave them home crying.

Walking home, she thought about what she might cook for dinner. At the market today, she bought a fresh loaf of bread and beef. Maybe she could make beef stew and use the last of the butter on the bread for dipping. It sounded perfectly appetizing to her, and it shouldn't be too difficult to make. All she needed to do was put all the chopped-up veggies into the pot with the beef and let it sit and cook. Easy enough. Then she could focus on other things, like her sewing. She could finally start getting around to making some clothes for the kids.

Katherine unlocked her front door and walked to the kitchen, set down the food, and got out a large pot. She set it on the stove and lit the burner. Something wasn't right. She felt like she was being watched. There was no screaming. It was too quiet. Turning around, Katherine let out a startled yelp. Lucius was standing at the bottom of the stairs. Had he learned to stand and walk all by himself? She had barely seen him crawl! Yet while she was away, he learned to walk already?

"G-go back upstairs," Katherine demanded.

She was thankful that Lucius turned around and waddled his way back up the steps. At least he wasn't fast. *Yet.* Who knew how quick he'd get as time went on! It was amazing he was even able to walk and stand at all, being so young. He was developing at a monstrous speed, far faster than any human child should, and the thought of having her two vampire children mobile and loose in the house filled her with terror. She had to fix this. She had to come up with a solution.

The next day, she installed a lock on every door and a lock on every window. She couldn't let them escape. She couldn't let them be seen. It was only getting harder to take care of these children, and it didn't help that Gelda was getting more and more pesky about wanting to come visit and see them. Katherine was running out of excuses and ways to say no. She often wondered just how long she would be able to hide them or if eventually she was just going to have to set them free and run away from the consequences.

They're going to be the death of me. I just know it. She installed the final lock on their new bedroom door on the outside. Then she walked both children to the room. Lucius strutted the best he could confidently alongside his mother, while Eileen shyly walked behind him, holding onto his hand for comfort.

Christ, Katherine thought, *they're inseparable. It's clear they're vampires, falling in love with their own siblings. How disgusting.*

"This is going to be your new room," she said in the most pleasant tone she could muster. "You're going to stay here every day while I'm at work, and you are not to come out. Do you understand?"

"What if I'm hungry?" Lucius asked, no more than a year and a half.

"Then you'll wait till I get home, and I'll give you some milk." Katherine narrowed her eyes at him.

"I hate milk! I'm hungry!" He was *always* hungry, and the lesser she fed him, the hungrier he got.

Katherine smiled as sweetly as she could. "I don't care that you're hungry, Lucius. I don't have any food for you. You'll just have to eat what I serve you at dinnertime."

"I hate food!" Lucius shouted. "It makes my tummy hurt, and then…and then…ewwww," he said as he rubbed his tummy in remembrance of throwing up last night's meal.

"Well, if you hate my food so much, then you can just leave," his mother said through an increasingly angry smile.

Lucius crossed his arms and stomped into his new shared bedroom. Eileen glanced up at her before joining her brother.

"Thank you, Momma. It's lovely," Eileen cooed in that soft little voice of hers. At least one of her children had the decency to thank her for her generosity.

"It's my pleasure," Katherine replied.

Time seemed to fly by. It was simple enough keeping the children locked in their rooms day in and day out, but when she was home Lucius insisted that they spend time in the family room. Where he pestered her about work, and about the world outside the house, and sometimes, when he was really daring, about his dad. Whenever his father sneaked into their conversation was always when she sent them to bed, however hard he protested. But as weeks turned to months to years, he only grew more impatient with her excuses and faulty answers. It only made her want to spend more time at work with Gelda.

For a time, she really was trying to be a good mother. She brought home all sorts of books and tried to teach them how to read. Eileen loved to read and read all the time. Lucius hated reading, always saying it was boring and it made his eyes see funny. *Maybe he needs glasses*, she wondered, but there was no way she could get him checked for them. So she just gave up on her attempts to teach him, and she focused on her daughter. Eileen was very smart, and in a way, she reminded Katherine of herself. She was quiet, curious, and had the same love for learning that Katherine had as a child. But every time she started to feel any love for her daughter, it was washed away by her pointy vampire ears and her snow-white hair.

"Math next," Katherine said, pulling out a new math book to learn from.

Eileen smiled, yanking the book away from her and opening it eagerly. She certainly was a fast learner. At the age of four, she had already learned almost every word she could come across and was able to do simple addition, subtraction, multiplication, and division. It really seemed impossible! No child should be this smart. She was smarter than any human her age, but then again, this was just another reminder. She wasn't human. And no amount of wishing would make her so.

Eileen read through the book with great speed, excited to start learning basic algebra, while Lucius sat on the bed and just stared out the window. *Why can't he be more like his sister?* Katherine thought. She knew how to deal with Eileen. She almost felt love for her even. *Almost.* However, Lucius was never interested in learning. He always daydreamed, dozed off, or just talked through every lesson, refusing to pay attention to anything she said. It was infuriating! If Lucius was determined on having paste for brains, why couldn't he just be quiet and let Katherine have this time alone with her daughter!

"When can we eat?" Lucius pestered.

"We just ate!" Katherine exclaimed, having fed them both less than an hour ago.

"But it made me sick!" he said, holding onto his stomach. "I threw up in the toilet. It tasted like badness," he whined.

Eileen sunk into the corner, as she always did when they started arguing about food or rather when they argued at all. And they were always arguing; it just seemed like it was always about food.

It was getting harder and harder to stay patient with her hungry, irritating child. At least when Eileen was hungry, she kept it to herself. Eileen hardly ever complained and was almost always silent. She never spoke unless spoken to, never made a fuss about the dinner Katherine made. But Lucius was just too much; he always acted as though she were starving them! And she couldn't feed him what *he* wanted to eat. It was barbaric! So Katherine spent more and more time down in the village just to get away, and the less she had to deal with her children, the happier she was. She missed Eileen, but Lucius made the trouble just not worth it. And as time went on, she found herself staying away from home as often as possible.

Chapter 3

LUCIUS

THE ESCAPE ARTIST

"It's so boring! Why does she have to leave! Why don't she want to stay with us!" Lucius screamed to his sister, who was reading a book in the corner.

"Why doesn't she?" Eileen corrected, not looking up from her book. "Mommy doesn't like us. Don't you know that?" Eileen said sadly. "She wishes we weren't around to bother her. That's why she leaves, and that's why she locks us in our room."

"That's stupid. If Mom didn't want us, why'd she have us? Mom must be really dumb."

Eileen just shrugged, seeming uninterested in the conversation.

"Whatcha reading?" Lucius asked as he trotted over to her.

"'What are you,'" Eileen corrected. "And I'm reading a book about kids. Mom had it in the family room. I took it for reading practice. You know? I think Mom was going to try to be a good mother before we were born." Eileen said as she pushed her unkempt hair out of her face.

Lucius looked over her shoulder. "Just looks like a bunch of boring shapes and pictures. It's dumb."

"It's not dumb, Lucy!" Eileen shouted. "It's interesting. At least I have something to do. You just walk around bored."

"I could read if I wanted to. It ain't that hard. I just don't want to 'cause reading is stupid," he said as he walked away from her book. "I'm getting out of this room. I've had enough."

"*Ain't* isn't a word," Eileen corrected stubbornly. "And you're going to get in trouble!" Eileen tried not to pay attention to her brother's bad behavior.

"Only if I get caught. So I won't."

"Won't what?" Eileen looked up and tucked her hair behind her ears.

"Get caught," he said, forcing the door open with a strong punch. Confidently, he looked to his twin. "Want me to getcha anything?"

"'Get you.' And no. I don't want to participate," she said stubbornly. "I'm not going to get punished for your actions."

"Oh, come on, you boring baby. You don't want anything?" He teased.

"No!" Eileen said, shoving her face back into the book, pretending not to see what her brother was up to.

"Not even anything from the sewing room? Like a ribbon?"

Eileen peeked at him from behind her book, and Lucius knew he had her interest. "A ribbon?"

"Yeah, a ribbon. Maybe red? I know you love the color red." He tried to tempt her.

She looked at her book and then at him. She knew she wouldn't leave the room, but if Lucy was leaving anyway, maybe it wouldn't hurt for him to grab a ribbon for her.

"Red...would be okay, if you got me a red ribbon for my hair."

Lucy smiled. "A red ribbon for your hair. Count on me!" he said as he confidently walked out of the room.

"This is a mistake. This is a *mistake*," Eileen said to herself. She had a very, very bad feeling about this.

Meanwhile, Katherine was on her way home after an evening out. The moon was high, so it must have been extremely late.

"Stupid Gelda," she said angrily. "She needs to mind her own business! Telling me how to live my life, raise my children." She thought back to her night at the pub. Gelda had been so insistent on meeting her kids and pressuring her into bringing them over so she could see them. When Katherine refused, it only made her friend frustrated. She accused her of being a bad mother, of neglecting them. She had no right to say anything of the sort. She didn't have kids, and she didn't know what it was like. As she stumbled up the forest, she thought about how it was unlikely either of them would remember this the next morning. Both of them were completely drunk.

As she approached her house, she saw that not only was the door unlocked but it was wide open. She peered inside, her stomach having sunk down to her toes. What had those monsters done now? She stumbled to their room as quick as she could and saw Eileen sitting down reading a book, her brother missing.

"WHERE IS YOUR BROTHER!" she screamed.

Eileen almost jumped out of her skin, then looked up with fear. "He...he left! I tried to tell him to stay. Oh, please, please don't be mad," Eileen said as she shrunk down into the corner of the room.

Katherine was surprised Eileen had spoken to her at all. She almost never spoke, especially not when she was scared, but she didn't show her surprise as she ran out of the house. "LUCIUS!" she screamed. "LUCIUS, COME HOME THIS INSTANT!" But there was no reply. She stormed out into the woods. "LUCIUS, COME OUT NOW, AND I WILL CONSIDER NOT BEATING YOU TO DEATH!" she screamed, more than mad.

As she stormed through the woods, she saw claw marks on trees that she was certain weren't there before. She followed them for what felt like hours into the dark. Where was he? He was a vampire! She now thought maybe it hadn't been the best idea to starve him as she had. What if he came out and attacked her for a fresh food source?

The farther she got from home, the less safe she felt. Soon, she felt like he must have been stalking her. Why hadn't she found him by now? Katherine started walking faster and then started jogging and soon broke into a full sprint. She was seeing shadows every-where! Where was he? Shaken to the bone with fear, she decided to run back home. She ran home, slammed the door closed, and locked everything up as tight as she could. Screw him! She didn't want a son anyway. Surely her life would be better without him!

After she calmed down, she walked to Eileen's room and saw two white-haired children asleep. He had come back and been here the whole time! Suddenly, in a great fury she had never felt before, she grabbed Lucius by his long white hair and yanked him to his feet.

"WHERE HAVE YOU BEEN!" she screamed in her blind fury. "I have been looking *everywhere* for you!" She said as she dragged him down the stairs.

"I don't know! I don't know!" Lucius cried. "You're hurting me! Stop, Momma!"

"DO NOT CALL ME THAT, YOU FILTHY VERMIN, AND DO NOT LIE TO ME!" she screamed, throwing him down onto the kitchen floor.

Lucius sat up and rubbed his head, having landed right on it. He looked up at the short woman standing above him and thought about how tall she seemed at that moment. "I went for a walk. It's so boring here," he confessed.

"When I tell you to stay, you stay! Filthy vampire, do you know what would have happened if someone found you and connected you to me? They would have killed you, and killed *me* next!" she screamed.

Lucius stood up. "I'm not afraid of you!" he screamed angrily. "And I wish they had found me. I wish they had killed you!"

Shocked by this, she shrunk away from him, feeling very small despite being much taller. He had never raised his voice to her. He had complained a lot, sure, but he'd never shouted. For a split second, his blue eyes flashed red, and he looked just like his father.

"And where would you go if I was gone?" Katherine asked in a voice smaller than she had meant.

"Anywhere is better than here. If you didn't want us, then you shouldn't have had us! We didn't ask you to have us!" Lucius said, walking toward her. He grabbed the table and threw it out of the way as if it was made of nothing but paper.

The table toppled over and smashed into the couch. He really was growing stronger every day despite her efforts to prevent it. He walked closer to her.

"Stay back!" she yelled, her anger replaced by fear. "Stay back!"

As she stared at him, she remembered what his father had looked like, coming at her like this—his eyes clouded by anger, his speed to catch her wherever she ran. It made her feel so trapped, and seeing Lucius in such a state was near enough to make her cry from fear.

"Lucius, please! Go away!"

Chapter 4

LUCIUS

WHAT AM I?

Lucius fumed with anger until he saw his mother's face. Red eyes turning blue once again, he stopped where he stood. What was he doing? He had been so mad, but now with his mom looking so scared, he couldn't remember what had made him feel that way. Of course, she didn't want to be killed. Why would anyone? She was only trying to look after him, wasn't she?

Maybe I am being stupid after all, he thought to himself as he bolted up the stairs and closed himself in their room.

Eileen was sitting upright in their room on the mattress on the floor. Her eyes wide, she stared at her brother with a similar fear he had just seen in his mother. Why was everyone so afraid of him? Or rather, was she afraid of what she had heard? Lucius walked over to their bed and climbed in. Eileen bolted up and grabbed him in a tight hug. He had no idea why, but he suddenly felt so tired, so he wrapped his arms around her and hugged her back. He didn't know how long they sat like that or when he fell asleep, but suddenly, without dreams, he was waking up the next morning.

Lucius knew he had to apologize for last night. So when he heard his mother stir awake downstairs, he sheepishly crept down.

She was cooking in the kitchen, looking over her shoulder every second, yet somehow, she still managed not to see him walk up behind her.

"Hi, Mom," Lucius said guiltily.

Katherine nearly jumped out of her skin and turned around in a flash, hand on her throat. "Oh, oh, Lucius, you scared me. Don't sneak up on me like that, you hear me?" she said.

"I'm sorry. I won't do it again, and I'm sorry for last night too. I'll stay in my room, I promise," Lucius said, looking down at the little holes in his socks.

"Good, I'm glad you've learned your lesson," she said as he nodded in agreement. "Now, are you hungry?" she asked, attempting to be kind.

Lucius nodded enthusiastically, even though he wasn't really hungry and the eggs and bacon she was cooking on the stove smelled sickening.

"All right, where's your sister? Is she not hungry?" Katherine asked, looking about the house.

"No, she's not hungry," he replied. She was never hungry, so he knew that was a more than safe answer.

"Humph." She sighed. "At least you pretend to like my cooking," she said as she put the hot breakfast on a plate in front of him at the table, now upright once again.

Lucius looked down at his plate, and his stomach gurgled for food but lurched at the smell. He swallowed thickly and shoved food into his mouth. It tasted as foul as always, but he forced himself to eat more.

After several vomit-inducing bites, he set down his fork. "Momma?" he asked.

"Yes?"

"What's a vampire?" Lucius questioned, and he saw his mother immediately tense.

"Did I call you that yesterday?" Katherine asked, having been too drunk at the time to really remember.

He nodded, eager for an answer. She was always calling them monsters and vermin, but he had never heard her use the word *vampire* before.

Katherine swallowed another bite of breakfast and waited for Lucius to eat another bite. "Vampires are wicked, horrible creatures who steal children and suck blood for food," she said, staring at him with an unknown emotion he couldn't identify. Was it fury? Fear? Hatred? All those he understood, but just as it appeared, it turned to sadness. Sadness was not an emotion she usually allowed herself to feel around him.

He looked down at his food, then back up at her. "Am I a vampire?" he asked, already fearing the answer.

"Yes, I think so," Katherine admitted, unable to look at him even when he asked a question.

"You think so?"

"Well, your father was anyway!" Katherine replied, growing impatient. She had given him a bigger answer than he had expected, obviously sounding shorter and angrier than she had meant to toward her own son.

Lucius sat up straighter. "You've never talked about Dad before," he said, determined to find out more about this missing father he had always wondered about. She turned and looked at him. He looked so much like his father that it almost hurt her sometimes with the memories—not memories of sadness, but memories of pain.

"Your father was a vampire," she said slowly. "He has white hair and sharp teeth and long pointy ears, just like you."

Upon hearing his father's description, he suddenly felt very self-conscious. He reached to his mouth and touched his teeth. Then he looked at his mother. It was true that her teeth weren't pointy and sharp like his were. Why hadn't he ever noticed? Then he reached up slowly for his ears. They weren't round. Just like she said, they were pointy and stuck up slightly through his hair.

Katherine stared at him while he inspected himself, and for the first time in his young life, Lucius really did feel like a monster.

"Do you understand now? Why I have to be so hard on you?" she asked. "If the townspeople found out what you were, if they found out I was hiding you, they would hang us both. That, or burn us at the stake. Is that what you want?"

Lucius felt like he was on the verge of tears as he looked down at his food and shook his head. He felt sorry for ever asking these questions, but at the same time, he was relieved to finally have some answers as to why his mother seemed to hate him so much.

"Good, now go to your room," Katherine ordered. "I have to go to work today."

He got up from his seat at the table and dragged each foot along until he sat in his room next to his sister. He looked over at her, immediately trying to notice how she looked. Just like him, she had white hair and sharp, pointed fangs. Her ears were smaller, though; maybe that was why their mom never got angry with her. They were still pointed, of course, but not as much as his.

Katherine came into the room and saw Eileen's new red bow around her hair. "Where did you get that?"

"Lucy got it for me," she said timidly. "It's from your sewing box. I can give it back if you want it. Do you want it back?"

Katherine hesitated before letting out a tired sigh. "No, keep it. It's just a ribbon," she said as she looked over at Lucius. "I will leave the door unlocked from now on so you can walk around the house, *if* you promise not to leave, under any circumstances."

He looked up at her. He had been so bad last night, and still, she was offering him a new form of freedom? *Maybe she does care!* Lucius thought, and he hastily nodded.

She smiled. What a pretty smile she had on the few occasions she decided to show it. "Then I'm off to work. Be good, you two, or I'll have to keep you locked in your room again," she said, walking down the stairs.

Lucius listened closely as his mother picked up her bag, checked its contents, and left the house. Then he watched as she walked down the forest pathway, no longer able to be seen in the distance.

Eileen picked out a new book to read, this one about some sort of aquatic creature. Lucius didn't really care. He got up. "I'm going to go downstairs. Don't follow me."

"Lucy, what are you doing? Please don't get in trouble again," Eileen said nervously.

"I'm not gonna to get in no trouble," he said. "I'm even gonna to leave the house."

"'Going to' and 'get into,'" she corrected and then pleaded with her older twin, "Lucy, please…"

Sighing, he turned to Eileen. "I'm not *going* to *get into* trouble," he said before turning back.

Walking down the stairs, Lucius went to the bathroom and threw up the breakfast he ate just a few minutes earlier. Why did he have to be born a monster? He wanted so badly to like the food that was given to him. He knew his mom was always angry at him for wasting it and being so hungry.

Flushing the old toilet, Lucius walked weakly into the kitchen. Throwing up always made his throat hurt and his legs feel too wobbly. He hated it! He hated everything about living here! He hated the food, he hated the mattress with no springs left, he hated the spiders in the corners, and he hated his mother most of all. He didn't hate Eileen, though. She was nice to him. She was all he had. If he was being really honest with himself, he didn't hate his mother either. He just hated how much she hated him.

He really did want to be a good son. He tried to never interrupt their lessons, staring out the window instead. He knew his mom wanted him to learn, and he really did his best, but the lessons were just so boring! Lucius lied sometimes and said it was just too easy, but in all honesty, he just didn't understand. It would be easier if the letters and numbers didn't move around so much. He didn't understand how Eileen had gotten so good at it all so fast.

But she wasn't as strong as he was. He could kick open any door and punch through any wall. In the woods, he even tried his luck at punching through a tree, and he knocked it right over! Right out of the ground roots and all! It wasn't a very big tree, but it wasn't small either! He was amazed no one heard him, but thankful too. Eileen couldn't punch down trees. She couldn't even lift up heavy books. But she was very fast and very smart. She could write and think faster than anyone; even his mom thought so.

Down in the kitchen, he grabbed a knife, holding it with shaky hands. *You've got to do this*, Lucius thought. *Momma will love you more if you do this.* He pulled the tip of his ear out, placing it to the blade of the knife. He took one very big deep breath and shut his eyes. With one swift yank of the blade, he gave a sharp yelp as the knife sliced through the cartilage of his ear. He stumbled backward, dropping the knife and clutching his ear tightly. It stung, and as he looked down at the knife, he noticed the tip of his ear lying next to it. Success.

With bloody hands, Lucius grabbed the knife. He wasn't done. "Just one more," he said aloud, raising the knife to his other side. Eileen rushed down the stairs and stared at him.

"What are you doing!" she exclaimed. "Stop it!"

She ran down the remaining stairs and over to her brother, but before she could reach him, he yanked the blade over across his other ear. Expecting the pain, this time, he made no sound beside a soft grunt.

Chapter 5

KATHERINE

But I Never Asked for Children

Coming home from work, Katherine was glad to see that the front door was still locked. As she opened the door, the first thing she noticed was blood. Blood everywhere. She wanted nothing more than to turn around and bolt back to the village, leaving forever right then and there. Instead she swallowed the lump in her throat and slowly followed the trail up to the children's bedroom.

Inside, she saw her son lying on his back on the bed, blood all over his face, and Eileen trying to use any spare cloth in the house to soak it up. She had used up several of her own dresses and had moved to empty food bags from the market.

"Momma, I tried to stop him!" Eileen cried. "But he cut his ears before I could reach him!"

Katherine went down to her sewing room and snatched up a needle and thread. Then heading back upstairs, she inspected his wound. She saw that he had in fact cut off the tops of his own ears, but in doing so, he had also cut a rough gash into the side of his head.

This is my fault, she thought. *If I hadn't told him about his father, about what he was, he wouldn't have attempted such a foolish thing.*

There was no way this was going to kill him, but it was making an awful mess. So she grabbed her needle and thread and started stitching up his head wounds first. After that was finished, she stitched the cuts in his ears closed before packing up her sewing kit.

Eileen was sitting beside him, much calmer now that the bleeding had stopped. Katherine inspected her passed-out son and noticed how much paler his already albino white skin was.

"He'll recover," she said to herself, getting up and picking up the remaining bloody cloth. "Somehow, he always does."

Eileen gave a relieved sigh as she held her brother to her chest. Katherine only looked away, disgusted by their closeness. It was stupid for Eileen to be so concerned. Vampires always grew back their parts as new, and Lucius's ears would be no different. But Katherine supposed that Eileen had no way of knowing that.

The next year, when the twins were six, Katherine made the decision. No more blood. If they died, then they died. Back in the castle, she knew the adult vampires could last maybe a year without any blood. She didn't know what would happen in a year, but she knew how horrible she felt when she gave those monsters the extra lining of her uterus. She felt disgusting. Watching those little vermin greedily suck out the blood in her pads reminded her of the days when vampires would forcibly hold her down in her cell to suck the blood out of her neck. Well, no more! What would happen in a year? Well, if they died she would be rid of them.

Walking to work, Katherine looked up at the beautiful morning sky. Was she really making the right decision? Yes, she hated giving them her blood, but was it wrong to deny them what they really needed? Even if they were monsters, they were still her children. Even though she was only acting, she really did want to love them. Sometimes, she acted so well she almost believed it herself, *almost*. But more than anything, she wanted to start a new life without them.

If they weren't in the picture, maybe she could meet someone, fall in love, live on her own. Even live with Gelda! She was her best friend, and if her kids died, she could always make up some story about them having an illness. She would get scolded for not seeking her out for help, but she knew Gelda would feel sorry for her and forgive her immediately and offer comfort and support for the "traumatic death" of her children.

If I keep feeding them, they'll keep living, and I'll be forced to live like this forever! Katherine thought. Every time she felt sorry, felt bad for starving them, for her decision, she thought of herself in the future. She thought of herself ten or fifteen years from now—older, maybe infertile, unable to get married anymore or start any sort of life, losing more and more blood every day as her kids grew taller and hungrier. Her kids would become the end of her with no more pads to suckle on for survival. At least at this age, she might still be able to fend them off if they got hungry enough to attack.

With that thought in mind, she had officially decided. The next month went by, and Lucius's stomach growled as he made his way toward his mother.

"Mom? Me and Eileen are hungry," he said, embarrassed about his need for blood. "Do you have any—"

"'Eileen and I,' Lucius. It's 'Eileen and I.' And no. I don't have any more blood for either of you anymore," she said, looking up from her sewing.

"Oh," Lucius said, eyes widening. He didn't know what to say. Was she not going to feed them anymore? He walked back upstairs, and Katherine continued sewing, as though it was no big loss to her.

The next few months went by, and Eileen was getting slower and slower. She didn't read or write as fast, and she didn't seem as interested in her books as she used to.

When Mommy used to bring us the red pads, Lucius thought, *Eileen seemed fine, but now, she's getting slower.*

It had been about three months since his mom had brought them her last pad, and he had to admit, even he was starting to feel the effects. He always felt sick, his head always felt foggy, and he always wanted to sleep but never could, even when he was exhausted. Even the books that Eileen could never pick up but he could lift with ease now suddenly felt very, very heavy.

Katherine, however, felt better than ever. Her son never had the energy to argue with her, and Eileen never asked for more lessons. All either of them ever did now was lie in bed and stare at the ceiling, unless she went into their rooms. It was like not having kids at all, and every day she went to work, hung out with Gelda, and went about her daily life as usual. Guilt-free.

Chapter 6

LUCIUS

BABY'S FIRST BLOODLUST

Eileen looked over at her brother. "Lucius, I don't feel so good," she squeaked. She seemed to be growing skinnier every day.

"Me neither," grumbled Lucius. He had to find a way to get some sort of food. "Ouch!" He heard from his mother downstairs, and suddenly, it seemed like the whole house was filled with the fresh smell of blood.

Lucius sat up, not feeling like himself. His head was all foggy, and he felt his body move on its own. Exhausted from starvation, he didn't even attempt to resist his natural urges.

Food. He walked downstairs, legs shaking. *Hungry.* He stumbled into the kitchen. *Starving.* Tripping over to his mother, wondering how he hadn't noticed how *delicious* she smelled before now.

Katherine soaked up the prick of blood from her finger with a piece of cloth. Why did she have to be so clumsy? Now was the time to be more careful about avoiding injury. She couldn't let the monsters smell her blood. As she soaked up the small rice-sized speck of blood on her finger, she heard footsteps behind her and swung around. Behind her, eyes red, Lucius was walking toward her in a zombie-like fashion.

"Stay back!" she shouted. "Lucius, go back to your room!"

But he could not hear her. All he could smell, all he could think about was the prick of blood infecting the piece of cloth she held to her finger.

I want it, he thought. *I need it!*

Katherine saw he wasn't listening to her. He was becoming more and more monstrous by the day. She backed up further into the wall and reached for anything she could use as a weapon. Reaching around desperately, she grabbed onto a hanging pan and brought it around on top of his head.

Suddenly, Lucy's world was spinning. What happened? He had just a moment to look around before a second hit came down onto his forehead. Lucius's eyes turned back to blue, and the bloodlust was gone as he fell to the ground, passed out.

Katherine panted. He almost attacked her! Over a speck of her blood on a ratty piece of old cloth! She had to be more careful, *much* more careful. Picking up her son, she noticed how frail he seemed nowadays, how small. She carried him back to his room and dropped him on the mattress next to his sister. Eileen didn't look up at her; in fact, Eileen didn't move at all.

As Katherine stared down at her two children, she felt a pang of guilt over her daughter. She might have never loved Lucius, but she did feel some attachment to Eileen. She always thought she could have loved her, if not for the white hair. But there really was no other choice if she wanted to move on, and besides, what would she feed her poor daughter once she got older?

Chapter 7

LUCIUS

I WISH IT WERE ME

When Lucius finally woke, his head was throbbing with pain. He rolled over toward his sister.

"Eileen, my head hurts," he complained.

She turned her head to look at him and spoke slowly. "You went to go see Mom because of the smell, I think. She knocked you out."

He felt confused as the world seemed to spin around him. He hardly remembered the event. But his sister must be telling the truth. His head hurt so bad he felt like he could hardly see.

Over the next two months, Katherine tried her best to stay out of the house completely. She spent every night at Gelda's, saying that her sister was watching them.

Meanwhile, when she was away, the children were getting hungrier and hungrier, weaker and weaker. Lucius could hardly control when his eyes turned red and could hardly control where his body went when they were. He often found himself shambling the house, only to wake from his hunger and wonder what he was doing.

But he never left; he didn't dare. Leaving the house meant he might be found, and his mother once said, "If anyone finds you, they'll hang you or maybe burn you." So even in his bloodlust shambles, something told him he had to stay.

His sister, however, hardly moved since their mother had stopped feeding them. All she did was lie on the bed and stare up at the ceiling. No matter how Lucius tried to cheer her up, she was almost always completely unresponsive, aside from the stray smile or a giggle at something funny he had to say. So most days, all he could do was cuddle her while she slept.

After three months, Katherine wondered if she was finally free from their burden, if she was finally able to go home. She was starting to miss her own bed, and it must be safe now. She hadn't fed them in over half a year. Saying goodbye to Gelda, she confidently made her way back up the path through the forest. She was happy to see that there was dust on the door handle, meaning they must not have tried to leave while she was gone.

"Surely if they were still alive, they would have tried to leave by now," Katherine said to herself as she unlocked the door. She walked inside, habitually locking the door behind her once inside her humble abode.

Lucius woke from his dreamless state to the sound of the door. He sat up as quickly as his starved body would allow. "Eileen, Eileen, Mom's back. Maybe she has some food for us!" he said with hope. Any hope right now would be enough to keep them going.

Eileen stayed silent.

"Eileen?" Lucius shook her softly. "Eileen, wake up" But still, she did not stir and did not move. "Come on, aren't you hungry?" Lucius asked.

His sister did not respond.

Lucius put his head to her chest. Was she sick? No. She wasn't sick. In fact, when he listened, he heard nothing at all. No breathing, no heartbeat, nothing.

Sitting up, he took a very close look at her face. Her eyes had started to sink in and were a light blue-purple in color, like she had two black eyes. She was the skinniest he had ever seen her and was completely still and colder than usual to the touch.

Eileen was dead.

Lucius couldn't believe it. She was gone? What was he supposed to do with her? He had to bury her somehow. But doing that meant leaving the house. Why had she died? Was she just too hungry? He wanted to understand, but this all felt so impossible. It all felt so fake.

"Wake up," Lucius said. He could feel his eyes turning red with fury. "*Wake up! This isn't real!*"

At that moment, Katherine climbed up the stairs. She walked to their room, disappointed to see Lucius sitting up.

So they're still alive after all. Maybe a few more months will fix this, she thought. Only then did she notice her son was shaking.

Tears running down his face, Lucius heard his mother open the door to peer in at them. He turned to look at her and forgot for the first time in months how hungry he was.

"You did this," he said softly as his mother turned to leave. Not hearing him, Katherine started down the stairs. "*YOU DID THIS!*" Lucius screamed at her as loud as he could.

She whipped around, and her eyes landed on the small boy with red eyes stalking her. He should be weak; he hasn't been eating. But at that moment, he looked stronger than he ever had, filled with rage.

In a blind panic, she turned and ran down to the kitchen, grabbing the pan that had protected her in the past. When she turned to him and swung, Lucius caught the pan before it hit his head. He yanked it out of her hand with one swift motion.

She backed up and reached for something else, but he pressed forward, backing her into the corner. "*You killed Eileen!*" he said. "*You killed my sister!*"

Katherine frantically looked around. There had to be something she could use to escape, something to stop her furious, bloodthirsty son. Above her, she saw a cabinet holding some brass serving plates. If she could get just one, maybe it would be enough to knock him out, as long as she could get to his face.

She turned around as fast as she could and reached up for the cabinet handle. In that small moment, Lucius jumped onto her and sank his teeth into her neck.

With a startled scream, Katherine punched him in the nose and flung him off her. "Get back!" she shouted. "Get back!"

Lucius landed on top of the table and then fell onto the floor. He was a little surprised. *She tastes delicious,* he thought.

His mother grabbed the serving plate and lunged toward him on the floor. As she hurled herself toward him, he rolled out of the way just in time, kicking her in the face as hard as he could. Landing the kick, he made Katherine fly backward; her head crashed into the ceiling. Now it was her turn to feel dizzy.

Katherine lunged at him again, barely able to see. Overshooting the distance, she landed on top of him, smacking at the ground. He punched her in the stomach, and she flew into the stove.

Scrambling to his feet, Lucius ran toward her as fast as he could. His mother tried to get up but couldn't will herself to stand. He had knocked the wind out of her, and her legs felt like no more than Jell-O. Lucius lunged onto her and sank his teeth into her neck eagerly.

"*No. No! Don't!*" Katherine whimpered. She pushed against his shoulders but couldn't manage to move him. She started to feel light-headed and weaker every second his lips were attached to her neck. "*Get off me!*" she pleaded. "*Please!*"

But her son couldn't hear her. He couldn't hear anything except the beating of her heart pulsing through his head. *Delicious. Delicious!* he thought with every gulp. This was the best thing he had ever tasted, far better than pads.

He drank and drank and drank. Katherine soon stopped struggling, having no energy to do so. Then she stopped moving. Lucius stood up and stepped away from her. His eyes turned back to blue. Before him, he saw what was left of his mother—a pale, small, dark, curly-haired woman who had lost all color in her skin and all blood in her body, making her look very similar to a raisin.

What have I done? Lucy thought to himself. *She's my mother, and I killed her.* Overcome with grief, he sat on her lap and wrapped his arms around her. Squeezing tight, he heard her back snap as he pushed his face into her chest.

All he could do was sob. Was he really the monster she said he was? Surely he must be. What kind of person would kill their own mother? He thought about how mean she had been to him, but also, the nice things she had done too. A large part of him hated her, but a large part of him loved her too. She was his mom after all, and now, with the only two people he had ever known having vanished from his life, he wasn't sure what to do anymore. After several hours of sobbing into the cold arms of her body, Lucius stood up. He wanted to remember her. He wanted to remember what he did. So he took a little golden band off her pinky finger and slipped it on to his thumb.

Running upstairs, he ran to Eileen and gave her a tight hug. He didn't want to forget her either. She had been his only friend in their times of loneliness and solitude. He took the red ribbon off her head and tied it around his hair, which hung down to the middle of his back.

After taking his memories as possessions, he was at a loss of what to do next. He couldn't stay. That much was obvious. But where would he go? Without making any plan, he ran out of the house.

I have to get out of here!

Chapter 8

GELDA

CHASING THE MENACE

Gelda made her way down the path to Katherine's house. She had never been invited over, but she knew where she lived. Katherine had described her home in the past, even if she never let her visit.

Enough is enough, Gelda thought. She knew her friend was struggling in ways she wouldn't tell her. And she had had enough with the constant secrets Katherine was keeping. *It's such a beautiful sunny day*, she thought as she stepped up the path.

She had made a good decision to walk instead of driving up the bumpy dirt road. Gelda loved the feeling of sun on her face, and it looked so beautiful as little rays shone through the trees. Feeling good about finally checking on her friend, she walked through the pathway, eyes closed, enjoying the natural warmth.

She bumped into something and almost tripped. *Watch where you're going, Gelda!* she said to herself as she opened her eyes. She didn't know what she expected to see, maybe a rock or a stump, but nothing could have prepared her for this.

Below her, having fallen into the dirt was a white-haired child at her feet, and immediately she noticed he was covered in blood. In a rush of memories, she thought of her father and how he had described the kidnappers of her sister. As he looked up at her, she couldn't help staring at his snow-white hair. His eyes were bloodred and his fangs needle sharp.

This boy, he's a vampire! Gelda screamed at the top of her lungs and shielded herself with her arms. *I bet I look like an idiot! I'm going to die alone in these woods!* She thought. *Is this what Katherine has been hiding? That can't be her son! No, it can't possibly. But maybe it was. Oh god, where's my friend!*

Were vampires real after all? Gelda was starting to believe it now. The child fit every description—white hair, pale skin, *blood.* Oh god, where was Katherine! First things first, she had to protect herself. But with what? All she had on her was a silly little handbag.

She brought her hands away and grabbed the first thing she could—a large stick. Then she whirled around, swinging it as hard as she could. But there was nothing to hit. She looked around, and the kid was gone. He must have run.

I have to find Katherine, Gelda thought, now sprinting through the wooded path toward Katherine's house. When she got to the door, she didn't even stop for a breath. She pounded on it as hard as she could.

"KATHERINE! OPEN UP!"

No answer.

"KATHERINE, IT'S GELDA!"

Nothing.

Trying the knob, it didn't open. Gelda stepped back, and took a running start toward the door, breaking it open with the bulk of her shoulder. Falling in through the door, she scrambled to her feet as quick as she could in search of her friend.

It took all of ten seconds to find her. Rushing into the kitchen, she saw Katherine's lifeless body lying on the kitchen floor. A knife was lying near her, and it looked like in her final moments, she had tried to grab it.

Katherine looked next to nothing like the woman who had become Gelda's dearest friend. This woman had two deep bite marks in her neck and blood all over her chest and shoulder, though she didn't appear to have any in her body. Her face and skin had gone completely pale, except for her hands, which were now a dark purple-blue. Her skin had seemingly tightened around her body, making her look like a withered husk of a woman.

Gelda resisted the urge to vomit. She couldn't stand to look any longer. She had to get help! Running away from her once-beloved friend, she bolted back to the town, feeling very foolish. All this time, she had mocked and belittled the townsfolk and her father for believing in such a thing as vampires. Now she had seen one for herself!

Was this the reason Katherine wouldn't share any details with her? Surely this must have been her big secret. Her child was a vampire! If she had only asked Gelda for help, they could have found something to do with him before he killed her. They could have done away with him themselves. Maybe that was what she feared, or maybe she thought the people would hang her with him.

Maybe Katherine didn't want them to kill her son at all? It would make sense. Maybe that was why she never spoke up. Even Gelda knew deep down it was wrong to talk of killing a living, breathing child. But he was a killer! It was just in his genes! Didn't Katherine know this was bound to happen eventually? She wanted to slap her friend for being so silly. But she couldn't. She was gone.

What of her sister? Gelda hadn't looked around the house very long, but she supposed she would have seen Katherine's mythical sister if she was there. Was that just another lie to cover up her tracks and give her an excuse to leave the house without being shamed for abandoning her children? It must have been. Gelda couldn't blame her, knowing what she knew now.

How had this all happened? Looking back, she remembered her friend was already pregnant when she met her. She seemed so clueless about the world, so out of place. It was obvious this life was forced upon her, however hard Katherine tried to dodge the questions. But where had she come from? Was there really a castle out there just filled with vampires and the missing townspeople? It seemed so far-fetched, yet it was the only solution Gelda could make at the time. Her friend must have escaped, and that was when she met her.

She ran back to town, feeling like a complete fool. She started screaming at the top of her lungs. "VAMPIRES! HELP!"

Everyone looked up, but no one reacted. Gelda expected nothing less. Surely they thought she was just making fun of them.

"Please!" she cried, shaking all over.

After a few noticed her tears, people started to jump into action. Wooden stakes were passed out, as well as torches, and guns with silver-tipped bullets! They even leashed their dogs, so Gelda knew that they were serious.

Everyone in town knew how to kill a vampire. Getting the supplies was easy since everyone was constantly ready to continue the hunt. But it occurred to Gelda that Katherine's son was surely only half a vampire. Would those sorts of weapons kill him? Of course, there had to be something. Maybe anything through his heart would be enough to do the trick, not just a wooden stake.

"Where did you see it?" a man yelled at her.

"I-in the woods!" she stuttered. "He killed Katherine! He's just a boy! He probably went back to her cottage in the woods!"

Upon hearing where he could be, the townspeople started making their way to the cottage on their own. Gelda felt very turned around from what she had just seen. Helplessly following, she watched as the townsfolk frantically pushed and shoved through the woods to her friend's old house.

Gelda ran in, desperate to know if Katherine did have a sister or if it had just been another lie. She averted her eyes from her dead friend as the townspeople screamed in horror over the body. She ran upstairs, wanting to be the first one to get there.

Upstairs was small, just like downstairs. It consisted of two bedrooms and a hallway. She peeked into the first bedroom and saw nothing. Then moving to the second, she screamed at the white-haired child she saw lying on the mattress on the floor.

"It's him!" she screamed. "It's him. He's up here!" she said, running over to the child.

The townspeople started coming upstairs, and Gelda grabbed the boy by the arm. He was cold. She looked down for a second. No, *she...she* was cold. Did Katherine have twins? That would have only made her life harder. Yet she had still said nothing! Gelda backed away from the girl, horrified by her lifeless blue eyes that seemed to stare on forever.

The people came upstairs in a mass flurry and, upon seeing the child, unloaded a series of silver bullets into her cold, already-dead body.

"It's not him!" Gelda shouted. "This one is already dead! He must have run off!" Not needing another excuse, the townsfolk swarmed outside the house, setting the dogs off on any sort of scent trail they could find. Gelda put the child back in bed, starting to feel regret for getting everyone involved in this situation, and then she followed the others outside.

Following the dogs was easy enough until they hit a river. After that, they lost the scent. It was hard to say whether everyone was on the right trail or not. She followed the townsfolk, conflicted about the actions she had just taken. Maybe there was more than just one side to this? Katherine had spent the past few months at her house, very clearly neglecting her children. How had she even been able to keep them alive for this long? What were they eating? Katherine never showed any signs of having wounds or being tired or anything of the sort.

And what about the girl? How had she died? Vampires didn't typically eat one another, did they? That seemed very unlikely. Perhaps Katherine really had starved her to death. Maybe that was her plan with the boy too. But she come home too early, and he hadn't died yet.

As distraught as Gelda was about losing her friend, it was hard to imagine her kind and timid friend starving her own children. She couldn't believe that there was so much Katherine hadn't been telling her. She was a very private person. That was obvious, but this! This was leading an entirely separate, secret life. Keeping your past a secret, your children a secret, your plans for *murder* a secret… Gelda felt a twinge of guilt. These monsters they were hunting were children. Despite being vampires, they were still *children*. And now she had accidentally led the town on a fox chase after the boy, and they were going to kill him if he was found!

Chapter 9

LUCIUS

THE SAIL AWAY FROM SHORE

Halfway down the path, Lucius ran head first into a tall woman with very curly dark-brown hair. He looked up at her, and she looked down at him, and for several moments, time seemed to stand still. Then she let out a blood-curdling scream.

Hearing her scream, Lucius turned around and bolted deeper into the woods. He had to get away from this woman. He had to get away from *people*. Lucius ran through the woods until he couldn't hear the townspeople. He ran and ran, day and night. He felt so strong now, having finally eaten, but he also felt scared.

He crossed a river and wondered if the running water would lead to somewhere different. Going down the river surely meant he would run into a large lake or something, right? The thought of water made him feel safe. Even though he had no reason to think this way. It was not like he had ever been on the run before, except for that time he ran from his mother through these woods. But he knew back then he only had to return home. He knew where he needed to go. Now he had no idea. He turned and ran down the river, on instinct, alone.

Finally stopping, he leaned against a tree. "I can't keep running forever," Lucius said to himself, slumping down to sit. He had been running for almost two days and still didn't feel even remotely hungry. It was getting dark. He hadn't even stopped to sleep during the night, and now he was feeling the effects. His legs hurt intensely, and he could barely keep his eyes open.

I killed her, Lucius thought. *I can't believe I killed her! I lost my mother and my sister!* Suddenly, it dawned on him, his whole family was dead. He leaned against the side of a tree and felt tears rush to his eyes. *I really am a monster, just like Mom always said!* He wanted nothing more just than to fling himself out of a tree just so he wouldn't have to think about what had just happened, what he had just done. Lucius felt his whole body seize up as he started to hyperventilate from the stress. His tears quickly turned into sobs. He curled up on himself and cried himself into a dreamless, exhausted sleep.

When he woke up, he wasn't sure how much time had gone by, but it was sunrise. No, it was *sunset*. He had slept a whole day away? He couldn't believe it. He had to keep moving. Getting up and walking more, Lucius got to the biggest lake he had ever seen. It was huge! He couldn't see the other side. He dipped his hand in and tasted it. Salty. This must be the ocean. How far had he run? After washing his hands and face of blood, Lucius looked back and forth. He heard the sound of chains and bells in the distance. Far off to his left, he saw a big dock and an even bigger ship. They looked so small from where he was.

Should I go see them? Lucius thought. *What if they're dangerous?* He couldn't just keep running. Already Lucius was starting to feel the effects of loneliness. So he started walking toward the ships. What was the worst that could happen?

After several hours of walking, he finally arrived at the docks by morning. He had never seen a ship before. How did it float? Why did it have to be so big? It looked twice the size of his house, maybe three times as large! Nervously, he climbed onto the docks. There were lots of ships, but the biggest one on the end was definitely his favorite, though the small ones were nice too. He must have run a long way because no one seemed to recognize him. That, or the woman he saw didn't tell anyone that they met, but that seemed unlikely.

The pier smelled strongly of fish, and Lucius wrinkled his nose at the disgusting smell. But the water was refreshing, and the breeze felt nice in his hair. He liked to sit on the edge and hold his toes in the ocean, and he liked to look at the sand and the blue of the sea. He decided right then that blue was his new favorite color.

As he walked through the pier, he looked toward the small market. It had loads of people—big people, small people—and everyone was shouting and pushing. It looked so busy and scary. Lucius decided not to go over there. He was supposed to be on the run, wasn't he? Even though it was early in the morning, you can never be too careful of being seen.

After walking around for a few hours, looking at the ships and enjoying the air, he noticed that the busier the docks got, the more people seemed to look at him funny.

Please don't notice me, Lucius thought to himself as he ducked behind a ship.

Two grown men walked by, and he stared at them. He had never seen a man before. His mother had spoken of his father only once. But he didn't know that they didn't have breasts or hips. He always assumed that his breasts would grow out when he was older just like Eileen's would.

I really should have paid better attention to Mom's lessons, he thought to himself, feeling very foolish. He turned and glanced into the water, staring at his reflection. What kind of person would he grow up to be anyway? Now that his mother was gone, it was his to figure out all on his own. As he looked through the water, he saw a little fish and thought of his sister. He wondered if this was one of the manatees Eileen had read about in her books. No, this fish was much too small.

While off daydreaming, a large sunburnt man walked up to him. "Nice hair you got, kid," he said in a thick accent Lucius didn't recognize. "What're you doin' out here all alone? Where're yer parents?"

Lucius jumped, then backed up toward the water. "Th-thank you," he stammered, not knowing what else to say. He had never been given a compliment before, at least, not from an adult and especially not from a stranger. "My mom and sister, they, uhh… It doesn't matter," he replied hastily.

"Hmm," the man replied, looking him over quizzically. "What are you so scared of?" he said.

Lucius noted that when he spoke, he was missing several teeth and that the rest were black.

"I've never been to the sea before. I've never spoken to a pirate before," Lucius said, suddenly feeling very, very silly.

The man laughed. "A pirate, huh? I guess I could be classified as that. Did you ever want to be a pirate, kid?" he said, brushing his black and graying hair out of his face.

Lucius shook his head. He didn't really know about pirates other than the fact that they stole gold and were missing lots of teeth, according to Eileen's fairy tales.

"Well, that's too bad. I was gonna offer to make you my first mate." The man smiled.

"Your first mate? I'll do it! I'll be your first mate!" he said eagerly. Going on a ship would surely take him far away from here. The farther he was from here, the safer he would be.

"Done. Now ya won't get paid, and ya have to do everything I say. Da?"

Lucius nodded eagerly. He didn't need money. What would he buy anyway? Lucius sat under the docks by the shore until the next morning. He didn't want to be seen, so he didn't bother going into town. It was wet underneath, but he enjoyed the sand. Lucius sat as close to shore as he could and played with the waves as they crashed against the beach. People passed above him busily, and he was thankful not to be noticed.

When morning finally came, he followed the man to his ship. Lucius was so excited he felt himself bouncing up and down on his toes. A new place, a new experience! And now with this man, he had a new family, or at least that was what he had hoped.

"Ready to go?" said the man, shuffling over to him.

He nodded.

"What's your name, kid?" the man questioned, packing the last of the stuff onto his very large ship.

"Lucius," he said, "but my sister used to call me Lucy." Suddenly, thinking back to his sister, he felt very sad.

"Don't cry, kid. Crying is for girls," the man said, climbing onto the ship and helping him on. "And Lucy is a girl's name. I'm going to call you Petya. An' you can call me Boris."

"Petya." Lucius sounded his new name out. "Pee-ate-ya." He thought it sounded like an awfully weird name. Like Peter, but not.

"Petya, where did you get your white hair?"

Tensing, he answered, "I…I… My mom says my dad gave it to me."

"Are you a vampire? I hear the nearby German village has some sort of vampire problem, and everyone is terrified of them," Boris said, eyeing him.

"I…I don't know. That's just what my momma said."

"Ya must be some sort of half-breed then. Maybe that's why you can go out in the sun."

That was the first time Lucius had heard that term half-breed. It sounded ugly. It made him sound less. But he didn't want to offend his new friend, so he said nothing.

All the crewmates arrived on the ship and started pulling down the sails. The whole boat moved and swayed. And before Lucy knew it, they were floating at sea toward a new life.

Boris watched everyone work before walking off, expecting Lucy to follow. "Let's go introduce ya to the rest of the crew."

Lucius followed. When they got down below deck, the crew was waiting for command.

"All right, you lot! Remember the rules! No talking back. No stealing. Hard work. And absolutely no messing with the cargo. No exceptions!"

All the crewmen nodded in agreement.

Boris leaned over to Lucius. "Kid, introduce yourself."

He stood up straight. "My name is Luciu—" And before he could finish, he was met with a sharp smack on the back of his head, pushing him forward. He fell onto his hands and knees.

"Petya. Remember that. Your name is Petya!"

Staring at the floor, he tried to shake the dizziness away as he stood up. "Petya. My name is Petya," he repeated back dumbly.

Boris looked back at the crew. "Petya is my newest personal slave boy! So I want you to treat him as if he was me when I'm not around. If I give him an order to give to you, you obey it. Understand?"

The crewmen all nodded.

Slave boy? Lucius thought. Wasn't he supposed to be the first mate? Wasn't he?

Boris turned and headed back up to the deck. Lucy followed, praying they weren't too far for him to swim. Maybe it wasn't too late to turn back.

The rays of sun stinging his eyes, he quickly ran to the edge of the deck. He was disappointed to see the amount of water surrounding the boat; he knew he was too late. Off in the distance, he could see the docks still. Could he still make it? He squinted and saw the woman he ran into in the forest. She seemed to be asking people questions, like she was looking for something or looking for someone.

Lucius turned back, deciding to stay after all. Petya was his name now. He just had to accept that.

"I thought I was going to be your first mate?" he said, turning to Boris.

"Da, that's what I told ya. But how old are you, boy? Six? Seven? Ya ever heard of a first mate that young? I certainly haven't. Besides, we too far from shore for you to be goin' overboard. So I suggest you stick around unless you want me to kill yeh. I can always find a different 'first mate' to boss around in your place."

Petya stayed silent. He hated this. He'd been tricked! Why should he have expected anything else? All grown-ups were terrible!

"Help the men put the last of the sails up."

Yanked from his thoughts, Petya was startled by the sudden command. "Where are we going?"

"*I'm* going to my office. You're putting the sails up." Boris said, sounding impatient.

"No, I mean, where is the ship traveling? Is it somewhere warm? I'd love to go someplace warm," Petya babbled nervously.

"Russia, and it ain't warm there. Now move! Unless ya want yer first beating," he said, pushing him forward toward the sails.

The way Boris went from calm to angry was frightening. It reminded him of his mother a bit. Petya ran over to the men and started helping with the sails. Boy, was it hard work! Luckily, he was very strong. When the other crew members realized how easy it was for him to move around the sails and to tie tight knots, they immediately chose him for each heaviest task.

"You shouldn't let them push you around like that. They should pull their own weight," said a boy. Well, he wasn't a boy, really. He was a teenager, but he didn't look able to grow a beard yet like the rest of the men. He only had some facial hair, and it was patchy at best.

"I don't mind," Petya replied. "It's something to do. Besides, I really like the fresh air."

"My name is Misha, by the way," he said. Misha had brownish-red hair that looked like it hadn't been brushed in months, and he was by far the skinniest of any of the crew members.

"Hi, Misha. I'm new to the ship. Do you mind if I ask you a question?"

"Shoot."

"What is the cargo supposed to be? And why aren't we supposed to touch it? Boris said we're going to Russia, but I don't know where that is. Is everyone here from Russia? Or just some."

"Whoa, whoa, Petya, slow down," Misha said. "That's too many. I don't have answers to all those. Besides, even the questions I do know, I don't think I'm supposed to tell yeh. But if I do, you have to promise that everything you heard you didn't hear it from me, all right? People can get in big trouble 'round here if they're caught spreading rumors. I don't want my head on the block. Got it?"

Petya nodded. "I didn't hear anything from you. I haven't even met you yet, if anyone asks," he said, trying to persuade some answers out of the teen.

"That's the idea," Misha said, taking hold of Petya's arm. He looked around cautiously before leading him down to the kitchen.

It was loud there, all the pots and pans banging from the cook. But Misha led him farther down the hall a little past the kitchen, where the noise was dulled and they were alone.

"No one will be able to hear us back here. Now I don't know what we sellin'—the cargo, I mean. All I know is, Boris goes down to the bottom of the ship's hold to check on it every morning and every night. Usually, he brings a big man named Luka with him."

Petya was confused. Why would he set that work only for one man and himself? He had a very bad feeling about this whole situation. He should have never boarded this ship! But what could he do now?

"And you were right the first time," continued Misha. "Everyone here is from somewhere in Russia. Most of us are here to try to find better lives in other countries but end up staying on the ship because it's the only work we can find. No one wants to hire a foreign smuggler."

"I thought we were pirates."

"Pirate, smuggler—what's the difference, really? I think *smuggler* sounds nicer, though."

"Are you from Russia?"

"You're awful slow, aren't you? Yeah, that's what I said. I have a little sister in Russia back home. She stays with my aunt."

"Why don't you stay with your aunt?" Petya asked.

"Because my aunt and uncle are poor and they said someone needs to earn extra money to take care of her. If they don't have the money, my sister will end up in an orphanage. I figured, if I made money here, I could send it home for them. And maybe I could even keep some for myself since they won't have to pay for my living expenses at sea. I used to get in some trouble for pickpocketing back in my hometown, but with the towns changing constantly, no one will be able to recognize me. Seems like an easy enough way to get some spending cash, eh? Anyway, enough about me. You got any family back in Germany?"

Petya hesitated. "No, not anymore." He looked down.

"Not anymore? What happened to them?"

"Well…I don't know who my father is or where he is. But I used to have a sister, and my mother used to…take care of us?"

"Why do you sound so confused? Is that supposed to be a question?"

"Well, no. But I would use the term 'take care of' very lightly. She just didn't come home very often."

"What about your sister?"

"She passed away. I guess we were poor too because she didn't get enough to eat," he lied. Petya didn't want to say quite yet that it wasn't money that starved her to death. It just seemed like too much information to say on a first greeting.

"Da, that's mighty messy. Awful sorry to hear 'bout your sis."

Petya nodded, not wanting to say anything else.

Misha looked around the corner. "Well, you can stick with me now! I was the youngest on board until recently, so you and I should stay close. But we better get back to work for now. Stay here a moment longer, so it don't look like we was talkin' 'bout anything," he whispered. "And remember, you didn't hear nothin' from me."

Petya nodded and waited while Misha walked out of the hall, back through the kitchens, and up onto the deck. After a few moments, Petya walked down the hall and through the kitchens.

"Yeh better be careful who ya trust," said a voice.

Petya whipped around to see a large, fat man standing in the kitchens.

"Are you…Luka?"

The man burst out a strong laugh. "No, no. My name is Oleg. I'm the ship's cook."

"How much did you hear?" Petya asked, nervous he was going to get in trouble and lose his only "friend" on the first day.

"Now, now, I ain't gonna get you a beatin'. I won't tell nobody. Just make sure you watch your back. This ship is filled with folks who would be more than happy to sell you out to make themselves look like the next guardian angel. At least in Boris's eyes."

Petya was relieved. He sat down at a bench. "So I can trust you, though?"

"Da, yer just a kid, hmm? I don't wanna see ya get into too much trouble. But don't push yer luck, understand?"

He nodded.

"Now off with yeh. There's work to do."

Petya went back up. Boris was waiting for him.

"Where ya been, Petya? I asked ya to help with the sails, not go snoopin' around the ship."

"I was with Oleg! He asked me to cut some…onions! We're having beef and onion stew today, and the onions needed cutting. So I helped! Because I finished opening up the sails," he said, making up the story on the spot.

Boris eyed him suspiciously. "All right, good. Now we need ya to clean the deck. Back in the kitchen is a bucket and mop. Come see me when yer done this time."

Petya nodded, happy his little lie worked out. He went back down to Oleg. "I need a bucket and mop for the deck. Boris said they're down here."

The cook pointed over to the corner. "Buckets over there, mop too. Bring them to me, and I'll show yeh how to fill 'em."

He grabbed them and did as he was told.

"It ain't that hard. Put soap in first, just about five drops, then fill it a few inches from full," Oleg said, doing the process for him. "I won't be doin it for yeh a second time, so make sure you know from now on."

Petya nodded. "Thank you, sir," he said, taking the mop and bucket.

"It's Oleg, I ain't no sir. Best not to keep the boss waitin'."

He ran upstairs to the deck, trying not to spill any water as he ran. Once he got upstairs, he ran to the front of the deck. *Best to go front to back*, he thought. *I don't want Boris to get mad at me, and get in trouble.* He dipped the mop in and, once it was completely wet, lathered it all over the ground. He was extra careful to make sure he didn't miss a single spot. It was hard to keep your balance with the boat moving back and forth, but he made do.

Right when the whole top deck was almost clean, the ship hit a particularly big wave. Petya grabbed for the railing of the ship, and the bucket went flying. It tipped over, and he dove forward, lunging for it to keep it upright. The bucket was faster and spilled the muddy ship water all over his nice, clean deck. Trying to put the bucket upright as fast as he could, he hastily looked around, making sure nobody saw. If nobody saw, maybe he could still clean it up on time. He grabbed his mop and started trying to soak up the dirty water. His hands got so dirty wringing out the mop over and over again. He had mud and dirt all the way up to his elbows, and his pants were completely ruined.

Oh well, he thought. *It's not like they were nice pants anyway, and it was probably going to happen eventually.* After he was finished, he dumped the water overboard, careful not to spill it this time. Then he returned the mop and bucket to Oleg.

"Thank you," he said.

"No problem. Go tell Boris you finished your mopping. And tell him the chum's ready, so everyone better come down if they plan on eating."

Petya ran upstairs and to the captain's quarters. "I finished, sir. Oleg told me to tell you that the…uhh…" He paused, not sure if he should use his exact words. "Chum is ready?"

Boris closed his book and got up. "Da, good. Go tell the other crew members," he said, walking out of his quarters and down to the kitchens to get the first meal.

Following him out of his quarters, he went down to the kitchens and turned into the living area for the rest of the crew. "Oleg says the food is ready!" he shouted over the crowd.

Everyone got up in a hurry. In the hustle to the kitchens, Petya got pushed out of the way onto the floor, narrowly avoiding being trampled by hungry shipmates. After everyone was gone, he sat up. Looking down to where he had been almost trampled, he felt his head, a headache threatening to arise from being stepped on. Something felt different. He reached up to his hair and found that it was missing. Where was his bow! Eileen's bow! He searched the floor in a panic. Nothing. He got up and looked around the corners. Nothing! Someone must have taken it!

Petya marched down to the kitchens. "Where's my ribbon!" he said, seething with anger. "Which one of you has it! Give it up now, and I won't kill you!" Petya knew if he was going to get it back, he was going to have to use either threats or force. He hadn't lived here long, but with how Oleg and Misha talked about the other people on board, Lucius knew the crewmates were all hard iron ship men. Force and threats were the way things that would work here, where no one seemed to care about anyone but themselves. The crew members stayed silent, acting as though they hadn't heard him. Why should they take him seriously anyway? He was just a stupid little kid. What was he going to do if they had taken it?

"You mean this?" said up a crewman, trailing the bow through his fingers. He was big, far bigger than any of the other crewmates. "Thought I'd use it for a napkin or maybe a spare piece of toilet cloth."

"Well, it's mine. Give it back!" Petya shouted, attempting to seem bigger than he was.

"Now what makes yeh think I'd do that? You were only using it to hold up that messy hair of yers. I think I would get far more use outta it," said the man.

"Just give it back to him, Luka," said Oleg. "It's not yours. Remember what the boss said. We're to treat him with just as much respect as Boris. So give it back to 'im."

"Da," he said. "We were to take commands from him." Luka sneered. "But only if they came from the boss himself. He wouldn't care if this shrimpy little kid lost a bow. In fact, I'm sure he'd let me have it if I asked. Maybe make the little twerp give it to me himself."

Petya scowled and walked over to Luka. "I'm not afraid of you," he said, eyes turning red with fury. "I'm not afraid to kill you, so give it back, or I'll get it back myself."

Luka looked at him, then burst out laughing. The rest of the crewmen joined him. "I'll tell ya what," he said. "If you can prove yer stronger than me, I'll give yeh back yer ribbon. But if ya lose, well, you have to…" Luka paused, taking a moment to think. He looked over at Oleg then at the rest of the crew. "Then you have to do all my chores for two months."

"Done!" he said, sitting across the table from Luka. Misha ran over to him. "Petya, are you sure this is a good idea? I mean, let's rethink this. How important is a stupid ribbon anyway? If you lose, you'll be the kid that was stupid enough to challenge Luka forever. Don't be stupid, just let it go."

"But if I win," he replied, "then I'll be the kid that *beat* Luka, and everyone will respect me. And besides, he has *my* ribbon. Once I get it back, no one will want to disrespect or steal from me ever again," he said, scowling at Luka as he put his bony elbow on the table, holding up a hand.

Luka smirked and grabbed his hand, putting his elbow on the table across from him. "When you lose, I'm gonna mop the deck with your face."

Oleg walked over. "Luka, that's enough." He looked to Petya. "If you're sure about this—"

"I am!" he shouted, cutting him off.

The cook let out a tired sigh. "All right then. Arm wrestling. You know the rules. Whoever can turn the other's arm down first wins. Are ya ready?"

He squeezed Luka's hand hard, pleased when he saw him wince then shoot him a look of disbelief.

"Go!" Oleg shouted. Petya pushed his fist down roughly, but Luka resisted him. His opponent was very strong but wasn't able to push his hand down immediately as he thought he'd be able to. Petya pushed down harder, and Luka's hand started falling toward the table. He was visibly sweating.

"You're just a stupid little brat!" Luka shouted.

This only made Petya want to win more. He might be a stupid little brat, but he was a strong, stupid little brat. He pushed his palm down as hard as he could, and Luka's hand hit the table with a loud thud.

For a few seconds, the kitchens were quiet. Then Misha was the first to speak. "You did it, Petya! You beat him!"

With a sudden energy, the whole crew erupted in cheers.

Maybe being the underdog isn't so bad, Petya thought, snatching Eileen's ribbon back and tying it around his hair.

Just when he was feeling truly triumphant, Boris opened the kitchen door with a loud slam. "What's all the ruckus!" he shouted. "Petya! Come here!"

Suddenly, he didn't feel that confident in his new victory. He walked over to him, trying to seem humble. Boris grabbed him by the back of his neck and held him to face level.

"My quarters. Now," he hissed, before releasing him.

Petya ran off as quickly as he could. Maybe if he was obedient now, his punishment wouldn't be so bad later. Boris was with him after a few short minutes.

"What's the big idea? Fighting on your first night here!" he screamed, smacking Petya hard on the side of the head before grabbing the back of the neck and squeezing hard, forcing him to look him in the eyes. "If you're trying to get on me good side, you ain't doin' a very good job. I suggest ya be changing that."

Petya nodded fearfully. "I'm sorry, sir. I'll be better, I promise," he whimpered, turning his head away. His nose wrinkled at the smell of alcohol on Boris's breath.

He eyed him suspiciously. "All right, I'll go easy on ya this time. Next time, I might not be so kind." He sneered, throwing him to the ground. "Get up!" he shouted, drunk with fury.

Petya hastily got to his feet.

"Hold out your hands."

He nodded and held his hands up, not knowing exactly what to expect. Boris grabbed them and turned them over a few times. He put the right one back down and inspected the left one with more interest. What did he have planned for him?

Getting up from his seat, he dragged him over to the fire. "No crying, or it'll be worse for you," the drunk man said. Petya couldn't take his eyes off the fire, and he didn't dare ask questions in a time like this. Boris grabbed his forearm tightly and shoved it into the coals of the firepit.

Running water, ice, Eileen's hugs. Petya tried to think of anything but what was happening. Something pleasurable. It burned! It hurt! *Don't make a sound, or it will be worse for you. What could be worse than this!* he screamed in his head.

Then Boris yanked his hand out of the fire.

"Da, you're tougher than I thought," he admitted. "That's enough for tonight. I'd say you learned your lesson, hmm?"

Petya nodded as quick as his neck would allow and heard a grunt in response.

"Off with yeh. The other crew members will show ya where the sleeping quarters are."

Not needing to be told twice, he left as quickly could, running down to join his crewmates back in the kitchen. But by now, everyone was gone—everyone except for Oleg.

"Didn't rough ya up too bad, did he?"

Petya looked over at the large man, hiding his hand, his eyes threatening tears. "No, but he said he might not be so nice next time."

"Da, you were lucky to get off so easy. That man ain't known for his kindness toward others," Oleg said, cleaning up after everyone's meal. "Bring me some of those dishes, will ya? I'd really appreciate the help."

"Oh," Petya hesitated. "I don't know. Boris said I needed to get to bed with the others."

"He won't mind if ya help me first, trust me. Then I'll take ya to the quarters."

"If you say so," Petya replied, grabbing some plates. Grabbing them with his left hand stung more than he could handle, his adrenaline and fear now gone. He dropped the plate onto the floor, wincing at the clatter it made.

The cook looked over at him and then down at the plate. "Slippery fingers, eh?"

Petya gulped. "Yeah, slippery fingers."

"Come 'ere, boy. Lemme have a good look at ya," Oleg said, more stern than usual.

Petya went over to him and dropped the other plate in the sink. He was nervous as Oleg looked him up and down and held out his hand. "All right, give it here. Lemme see your hand." Petya put his hand in Oleg's and watched as he turned it back and forth. "Yeh got horrible burns on your palm! Did Boris do this?"

Petya nodded, glancing at his feet.

Oleg let out a long sigh. "Let yeh off easy, huh? I'd use the term *easy* lightly, but I guess he's been known for worse. All right. I'll fix yeh up. Just sit on the bench over there."

Doing as he was told, he set his hand on the counter. Petya watched as the half-bald man tossed a cold rag onto his blistering hand. Oleg went to get a metal can filled with all sorts of things. Rummaging through it, he found what he must have been looking for. Bandages. He got up again and grabbed a bottle filled with some strange thick golden liquid.

"What's that?" Petya asked.

"Honey," Oleg replied. "Learned from my ma when I was young. Honey will keep the burn from getting inflamed and infected and will take away some of the pain. After we clean it, of course," he said, taking the cloth off his hand and wiping away as much dirt from his palm as he could.

Petya winced. Why did it have to hurt so badly? He had never faced any sort of burn before. This was a new kind of pain, and he didn't find that he liked it very much. After Oleg cleaned the dirt from his palm, he tried to peel off any dead skin that he could.

"Now hold still," he said. "I just have to put the honey on, and bandage it up."

The honey felt sticky in Petya's hand. But it did make it hurt a little bit less. It felt so thick and smelled far too sweet. After the honey was rubbed onto his wound, Oleg bandaged his hand, securing the wrappings with a safety pin. Petya inspected his work, impressed with the man's resourcefulness. He gave him a thankful smile.

Oleg gave him a weak smile back, but then his face turned a little grim. "You know," he started, "he wasn't always this way. You don't have any reason to be understanding, but maybe it'd help if you knew more about Boris."

Petya looked at him quizzically.

The cook handed him a wet, soapy sponge. "Get scrubbing, and I'll tell you. Try not to get yer bandages wet. Just promise to keep this to yourself, eh?"

Petya nodded and started scrubbing with his right hand.

"He ain't a kind man, but you know that. I don't know if he was always as harsh as he is now, though. I met him right before he started this whole captain business, after Luka and him were together."

Petya finished the plates and moved onto the silverware.

"Da, you're pretty quick at that. Could use your help more often," Oleg said, finishing the biggest pot and putting it away to move to the smaller pans. "Anyway, when I met him, his wife had just left him for a richer man, takin' their only daughter with her. And he's only been gettin' worse since then."

Thinking on it, Petya felt bad. He knew what it was like to lose family. Maybe not in the same way, but he imagined it must have felt similar.

"So what about you? What's your story Petya?"

"Huh? My story?"

"Da, that's what I asked. Yeh been awful quiet, except when yer gettin' ready for a fight," Oleg said, bursting out with a loud laugh. "But what about when yeh ain't pickin' fights with the biggest men on ship? Or before yeh hopped aboard?"

"Oh," Petya replied. "I don't know. I mean, I didn't have much of a life before. I lived with my sister and mom in our house in the forest."

"Hmm." Oleg nodded, focusing down on the grime on a particularly old pan. "And this sis and ma of yers, they still live in Germany? That's where you're from, ain't it? You speak it good."

Petya nodded, finishing the silverware and putting it away. "I didn't know it was called Germany until this morning, but that's where I'm from, yeah," he said. "As for my mom and sister…" He paused. "They just…aren't around anymore."

Oleg stopped scrubbing for a moment and looked up. "I'm awful sorry to hear it. Must be hard to lose your family, and at such a young age."

Petya could only shrug. "What about you?" he asked, looking to change the subject.

Oleg let out a hearty deep laugh and scratched his balding head. Then he stroked his rough patchy graying beard. "You wanna know the life of an old goat like me? That's a joke, ain't it?"

He shook his head.

"All right, I'll tell ya. But don't blame me if ya get bored. I didn't always lead an exciting life," he said. "When I was younger, less fat, stronger, I wanted to be a top chef, maybe own my own restaurant. None of this greasy sea slop I serve now. I'm talkin' top cuisine," he said grinning, envisioning his own place and his own business. "But," he continued, looking back to his pan, "I ain't rich enough to get no fine education, and by the time I thought to do it, I was already married, with a kid on the way. If I could do it over, I think I'd plan my life out better before I went on livin' it."

"Why don't you just go back and go to school now?" Petya asked.

"Kid, I know ye ain't never been to Russia, but things ain't always all great up there. It's cold, so cold it'll freeze ya solid. And unless you got schooling or are signing up for a war, there's no place for the poor to go. If ya poor, ya stay poor. That's just how it is in most places of the world, I bet. So when Boris was looking to hire a crew for the smugglin' business, I hopped on, hoping it would at least feed me family."

Petya thought it must be hard being an adult and having to take care of others, along with yourself. "How many kids do you have? Er…family members."

"I got seven kids, one wife." Oleg laughed. "Don't think I could ever handle another. One is more than I can manage. But if yeh saw her, yeh'd know I wouldn't trade her for any other woman in the world. She's a big, thick woman. Strong, busty, and beautiful, but she's got an attitude that'd scare off bears! I don't make it a habit to get in 'er way," he said, chuckling to himself.

Petya liked when Oleg he talked about his family. He seemed really happy, less troubled. Putting away the final dishes, he watched as the man got off his stool.

"Let's hit the hay, kid," he said, leading him down the hall to a series of rooms with several beds nailed and screwed to the walls. "You can have yer pick. Mine's that way," he whispered, pointing to a bed and walking toward it. "Just make sure you keep track of yer stuff. Don't want to see yeh get into another fight, and when yeh wake in the morning, come see me about changing them bandages."

Petya was about to continue following Oleg when he heard a loud "Psst!" He looked around and saw a little tuft of red-brown hair poking out of the covers. When he walked into the room to get a closer look, he saw Misha's green eyes reflecting back against his own.

"Petya!" he whispered loudly. "I saved you a bed!" Petya crept to him as quietly as you could. "I tried to save you a bed before all the good ones were taken. You can have the one next to me!" he whispered noisily.

"Misha, be quiet! You're going to wake the others!" Petya hushed much quieter than his new friend, trying not to wake the already snoring crewmates around them.

Misha pouted. "Fine, fine, you could at least say thank you."

Petya smiled and pulled down the covers to crawl in. "Thank you. I really appreciate it. I do."

The teen grinned. "Tomorrow will be better Petya, just you wait. After we go to the deep ocean, things get pretty repetitive and boring. But it'll be funner now that we're friends!"

Petya tucked himself in. "More fun," he said.

"What?"

"I think the way to say it is, more fun. Not funner. My sister used to always correct me when I talked. Mom did sometimes too."

"Oh, more fun. I'll try and remember that."

"We better go to sleep." Petya yawned, exhausted from the tiring day.

"Yeah," Misha agreed. "Good night, Petya," he said, passing out before he could even hear a reply.

Petya lay in bed, trying to sleep. He thought about his day and tried to ignore the stinging in his palm. He remembered what his sleeping friend had said about their sister. How old was he anyway? Misha didn't look that much older than him. It seemed amazing how much could happen to a person in such a short amount of time. As Petya thought about all the things that had happened recently, he forgot about the pain in his hand and then sleep came easy.

Chapter 10

PETYA

THE CARGO

He awoke the next morning to shouting; everyone was getting up before dawn to eat breakfast. If he thought he was tired, he wondered when Oleg had any time to sleep, considering he had to wake up even earlier to cook the food.

Petya stumbled out of bed and, with a big yawn, tied his hair up and slipped his underpants on. Not having any other clothes, he made his way to the dining hall. He must have been the last one there because it was mostly empty except for a few straggler crewmates. With a big stretch, he found a seat and plopped down next to Misha.

"Hey, wondered when you were going to be waking up," Misha said, taking a long drink of some funny-smelling brown liquid.

"Sorry." Petya yawned. "I guess I was really tired."

Misha handed him a plate of food. "I saved this for ya," he said, looking proud. "Had to defend it from a lot of the other crew members. Food goes fast around here. You have to get your fill early."

Petya looked down at the plate in front of him. Eggs, bacon, and an apple. He tried to look thankful.

"I even got an apple for yeh," Misha said proudly. "In a few weeks, all the fresh produce will be bad, and we'll have to toss it.

That's why it's important to try and get your fill in now when we haven't been at sea too long."

"Thank you," he replied. Petya took a fork and scooped up a bite of the egg. *Deep breaths.* He shoved it into his mouth and, without chewing, swallowed it whole. *Better not to taste it,* Petya thought. This was how he choked his mother's food down back home. Surely it was a transferable skill.

Swallowing the whole meal down without chewing, he gave his friend an appreciative smile. Some of it was easy, like the eggs, but the bacon and apple was a bit more challenging to get down without the use of his back molars. Misha talked the whole time, which was a good distraction.

"You know, I think yer gonna like it here. I was thinkin' after our talk yesterday, even though you technically belong to Boris, when he's not using ya, maybe we could be friends, you and me."

Petya nodded. He didn't want to say it, but he had already thought of them as friends, though Misha saying it was a nice bit of reassurance.

"So," Misha started, taking the last bite of his own food, "you're just a kid. How did you get yourself into the position of Boris's personal slave, huh?"

"Oh, he told me he was going to make me his 'first mate,' but I guess that was just a trick," he admitted, feeling very stupid.

"You must not have any family then. I've seen the boss take other kids as temporary slaves—that is, until he sold them to other people. But he always tries to make sure they don't have a family that's gonna come looking for them first. And always under six or seven."

Petya tried to remember back to their first conversation. He did remember being asked if he had a family. And he foolishly told him that it wasn't important. That *they* weren't important. He felt so stupid! He was so nervous at the time he fell right into the trap. He should be more careful about not revealing his personal details to total strangers. And now he might be sold off to someone else when they landed ashore? It was too much to handle. Trying for a distraction from the panic he felt within, he changed the subject.

"What about you? You mentioned you had a sister and that you came to be a smuggler to feed her. But what did you want to be before that?" he asked.

"I was going to become a painter. I always practiced with whatever I could get back home. When I had lots of yellow, I painted bananas. Lots of red, apples. I think I was pretty good. But you know the situation with my sister. Maybe once my life gets back on track and I got some savings, I could to start an art gallery. Then everyone will see my paintings!" he said hopefully.

Petya listened intently, it seemed everyone on the ship has some sort of dream waiting for them back home, or some sort of dream they had to put aside.

After helping clean the dishes, Petya got his palm looked at. He was amazed by how much it had healed overnight. By the look on his face, he could tell Oleg was amazed as well.

"Mighty fast healer, aren't yeh?" he questioned. "I was sure it'd take yeh weeks to get rid of the burn. But it's only been a day, and yer already almost cured! Yeh will be showin' some scars, though."

Looking down at his hand, it really did seem an awful lot better. That was good. It meant he could get back to work sooner! For good measure, Oleg put more honey on his wound and bandaged it up again, then sent him off. Petya liked Oleg. He was kind, and he seemed to really care about the well-being of others—not like his mom, who he often thought was only loving him because she felt for some reason she *had* to.

Going up to the sails, he grabbed a rope and started helping the other men untie the knots to pull them down. The nice thing about working on a ship was that it was never boring. He did find himself wondering why Boris hadn't invested in a motor to make the ship move faster. Either way, there was always something to do. When he wasn't swabbing the deck, he was stocking ropes, cleaning guns, helping cook, and doing countless other menial daily tasks. As days turned to weeks, it seemed as though there were endless chores. But at least he got to hang out with Misha and help Oleg whenever he could. Jobs involving his friends were always his favorites. But of course, with every pleasant job came an unpleasant one, like cleaning up Boris's quarters every now and again. That was definitely his least favorite. He never knew when the man was going to have his next outburst! He did his best to always avoid punishment, but sometimes he found himself taking punches and hits no matter what he did. Petya quickly decided his least favorite punishment was getting whacked with the belt, though it had never been as bad as the burning. Maybe he only did that to make sure he knew who was boss.

But aside from Boris, ship life was nice! Until the day Luka got sick. He thought it would be a blessing until he realized that with Luka's sickness came Luka's duties, all of which now fell into Petya's hands. Boris seemed the least thrilled with the whole idea as he handed him a bucket filled with cooked meat and leftover food.

"Go down, and toss the meat in the cage. Bring up the buckets down there, and throw the contents overboard. Then wash 'em out real good, and return 'em," Boris commanded. "Nothing else. Yah hear?"

Petya nodded. He didn't really understand all this. Wasn't the cargo forbidden? He didn't feel welcome to go down there, yet it was being ordered of him now, just for convenience. Walking down the hall past Oleg's kitchen, he turned the opposite way of the sleeping quarters. They had been at sea for several weeks at least, and Petya had started to grow hungry again. As he looked around the dark damp wooden hallway, he wondered what could possibly be down here and why no one was ever allowed. It was so dark down here. Luckily, he didn't need to struggle to see. Even though he could go out in the day, he always thought that the night was much more suitable for him.

Much more suitable for a vampire, he thought.

Reaching the end of the hall, he opened the large black door at the bottom of the floor and followed the stairs to the ships lowest level. He expected to see dogs. Dogs ate meat, didn't they? Maybe they were fighting war dogs. Oleg mentioned war once. At the bottom of the stairs, Petya dropped the bucket, stunned at the sight before him.

Children. He looked around at the cages of children. There were three or four cages at least, each with maybe ten kids. No, fifteen! Every kid was younger than six, the same age as him. And the smell was awful! As Petya covered his nose, the bucket tipped over with a loud crash.

The kids all ran to the front of their cages, reaching out for the food. It was obvious that the kids hadn't been getting enough to eat. He supposed that made sense. With him and maybe twelve other crew members, including Misha and Oleg, it would look suspicious if too much food was disappearing.

Oleg! Misha! Did either of them know about this? No, they couldn't! They were his friends! Kind people who wouldn't ever do this!

Petya quickly passed out the meat the best he could despite the awful smell coming from each cage. Some of the children spoke in strange tongues he couldn't understand, but some he understood perfectly.

"Have you seen my younger brother? He looks just like me! His name is Edgar! We were separated. Please! I'll do anything if you tell me!" said a girl about his age. Her hair was messy and red, but it was hard to tell with how much dirt was caked into it. He shook his head and handed her some food. When he got too close, she reached out and grabbed his arm. He felt himself jump as she dragged him closer.

"Please! You have to find him! He's only a little boy, he'll die without me!" she screamed desperately.

"I…I don't know where he is!" Petya stammered, too shaken up to think clearly.

"Promise me you'll find him," she said, squeezing his shaking limb with more urgency. "Promise me! You have to promise me!"

Frightened by her urgency, he yanked his arm away. "I…I'm sorry!" he shouted, backing away from her.

The look on her face was sad enough to make anyone burst into tears as she slunk away to the corner. He knew he shouldn't be talking to any of them, but as he heard her cry, he wanted nothing more than to reach out to her. Now he understood why Boris made it strictly forbidden to be here. He grabbed the empty bucket and the other buckets just as he was told. Above deck, he dumped the brown smelly contents overboard, washed them out, and returned them all in robotic-like fashion.

Upon returning the buckets, he made his final leave. As he walked up the stairs, his mind wandered. What made him and these other kids so different? Why were they in cages and he was allowed to walk around on deck and play pirate? He was supposedly a slave too, yet he hardly noticed it at all. Misha had mentioned that Boris would use a kid as a slave for a time, then sell them. Was he really going to be sold with those children when they finally reached their destination? Did everyone know this, and he was just too naive to believe it?

Petya walked to dinner. This one task having taken him all day due to the burden it bore on his morals. Misha smiled at him when he walked in and waved him over.

"Oh god, you smell awful!" he said, plugging his nose. "You didn't at least clean yourself up a little before coming down to eat?"

Petya looked down at himself. All his chores had left him dirty, and his pants had stains. He hadn't even thought to clean up, being nose blind to the smell after a day of filth. Embarrassed, he immediately got up and ran to the side of the ship, hoisting up a bucket of water to dump over himself, trying to get rid of any evidence of where he had just been. Misha came up on deck to join him, carrying two plates of food. It had become a habit for his friend to save him food. Petya was always late, being the smallest crew member, so he was easy to push around. No. He was the *only slave* above cargo, so they *were allowed* to push him around.

"You look troubled. What's eating at ya?" Misha asked, handing him a plate after he got cleaned up. Petya didn't know what to say. He took his plate and looked down at the contents. They only ever ate meat now. All the produce was long gone. The meat he found, while not ideal, was easier to get down. And didn't always end in vomit. But it still caused him to feel sick.

"Misha? This is under our code, so..." He paused, watching as his friend gave him a funny look. "No telling."

The green-eyed teen swallowed down a bite of overcooked beef before giving him a trusting smile. "All right, I won't tell. What's going on?" he asked.

Petya wasn't sure how to word what was troubling him, but he had to start somewhere. "I did Luka's job today. Boris said I had to. I saw the cargo," he said, trying to just spit it out.

Misha stopped eating and looked over at him. He looked around and scooted closer, whispering loudly, "Really? What is the cargo anyway? I always assumed we were carting around dogs or horses for fighting back in Russia. Was I right? Or was I right?" he said, feeling more than confident in his assumptions.

Petya felt a little relief. At least his friend didn't know the truth. But how didn't he know? He knew that Boris sold his personal slaves. Why wouldn't he know about the slaves under the ship?

"You said you had seen Boris take slaves, then sell them? What do you know about that?"

He shrugged. "It just seems like every time we do a cargo run. Boris takes a kid with him to clean his quarters and help on ship. Then by the time we go on the next run, the kid is gone. He always says that he sold them to a rich family to do their cleaning or something. I assume the same thing will happen to you, but it's not so bad. I mean, cleaning for a rich family? Sounds like easy work, and you get to enjoy the benefits, right?"

Misha was older than him but much more naive. "No!" Petya shouted. Then he looked around. *Be careful, stupid!* he thought to himself.

"No? It can't be that bad, Petya. At least you'll have a home to stay in."

"No, it's not like that," he whispered. "The cargo isn't dogs and horses. It's other slaves. Children slaves. How could you not know?"

"What? Children slaves? How many?"

"At least thirty, maybe more!"

"Whoa, I would have never guessed," his friend said, looking over the sea. "Do you think he took them from families? Or do you think they are like you and his other personal slaves, where they had nowhere to go?"

"I don't know. One of the girls, she was begging me to find her brother, uhh." Petya tried to remember. "Edgar, she said his name was. So they must have families. Misha, this isn't right."

The taller preteen looked down at Petya, then looked at his food. Food that didn't sound so good now. "I…I don't know. I mean, I do. You're right. It's not right. But…I mean—"

Petya grabbed the plate out of his hands. "It's not right, Misha! It's not right!"

"No, no, I know that. I just…this is going to sound selfish. But if I don't help Boris take them to our destination, I won't have any more work, and I won't be able to help my sister and start my gallery. What other choice do we have? Do *I* have?"

Petya felt his face grow hot with fury. "How did you not know this whole time, Misha! How long have you been doing this, been helping the crew? Helping him!" he said, doing his best not to scream.

Misha looked over at him, and Petya knew he had made a mistake. His friends normally bright green eyes were now dark and full of hurt. Even though he was older, sometimes Petya forgot that Misha was still a kid. He was no older than thirteen, after all.

"I'm sorry," he apologized. "It's just…I don't understand how you couldn't have known this whole time."

"Well, I never was put in charge of the cargo. That was always Luka's job. And when we sail into Russia, Boris always lets us off duty immediately. Then a different crew of people are in charge of the cargo we brought over."

Petya grew silent and looked over the ocean. It really was a beautiful night. The stars were so gorgeous and bright in the open sea. With a clear night like tonight, it was sad to have such disappointing news looming over them both.

"I know you're worried about your sister and what will happen if you lose this job, but what if one of those slaves was your sister? How would you feel then? We shouldn't be making money at the expense of kids."

Misha looked down at his toes and leaned against the mast. "I know you're right. But unless you have an idea of how to free them and save the day," he said, waving his hands up in a sarcastic fashion, "then I don't know what you propose we do."

Petya sighed. "I don't know, but I'm sure I'll come up with something," he said, tugging at his ear as he tried to think.

Misha nodded and took his plate back, finishing the last bit of food on it. "I'm going to bed," he said coldly. "This seems like enough bad news for today, and I need to think." He took his plate down to the kitchen.

"Good night," Petya replied.

He really didn't want to hurt his friend, and he knew this was a hard choice to make, considering the safety of his sister. But when he thought back to the kids down there, to that girl asking for her brother, he couldn't just let this happen. Misha didn't see what he saw; he didn't understand. After thinking for the better part of an hour, he went down to help Oleg clean. Maybe he knew something. Putting the dishes into the sink to soak, Petya walked over to him.

"Oleg? Can I talk to you about something?"

"What's on yer mind?" he replied, washing the pan he used to fry up the meat for this evening's meal.

"I did Luka's job today," Petya started, not eager to have this whole conversation repeated.

"Uh-oh, am I about to hear somethin' I ain't gonna like?"

He nodded and looked down. "I did his chores and went down to the cargo. Boris is shipping slaves! Children slaves! And we're helping him!"

"Shh!" Oleg hushed in a panic. "Keep your voice down."

"Did you know about this, Oleg?" he asked, feeling the hot tears rush to his face. He sniffled and tried to choke back a sob. "Please tell me you didn't know about this."

"Shh. Calm down," he said, trying to comfort him.

"No! Answer me!" he said a little too loudly, not wanting the comfort.

"All right, all right!" Oleg hushed. "Well, I knew we was doin something illegal, but I didn't know what."

"Are you surprised?" he asked, wiping away a tear as it rolled down his cheek.

"I'm not surprised. But I can honestly say I didn't think Boris would go this far."

"If you aren't surprised, why didn't you go down to see for yourself?"

"Because I value my life, Petya. I like my head, and I intend to keep it on me shoulders. You've seen that man's outbursts these past few weeks. You know how his temper flares. I don't want him to start spitting fire in my direction," he confessed, scrubbing his pan harder in frustration. "I think it's best you just forget what you saw."

"Forget what I saw? Forget what I saw! Oleg, those are children! There were thirty of them at least. What if one of them was your daughter? How would you feel then? It isn't fair!" he shouted, slamming his fist down on the counter. Petya left a considerable dent in the wood, but he didn't care.

He couldn't believe his friends were such cowards. How could they not want to do the right thing immediately? Then again, they had built an actual life here; they were invested in this life. Petya had only been here a few weeks at best.

Oleg sighed, putting a clean pan away and moving to the soaking plates. "Petya, I know it's wrong. I ain't a fool. I wish there was something I could do, but I got a family back home. Remember when I said this was the only job I could get? Well, what happens when I don't have it? Who's gonna feed all those girls? Besides, life isn't fair, kid. You should just be thankful it isn't you down there."

Petya felt the blood rushing to his face in fury, and he crossed his arms tightly to his chest. Oleg and Misha were only thinking of themselves! But when he stopped to think, perhaps it made sense. It was always easier to care about someone you knew versus someone you didn't. Could he really blame them for wanting to look out for themselves and their own families?

With a big huff, Petya continued cleaning the silverware and put it in its respective drawer. "I know you're worried about your own family, and I understand. I don't have a family or people I have to worry about. So I'll do what I can for them by myself. I don't want to burden you and Misha about this."

Oleg looked troubled by his words and stopped working. "Petya, I really don't want yeh to get hurt. Yer a kind boy, and I know yeh want what's best for everyone. But trust me when I say, yeh just can't save everybody."

"But—"

"Don't start. Listen. I had no intention to tell ya this since it probably won't work out anyway. But I was gonna see if at the end of this trip, maybe I could convince Boris to lemme have ya. Take yeh in with my wife and me girls. I know it ain't a big chance he'll let me have yeh, but it's still a chance. Don't screw it up, Petya. Just take a moment to think tonight while yer tryin' to fall asleep. Hmm? Now off to bed," he said, ending the conversation.

Chapter 11

PETYA

THE RIGHT DECISION

Petya was shocked. Oleg? Take him in? As he headed to bed. Misha wasn't waiting for him awake like usual. He was asleep, turned toward the wall. Perhaps he was angry at him for calling him selfish. The thought of Misha being angry with him made his heart hurt. He wanted to wake him up and apologize for being so mean earlier. But he decided it was best to let him sleep and apologize tomorrow.

What had Oleg been talking about? Taking him in? He couldn't imagine what it must be like to have a nice home, a family that cared about you. He remembered Eileen. Petya could have seven Eileens! Seven sisters! No. That couldn't be. He would hurt them; he knew he would. If he wasn't able to find a safe food source, he would surely hurt them. He needed to eat, *to really eat*. Once every month at least, even if it was only old dead blood. That was one thing his mother had taught him.

He needs to eat *something* once a month.

It had been two months since he had last eaten, and he still didn't feel all that hungry. The only difference he could imagine was the quantity. He had as much food as he could have ever wanted at his last feeding. But the thought of it made him want to cry all over

89

again, so he turned his thoughts back to Oleg. He wanted to have a family; he wanted it more than anything. Perhaps the mother was still having regular periods he could feed on. With a little effort, he was sure he could find some way to work it out. The thought of not having to be alone filled him with a warm, fuzzy feeling he could only describe as the happy sensation of companionship with his sister.

But what about those children? He was sure to get in trouble if he found a way to set them free. Now it was him being selfish. He didn't want to lose the promise of a family, but when he lay in bed, thinking about it, as much as he wanted to be with Oleg, he just had to do what was right. What about those children? No one would stick up for them.

So it has to be me, he thought.

The next day, Misha went down to breakfast, and Petya followed shortly after him. When everyone ate and left to do their morning chores, his friend turned to him. "You know, I was thinkin' last night. I was so mad at you, but maybe you're right," he said, rubbing the back of his head, feeling a little embarrassed. "But if we're going to help them or set them free or whatever your plan is, we have to do it carefully. I don't want to lose my whole future 'cause I decided to do the right thing."

Petya couldn't believe what he was hearing! Misha was helping him! He was glad to know that his friend had a conscience. Overwhelmed with joy, he gave him a tight hug, trying to ignore how good he smelled having not eaten in two months.

"Ow! Not so tight!" Misha gasped, trying to breathe beyond his friend's strong grip. Sometimes Petya forgot he was stronger than most humans. He let go.

"I can't believe you're going to help me! Thank you, Misha," he said, unable to hide his smile. He was so happy. He could have kissed him.

"Do you have a plan?"

"Well..." He paused. "No, not at the moment," he confessed.

"But I do," Oleg said, taking their plates and dumping them in the sink.

Petya looked over at him. "You do?"

"Yes, but we need to talk tonight. I'll explain then. For now, both of you get to yer posts," he said, glancing toward the stairs to the deck.

The two boys nodded and ran to their posts. Misha cleaned and counted the rope and guns. Petya went to Boris's chambers to clean like always—dusting his cabinets, folding his clothes. Maybe he could find something useful in here. He looked around his desk. If only he had listened to Eileen and learned how to read! He dug through the papers, trying to remember the order of them so he wouldn't suspect anything. He found a document and tried his best to make sense of the letters on the top of the page. It was no use, but it was better than nothing. He yanked it out of the drawer, folded it up, and shoved it into his pants. Then he finished his cleaning as quick as he could.

Later that night, after the crew had gone to bed, Oleg and Misha met with him.

Oleg handed them both pots and dishes to clean.

"Best look busy," he said, scrubbing the countertop. "Petya, last night, I was tryin' to fall asleep, thinkin' about what yeh said. And I realized the whole reason I liked yeh so much and I wanted to take yeh into my home in the first place is because you think of others first. You are always helpin' me clean after dinner without bein' asked, and yeh always help a crewmate when no one tells yeh to. So how could I fault yeh for the trait I liked best in the first place? So I decided teh help since I know yeh'll do it without me either way," he said, giving him a small smile.

Petya felt himself grow taller with pride. Oleg thought he was good! "Thank you, Oleg," he said, not used to getting compliments very often. They felt nice. "What's your plan?"

"We should be landin' in Norway in a few days. When we do, the crew will be goin' to stay in town, while Boris and his trusted transporters sort out some of the cargo. I imagine they'll be selling some of 'em and doing upkeep on the rest, which means some of the kids will be going out and the rest will probably be cleaned, fed, and checked for sickness. When they do that, Boris is probably going to want to keep you with him, Petya. You and Luka. He'll try and scare yeh, I'm sure. But you need to pretend to be scared, and you need to keep his attention. Can yeh do that?"

Petya nodded, he had spent weeks with Boris and thought he at least had a decent idea how to keep him occupied.

"Good, Misha, this is where you come in. Yer small, and what's more, yer quick. Quicker than any of the other crewmen that's for sure. I've seen you scurry up the mast to let down and pull up sails, I know you can do what I'm gonna ask of yeh."

Misha nodded and listened closely.

"When Petya is distracting him, you pick the locks on some of the cages and let the kids free. Make sure it's around evening time when Luka goes for his drinks. Then send 'em my way. I'll make sure they go out into towns, maybe families. I got a few cousins in Norway. They'll take 'em in. Do you think yeh can pick the locks?"

Misha grinned big. "I can pick any lock with my eyes closed. My hands are quick, and my ears are good enough to listen to the clicks and taps through any racket."

Oleg smiled. "Good, though I might not be sayin' that too loudly. Remember, you two, the most important part of this whole plan is timing. Petya, you need to distract him between two sales. No doubt we'll be there for five days. The sales will probably be between multiple days. If yeh can get the job done then. Misha, when you get them out, try to make it look like they escaped by themselves. The last thing we need is for Boris to get suspicious and track it back to us. I only wish we knew how many he had for sure so we could know how many it was safe to free."

Petya reached into his pants and yanked out the paper. "I found this in his office. Maybe it'll help," he said, handing the sheet to Oleg.

Looking it over, his face lit up. "Yes, yes, perfect! This is exactly what we need! It says there are thirty-five slaves down below. He has plans for five of them in Norway and twenty in Russia. But an extra ten don't have any plan. I bet yeh he's hoping to sell 'em off on the customers who are buying more than one when we stop. Those ten we can free for sure. But with them, maybe we can free another ten with buyers in Russia. If we are careful. When Boris finds out slaves are escaping, he'll tighten down on security. So it has to happen all at once. After we free them, Boris will probably start panicking and canceling sales. Petya, this is where it gets hard, but only for you."

Petya felt puzzled as he looked over at Oleg. Get hard only for him?

"After Boris finds out the slaves are missing, he'll panic. As you know, that man isn't known for his kindness. He'll probably lash out at you, take his anger on you, hit you, or worse. With that in mind, are you sure you can handle this? Do you really want to do this?"

Nodding, Petya was certain he could handle a little roughing up. His mom hit him every now and again, and he knew what a drunk Boris was capable of. He could handle this if he had to.

Oleg let out a long sigh and handed the paper back to him. "Return this where yeh found it. Exactly where yeh found it, as soon as yeh can. Fifteen is probably all we'll get away with for now, twenty if we're lucky. But after we free who we can, when we get to Russia, we can turn Boris in, tell the police he's illegally trafficking children. After that, finding the rest of the slaves he sold and their families will be out of our hands," he said, rubbing his hand over his shiny head nervously.

Misha and Petya nodded. This sounded like a decent enough plan. The next day, Petya returned the paper before it was ever missed. Three days after that, they docked in Norway. He was amazed. Just like Oleg had said, Boris was eager to hurry the crewmates off the ship. But he kept Luka and him close. Petya was ordered to sleep by Boris at all times. Luka could go wherever he wanted. But Luka wasn't very smart, and Boris obviously trusted him more. Petya felt a little uncomfortable having to be around him all the time. Sometimes the drunk man gave him weird looks that sent shivers down his spine. But one thing stayed consistent as when they were sailing. He drank every night.

"I've been nuthin' but good to you," Boris said, taking another long swig from his bottle. Petya had learned that it was best to stay silent at times like these. "Nothing but good and kind to you, ya stupid little brat. What's the matter? Got nothing to say?"

He shook his head, making extra sure not to look Boris in the eye.

Boris grunted. "You never have anything to say. Wonder who taught you so well. Certainly wasn't me. Yet, I hear you got more than a lot to say to Misha and Oleg."

Petya looked up, startled.

"Yeah, that's right. I know about your little friends. I know how much time ya spend with 'em, and I know what you say to 'em too."

Panicking, he tried his best not to show what he was thinking. No. He couldn't know about their plans for the children underneath the deck? *He just couldn't?* He's not that smart. Is he? Petya studied the man, trying to get any answers he could from his slack drunken body language. He didn't think he knew? If he did, he might try looking a bit more smug.

Boris sat upright and grabbed Petya by his hair, yanking him closer. "But a part of me thinks that there is still stuff that you're managing to keep from me. What is it? What are ya hiding? Hmm?" he said, using the whiskey bottle to trace under his jaw.

"I'm not hiding, sir. I would never keep secrets from you," Petya said with absolute certainty. He learned the hard way that if he didn't sound completely certain at all times, Boris would get suspicious.

Eyeing him, he finally let his hair go. "Fine then. But I'm watching you, ya little shit."

Petya only nodded obediently, eyes fixated on the fancy tan rug under his desk. The next day, the first slave trade went by smoothly. He tried his best to say nothing, to stay completely obedient. One, two, three were sold. But the fourth was the little red-haired girl. Petya watched as she got dragged out of her cage. It was almost enough to set him over. She frantically looked for her brother as they grabbed her arm and roughly yanked her forward. Petya couldn't do anything as they dragged her to her new "owner." While she was being pulled, something must have caught her eye—another little red-haired boy, being pulled in the opposite direction, much younger than her, only four at best.

"Edgar!" she shouted at him.

The boy frantically looked around until he spotted his sister. He reached out to grab her before being yanked out of her view. Maybe forever. The girl cried and screamed as she kicked and fought to get closer to her brother. Petya averted his eyes and heard her new master give a hard smack across her face. He shut his eyes tightly and thought about his own sister. What if they had been in the same situation? He imagined it might go a similar way.

After the few children of the day were sold, Boris ate dinner, while Petya sat and watched. Boris knew what he was, so there was no point in pretending to like the food he usually forced down, only to throw it up in secret later. Boris was eating his steak and drinking more alcohol. Alcohol, alcohol, alcohol, he was always finding a way to shove more of it down his throat. Petya hated the smell of it, or maybe he just hated the smell of Boris.

This was the night he knew that he needed to work on distracting him. If Boris got too smart, then their entire plan would be foiled. Maybe if he could get himself punished, it would be more than enough to distract him. If there was anything he loved more than drinking, it was beating him up; that much was obvious.

"Are yeh gonna be quiet all night again? Yer awful boring," the man said, scanning him up and down in his usual way.

Petya looked back at him. He knew he hated being looked in the eyes. To Boris, it was like a challenge.

He grunted, "Feeling daring today, are we? You hardly ever look at me anymore. Come here, you stupid little shit."

Petya complied, determined not to fight back, only egg him on. If he fought back, it would be unnecessarily hard for him. Boris wrapped his hand around Petya's neck and squeezed very hard. Trying his best not to gasp for air, he stared into his eyes. But as one minute turned to two, he felt himself gasping. His head started to feel light, and his throat started to burn and itch. He could feel his pulse beating in his neck all the way to his head and could hear the noise around him, but he couldn't make out what it was. It felt like he couldn't feel anything other than how much his throat hurt. Two minutes turned into three, and finally, he let go.

Petya dropped to the floor, gasping and clawing at his throat for air. After coughing for several minutes, he finally recovered enough to stand up. His ears finally picked up on the noise around him. It was Boris, laughing. Petya looked at him, and Boris was gasping for air between his big booms of laughter.

He's laughing at me, Petya thought. *He's laughing at my pain, like it's the funniest thing in the world. Well, keep laughing. You won't be laughing tomorrow.*

After finally calming down, Boris looked back to Petya. "Yer face got so blue." He snorted, letting out another laugh. Petya only stared at him, not challenging him verbally, but with his eyes.

"Hungry for more? I almost swear yeh like the pain. You would, wouldn't you?" he said, grabbing Petya's arm.

It was true. Petya did have a weird relationship with pain nowadays. It started after his burn accident. Being beaten again and again, eventually, he didn't dislike the pain anymore. He didn't love it, but it just seemed to be a fact of his life. Maybe he was just tricking himself as a way to escape from what was really happening, or maybe it was from the lack of physical contact he had with others that made it so bearable. He hadn't ever really hugged anyone since Eileen, even though he supposed he could hug his two friends. But he didn't think they really liked to be hugged, and he felt a little embarrassed to ask.

As Boris got out a long sharp knife, Petya tried to remember the last person he had hugged. It wasn't Eileen. No. It was his mom. His last hug was from his mom when he had killed her. He wrapped his arms around her tight so she couldn't escape. Maybe that was why he didn't hate the pain. Maybe it was all just the effects of trauma. Perhaps the reason he could bear the pain was because he thought he deserved it.

Boris slit the knife into Petya's finger, and Petya watched as the blood appeared. Dragging the knife, Boris slowly and surely yanked the knife all the way up his arm and into his shoulder. Petya watched with unfeeling eyes. This only seemed to anger Boris further as he repeated the process on a different finger in a different part of his arm.

"Won't this kill me, sir?" Petya asked, feeling no real fear at the notion.

Boris only grunted. "Doubtful. I've seen how fast you heal. You'll probably heal before morning, dare I say it."

Petya was happy to hear he wouldn't die from this event, but with death no longer a threat, he hardly felt the need to feel any emotion about the events playing out on his arm. The whole night went along like that. Petya felt less and less worried about the pain. Meanwhile, Boris just got more and more frustrated by his lack of fear. Finally, while trying to shove his head in a bucket of excrement he took from the bottom of the ship where the "cargo" was kept, Boris fell asleep.

Coughing as he pulled his head up, Petya grabbed a towel and looked down at the drunk man on the floor. Petya's work for the night was finished. Feeling a wave of relief, he cleaned himself off and slept in the corner of the room. The next morning, Boris went to go and check on the cargo count. Walking along beside him, Petya expected his fury at any moment.

When the cages came up empty, he desperately reached for the paperwork, trying to see if they had sold too many. They hadn't. Luka, Boris, and Petya spent the remainder of the morning frantically searching for how this had happened. Petya discovered that his clever friend had put a rock in the cage and bashed the locks of several of them open.

Smart Misha. Clever Misha! he thought. When he went and told Boris how the slaves "escaped," he was furious just as predicted, kicking and screaming and shouting his dismay for the situation.

Luka ran around frantically trying to frighten the other slaves into staying put. Meanwhile, Boris grabbed Petya by the back of his neck and held him up. His breath stinking of egg, the breakfast he had earlier that morning.

"*You* did this, *didn't you!*" Boris screamed, shaking him so hard he could feel his head spinning.

Petya shook his head no and stared him in the eyes so he'd know he was telling the truth.

"Liar! I should have known!" Boris shouted. "I let you do Luka's job once. Once! I've never had a problem with escaped slaves in all the years I've been doing this. Congratulations, Petya, you just lost your rights above ship," he said, throwing him into a cage of his own and locking him inside.

"I'll see you in Russia." Boris sneered, stomping out of the cargo hold with Luka before slamming the door behind him. This Petya hadn't predicted. He foresaw the anger and the beatings. But he didn't ever think that he would get thrown into a cage of his own. He looked at the remaining ten slaves. Misha had really done a good job. Boris would have to withhold a few slaves from buyers in Russia, but still, it was enough of an impact to make him angry. He wondered if Misha and Boris would know he was down here or if they would try to get him out.

No, don't be stupid, Petya thought. *If they rescued me, it would only get us all in trouble. I hope they think of themselves this time. I hope they stay safe.*

He looked around at all the others; every one of them looking scared—all except one. A young girl with beautiful blond straight hair, who reached out into his cage and grabbed his hand. She didn't speak German, so he couldn't understand what she was saying. But he understood the message. She was thanking him. She knew he must have been a part of this, or she was only looking to provide comfort. Either way, he felt thankful.

After a few nights, Petya felt the ship set sail again. After that, it was hard to estimate the passage of time. It was always dark down here, and he could only tell how long it had been by how often Luka came down to feed them. But he was never fed, and it made sense. He ate people. But he found that by being down here, he was learning a new side of this large man. Not a side he liked. He had never noticed it before, but Luka was not very old. Only being maybe twenty-five or thirty, with dark-brown greasy hair. But that wasn't what he disliked. No, what he disliked was the way he looked at the slaves, especially young girls. He stared at them like he was hungry, but not to eat them, hungry in some other way that Petya didn't understand, the same way Boris stared at him sometimes when he got really, really drunk.

The children were all terrified of him. Even when he held out food for them, none of them dared get close enough to take it. Luka tried and tried again to get one of the children to come close enough for him to give them some food, but none of them ever did. Finally, one of the young boys inched too close to take the food, and in a flash, his hand shot forward. Suddenly, Luka had him by the throat, squeezing tighter and tighter. The young boy choked and coughed and clawed at his hand. The slaves all screamed at him, most likely telling him to stop. But he only laughed. After several minutes, he finally let go. Petya sat there, unable to do a thing to stop the situation. He was trapped in his own cage. But that wasn't what infuriated him the most. After the boy had recovered and gone back to the corner, Luka stared at him and smiled big.

"Just like you and Boris, eh? Little man?" He smirked.

Petya wanted to scream he was so furious. But instead he said nothing, and Luka wandered back upstairs. The next few weeks and then months went by with few other events.

Petya found, with no friends to distract him and no chores to do, his hunger was becoming all the more apparent. His stomach grumbled, and with roughly five to six months between him and his last meal, Petya could feel his eyes turning red more and more often. He had to find some sort of food.

Every time his eyes turned red, the other children seemed more afraid of him. He found himself nearly uncontrollable like this. He was banging his hands against the cage, pacing, growling, becoming more and more animalistic. It was all he could do not to bend the bars with his insane strength and help himself to the delicious smelling bodies of meat in the cages surrounding him.

One night, he heard the children talking. They seemed to be discussing something very important. Petya could not understand what they were saying, but he tried to listen anyway. After several moments of talking, the girl that held his hand crawled as close as she could to his cage, trying to find the words to speak his language.

"You, hungry?" she questioned. Her German wasn't half bad, but it had a lot of weird pacing and pauses. Like she wasn't quite sure what she was saying.

He nodded.

"Drink from me," she said, holding out her hand.

Petya frantically shook his head. He didn't want to hurt her. He didn't want to hurt anyone!

"Will not die. Only take little," she said, grabbing a piece of sharp metal from the broken cages on the ground and cutting the back of her hand with it. The smell instantly flooded his nose. It was almost overwhelming, and he felt his eyes involuntarily flash red. He wanted it. He wanted her. She held her hand out once more.

"Only some," she commanded as he bolted over to her hand and pressed his lips to her skin. He had to be as careful as he could not to bite her. He didn't want to cause her more pain than she had already endured for his sake. He sucked and sucked and sucked. She tasted so good! Different from his mom, but still delicious.

Finally, she spoke up. "That enough," she said, but he couldn't stop. He sucked more. No! He thought. Just a little more, I'm still hungry!

"That enough!" she shouted, yanking her hand away from him with all her might and covering her wound with her other hand, masking the smell of blood. Petya felt his eyes turn blue again and stared at all the small, tiny faces around him. They all stared back, judging him with their eyes.

Going to sit in the corner of his cage, Petya tried to cover his face by turning toward the wall. Never before this moment had he felt such shame. She had offered the blood to him, yes. But that wasn't what made him ashamed. At this moment, with everyone watching, everyone staring, he felt like a freak on display. *A monster*, rang his mother's words in his mind as he shut his eyes tightly and fought the threat of tears wanting to emerge.

Petya wiped the blood from his mouth and tried to pretend like this new turn of events didn't bother him. He looked over at the little girl and nodded to give his thanks. She nodded back. With his hunger lessened, he was certain he could make it to Russia. Surely it wasn't that much longer.

In less than a month, they finally arrived. At least, that was what he had thought.

Boris came down and laughed at Petya when he saw him.

"My, my, you've really gotten filthy down here, haven't you? Covered in your own shit, you're disgusting!"

Petya looked down at himself. If truth be told, he had been so preoccupied with the worry of his friends, and his hunger he had hardly even noticed.

"I've decided to give you one more chance, but this isn't the last of your punishment for your little stunt," Boris said, unlocking the cage and grabbing his arm. He yanked him out and dragged him upstairs.

The light hurt Petya's eyes as they walked onto the main deck. He tried to make the adjustment quickly. When he looked around, he could see vague shapes. Lots of tall crew members, but he couldn't see Oleg or Misha. Oleg was probably in the kitchens anyway and Misha counting rope; it was his favorite job after all.

When his eyes adjusted, he realized he had been wrong on both accounts. Looking around, something caught his eye up above the crew. On the mast, above the deck, were two strings of rope hanging off it. At the end of those ropes were Misha and Oleg, dangling by their throats, dead-eyed, and slack-jawed. Petya stared, hardly able to hear the loud laugh of Boris as he mocked the pain of losing his only friends.

"Ya shouldn't have been so careless." Boris sneered at him. "You were the only new crewmate this year, so it had to be you that set them free. But I had my eye on you all the time, knowing you must have had help. Who else would help a stupid little kid like yourself, except for your two most loyal friends? The nimble-fingered boy thief and the sad chef."

Petya didn't feel rage at Boris's laughter like he thought he would. This wasn't the same as his sister. He couldn't attack him in front of the rest of the crew or they might kill him. He felt only despair, staring up at the bodies swaying in the wind.

He thought back to Misha's sister. Who would take care of her now? Who would send his aunt and uncle money to feed her? By dooming Misha to death, had he accidentally doomed a little girl he had never even met? He thought about Misha's hopes and dreams of becoming an aspiring artist, of owning his own art gallery for people to come and visit from countries all around the world. That would never happen now, he realized, as he stared at Misha's dead green eyes and greasy brownish-red hair blowing in the wind. Seeing his beloved friend's happy eyes so changed like that made him feel like his heart was going to burst. He loved Oleg like he was a dad. But he really felt attached to Misha. He was his best friend, though Petya always thought he might have liked him a bit more than that. Maybe he loved him like a brother.

What was he to do now? He was going to stay with Oleg. It was a slim chance, but still, it was a chance of a future. But with Oleg gone, now it wasn't only Petya who would suffer. Oleg had a whole family waiting for him in Russia. Seven daughters! Seven! Would Oleg's snarky spitfire wife be able to take care of them all? What would she say to him if she realized that he killed her precious, loving husband? What would she say to Oleg if she realized he had died for some stupid little white-haired brat?

Chapter 12

PETYA

FOLLOWING BORIS

Petya barely listened as Boris took him up to his cabin quarters.

"You know, I think you might be the first slave I decide not to sell to a richer buyer. I might keep you for myself."

Petya tuned in softly, trying to remember who had told him that most of Boris's personal slaves would get resold. He thought it was Misha, but in the haze of panic, he wasn't quite sure. Every time he thought of his friend now, all he could remember were his dead green eyes. How long had the two of them hung like that before Boris decided to bring him up to see? Had they struggled? Had it been painful? They were both right when they decided not to listen to him the first time. He should have listened to Oleg and just forgot what he saw down in the cargo hold.

"You're mighty strong, and I think I can use you to make an even bigger profit, especially now that because of you, I'm gonna have to quit the smuggling business. Don't know where you put those stupid slaves, but they're sure to rat on me," Boris continued, not caring if the small grief-stricken boy was listening or not.

Petya felt happy he had at least made it difficult for him to continue his illegal practice. That was the only good thing to seemingly come out of this. At least now, it was over.

"Since you're mine now, I'm going to make sure everyone knows it," the greasy man said, pushing him into his personal quarters. "From now on, you are to stay in my quarters with me. I don't want you scheming with the remaining loyal crew that I have left." He turned him toward his desk and doubled him down over top of it.

Petya hadn't been listening, distracted by what he just saw. He heard Boris rustling behind him but didn't dare try to see what he was doing. He was expecting to be hit with the belt around his pants, as he had done in the past. Instead he felt his own pants get forcefully yanked off him. Then came sharp pain down at his backside.

It was rough, and it burned! He yelped at the sudden sensation of pain. He almost turned around before he felt a hand grab the back of his neck and force his face roughly into the table. He felt a smack up against his hips. He could only compare to the sensation of a spanking. But this was more than that. This hurt more than that, in places he didn't expect it to. Was this the punishment he deserved for setting the slaves free? No, Oleg and Misha paid in full for that mistake. This punishment was for getting two innocent men killed for no reason other than his own agenda. Surely Boris was punishing him for that, for making him lose two of his crewmates and ruining his slaver's business.

Petya supposed at any time he could have forced himself up. He knew he was a lot stronger than Boris, but with recent events, he didn't want to risk his life being taken should he fail to escape. And where would he run to? They were at open sea! It felt like he was experiencing the whole situation from far away. Shutting his eyes tight, he desperately tried to think of anything besides the pain and the situation he currently faced. He couldn't imagine anything good right now, so he wondered about the families of his friends. Where was Misha's sister going to go when his aunt and uncle couldn't afford to take care of her? *Smack.* What was going to happen to Oleg's daughters if his wife couldn't afford to feed them? *Smack.* What was Boris going to do to him once they got to Russia? *Smack.* What would

Eileen say if she could see him now, in this awkward, uncomfortable, embarrassing position?

With a loud, low series of grunts, Boris pulled himself out, and the pain ended. Petya felt his head get released from the sweaty hand and tried to stand. His legs were wobbly, and his backside ached. As he got to his feet, immediately his knees buckled under him, and he fell to the floor. He felt himself throbbing down below and decided he didn't much care for the sensation.

As he turned around, he saw Boris zipping up his fly and refastening his belt. Petya felt oddly numb to everything happening around him. He looked around the room, noticing how everything seemed to be covered in a foggy, hazy layer. Paper cuts littered his chest from where he was pinned to the desk. The doorknob of the room had been polished this morning, and the brass was shining a bright yellow. As he lay on the floor, he couldn't help but notice every small detail in the room around him. Even as the man who just finished raping him dragged his limp body to the fire, he noticed how dusty the iron fireplace seemed to be. Then Boris yanked a metal rod from the flame. Petya saw letters on the end of it, but he couldn't tell what those letters were. It was red with heat. Then Boris pushed him onto his side and pressed the red hot metal to his hip.

Petya felt like screaming but found no voice to do so. Besides, Boris hated when he screamed or more likely loved to punish him for doing so. He shut his eyes tightly again and tried not to feel the burn. Just when he heard himself begin to make involuntary noises of agony, the metal rod was removed from his skin. After it was finished, Petya lay there, not making any attempt to get up, until he was forcibly dragged to his feet.

"Put your clothes on," Boris commanded.

Without another thought, he did as he was told, noticing how difficult and painful it was to lift his legs into his pants and how badly his new burn hurt underneath them. When he was fully dressed, the greasy man yanked Eileen's ribbon out of his hair and the golden ring off his finger.

"Those are mine," he heard himself say dully. It was strange. This was all happening so fast, yet he felt like it was all moving at a snail's pace. He couldn't remember how he had ever gotten himself here. Why was he on this ship? Where was his mother? He felt like his brain was shutting down, and it frightened him.

"Not anymore," Boris grunted. "A slave has no need for personal possessions." He shoved them into a small box and locked it away in his desk.

Petya only watched as he did so, not having the energy or feeling the drive to do anything. Was he in shock? He certainly wanted his things back. He just felt so powerless, unable to get them.

Not knowing what else to do, Petya made to leave for the deck, wanting to start on the chores.

"Where are you going?" Boris said angrily.

"Don't you want me to help the other crewmen with the chores?"

"No," Boris said sternly. "No, you lost that right. For the remaining two days, you are going to stand in that corner, facing the corner unless I tell you otherwise. Do you understand?"

"Yes, sir," he replied, turning to face the corner as instructed. He remembered Oleg mentioning that the man behind him used to have a wife and a daughter. Remembering how bad he used to feel, he looked back on it. Was this was the reason they had left him? He only hoped that Boris's daughter, whoever she was, hadn't had to suffer as he did.

As time went by, Boris worked on the paperwork in his office in silence. Petya thought about his sister and mother. He would have given anything to be back with them. To be away from this situation. But that life was long behind him, and there was no way he could go back.

The remaining one night and two days went by slowly. He had known how boring it was, doing nothing from his time in his mother's house. But never had he not been forced to stay completely still. He found that it was difficult on his legs, especially with the recent turn of events. As he stood, Lucius tried to comprehend what had just happened to him. With every passing moment, it felt like worms were crawling around inside him, down his legs, and up his back from where he was touched. Not to mention the side of his hip burned painfully from the mark he had received hot metal. He wanted to scream and scrub his skin off with hot water. Instead he clenched his fists tight so tight that they started to bleed where his nails hit his palms. Why was this happening? What did all this mean?

With a loud couple of bumps, the ship docked. Boris stood up, tucking his papers into a bag. "We're leaving. Don't make a fool of me, and I will see fit you don't have to suffer too badly."

He nodded, walking over to the smelly man who pulled something unfamiliar out of his desk drawer. It was like a belt, only a lot smaller.

"Hold still," he said, fastening it around his skinny neck. Petya didn't bother trying to struggle and didn't attempt to touch it once on securely. It itched, and it bit into certain parts of his neck. But he had known worse. Boris put a rope through the loop on the collar and attached the rope to a belt ring on his pants. Petya was made to follow him out of his office and onto the deck. All the men had gone already, and a different crew was transporting the kids. Now out of cages, they all wore collars and leashes.

Now I really am no different, he thought. The collar burned his throat and seemed to tighten with every passing moment.

Petya tried not to look up to where Misha and Oleg hung. But when he found he could finally stand it no more, he glanced up, and they were gone. Perhaps their bodies had been dropped off at sea? Maybe Boris only kept them there long enough to show him—to show him what he had done. Walking off deck over to several men, Boris started rambling to them in a language he couldn't understand. It sounded like their conversation was serious. Then the man he was talking to handed him a large wad of unfamiliar money, and they started walking again.

Turning to give it one last glance, Petya knew they were done with the ship, and with the slave children they had transported. He single-handedly ruined the business for him. At least he could feel proud of that.

As they walked through the docks toward the city, he noticed a woman frantically looking for someone. She spoke the strange language, so he couldn't tell what she was saying. Every few words, she did speak one familiar word.

Oleg, he thought. *She's asking for Oleg.* Suddenly, Petya felt like he was going to be sick.

Stopping to rest for a brief moment, he tried to avoid throwing up the little food he had in his stomach. The weight of what he had done falling heavier and heavier upon his shoulders. He never imagined he'd have to see the immediate effects of his actions like this.

"Keep moving!" Boris shouted, yanking on the rope attached to his neck.

"Ggkk!" He choked, trying not to be sick from the added pressure around his throat as he hastily followed.

They walked through the poor areas of town for quite a while, taking only back streets and alleys. Finally, they got to a smallish house. Unlocking the door, Boris dragged him inside. For someone who supposedly made so much money in human trafficking, Petya was surprised to see how small the place was. But Boris also drank a lot and did whatever else he wanted. Petya had no doubt there were plenty of ways to waste money instead of taking responsibility.

Entering the building, he looked around. The whole house was coated in wood paneling and had the ugliest purple-brown shag carpet he had ever seen. It felt crusty and dirty under his feet, like something sticky had spilled and then dried a long time ago. Boris very clearly didn't care about his place very much, because the whole area was an absolute pigsty. Magazines of naked women and children's catalogs from over a year ago littered every table. There were socks on the floor and shoes covered in mud on the kitchen counter. Petya couldn't imagine anyone living like this. His office on board had been so clean. But it had always been him cleaning the room. He never once recalled seeing Boris clean up his own mess.

Grabbing Petya by the back of his neck, Boris opened a small room coated in dust. "You sleep in the pantry for tonight. I trust you not to touch any of the food or try to escape in a country where you can't even speak the language. But just to be sure, I will be locking you in. Understand?"

"Yes, sir," he replied. He was shoved into the small cramped pantry filled with hardly any food except for rice and bottled sauces.

"Tomorrow you will start in the fighting rings. Have you ever heard of a fighting ring?"

Petya shook his head.

"You're strong. I'm more than sure you'll do well. It's held in an abandoned building. They put together two slaves, and they fight to the death."

Petya felt horrified. He was going to kill him? Why even bother dragging him all this way if he was just going to kill him?

"You aren't going to die. Settle down," Boris said, seeming to read his mind. "You're going to fight. I saw you beat Luka in an arm wrestle, and I'm sure you have the means to do a lot more than just that. You'll fight, and unless you want to die, you'll win."

Petya stood silently. He didn't want to kill. Death was starting to become all too familiar to him, and the more he saw of it, the less he liked it. He didn't want to make a living in killing, but then again, he didn't want to make a living in slavery either.

I'm a vampire. Is there any other option for me than a life of killing and death?

"Tomorrow you'll be up against someone new. The new always end up on the bottom, against the other easy opponents unless there are special circumstances. Trust me, a vampire like you will get a taste for it before you even know what hit you," he said with a laugh, locking him into the pantry. "And I'll have a proper cage for yeh when you win. So just endure your sleeping quarters for tonight."

Hearing the heavy bolted lock slide across, he glanced around the room. Had he kept other slaves here? None as strong as he was; that was certain. Maybe that's why he would be getting his own cage. After Boris walked to his own bedroom to sleep, Petya started clawing at his neck. He hated the collar. It itched, it stung, and it choked him. Every time he touched the collar, his hands burned along with his neck where the buckle was, and his arms felt too weak to yank it off. What was this thing made of? He pulled at it and yanked at it until his hands and neck hurt so bad that he burst into tears.

He wished he had been alone to do this when it was first put on. But Boris had been watching him the whole time like a hawk. This made him feel like he couldn't breathe or speak. He clawed and clawed at his neck until red gashes, blisters, bruises, and cuts ran down to his chest. Once he saw blood, he was too scared to continue. Flopping over on the floor of the pantry, Petya breathlessly sobbed for the first time since the recent events.

He cried for Misha, he cried for Oleg, he cried for the slaves he surely got killed, and lastly, he cried for himself. Petya sobbed until he couldn't force any more tears out of his body and struggled to force air into his lungs. After he finished, he lay on the floor and stared at the ceiling. Every time he fell asleep, the choking and burning of the collar was enough to wake him.

Chapter 13

PETYA

THE FIGHTING PITS

The next day, the door swung open, and Boris looked down at the white-haired boy, eyeing his bloody neck. "I forgot that collar had silver in it. I'll get you a new one when we go to the rings," he said, hooking him up to his belt.

Petya had to stand next to the greasy man as he cooked and ate his breakfast. Scrambled eggs and bacon. Boris and his food smelled disgusting, but by now Petya was well used to human food smelling rotten to him. After he was finished, they headed out. Down through the alley, they finally reached an abandoned building. It looked roughly patched up, and inside were several rings and tables. Each ring was made of sand, brick, or wood. Each table had a person at it, collecting money for the fights and wagering bets. Petya looked around as he followed Boris. The roof was leaking just a little, and the floor was made of pure concrete, with a few cracks here and there. In the corner of the building was a cart full of dead people stacked onto it. Those must have been the losers. The smell made his stomach growl much to his shame and dismay.

Speaking to another man, Petya tried to listen. They both looked him over, and he suddenly felt very self-conscious before Boris paid the man a small fee. The man walked over to the corner, and Boris followed, dragging Petya along by the rope attached to his neck.

He watched as Boris dug through the dead slaves, plucking a collar off the neck of one of them and replacing it onto Petya's neck. This one didn't hurt at all, and he took a huge breath as he felt the oxygen return to him, finally able to breathe again.

"Better?" Boris grunted.

Petya doubled over and gripped his knees, nodding weakly as he tried to regain his breath. He never thought he would miss air so much.

"Good, yer probably a better fighter with decent airflow," he said, looking back out to the crowd of people. "There," Boris said, his shorter stature making it hard for him to look over the taller people in the building. "You'll be fighting him," he said, pointing to a medium sized man, about twenty years old.

Walking over to the table, his greasy housemate started talking to a different slave owner. After several minutes of talking, people started coming to the table to wager money. Petya found himself getting pushed around and tossed about till suddenly, the loop came off his collar and he felt himself get pushed into the ring across from the twenty-something pasty black-haired man.

Petya was horrified! He was so much bigger than he expected. How was he supposed to kill a man almost twice his size! Boris mentioned earlier they were both new to the fighting pits. But now this brought him very little comfort. Maybe, since they were both new, Petya would have more experience with killing, but he wasn't sure if that would be enough to make up for their size difference.

They shared a brief glance before his opponent dropped low to the floor with his arms held out, looking ready to tackle him at any moment. Petya looked down at himself, unsure of what to do. He did his best to mimic the same pose. A different man, older than the rest, went to the side of the ring and started to speak.

"Tri!" he screamed. Petya watched as his foe get lower to the ground, eyeing him in a way that made him uncomfortable.

"Dva!" His opponent went completely still and stared at him with determined eyes. Petya paused, thinking about how this man really meant to kill him.

"Odin!" he heard the announcer scream. Petya couldn't blame him. It was clear that one of them was going to die, naturally, he didn't want to be the one to face that fate.

"Bor'ba!" he said with a last shout. And in an instant, his opponent lunged at him, forcing him to quickly dodge out of the way.

Stumbling, the midtwenties man regained his balance and turned as quickly as he could. Petya wasn't sure what to do. He had seen the other crewmates fight on occasion, so doing his best to mimic what he remembered, he stood rigid and brought his fists up. Immediately feeling foolish, he glanced around. No one else stood like that; no one else was fighting with fists.

The man grabbed onto his wrist and lifted him up before pushing him down onto the ground again. Petya felt his breath escape him and rolled out of the way just before another punch came down where his chest had been. He could hear people screaming. He could hear Boris calling him names and cursing him, though he could barely make it out amongst everything else.

I have to win! Petya thought, *Or he'll kill me!* He scrambled to his feet, wishing he was a better fighter as he dodged and ran from the man. He wasn't sure how to kill him! He was twice his size for crying out loud! Petya tried to remember the last person he had killed. Did Oleg and Misha count? No, he had gotten them killed, but he didn't do it himself. He remembered his mother, how animalistic he felt when he ate her.

I have to be like that! he thought. *Turn red! I have to turn my eyes red!*

As the man lunged at him again, he ducked underneath his grip and tried to focus on the smell of blood. He could smell it in the corner of the room from the dead bodies. He tried to think of his hunger, of meat.

Pretend he's a piece of meat! He's just a piece of meat!

Then with a sudden urgency, he felt his eyes turn red. Now it was just a matter of controlling the blood hunger. He focused all his attention on the man chasing him around the ring. Stopping and turning to face him, the man grabbed Petya's shoulder. Reacting quickly, he grabbed his wrist, and in one fell snap, brought his other hand up and roughly pushed it from one side of his body to the other, through the dark-haired man's arm.

A scream echoed through the building as his elbow snapped backward. He backed up and cradled his arm the best he could. Petya stared at him and saw the fear in his eyes. He felt his eyes flicker blue and saw for a brief moment his mother's fear.

I'm going to kill him, he thought. *No, I don't want to kill him! He's in the same situation as me!*

When Petya backed up, his opponent rushed back toward him, seizing the opportunity. Petya felt the back of his hair get yanked to the floor. The man had a fierce grip on his hair with his still functioning arm. His world spun as he felt his head get pounded into the pavement again and again.

Trying his best to reengage his bloodlust, Petya closed his eyes tightly. He remembered how hungry he was, remembered all the blood he had tasted, and opened his red eyes ready to attack. The man was about to smack his head into the pavement again before Petya caught himself with his hands, pushing against the pavement. His head ached, and his arms felt wobbly against the pain. He was stronger than this! He had to be stronger! As he wrestled his body to face his opponent, Petya kicked up as hard as he could. The man shot up toward the roof and landed back in the ring head first, emitting a loud cracking noise. For a moment, everyone surrounding his ring went completely silent. Then loud roars of applause and cheering surrounded him.

He didn't hear any of it. His eyes still red, all he could think about was how hungry he was! And now there was a perfectly good meal sitting right in front of him. He dived down toward the body and grabbed his arm, sinking his teeth into the flesh. *Delicious.*

Petya drank and drank until he felt Boris yank him off the body.

"Not too much, eh? Too much and you won't feel like fighting tomorrow. I need you to stay a little hungry at the least." He laughed.

Shutting his eyes tightly, he desperately tried to regain control as Boris went around and collected the wagers and bets from the fight he won. When Petya opened his eyes, he looked down at the body before him. Not as drained as his mother had been but still very pale. *Monster.*

Leading him out of the ring, they dragged the body off to the cart. Boris attached the rope back to Petya's collar and gave him a hard pat on the back.

"You did good, kid. Now that you got a taste for it, how did you like it?"

Petya stared up at him, feeling a little shocked that Boris was asking him an honest-to-God question about his personal opinion. He felt compelled to reply. "I didn't like it. I mean, a part of me felt so good when I finally killed him. I got to eat! But another part…felt very bad. He didn't deserve that, but it's not like I knew him. What if he had a family or people that cared about him?"

Boris chuckled. "Kindness has no place in this world. You'd do good to remember that. They won't win you any of these fights, and they won't keep your stomach full. You're a monster who feeds on humans. It's past time you accepted it. So if you want to eat, I suggest you keep killing."

Petya nodded. He knew this was something he had to face eventually, but a part of him still wanted to think he was good, that he wasn't a monster, that he was *human.*

"Besides," Boris continued, cutting off his train of thought, "he didn't have a family or people who cared. He was a slave, just like you are. None of the people you'll be fighting really matter. They're all just property and outcasts. So you have no reason to feel guilty."

Petya tried his hardest to convince himself that wasn't true; everyone had someone. But the thought of his meals having no one to go home to did make him feel the slightest bit better, even if he knew it was still wrong in the grand scheme of things.

Walking around the building, Boris inspected the cages as Petya was forced to follow him. "I'll tell you what, since you did so good today, you can pick which cage you'd like."

But he didn't really want a cage in the first place, although he could hardly say that, and just walk off. Better pick a nice one, he thought, trying to make the best of a bad situation. Looking around at the empty slave cages that used to belong to some of the victims of the matches, he thought about which would be most suitable.

Some of them were very big; some of them, very small. He knew he didn't want one that was too big. If they couldn't fit it into Boris's house, then he would be forced to sleep outside in the yard. That, or Boris would just say no and choose for him, taking away his opportunity for at least a little comfort.

After glancing over all the cages, and thinking very hard, he finally decided on a medium sized cage, five feet long, three feet wide cage. It was the same in height as it was in width, but it would only be used for sleeping anyway, right?

Boris looked it over and tested the bar strength before agreeing. "You're gonna carry it home. I know you're strong enough. We'll wait till it's dark."

Petya nodded.

They spent the rest of the day in the pits. He felt glad he didn't have to fight again, but Boris made bets and wagers on several other slaves, winning many, losing some. Mind drifting, he thought about this new life. It seemed like his world was changing all the time. It was hard to imagine that just a little under half a year ago, he was still living in that room with his sister. It felt like a lifetime away now.

And what of the people in the town? Surely they found Eileen and his mom. They must have known what he did. He saw that woman looking for him as the ship sailed away, but did they really know who he was? No, surely not. If the world went by this fast outside his room, where would he be in a year? Or two? It was impossible to say. Even though it felt like so long ago, Petya remembered his sister. He missed her so much, and he couldn't help but wonder what she would think if she saw him now. No doubt his mother would think him a monster, as always, not that he could blame her. But Eileen, maybe she would feel sorry for him. She loved him after all, and he loved her. They were all they had. Just a brother and sister against it all. But perhaps she wouldn't feel pity for him. Maybe she would hate him for what he had become, hate him for killing their mother and for killing his friends.

He wanted so badly to do good, to do right by others. He didn't want to kill his mom or Misha and Oleg. He only wanted to free those children, to give them a chance at a better life. How would he be living now if he hadn't made that one seemingly selfless decision? Would Oleg have been able to convince Boris to give him up? No, it seemed foolish now. Surely Boris had this plan from very early on. Petya imagined he must have thought it up as soon as he discovered his incredible strength.

When the day was finished and it got dark outside, he picked up the cage with ease. Boris led them through back alleys, till they got to his house. It made sense, it looks a little odd to have a man carting around a kid on a leash carrying his own cage. Once they got home, Petya tried his best to fit the cage through the door but stopped when he was told otherwise.

"Put it in the cellar. No one goes down there, and it's only used to store things. Besides, it'll fit through the latch doors more easily," he said, taking him around the back.

Petya opened the doors after they were unlocked, and he squeezed the cage through them, setting it on the floor. It was very dark down here, and as he breathed in, he coughed at the dust in the dry air.

"I will come down to let you out during the day if I need you for something, but other than that, you'll live in your cage."

"May I have a pillow? Or a blanket?" he asked. It was sort of cold, and he didn't want to freeze to death.

"Vampires are immune to the cold. Yeh might feel it, but it won't kill you. If yeh keep fighting well, maybe I'll consider it. Use that as motivation to win," he said. "Now come here."

Obeying the command, Petya walked over, watching Boris as he pulled out a knife. "Hold still," he grunted, turning his body to face away from him. "Yeh got grabbed by yer hair during the fight today. I want to make sure something stupid like that won't be getting yeh killed."

Petya felt the cold of the knife touch the back of his neck and heard the soft sounds of ripping and cutting as Boris sawed off his long white hair with his too-dull blade. Watching as the strands of his waist-long white hair fell to the floor, he felt sad. He rather liked his hair, even if it was a vampire trait. It was just like his sister's. But seeing it all on the floor, it hardly mattered now.

"Now get in," Boris commanded once the deed was done.

Petya had tried to put his cage in a place where he thought would be comfortable. He ended up setting it in the corner as far from the door as he could. It felt warmest there and safest. It meant he only had to keep his eyes trained one way and nothing could sneak up on him from behind. Crawling in, Boris tossed a bucket in after him and padlocked the door of the cage, putting the key in his pocket.

"I'll see you in the morning," he said, turning around and walk- ing up the steps. With a heavy thud and a series of clicking noises, Boris locked the cellar door behind him.

Petya looked around the underground room. It was very dark. Even more so now that the moon wasn't shining in. Was this really how he was going to live? It reminded him of when he was in the cargo hold of the ship, except now he had no company, aside from a few rocks and mice.

He sat in the corner, bringing his knees to his chest. As he felt the bottom of the cage, he was thankful he chose one with a smooth base that wouldn't cut up his skin. For the first time, it dawned on him that he might be living like this until either Boris or another slave killed him. He didn't want to live the rest of his life like this. He reached up to inspect his new haircut. It was short, almost too short. Parts of his scalp were showing and every strand of hair was a different length. This definitely wasn't a haircut for fashion but for convenience.

His hair was so dirty, this place was dirty, and being with Boris made him feel dirty. He still hadn't showered since his time on the ship, and staring down at his hands, he saw that they were covered in blood, dirt, and who knew what else? Petya thought back to what had happened. He thought about how disgusting Boris had made him feel. He didn't want to think about it. He didn't want to think about what happened! Covering his ears, he tried to block out the thoughts that effortlessly flowed through him in his newfound solitude. He had been alone since the incident, but this was the first time he was without a distraction.

Falling over in the cage, he tried to get comfortable lying down, anything to take his mind off what ailed him. *Just shove it down! Don't think about it!* But Petya was struggling now to think of anything else. It was not like he had a surplus of good memories to fall back to. He tried to remember his friends and his sister.

Eileen. What sort of books had she tried to read to him? Petya remembered a book on aquatic life. He remembered how much she loved the funny sea cows. Man-a-toes he thought they were called. Something like that. He remembered her flower phase, when she read books on flowers and asked their mom to bring her home a new flower every day. Petya always liked to touch the petals. They were so soft and so fragile. His sister was always determined to keep them alive forever, but that never happened.

He reached for his hair bow before remembering it was gone. Boris had taken it. Eileen was so happy when he brought that back for her, but she was so scared their mom was going to punish them for it. She was so scared she didn't even wear it the first night she had it. She waited until the next day. His sister was always smarter than he was. She knew how to manipulate their mother's emotions much better than he did. He only served to make her angry, but she always tried to calm the situation. That, or remove herself entirely from it.

Petya couldn't blame her. His mother's wrath was definitely something to be afraid of. Back then, he would have done anything to leave. But now, he missed his old house. He missed his old bedroom, he missed his sister, he even missed his mom. He shut his eyes tightly and covered his face as he tried not to think about the good life that was stolen from him. But he had no other pleasant things to think about. As he sobbed, he gradually felt so tired his body forced him to sleep.

Chapter 14

PETYA

A BETTER FIGHTER

"Lucy."

Petya looked around, surrounded by trees.

"Lucy!"

He turned, and behind him stood his white-haired sister.

"Eileen!" he shouted, running toward her before stopping short.

This wasn't the girl he knew. This girl was covered in blood, smiling. It wasn't her normal soft, gentle smile. This smile was insane, deranged, *hungry*.

"Lucy, she tastes so good." She grinned, taking a step forward.

Lucius took a step backwards and turned around to see his mother's cold white corpse. Her chest was opened up and her ribcage was poking through her skin. It looked like someone opened her up for dissection and left her mangled cold empty body in the woods.

"Eat, Lucy, I know you're hungry. You're a killer. This is no different. You killed her. You killed her for me, didn't you? Or did you kill her for yourself?" she said, voice devoid of emotion.

Lucius backed up, feeling such shame at the sight before him. His mother's head then turned, making a horrible cracking noise as her dead unfeeling eyes seemed to stare right through him.

120

"Monster" she whispered, holding up a hand to weakly to point in his direction. Then, she spoke in a dry hoarse voice. "Monster!"

Lucius turned back toward his sister, who was still smiling and was now walking toward him with heavy, dead-sounding steps. He ran, not sure where he was going, only knowing that he had to run!

"Monster!" he heard his mother scream. Then her voice turned into the voices of many, all shouting the same thing at him. "Monster!" He saw the black curly-haired woman and his mother and sister, all chasing him.

I have to get away! Leave me alone! Lucius thought. As he was running, he noticed strange shadows in the trees and looked up to see Oleg and Misha hanging from the branches.

"Vampire!" they shouted. "Petya's a vampire! A monster! A killer!"

"I'm sorry!" he screamed. What else should he say?

"You tricked us. We thought you were our friend. We had families. Yet you got us killed!" they accused.

Petya didn't know where to go. He just wanted this to stop! He didn't mean to hurt anyone! He wanted to go home! He wanted to be with Eileen! The real Eileen! If only he had known how easy his life was back then before he lost it all. He screamed, hearing his name over and over again, each voice mingling with the next.

"Petya, Petya! Petya!"

"Petya!" Boris said, shaking him awake.

Screaming, he sat up.

"It's just a dream, kid. Get up. We have another day ahead of us," he said, standing up.

Petya panted and nodded. It was just a dream. It wasn't real. Struggling to his feet, he was careful not to fall over. Boris attached him to the leash as soon as they left, like usual.

"Today, I have another fight set up for you. You'll be fighting someone a little older, but much stronger. *And* you'll be making me twice the profit."

He shook his head, still shaken from his dream. "I don't want to fight today. I don't feel good." He whined, grabbing his stomach.

Boris's face went blank, and he looked down at him. "You don't feel good. You don't want to fight because you don't feel good?"

He nodded tiredly.

Boris turned to face him completely and reeled a hand back. Petya braced himself, feeling the sting as he was slapped hard across his face. Then he was grabbed by the collar and held up to Boris's eye level. The scent of stale coffee on his breath was enough to make him want to wretch.

"I didn't ask if you felt good. You'll fight, and you'll win. You ate yesterday, so I know you aren't sick, you little shit," he said, dropping him back down to the floor.

Scrambling to his feet, he tried to stand as quick as he could. He didn't want to get punished beyond a bit of choking. He could always fake sick, throw up just for show. Couldn't he? Before he had time to consider such an option, Boris yanked him forwards, and he was forced to follow him out of the cellar.

Down in the fighting matches, Petya saw the man he was meant to fight. He was big, very big. Over six feet tall at least and very muscular. Was he really expected to fight this man? He looked much more experienced than the boy from yesterday!

Boris only laughed at his fear. "Scared?"

He nodded, finding his tongue-tied in his mouth.

"I would be too if I were you. This man has been in the fighting rings most of his life. But you can beat him. You kicked that other twerp almost through the roof. Just make sure to focus on your strength, and you'll be fine."

Petya felt his knees shaking, he didn't want to do this. This opponent was just too big! He'd kill him for sure! His eyes looked like they had no soul left within, only the urge to fight and kill. Fearing for his life, he knew that emotion all too well; he felt it himself whenever he was hungry. But he had never seen it in another person before. Was that what people saw when his eyes turned red? Did they see dead, hungry, murderous eyes as this man showed to him? He hoped not.

The man stepped into the ring, and his leash was taken off him. Petya wondered for a moment why he didn't just escape if he was this strong and large. Why didn't he just run away? Maybe he was so used to being a slave, he didn't feel comfortable on his own anymore. Petya could understand the feeling. It was the same fear that kept him tied to the collar around his own throat. He couldn't imagine being alone in this strange country, where no one spoke German. He hated Boris, but he hated even more the thought of having nowhere to go, running from the murderous townsfolk.

Boris took the rope off his collar and pushed him into the ring. Petya turned around, facing his opponent, waiting for the match to start.

"Bor'ba!" the announcer screamed, and his opponent raced toward him.

Petya ducked, pulling his arms up to his head, trying to shield himself from any attack. The man tripped over his body and landed on his arms. Standing up as fast as he could, Petya took a whack at his side. It was a weak whack. He wasn't trying at all! All he heard from the man was a low grunt. He knew he should punch harder, but his fear made him feel paralyzed.

His opponent stood up and held his hands out, slowly walking toward him, trying to corner him for an attack. Petya foolishly backed up, directly into his plan. When the man grabbed his arm, Petya bit down onto his hand as hard as he could, ripping out a chunk of flesh.

With a loud scream, the man let go of him and clutched his hand that was now that was bleeding profusely. Petya heard screams and chants of encouragement. Feeling a bigger surge of confidence, he ran toward him, attempting to take a punch. But his opponent stood up and dodged before he could get the chance. Before he fell, he turned around, catching himself. He had to admit, he was a better fighter than yesterday. He felt like he at least had an idea of what he was doing as he took a defensive pose. His opponent did the same, trying to decipher his next move. He was smart, so Petya had to be careful, or his next move could be his last if it was predicted properly.

He looked around, then spotted the man's left leg. His ankle had a slight bump in it. No doubt he had injured it before. A weakness! He could exploit that weakness! Then looking up at his opponent, he noticed that he was overcompensating for his past injury. He leaned most of his weight on the right side and made sure to overly defend his left ankle to decrease the chances of attack to that area.

Deciding what to do in an instant, Petya ran toward his opponent, and just like he predicted, his left leg vanished behind his body in defense. The man reached toward him as he ran, bending his right knee and getting low to the ground for a better defensive position against his past injury. It made sense. Petya was short. It would only be natural for him to attack from below. That was why he decided to attack from above instead.

As the man leaned low to grab, holding his left ankle behind him, Petya jumped up and kicked the man in the face. He knew his opponent would expect him to go for his obvious weakness.

With a kick to the face, he fell onto his back. Petya turned in the air and landed, one leg on each side of his opponent's stomach. He grabbed the man's right leg and yanked it up to his chest. With a loud crack, the man let out a horrid scream. Petya punched his fist through the man's leg, breaking the bone and causing it to break through the skin. The smell of blood instantly turned Petya's eyes red with hunger.

"Finish him!" Boris screamed. "Kill him!"

He felt his stomach gurgle. The more blood he ate, the more he wanted. He shot up and stepped on his opponent's chest. He grabbed ahold of his arm and yanked it from its socket. Then he dropped down on top of him and sank his teeth into the crook of his neck. He felt his opponent try to yank him off, but he was losing blood. As he clawed at Petya, he could tell that the man was getting weaker and weaker with every passing second until he fell still and Petya no longer felt the pulse in his neck through his teeth. He had won.

The crowd let out a loud roar, Boris was screaming in delight louder than all the rest, as he collected every wager. Maybe now, Petya could get a blanket. Boris yanked him out of the ring once he had collected all his money.

"Yeh did great, kid! I can't believe yeh actually did it! I knew you could, but it's still incredible! Breaking his legs that smoothly? I've been giving you opponents too easy!"

Petya started to feel dizzy. Boris was roughly shaking him and the screaming wasn't helping. The adrenaline finally slowing down, he really did feel sick. He leaned away from Boris and threw up a good portion of the blood he just drank onto the floor.

"Guess you weren't lying about feeling ill. If you can fight that good while sick, imagine the profits you'll bring at full strength!" He laughed.

Petya said nothing, trying to catch his breath after throwing up. Boris tugged him along despite it. Yanking him to and from every fight to make wagers. But never forcing him to fight again that day.

On the way home, he finally felt enough courage to ask. "I won today. Can I have a pillow?"

Boris grunted and looked down at him. Petya imagined he was a very sad sight, still partially covered in his own bloody vomit, not to mention the blood he had from his last kill. His pants were without a doubt completely ruined, not that it mattered.

"Fine," he grunted. "I'll get you one after I clean you up."

Upon arriving home, he led him into the backyard and tied his rope leash to a rusty nail on the wooden fence.

"Hold still," he said. "And stay there."

Obediently, he complied as Boris walked off to get a bucket filled with water. Upon returning, he held Petya's arms out to both sides and dumped the water over his head. It was freezing! Just like the rest of the climate in Russia. The process went on, bucket after bucket until finally, Petya seemed at least halfway clean. The blood from his pants was faded, and the dirt and vomit on his skin was gone. He still smelled, because he didn't have any soap. But he didn't smell as bad as before. He imagined Boris probably wanted him to smell as a reminder of what he was. A slave.

"Get to the cellar," he grunted, untying his leash. And he happily obeyed.

It was freezing out here in the yard past dark. After a few minutes alone in his cage, Boris came down, carrying a big heap of cloth. He dropped them in the cage, and Petya realized it was a towel, two blankets, and a pillow.

"That should be enough for now," he grunted. "Use the towel to dry yourself, then set it out, or else it will stay wet all night. If it stays wet, you can't use it to dry yourself should I decide to clean you tomorrow."

"Yes, sir," Petya replied, doing as he was told.

"Yeh did good today, kid. Get some sleep and get better for tomorrow. I'm not making enough money if I'm fighting with a sick little brat," he said, walking up the steps and closing the doors behind him.

Petya finished drying and set the towel out to dry as he had been told. As he started taking off his pants to dry but thought better of it. What if Boris came down to wake him up and saw him naked? He didn't want to tempt him into committing more unwelcome sexual acts.

Fluffing the pillow and setting it at the end of his crate, he laid one blanket on the floor and one over top of him. Sleep came much easier tonight.

Chapter 15

PETYA

THE UNWELCOME COMPETITOR

The next day, Petya woke on his own, feeling much better. His stomach didn't hurt, and he didn't have any nightmares. He didn't have any dreams at all actually. About an hour after waking, Boris came down.

"You look like you're feeling better," he said.

Petya nodded and tried to give a little smile.

Boris laughed. "Yeh look ridiculous when you smile. Your sharp teeth show through, like a mutt."

Petya stopped smiling and covered his mouth. Did he really look like a dog? Unlocking his cage, Boris yanked him out. "I'm glad yer feeling better. We got another day of fighting ahead of us, and yer going to make me a lot of money today. I dare say you'll make me more profit this year than any year I made in the trafficking trade," he said, giving a small delighted chuckle.

The next three years went on just the same. Petya was very obedient and fought a new person every day. He was amazed, as many people as he battled, they never ran out of opponents for him. Sometimes they would call off the fight before he could completely kill them, and then he would end up fighting the same person twice, but it was very rare.

Boris had been right. He did make a ridiculous amount of money, so much so that sometimes he allowed Petya to take a week off. But those weeks were always very boring. His housemate still went out for activities, while Petya was stuck at home alone in his cage. He didn't like solitude. He hated the ringing in his ears from the quiet. However, after complaining about this enough times, he was finally allowed to have a small rubber ball to play with. It wasn't much, but at least he could roll it around or bounce it. It had been a very uneventful three years, filled with nothing but violence and solitude. He no longer tried to act out. He had no more reason to fight with Boris because he had no friends to bother trying to protect.

Petya had grown almost a foot taller with Boris and was just over ten he guessed. It was in the middle of winter and very cold. However, just as Boris had said, the cold didn't really bother him. It might be uncomfortable at times, but he never felt like he would freeze. He never even shivered. Vampires were immune to cold.

The only thing Petya really felt he had accomplished during this time for himself was that the immersion in this new country helped him to really learn the Russian language. Now there really was nothing stopping him from leaving. But why leave? He didn't know when or how he would be able to eat if he left, and he didn't know where he would go. Besides, what if Boris somehow managed to find him?

So he remained in the fighting pits and never lost a match. He had to admit, there were a few times he had come uncomfortably close. Someone might have broken his hand, his arm, his leg. One even managed to rip off some fingers on his right hand. However, Petya was amazed when his fingers started to grow back much like a tail grew back on a lizard.

Were vampires really that difficult to kill? Petya wondered what his weakness might be if any. Surely there had to be a weakness that could be used to kill someone like him. Boris had said he was immune to the sun because he was only *half* a monster, which made him all the stronger. The only weakness he knew was to silver. It burned him worse than fire did. Fire hurt, sure, but it never stung and burned as badly as silver did when he touched it. And silver didn't seem to hurt anyone else from what he had gathered.

As they headed down to the abandoned building toward the fighting rings, Boris quaked in the cold. In the middle of winter, it was freezing at the dawn of morning. Boris had on layer after layer of sweater and winter coat, along with thick boots to insulate his feet from the snow. Meanwhile, Petya had none of that. All he wore was a pair of very dirty, growing-too-small pants, the same ones he started with.

Even so, he liked the feeling of the snow under his bare feet. It was cold, yes, but it was also soft and fluffy. He liked the way it felt when it melted and how it felt when it landed on his face. It was like being kissed by tiny little fairies, that melted away and flew off before they could be seen. Petya enjoyed the winter more than most despite his occasional discomfort to the extremities of the weather.

As he looked up at the bright orange of the sunrise, Petya closed his eyes. He could feel the sun shining down through the gaps at the top of the street where the buildings spaced. This was always his favorite part of the day. The part before the violence. It was so peaceful, if he ignored the tugging at his collar. He could hear the small birds chirping, and feel the fresh air of the outside. It seemed as he got older Petya was allowed to be outside less and less. So during the time he was allowed to be outdoors, he made sure to fully enjoy himself. But like always, just as he began to feel truly happy, they arrived at their destination.

As they entered the building, he looked around at the lack of people. Winter was always the slowest time for fighting. New shipments of people were always being brought in by human traffickers, but during the winter months, the ships couldn't break through the ice to make many deliveries. So it was slow until spring in a few months.

Still, Boris was greedy, and his spending habits were high. As Petya walked through the building around the sandbag circles, he tried to guess whom he would be fighting today. Most of the men were gone. So he would probably be fighting a woman today. He wasn't a fan of fighting women. Whenever he won, people would scream at him and Boris that fighting girls against boys was an unfair fight.

Boris let Petya off his leash and led him to the sandbag circle, then turned him to face him.

"We're trying something different today." Boris shivered, rubbing his hands together in an attempt to warm himself up.

Petya tilted his head and gave him a puzzled look. He tried never to speak to him anymore for fear of saying the wrong thing. A look was usually enough to get his point across.

"Don't give me that look. It'll be easy. Yeh won't even have to fight. Just make a show. People love a good show," Boris said, removing his hat once his body temperature started to rise.

Petya didn't know what he meant. Give them a show? Wasn't the fighting pit always a show? At least, that was what it was for the slave owners and the viewers. Why would this fight be so different? And what did he mean he wouldn't be fighting? Wasn't that why he was here?

Boris continued speaking at length. "No one here is strong enough to fight yeh, and no one wants to put one of their mediocre fighters up against yeh since it's obvious you'll win. So I worked out a little thing. See, I bought a slave from a friend of mine. There is no way they'll be able to beat you with your strength and all. However, people are paying good money to watch you beat the shit out of 'em to kill and eat them. I don't know why, but people seem to get really excited by the fact that yeh eat all your opponents. I think it's disgusting."

Petya was stunned. He was going to fight someone? And they wouldn't even fight back? He didn't want to do this. It didn't seem fair! He can't just take the life of someone who wasn't even trying to beat him. This was too much. This was too far! Behind him, Petya heard a loud thud of skin hit the concrete floor of the fighting ring. Turning around, he was stunned at what he saw.

A little girl, the same age as him, with beautiful blond straight hair, although it was fairly muddy. She had her hands tied behind her back and her mouth bound and gagged. She tried to scream, but nothing came out. Looking at him, her eyes filled with fear and sorrow.

Petya recognized her instantly. It was the little girl! From the ship! She held my hand! I drank her blood! He turned, feeling immediately disgusted. How could they expect something like this from him? Fighting was one thing, but killing and torturing an innocent tied-up girl for the pleasure of viewers just because business was slow was another. When he looked into her frightened blue eyes, he saw Eileen.

Boris scowled when he turned away. Everyone was surrounding the sand pit, yelling and screaming. "Kill her! Rip her hair out! Cut her leg off!" And other horrible methods of torture and violence.

"No," Petya said, and Boris's face twisted into an ugly look of rage. He grabbed Petya by the back of his neck and brought him uncomfortably close to his face.

"Don't make a fool of me, boy. Do as the crowd says, you little shit. Or you'll be punished for it, I swear on my life. You will feel pain and humiliation like you've never felt before."

For the first time in three years, Petya felt truly strong. Strong enough to stand up for himself. "No! I won't!" he screamed.

Boris was clearly furious, grabbing Petya's wrists and shouting for help. Several of his friends and gambling companions grabbed his wrists as well and held them still and tied them together. Petya didn't resist and only scowled at Boris, staring into his eyes the whole time.

As he was pushed into the ring, hands tied up. Petya stared harder. "You know this is wrong, Boris. Fighting and slavery are wrong, but killing an innocent girl who can't even fight back? I don't know why I expected more from you."

"Shut up," Boris said, waving at the others to re-cage the girl.

"Didn't you have a daughter? What would you do if it was her I was up against? Would you have me kill her if it was good for profit?"

Boris's head snapped around. "Who told you about her? It was Oleg, wasn't it? Fool, I knew I shouldn't have shared that with anyone," he said, ripping his belt free from his pants and balling it around his fist.

"You and Oleg were friends, weren't you? How could you kill him."

"Oh, so three years later, you decide to finally find your voice? I thought I had broken you. Well, when I'm done with you, you won't ever feel the need to speak or disobey me again!" he screamed, swinging the silver buckle of his belt around and whacking Petya in the face.

It knocked him over and stung worse than any bee sting. The sharp edge of the belt hit him so hard that it left a cut across his eye that was quickly starting to swell. He quickly turned onto his stomach before the next hit could come. It landed on his shoulder, and Petya held back a scream, the belt breaking skin again.

Boris never used the buckle to beat him before, only the leather. He couldn't believe he had never noticed that his buckle was made of silver and now wished he had paid better attention. Not that it would have done him any good anyway. With every whip and whack to his back and sides, Petya refused to scream. He wouldn't let Boris have the satisfaction. He didn't want him to feel any glory from this.

But as he predicted, this only served to make Boris angrier. As he was whipping and beating him, Petya closed his eyes and thought back to his friends so long ago. He thought about the kids he had saved from slavery and how proud his friends were that he was willing to risk his life for the sake of others. It occurred to him then. He didn't kill Misha or Oleg.

Boris killed them. It was him; it was all him. Boris was the human trafficker, Boris was committing the crimes, and Boris had killed his friends. It all felt so clear now. He couldn't believe he had blamed himself for so long. Boris was cruel. Oleg was right. Maybe he had been kind once. But that time was long ago, and that Boris was past dead.

Finally, the lashes quit from exhaustion. Boris's hands clutched his knees as the overweight man tried to catch his breath. Petya stood up, and Boris strode over to him, leashing him and fastening him to his belt. Petya was shaking with rage but fought the urge to kill him. Not here. Not now. Not surrounded by enemies. He hung his head low in an attempt to look sorry, but in reality, he didn't want anyone to see his eyes rapidly trying to turn red. Petya fought it with all his might as Boris dragged him through the snow back home.

Going down into the cellar, he allowed himself to be tossed back into his cage. "Yer done for today, maybe even done for the week. Just sit down here in your little cage, and think about what yeh should have done," Boris said sternly, his voice filled with anger and frustration at Petya's earlier disobedience as he walked up the cellar steps, closing the door.

He sat in his cage for a good hour, trying to bandage up his wounds with his sheets the best he could. Ripping them up, he knew wouldn't need them anymore since he was determined to leave tonight. He had enough. He was sick of Boris blaming everything on him as though he weren't committing his own terrible acts. He was sick of blaming himself for what Boris had done to his friends and what he had been made to do to those innocent people.

After waiting a few hours, Petya felt certain Boris was asleep in his bed in the upstairs. He grabbed the bars of the cage and easily bent them open. He could have done this any time, but only now did he realize he couldn't stay here any longer. He had accepted the truth of things, and he needed to escape, now that he was no longer plagued with guilt.

Walking to the cellar door, he pushed against it. Locked, as usual. He looked around for something he could use to quietly open the door, but Boris had taken everything and anything useful out of the cellar over the years he had been sleeping down here.

Pressing his ear against the door, he knocked on it up and down the crack between the two, trying to find where the lock was holding the door shut. Finally, he heard the clunk of the metal lock on the other side. Petya knew where to aim. He punched through the door where the lock was held and ripped it off. It caused a lot of noise, and he stood completely silent for a moment while he listened for any signs of Boris coming down to investigate. Inside the house, he heard no footsteps. Safe. For now.

He opened the door as gently as he could, picked it up, and set it back how he had found it. The hinges made a terribly loud squeak. Everything sounded loud when you were trying to be quiet.

Carefully, he made his way around to the back door of the house and jiggled the handle. Also locked. Punching this one was too risky. Boris was inside, and he knew he would surely wake if he heard his house door open.

Petya looked around the yard. A bucket? No, that wasn't useful. Some laundry? Probably not. A workbench with a hammer and some nails? He could work with that. Petya grabbed the hammer and one of Boris's shirts off the laundry line. He went to the handle and wrapped the shirt around it as many times as he could. Then in one swing, he hammered the knob off the door.

As the knob on the other side fell, Petya reached through the hole as fast as he could and grabbed the knob on the other side. It was a very close save, and he felt very thankful for his small nimble hands. Petya pushed his way through the door and put the knob on a nearby table. Time to find that bastard!

He walked on the balls of his feet, trying his best not to make any noise. He heard snoring in the room down the hall and cautiously stalked down the hallway. Peering in, he saw the man lying on his back. He moved in closer and, in an instant, pounced on top of him and wrapped his hands around his fat neck.

Boris's eyes shot open, and he stared at his killer. "Pet...ya!" he gasped, struggling for air and clawing at his hands.

Petya's rage took control of him, and he squeezed tighter. "My name is Lucius!" he screamed.

Boris gasped and clawed for what felt like hours, even though in reality it was only a few minutes at best. Petya squeezed even harder and watched as his owner's eyes rolled into the back of his head, but he didn't let go. After holding on a few minutes longer just for the satisfaction, Lucius finally released his grip.

For the first time, he felt no desire or urge to eat. Boris was disgusting. He didn't want his blood anywhere near him. Hopping off, he scrambled to look for his old belongings. He ripped open drawers, tore up cabinets. But he couldn't find the small box he was looking for.

Thirty minutes and a destroyed house of searching finally led him to a hidden compartment under the desk. He opened it and sighed a big breath of relief to see his red ribbon and golden ring. In the box was also a fair amount of money. Money! Boris had to keep all his money somewhere! This was just a few simple rubles; it wouldn't last him long enough to leave this horrid place.

After tying his ribbon around his head and putting the ring on his pinky, Lucius started digging through the desk for more cash. It had to be somewhere. Finally, in the kitchen drawer, he found a huge wad of cash. It must be all Boris had, as he wasn't known for his saving techniques. He ran out into the yard and looked down at himself. He still looked like a slave, wearing ratty pants and nothing else. Thankfully, there were still clean clothes on the line.

He grabbed a long-sleeved black T-shirt. It was very big but would do for now. The jeans, however, were just too big. Lucy kept having to pull them up, and when he did, they would only fall back down to his knees. He turned and waddled like a duck back inside to the dead body in bed. He looked around the bedroom and found the days clothes in a heap in the corner and his closet door wide open. Digging through the clothes on the floor, he found the belt and put it through the belt loops in his new pants. He was very careful not to let the buckle touch him, but it wasn't difficult since it was on top of the pants. Then, going to the closet, Lucy picked out a nice pair of boots to wear and also a coat. The boots and coat were both made of leather and a bit too big. Everything was too big.

After getting comfortable in his new clothes, he put the rubles in his coat pocket and left the house, happy he would never have to see the dreaded place ever again.

Chapter 16

LUCIUS

A New Friend?

Lucius shuffled through the cold. The snow building up in the streets as he trudged as far away from the slave rings and Boris as he possibly could. He was very thankful he had stolen clothes to wear. Even though he liked the cold, now that it was the middle of the night, he wasn't sure he liked it *this* cold.

With snow flying into his face at what felt like one hundred miles an hour and winds that seemed to blow through his layers, Lucius ducked behind a large house and rubbed his hands together to try to generate any sort of warmth. It was so dark in the city at night. He had moved neighborhoods at least four or five times since he left, but he couldn't find anywhere to stay. As he moved farther and farther from Boris's small shabby home, he found the houses kept getting bigger and nicer.

"Psst! Hey, kid," said a man in Russian, standing behind the building. He was dressed in thick, warm clothes, standing by a back door.

Lucius turned. "What?" he barked, feeling grumpy due to the snow melting through his boots.

"You look really cold. What's your name?"

"Pety—" he started before realizing, *No, that's not right.* He was his own person now. "Lucius."

"Lucius, that's an interesting name. What are you doing out in the middle of the night?"

He smiled and let out a little laugh. "I could ask you the same thing."

The warmly dressed man held up the cigarette. "It's a nasty habit, I know. But I couldn't fall back asleep unless I had one. My name is Adrik."

Lucius turned toward him cautiously. "It's nice to meet you, Adrik."

"Do you need a place to stay for the night?" Adrik asked.

"What's in it for you?" he questioned. Lucius wasn't a stupid little boy anymore; he had learned the hard way that nothing came free from strangers. You should never expect someone to give you something for nothing.

"In return, you can come with me tomorrow. You have nowhere to go, right? I have a group that would love to meet you."

Lucius wasn't about to fall for that trick twice. Traveling with strangers was what got him into slavery in the first place! Still, the temperature was rapidly dropping, and he felt his body beginning to sag with exhaustion. "Where I go is none of your business. But if you give me a place to stay, I'll follow you to your 'group.' But the second I smell trouble, I'm gone."

Adrik laughed. His laugh wasn't hard and heavy like Boris's but rather lighter and softer. Everything he said was in a soft gentle voice, like talking to a cat. "You are awful suspicious for a little kid, aren't you? I'm not going to hurt you. But sure, come in if you want, and if you want to leave tomorrow, feel free," he said, snuffing out his cigarette and opening the door to walk inside.

Lucius followed, suddenly thinking he should have taken a knife from Boris's house to defend himself with. Unzipping his coat and taking off his hat and mittens, Lucius noticed that Adrik was extremely tall and inordinately skinny. His hair was a sleek blond color, which hung to his shoulders, and his eyes were a dark brown.

Adrik led Lucius to a spare bedroom. As he looked around, he noticed the whole place was kept ridiculously clean and organized to a fault. He owned lots of shelved books all in alphabetical order by genre. And even though he was a smoker, his house didn't smell at all of cigarettes. He could tell this man was much different than Boris, but he still didn't trust him. Not yet.

"This will be your room for tonight," Adrik said, leading him to the guest bedroom.

Poking his head in, he eyed the room left and right. "Thank you," he said, cautiously walking in.

The man laughed. "Still don't trust me? That's fine. I sleep in the room across the hall, so if you need anything, don't be hesitant to ask. I'll see you in the morning, yeah?"

Lucius nodded and closed the door. Immediately after closing the door, he listened to his new housemate quietly walk away. Everything about him was catlike. His quiet talking, walking, his neat and perfectly organized home, even his tall and skinny frame somehow seemed to resemble that of a cat. It made Lucius uncomfortable. He was used to loud, heavy-walking sailors with bad breath.

Turning, he took off his clothes, except for his ring and his bow, and crawled into bed. It was so soft he instantly felt himself melting into the mattress. No! He had to stay alert! He was in a strange man's house! He tried to stay focused on his surroundings. Blue wallpaper, white carpet. The warm heat vent. The ceiling fan above going around from the draft. The creamy yellow colored blankets. They were so heavy, and the mattress was soft, sweet, and comfortable. Before Lucius could think much else, he had drifted into a deep slumber.

Waking the next morning, he sat up in a panic. He had fallen asleep! As fast as his body would allow, he hopped out of bed and dressed himself up. Then he bolted out the door to look for Adrik.

The man was standing in the kitchen—in a suit?—cooking eggs and bacon for breakfast.

"Good morning, Lucius," he said, smiling. "Want some breakfast?"

He shook his head. "Why are you wearing a suit?"

Adrik gave him a puzzled look and glanced down at his clothing before he started to laugh. "No, no, this isn't a suit. These are my pajamas. They're black, yes, but they're only silk pajamas."

Lucius had never heard of silk pajamas before. It seemed much more comfortable to just go to sleep naked, but he didn't say that.

"Please, sit, sit. I have breakfast almost ready."

"I said I'm not hungry," Lucius persisted.

"Fine, fine. Suit yourself. But you should sit. I still have to eat despite your lack of hunger."

He sat down. The table was made of fancy dark wood, and the chairs matched perfectly. Everything this man owned seemed to be of some level of elegance. Yet the house itself seemed very empty, like it had been built for only one.

The man sat down and ate quietly, chewing with his mouth closed—yet another difference between him and Boris. It seemed silly to compare the two at all. It was like they were both completely different creatures altogether. Boris was a huge ugly bull, and Adrik was a sweet, sleek, loner house cat. It all seemed very odd.

"Do you have any family?" Lucius asked, thinking the answer was probably no due to his living conditions.

"No, I live alone," Adrik confirmed. "I was never lucky enough to find that special someone. But believe me, I looked." He smiled. "I guess I was just too stubborn to change my ways for another person. Sometimes, I think it's no one's fault but my own. But that's okay. I'm happy living alone. It's quieter this way."

Lucius nodded. He really did like the quiet. He was very used to that sort of environment from his time spent in the cellar. The lack of noise was somewhat comforting to him. No, comforting wasn't the right word. *Familiar* was more accurate.

Lucius looked around the house. It wasn't as little as Boris's, but this was a nicer part of town. This house had two bedrooms, an office, a nice big kitchen, three bathrooms, a dining room, and a basement that didn't require an outdoor trip to get to. Not to mention it was heated. That must have been nice. The walls of the dining room were painted a nice pastel green color. In fact, all the walls were pastel of something or another. It gave the whole house a very light and airy feeling, like you were living in a dream. Looking up at the light, he saw that it was actually a small chandelier of lights. Little light bulbs were hanging on a brass chandelier above the table. He had never seen anything so glittery and beautiful.

"Like the lights?" Adrik said when he noticed his staring.

"Oh, yes. They're very pretty."

He smiled and looked up at them. "I think so too."

Trying to focus back on his original thought, Lucius broke his vision away from the twinkling bulbs. "So where are we going?"

"To my work. I like it. So can you keep a secret?"

Lucius narrowed his eyes, then gave a curt nod.

"You seem like a sensible kid, so I want to be honest with you. What I do isn't exactly a legal profession, but it doesn't cause anyone harm either. Well, maybe to some, but no one that doesn't deserve it."

Lucius didn't like the sound of this but was glad the secret was finally coming out. He knew something was wrong with this situation. What was it, more human trafficking? Sex slaves? Killing for profit? Maybe Adrik and Boris weren't so different after all.

Adrik continued, "I work in the drug trade. I sell legal drugs from other countries that are illegal here in Russia. I sell dangerous, seriously illegal drugs as well. Some of my medicines help people get better, but not all of them. That's just business, though. I never force any of my medicines on people. If they are choosing to take drugs they know are bad for them, I won't say they can't."

Medicine? That didn't sound so bad. It didn't sound bad at all. Lucius felt so silly; he had gotten himself all worked up over nothing. If the medicine was helping people, that was great! He supposed the bad drugs hurt people, but they shouldn't be so stupid with their decisions. Why was he telling him all this?

Finishing his breakfast, Adrik picked up the plate. "I'm sharing this information with you because I work for a higher boss. He has been looking to hire someone small who can carry medicine and drugs from one place to another without getting caught. Do you think you can do that? If you do, you can live with me, and you'll make quite the profit out of it. He'll have more details if you want to talk to him first."

Lucius felt skeptical, not thrilled by the idea of escaping illegal activity only to jump right back in. But it was not like anyone else would hire a kid, and he didn't want to end up in an orphanage like Misha's sister surely was now.

"I'll meet with him, and then we'll see," Lucius said. It seemed like a safe answer to give. Not a yes, but not a no.

Adrik smiled and gave an affirmative nod. He got up to take care of his dishes in the kitchen, then walked to his bedroom to get dressed.

After he got dressed, Lucius stood up, and they headed outside. It was warmer now, and the sun was shining gently over the horizon, making the sky a strange mixture of blue and yellow without mingling into green. He thought it was very beautiful, although not unfamiliar. On the ship's deck, he was used to getting up early and watching the sunrise. He couldn't see the sun. There were too many buildings blocking the view, but looking up at the sky did give him some comfort.

Adrik walked into the garage and opened up the door. He had a small fancy blue car with enough room for the two of them. Lucius walked around the other side and hopped into the passenger seat. He had never ridden in a car before. Most people in his fighting town didn't have enough money for cars. It was why he and Boris walked everywhere.

Adrik climbed into the driver's seat beside him and noticed his discomfort.

"Never ridden in a car before?" he said, smiling at him.

"Maybe I have maybe I haven't," Lucius said, turning to stare out the window. He was getting very tired of Adrik's fake kindness. He was giving him too much, too soon. Anyone could see it was a trap. Lucius was just curious how long he could keep it up, then he would make a better judgment once he learned more about this 'business' of his.

"I didn't ride in a car until I was twenty-four years old," Adrik said, starting the car.

Lucius jumped from the sudden noise beneath him and turned to look at Adrik. "How come?"

"Well, my family was poor. I had to work really hard to be able to afford all that I can now," he said as he pulled out of the driveway.

Lucius only nodded, staring out the window as they drove away from the small, alphabetically organized, elegant house.

After driving the better part of a half an hour, Adrik pulled into a large parking lot connected to a warehouse building. Lucius looked up at the building, suddenly feeling queasy. It brought back too many memories of the fighting rings. It was big, not surrounded by too many other buildings and didn't have many windows attached. Though he had to admit, it looked as though it was better taken care of.

So distracted by his thoughts, he didn't notice Adrik had gotten out of the car until he heard the loud slam of the car door beside him. Snapping back to attention, Lucius opened the car door and exited with him. Following him to the front of the building, he made sure to stay a good distance from Adrik and everyone else walking in to try to have a decent chance at running away should something happen.

This didn't work, however, when Adrik walked to the two double doors at the entrance, opening one for him.

Lucius scowled, feeling defeated by the man's courtesy, as he walked inside. The building was much different from the old warehouse where he fought. The ceilings were still high, but the whole place was packed to the brim with different bags, bottles, and jars filled with different tablets, liquids, and powders. Despite the building being so large, it seemed much smaller due to its fullness. The floor was made of only cement, and all the walls were a boring white. In fact, he noticed there was no sign of decoration anywhere, aside from a stray poster about safety hanging by the doors.

"Are you coming?" Adrik said, a few steps up the stairs by the wall leading to the split-level upper floor.

Lucius nodded and ran after him.

Up the stairs was a big balcony like setting. It had a railing that made it able to peer down at the bottom floor. It looked so high up from above. He clung to the railing, afraid he might fall if he moved too quickly. Upstairs, there was also a walled-off section behind another set of double doors.

"That is where I work," Adrik said, pointing to the office section behind the doors. "I manage our clients and the money. It's important to make sure you are paid on time in any business. Remember that, okay?"

Lucius nodded. "Don't you sell the medicine?"

Adrik laughed. "Well, the business sells medicine. We have salesman for that. They seek out the sick. I don't sell the drugs. I just manage the money. I'm more of a"—he paused, thinking of the right word—"company accountant," he said with a smile, walking through the second set of double doors.

Lucy followed him. All around him were different office desks, each one seating a man working furiously on paperwork. "What are they all doing?" he asked.

"They're trying to manage the clients or bring in new clients for us to sell to. Some of them are trying to deal with the companies that sell and trade with us. It takes a lot of gears to make a clock turn, Lucius."

He nodded, believing what he said. Their ship had taken a lot of men to hoist the sails and to make the ship move smoothly over the water. He imagined this company worked a lot like that. The men downstairs must be working to ship out these "drugs" Adrik kept mentioning.

Walking to the back, there was another small room attached to the corner. This one had a regular singular door. Lucy followed him as he walked through.

"Feliks, I think I found us the worker we needed!" Adrik said proudly, grabbing Lucy's hand and pulling him forward gently. "This is Lucius."

Lucius said nothing. He knew sometimes in situations like this that it was best to remain quiet and keep your information to yourself. Feliks looked up from the papers he was working on. Lucius quickly and carefully observed the man sitting at the desk, trying to know him before he even had a chance to speak.

The man had thick white hair, no signs of gray, and was very old. He sat in a chair that, glancing under the desk, Lucius knew had wheels. He wore glasses on the end of his nose and looked up over them before speaking in a calm, cool voice.

"And has Adrik told you what the job entails, Lucius?"

"He said I will be transporting medicine and drugs from one place to another because I'm small and not likely to get caught doing so," he repeated, exactly as he had heard it.

"Yes. Very good," Feliks said, looking back to his desk and opening a drawer to rummage through some papers and items. "But that isn't all you'll be doing. We have lots of people for that. It will be your main job at first, of course. But if you can prove yourself trustworthy, I have bigger and more important jobs for you."

Lucius listened carefully, bigger more important jobs could mean a better, richer life. But he didn't want to participate if it meant he would be harming innocent people.

"You are how old? Ten?"

Lucius nodded. "Ten or eleven. We never celebrated my birthday, so I'm not exactly sure."

He nodded and gave a short grunt. "Very good. Either way, you are young and small. Prove yourself quickly, and you would be a great way to gather information. People are more likely to share things with you or speak around you since they don't think you will understand. Any information you hear, you report back to me, and I'm sure you will do very well for us. Yes?"

Lucius nodded. "Yes," he agreed. This place didn't seem so bad really. Selling and transporting? That was easy work, and it would make him money. He needed to make money somehow if he was going to survive. Not to mention he could only live with Adrik if he worked for the company. Thinking on it, he wasn't a big fan of being homeless again, and anything was better than a cage in the cellar, wasn't it?

"Excellent," Feliks continued, cutting off the boy's train of thought. He pulled out a piece of paper and handed it to him from across the desk.

Lucius came and took it, looking at it. It was covered in words and writings. He stared at it for a good two minutes, trying to decipher the code, before looking up at Feliks, who was offering him a pen.

"Well, take the pen, and sign your name. Did you read the general basis of the contract?" he asked.

Lucius looked back at the paper, cheeks turning red with embarrassment as he shook his head no.

"Can you read?"

Lucius paused, staring at the paper for a few seconds, before shaking his head no again.

Feliks took back the paper. "All the better. I'll tell you what it says."

"Thank you," he replied. For a moment, he was afraid they were going to make fun of him, but now he was glad to see his fear was all for naught.

"It says, in summary, that you are not going to work for any other drug cartel. You will not be sharing the secrets of our company with others or talking about it outside of work unless instructed otherwise. And you will remain loyal to us until your contract ends in a year. We will be paying you 10 percent of every sale you are involved with, but that percentage will increase the longer you stay in the fold. Does this sound agreeable to you?"

Lucius nodded, this all sounded like a good, easy, and loyal way to make a living.

"Very good," Feliks replied, turning the paper and pointing to the line at the bottom. "Can you write your name?"

Lucius shook his head. He only knew some of his letters. "I can write maybe some of it?"

The boss gave an affirmative nod. "Then just write what you can, and you'll start today."

Lucius grabbed the pen and leaned over, staring at the line on the sheet of paper. He wrote a big *L*, then a *U*, then *S. Lus*. He knew he was missing a lot of letters in there, but that was the most he knew of his name's spelling. It seemed so incomplete. So he added a *Y* on the end for good measure.

Feliks took back the paper and looked it over. "Lusy, huh? It's good enough. Do you want us to call you Lusy instead of Lucius?"

Lucius paused, thinking for a moment. No one had ever called him by his nickname, except for his sister. "You can if you want. Only my sister called me that."

Feliks nodded and handed the paper to Adrik. "We'll stick to Lucius for now then. Mister Kilesso, go show him around and bring his contract to Rupert."

Adrik nodded. "Yes, sir," he said, taking Lucius's hand and walking him out of the office and back down the stairs. Then, he turned to face him with a smile.

"Welcome to the company! You did good!"

"Thank you," he replied, looking around. "So how am I supposed to do this?"

"Well, it's easy," he said, leading him to an office in the back. A dark-skinned man with big glasses and dark black hair was staring down at some papers, trying to work. "This is Rupert. He's in charge of the warehouse employees and their shipments."

Rupert looked up as Adrik handed him the paper, which he put it into a new folder. His eyes were a light greyish color, and his nose and fingers were red. He looked very ill.

With a sniffle, Rupert started talking. "It's nice to meet you, Lucius," he said, sounding very congested.

"You too," he replied. "Are you sick?"

Rupert nodded and grabbed a tissue to wipe his nose. "It's no big dilemma. I get a cold every winter."

"Every. Winter." Adrik laughed. "You should really bundle up if you know the cold is coming."

The dark-skinned man nodded. "Probably. But that's not why you came to bother me, is it? Back to business matters. So, Lucius, you're new to transporting. Have you ever moved things from one location to another? How long have you lived here?"

"Oh, um, no, I haven't transported things before. And I just moved here yesterday."

Rupert sighed. "So you've never been to town before. Adrik, what am I supposed to do with a kid who doesn't even know the streets?"

Adrik gave a lighthearted laugh. "Well? Teach him! He's going to be great at his job. I just know it. It shouldn't be that hard, Lucius. Rupert here will teach you the town, and you'll be transporting in no time."

Rupert gave Adrik an irritated look. "Fine, fine." The tall cat-like man gave a satisfied nod. Rupert rolled his eyes. "Lucius, after you learn the city, you'll be taking small amounts of the prescription drugs to sick parts of towns. Do you think you can handle that?"

He nodded.

"Good. We'll put you to work by the end of the week. Today, I want you to make yourself familiar with where everything is. We have a table with scales next to my office where you can weigh out some of our products. But most of it comes prepackaged. Tomorrow, I'll give you your first out-of-building assignment," he said, handing Lucius a paper. "Judging by your signature, I'm guessing you can't read. This shouldn't be too much of a setback. We've had illiterate workers in the past. Just find every drug on that list. Each drug is labeled with the same name on its packaging. Can you do that?"

He nodded. It shouldn't be too difficult, just like a hide-and-seek game or a scavenger hunt.

"Good. Spend the rest of the day doing that. If you have any questions, feel free to ask me or another worker. Do you have a place to go after the day is out?"

"I'm living with Adrik."

"Perfect. You'll leave with Adrik when the day is done. And like I said, if you have any questions, just ask. We're all a family working for the same place here. Don't be afraid to ask for help if you need it. Better to work quickly with others than slow by yourself," Rupert said, turning back to his paperwork.

Lucius nodded and followed Adrik out of the office.

"I have to get back to work situating out the income upstairs. You'll be on your own for now. Are you all right with that?"

"I'm not afraid of working by myself. I'm not a child," Lucius said, standing up tall and looking as independent as he could manage at ten years old.

Adrik only smiled in response. "I'm glad to hear it. I'll come back and get you at six," he said, pointing to the clock up on the east wall. "Just listen to Rupert, and find everything on that list. Memorize where things are in the warehouse. It'll really help you later on once you need to start delivering."

Lucius nodded, and Adrik walked back up the stairs, vanishing from his line of sight and leaving him to his job. As he looked down at the sheet of paper, he tried to figure out how several of the excruciatingly long words were pronounced based on what he heard others saying around him. The workers said several of the drugs the list were simply very strong painkillers or dietary supplements. A few were vaccines, and every now and again, he would find a cure for a serious disease. Then he got to the part of the warehouse with things Lucius thought must be illegal, drugs like heroin and cocaine. These were all things he felt vastly unfamiliar with.

As he worked his way through his list, the day went by in a flash. Before he knew it, his blond haired friend was walking back down the stairs toward him.

"Ready to go?" he said.

"Yeah, I'm ready," Lucius responded as they headed out back toward the car.

On the drive home, Adrik looked over to him. "How did your day go? Did you find everything on the list?"

"Of course, I did!" Lucius said he didn't want anyone to think he was incapable of doing things this early in his new career. "I found every last medicine and drug. Some of them have very, very long names."

"Yeah, some of them do. You'll find, the more uncommon the drug, the longer and more scientific-sounding the name is," Adrik said.

Lucius nodded and looked out the window.

"What would you like for dinner tonight? I can make piroshki. Or beef stroganoff? Which sounds better to you?"

"I'm not hungry," he replied dully.

"You have to eat. You didn't eat this morning, and I didn't pack you lunch, so I know you haven't eaten. What sounds better?"

Lucius thought to himself which he was more likely to be able to choke down. He didn't know what either dish was, and he didn't want to expose himself this early into their relationship. Or should he say their agreement.

"Beef stroganoff," he said. He didn't know what it meant, but he remembered his time back on the ship. The beef was always easier to get down, and half the time, he could even keep it down. Despite the stomach pains.

Adrik smiled. "Beef stroganoff, it is," he said, pulling into the driveway. Climbing out of the car, he immediately headed to his room. His housemate started cooking dinner, while he went through the drawers of the nightstand. Inside, he found a notebook, a pencil, some tissues, and a book. *The Twelve Chairs*, it was titled. He ignored the book and grabbed the pencil and notebook. He opened the notebook and found a blank sheet. He felt so pathetic today, not even able to spell his own name.

Lucius, he thought. *My name is Lucius! I can do this!* Writing out the *L* much too big on the line, he then wrote a large *U. Lu.* After that, he needed help. He didn't know what letter made the "shhh" noise. After thinking on it for over ten minutes, he admitted defeat and walked out to see his new friend.

"Adrik, I need your help," he said, crossing his arms, still defiant despite his request.

He looked up from the pot he was stirring and turned to face him. "Hmm? With what?"

Lucius held out the notebook. "I want to learn to spell my name," he said, sitting at the counter on a stool.

"Ahhhhh, yes, that would be a good thing, wouldn't it? Then you'll know how to sign papers and know when people are writing about you. Say, why don't you go to school? Christmas break is sure to be over soon. January is a few days in after all."

School? He had never heard of such a place. He looked down at his book. If school was where he had to go to learn to read and write, then he would go. If he got paid less, it wouldn't be for too long.

Lucius looked up from the notebook. "What's"—he paused, feeling a little embarrassed—"school?"

Adrik took the noodles off the stove and drained them before looking over. "You've never been to a school before? I guess that makes sense since you can't read. It's a place where children go to learn. Children get taught how to read and write there, how to do math, and all sorts of things. It's fun. You should go if you want to," he said, putting the noodles into a bowl and pouring the stroganoff mixture over them. "I'll take you in two weeks. How's that sound? Then if you don't like it, you don't have to go back."

Lucius nodded and choked down the food that was put in front of him for dinner.

Chapter 17

LUCIUS

ON THE TOWN

The next day, they went to work. Adrik went up to his office, and Lucius reported back to Rupert.

"Did you figure out where everything is?" he asked after leaning forward to sneeze.

"Yes, I did. I'm ready to transport," Lucius replied with certainty.

"I like your attitude. But hold on to your horses. Do you even know the neighborhood?"

Lucius shook his head.

"Then it's time for you to start learning the town. Here," Rupert said, handing him a folded-up piece of paper with lots of squiggles, lines, and names on it. "It's a map. Go find every street and every house. I want you to have every place memorized in a one-mile radius in two days. Think you can handle that?"

He nodded, putting the map in his leather jacket pocket.

"It's pretty cold outside. You might want to ask Adrik for a warmer jacket. Need to bundle up in this weather," Rupert said, blowing his nose.

"Maybe you should take your own advice," Lucius shot back, giving him a quirky "I know better than you" smile.

"Hey, hey, watch it! I'm supposed to be your boss, you know. Get outta here, kid," he said with a small chuckle, pushing his glasses up his fat little nose.

Walking out of the building, he unfolded the map. He liked Rupert. He was funny, and Lucius could tell that he was never going to be a physical threat to him. He was too sick and seemed to favor taking the easy route over the harder, more violent one.

As he walked out of the parking lot, he looked left and right. On the left side were lots of smaller houses and a few businesses toward the middle. On the right were bigger houses. clearly better taken care of and housing richer clients. There were no businesses on that side. Maybe they all had servants to take care of things like shopping. He turned to the left, feeling more comfortable dealing with poorer parts of town. It was familiar to him, and he at least knew where to start. One of the first things he noticed was that no one on this side of the street had a car. Lots of children were running around and playing, every single one dressed in layer after layer of clothing—snow pants, mittens, coats. He wondered how some of the kids managed to breath under all those layers.

As he marked down each street on his map, he turned into the business part of town. This part was much easier. Every business had a huge sign above their door, saying the name and often what they sold. He walked by a group of kids his age all huddled around a shop and decided to look in. Inside, he saw all sorts of toys. Small wooden race cars, little plastic dolls, and tiny replica houses.

Staring inside, he reached up and touched his bow, wondering if Eileen might have liked to play with toys like these. He wondered if it was really all that fun to play with and paint those simple wooden cars. The children around sure seemed excited about them. He watched as a little blond-haired boy and his dark-haired mother walked out of the store, carrying a bag. The boy seemed so happy, and the mom held his hand. They smiled as they talked about the dinner they were going to eat when his father came home.

Lucius felt his stomach sink to his feet and his ears burn up with envy. Maybe in a different life, he could have been that boy. His life could have been as simple as shopping with a mother that loved him and what they would eat when they got home. *If only I hadn't been born a monster,* he thought to himself, turning away from the store and the life he knew he would never have.

Lucius opened the map once more. This was his life, a life of working and of making enough money to survive. He turned the corner, looking into the next window. A motorcycle shop. It held all sorts of bikes of all different colors. They looked so small and convenient. He thought maybe if he saved up enough money, he could buy something like this when he was older, a blue one, something fast that could take him far away from whatever he disliked.

The next business street held fewer shops for children and less bikes. Every building on this street was a restaurant of some kind. He walked through the street, trying not to notice the disgusting smells of the human food as he searched and spotted every place on his map. Was this what Oleg had been talking about? He always spoke of the restaurant he wanted to own when they were cleaning dishes together. Maybe he could have had something like this if he hadn't married so young and gotten trapped in ship life. Lucius missed his friends. It was sad to think about. He felt he knew so much about them. Yet because of his shame, they hardly ever got to know him in return. He wouldn't tell them about his mother and his sister, only that they weren't in the picture. They never even got to learn his real name. It made him suddenly feel very guilty.

As he finished looking at all the shops, he turned and headed toward the richer part of town. There was no business here. Well, hardly any. As he walked through the streets, he noticed that, unlike the poor residential area, which had playing children and happy adults spending time with their families, these houses were all quiet. The lights inside made it easy to tell that people were home, but no one was outside playing. He walked up to a house and peered inside, trying not to be seen.

He saw two children sitting in front of the fire. A boy and a girl. They were playing with toys together and watching TV while the mother was reading a book. A maid was in the kitchen, working busily, cooking something for dinner. Lucius crawled around the side of the house, and in the next room, the father was at a desk in the study, doing paperwork. This was a whole different sort of life. It didn't seem as merry as the lives led with less money, but it did seem more comfortable. Lucius shivered as he watched the fire crackle.

These kids, this family, they have no idea how lucky they are, he thought as he left the house.

After several more hours of searching, Lucius felt as though he had properly explored the area. It was starting to get dark anyway. Adrik would be wondering where he was if he didn't return soon, and he didn't want to be left behind.

Arriving back, everyone was gone, except for the tall blond man who was waiting in his car. He honked and rolled down his window.

"Lucius! Come on!" he shouted.

Lucius ran to the car and hopped into the passenger seat, buckling himself in.

"So? How was the town?"

Lucius crossed his arms tightly in front of him. "It was fine," he said bitterly. Adrik nodded, leaving him alone for the rest of the car ride. Lucy was happy he knew how to take a hint. Once they got home, Adrik started cooking dinner as usual. Lucy beelined to his room, closing the door. He undressed himself and crawled into his bed. He didn't think it would hurt so much to see the life of a normal child. It was like glimpsing into the world he wanted but could never have.

Trying not to cry, he buried his face into the pillow. Those stupid kids. They didn't know how good they had it. They never had to be sold, never had to be exploited, and had probably not once witnessed death. Lucius had more blood on his hands than a butcher, and he felt enraged by the thought of it.

He missed his sister. He missed the little house in the woods. He thought it was so boring when he lived there, but now he would give anything to be back. If only to see Eileen again. He even missed his mom. She was never kind to him or his sister, but she was still their mom. He thought maybe if he had been a less troublesome kid, his mom wouldn't have hated him quite as much.

Adrik knocked on the door. "Lucius, food is ready. I made chicken kiev."

"I'm not hungry," he replied shortly.

"Are you sick? Did you catch a cold? Why don't I get you some medicine? I keep some in the bathroom, in case—"

"No, I just want to sleep!" he barked, cutting him off.

Adrik fell silent for a few moments. "All right," he said, leaving to go and eat.

The next morning, he got up and found his clothes missing. He looked around and felt up to his hair. His bow was left untouched; that was a relief. Getting out of bed, he walked to the kitchen naked. Adrik was at the counter, cutting up some bread to make grenki for breakfast. He jumped a little when he looked up to see the boy in his birthday suit.

"You're naked!" he exclaimed.

Lucius looked down at himself. "Well, yeah, you took my clothes. Where are they?"

"They're in the wash. I left you some spare clothes on your bed to wear."

Lucius remembered seeing the clothes but didn't think to put them on. He walked back toward the bedroom, slipping into them. The pants were a solid black, and they fit him much nicer. Adrik must have gone out and picked up some clothes his proper size. The shirt was a red long-sleeved shirt with a plaid pattern. Lucius thought it looked stupid. He couldn't help but think the pants were uncomfortably tight. They rose up past his belly button, and the shirt seemed too baggy and without shape. He walked out toward Adrik and held his arms out, waiting for a response to the outfit.

Letting out a light chuckle, he gave comment. "You're supposed to tuck the shirt into the pants."

Lucius looked down at his clothes and undid the pants to tuck the shirt in. "Why are the pants so high? I feel like they're squeezing me to death."

Adrik went back to eating his breakfast. "They're high-waist pants. All the boys nowadays are wearing them. Didn't you see any boys wearing pants like those around town?"

Lucius shook his head, zipping up his fly. "Everyone was wearing coats on top," he said, sitting across from him at the table.

"Ahhhh, that makes sense." He chuckled, passing him a plate full of fruit, bacon, and breakfast grenki.

Lucius tried not to let his face twist at the awful smell of the food in front of him as he gobbled it down without a word. As he ate, he couldn't help but notice how itchy and uncomfortable these new clothes were with every movement. But once breakfast was done, he said nothing as he put on his old leather coat and walked out the door behind Adrik.

Once they arrived at work, Lucius went to Rupert, as usual.

"I see Adrik got to pick your clothes today," he mused. "He's always about the latest trends and styles. I think he just wants to impress the ladies or, if rumor is correct, wants to impress the men." Rupert laughed before falling into a series of coughing fits.

Lucy looked down at himself before looking back to the hacking man. "He likes boys?" Maybe that was why he was being so nice to him?

"No, not boys. Adrik has always been nice to children but has never been sexually abusive toward them. I don't think he'd ever do something like that. But rumor around the warehouse is, he does like a good strong, burly man," he said, giving a soft chuckle. "That's why he never married, you know. A while back, we all thought he was involved with one of our warehouse workers. Um…Abram was his name, I think. But neither of them would confess to anything despite how we pressured them. Then one day Abram just up and left, never gave a note or anything. The second his contract was up, he was gone. Adrik seemed very upset, but he wouldn't ever admit to it," he said, flipping through the files next to his desk.

Lucy felt bad. He had never been in love before; well, he had loved Misha. But that was just a childish love. He imagined it must really hurt to trust someone and then have them betray you. Rupert spoke about this like it was a bad thing—loving the same gender as your own. But Lucius felt a little confused. He didn't see why it was bad. After Boris, he knew much more about sex and lust, though he didn't exactly want to learn the way he had. But that one bad experience didn't mean it was all bad, did it? Maybe only people like him were bad.

"I explored the whole area in a mile of the warehouse. I'm ready to transport," Lucius said, moving back to the topic of business.

"Already? Didn't I give you two days to do that?"

"Yes, but I did it in one. I'm eager to start working and get paid. Besides, the map you gave me was easy. Anyone could have cleared it in the time I did."

"All right! I'm liking you more and more, kid. Keep up the good work!" Rupert said enthusiastically. "Keep working like this, and you could be my ticket to a raise and a promotion. Assuming you get one yourself, of course."

Lucius nodded. He liked the idea of moving up. It meant his life would only get easier, right?

"All right, let me see your map," Rupert said as he handed it over. "You are going to deliver two hundred milligrams of morphine to this spot," he said, making a small red X on the map. "We have it already measured out, and they prepaid for it about three days ago. Make sure you grab the right one. Morphine. Two hundred milligrams. Ask if you need help. Got it?"

"Got it," Lucius said.

"Make sure you tell them it's from Dixie Drug Cartel. All right?"

"All right!" he said, already walking out of the office to grab what he needed.

Lucius stalked down the aisles until he found what he was looking for. Morphine. He was thankful he remembered how it was spelled. Then he found the bottle with two big zeroes on it. Two hundred. Grabbing the bottle, he shoved it into his coat and walked out. The X was in a poor part of town. As he walked down the streets, he watched the children. Then he finally stopped in front of the house he was to deliver to. He paced up to the door and knocked very loudly.

A small woman answered the door. She looked very unkempt and unwashed. "Hello?"

"Hello," Lucius said, trying to sound professional. "I'm with the Dixie Drug Cartel," he said in a low tone, careful not to let others hear.

The woman opened the door and looked around. She had dark black hair and skin and was very skinny. "Come in, come in!" She beckoned to him.

Lucius did as he was told. There were no kids in this house. He took the medicine out of his coat, and she snatched it away from him.

"Thank you. Oh, thank you," she said, running down the hall to another room. Following her, he saw a sick old man lying in bed. The woman helped ease him up to a sitting position. She took the bottle and opened it, popping a pill into his mouth. Then she gave him some water. She turned and saw Lucy standing at the door.

"He is very sick," she said. "He has cancer. Thank you for bringing the medicine."

"Will the morphine help make him better?" Lucius asked, thinking the man looked awfully sick to suddenly spring back to life because of a tiny little pill.

The woman shook her head, tucking the man in and closing the door. "No, but it will help ease his pain until it's his time. Sometimes, that's all you can do for a person—help them toward a comfortable ending."

Lucius stared at her in disbelief. He had never thought of it like that. Whenever he saw someone destined to die, he only thought of how to save them. He never considered the kindness of putting someone out of their misery in a gentle way, but there was truth to her words. He never thought of death as an act of mercy.

The woman walked back out to the house, setting the bottle in a kitchen cabinet. "Tell Dixie that we won't need another order. I'm sure what you delivered will be enough."

Suddenly, he felt sad. These seemed like nice people, and there wasn't anything he could do to help them. "Are you alone?"

The woman looked up, puzzled by his concern for a stranger. "Yes, I never had any children. Papa got very sick when I was young, and I never took the time to go find a husband. Why do you ask?"

"I was just wondering, what will you do when he's gone?"

"I will move on. Everyone has to move on from what holds them down at some point. That's a good lesson to learn, little boy. You should remember it," she said, giving him a small smile.

Lucius looked down at the floor and kicked at the wrinkle in the dark-purple rug. "Lucius," he said, looking back up. "You can call me Lucius."

She smiled. Some of her teeth were brown and rotting, probably due to the money they didn't have. It reminded him of Boris, though it was clear they were nothing alike.

"Lucius, thank you so much," she said, walking over to the dying tree in the corner. She grabbed a red and white hanging thing among the other bright and shiny bulbs and lights, and handed it to him.

"For you," she said, "because you are such a nice boy."

He took it. He didn't know what it was but was thankful anyway. These people didn't have much, but still, they were giving him something to take with him. "Thank you," he said.

She walked to the door and opened it. Lucius knew Rupert would be expecting him back soon, and walked out the door, putting the funny red and white cane in his pocket.

"Be safe now, okay?" the woman said, giving him a small pat on the head.

"I will. Thank you, ma'am," he replied, turning and walking down her driveway.

Chapter 18

LUCIUS

ADRIK'S SECRET

When he finally got back, he returned to Rupert.

"You're back! Did your first delivery go all right?"

He nodded. "The man was dying. His daughter said she only wanted to give him a quick, comfortable death so they won't be needing another shipment."

"Pity, but sometimes life is just like that," he said, pulling out a folder and crossing a big X on it before putting it in a completely different file. "Life is hard, Lucius. Sometimes, the only thing left to do in life is die, as sad as it is."

"I know," he said, reaching up to scratch the scar around his ear.

"Then you know that sometimes people die and there just isn't anything you can do to save them. That's just life. At least we were able to help make the end of his life an easy departure. Yeah?" Rupert said, removing his glasses to itch at his red cold-ridden eyes.

"Yeah," Lucius agreed, feeling good about helping the poor family with that much at least. "The daughter gave me this," he said, taking the candy cane out of his pocket.

"Ooooooh, a candy cane! Kids usually like to eat those around Christmastime. Well, Christmas is over, so I guess they gave an extra one to you, hmm? Enjoy your treat, kid. You've earned it. I'll send you on another trip tomorrow."

Lucius nodded. "Thanks," he said, inspecting the candy cane. This was supposed to be food? It seemed awfully hard to chew.

Suddenly, he felt a twinge of guilt. She gave him a gift to enjoy, and he didn't know if he would even be able to eat it. He could try at the very least. He took the wrapper off the longer end of the cane. It didn't smell too bad, and the red stripes were very intriguing.

He stuck the treat into his mouth. It didn't taste horrible; it didn't even taste bad! He couldn't stand eating vegetables, and eggs were just god-awful. Anything involving garlic was enough to make him throw up in less than two minutes, if not immediately. But meat, he could usually stomach for at least a day, if not keep it down entirely. And this small candy cane? Well, the more he ate, the tastier it seemed. When he finished climbing the stairs, he went to an empty bench overlooking the warehouse and sat. Since he was done for the day, all he had to do was wait for Adrik to get out before they could go home.

When Adrik came to him, he greeted him with his usual sleek cat-like smile. "Ready to go?"

Lucius nodded, having finished his candy cane.

"I'm glad you're feeling better today," Adrik said as they walked to the car.

"I just didn't have a very good day yesterday," Lucius said as they climbed in.

He felt bad for being so mean.

"It's all right. We all have bad days," he said with a smile.

As soon as they arrived home, Adrik got out and headed toward the kitchen. "So I was thinking maybe kotlety for dinner tonight."

"Okay," Lucius agreed, following him. "I have a question."

"All right?" He replied, pulling minced pork out of the fridge. "I'm all ears," he said, flashing him his usual smile.

"Well, I don't mean this in a bad way, and if you are, I don't care. You're very nice to me, and you drive me home. I will still like to be around you either way," Lucius started, not wanting to give off the wrong impression. "But do you...like men?"

Adrik paused before continuing to get things ready for dinner. His smile disappeared. "Who did you hear this from?"

"Rupert," he said, thinking now was probably best to be honest.

Adrik said nothing as he turned and put the balls of meat onto the stove.

"I don't think any less of you if you do! I promise. Rupert acted like it might have been a bad thing, but I don't see what's so bad about it."

"There's nothing bad about it," Adrik said. "It's just that sometimes, being gay is associated with being perverted around here. People find out you fall in love with the same gender, and they immediately think you're trying to have sex with children or something."

Lucius nodded. "Well, I don't think that. I'm happy I know. Now I think we can be better friends, right?"

Adrik turned, facing Lucius. He got out a cutting board and started to cut up the vegetables for the side. "Right," he said, his usual smile slowly returning to his face. "Can I share a secret with you?"

"Of course!" he replied, eager to know more about his new friend. "Anything you want. I won't tell anyone, I promise."

He let out a small laugh. "You really are a funny kid, you know that?" he said before looking back at the steaks. He paused, sounding a little uncertain. "If you want the truth. well, I've only ever told a few people, but I'm actually a trans-man. Do you know what that is?"

Lucius shook his head.

"A trans-man is someone who was born as a girl but decided they didn't feel right like that. So they changed to being a boy. The same applies for me. I just feel more comfortable as a boy. Have you ever wanted to be something other than you are, Lucius?"

He only stared at him. He had always wanted to be human, so he knew what it felt like. But being a girl? Lucy would have never predicted it! How did he hide his breasts? Did he have them at all? Was he all boy now? How did he get new parts? There were so many questions on Lucius's mind, and half of them seemed rude.

Adrik turned and stared at him. "You look like a fish with your mouth hanging open like that." He laughed. "I guess, technically, nothing's really changed. They don't offer surgery to change my gender, so I just change how I dress to accommodate it," he said. "But I don't want you to think of me as a woman. I've always been a boy in my heart, you know? All I can do is try and hide it the best I can—that is, until we live in a society that's accepting of people like me." He cut up some potatoes to go with the meal. "Do you promise not to think of me any different?"

Lucius nodded and got up to give Adrik a big hug.

"Please don't tell anyone. I don't want other people thinking the wrong thing."

"I won't," he promised. "And since you told me a secret, I'll tell you a secret, okay?"

Adrik smiled. "Okay."

"But you can't tell anyone, and you can't be upset with me. Promise?"

"I promise."

Lucius nodded, going back to his seat. He played with his fingers under the kitchen counter nervously, looking down at them. "Well, it sounds kind of crazy," he started. "But...I mean, I don't really eat people food," he said.

Adrik gave him a puzzled look, and he stopped cutting the potatoes.

"I'm from Germany."

Adrik smiled and laughed. "Well, I knew that. You have a very strong German accent."

"Well, in Germany, they have these things called vampires. I don't know much about them since I've never met another besides my sister."

"Vampire, huh? I've heard of them, only maybe a handful of times. I know they're some sort of myth around Germany and England, but I've never heard of them in Russia. Don't they drink the blood of humans? I never really believed in such fairy tales."

Lucius tensed up a little, then gave a curt nod. "But depending on how much I eat when I get the chance. I can go for as long as three or four months without food. I just have to be careful."

Adrik nodded. "Well, that explains the funny faces you've been making at my cooking!" He laughed. "I guess I'll save some of this food for leftovers. When was the last time you ate?"

"About a week and a half ago. So I should be okay for at least another two or three months at least."

"Well, that's good. Is the white hair a part of this? I've always wondered, but you seemed too unlikely to answer if I asked. I didn't want to scare you off."

Lucius nodded. "My father was a vampire, but my mom was human. She said this was a trait from him, but I never met him myself."

Adrik took a long sip of a glass of water he poured for himself. "How did you get so far from home anyhow?"

Lucius fidgeted under the table. "I was snuck into the country as a slave without realizing it until it was too late. I fought in the fighting pits and had just escaped the night you found me."

"Ahhhhhhhh…human trafficking. That would explain why you were so hesitant to trust me. But that leads to a bigger problem. How are we going to get you food when you get really hungry?"

Lucius shrugged his shoulders. "I, uh, I haven't figured that out yet."

Adrik thought for a moment before speaking again. "Sometimes people die in the drug cartel. Some of our clients, I mean. Those who take our goods but can't pay usually end up either owing us or paying with, well, with their life. I'll see if there isn't a way we can get you the bodies in secret. Do you care if I tell Feliks about this? That way, we can work out some sort of system."

Lucius shook his head. "No, I don't mind. Thank you, Adrik. This really means a lot to me."

Adrik smiled, putting food on his plate. "It's no problem. We're friends, after all. You said so yourself."

"Friends," Lucius agreed.

Heading off to bed after the meal was over, he lay on his back, staring at the ceiling. So Adrik had been a girl this whole time? He couldn't believe he had been so deceived. Then again, he supposed everyone had their secrets. He reached up and touched his teeth. If only it were as easy as saying he wasn't a vampire, to make it come true. He thought about how much he wished he could be someone else, someone who didn't have to kill to survive. Adrik must have felt the same way as a kid, wanting to be a boy instead of a girl. It was then that Lucy decided he would always respect his friend's wishes. If he wanted to be a boy, then he would treat and think of him as one. The secret of Adrik's birth gender, he would take it to his grave.

The next day, he got another transport, more medicine to people who were struggling in life. Lucy felt good helping people who were struggling but felt bad he couldn't do more. After the drive home, Adrik cooked himself dinner. For the first time in a while, Lucius actually felt pretty good about the direction he was headed.

Then Adrik spoke up about a week later.

"Are you still interested in going to school? They could teach you to read and write and do numbers and math. All sorts of things. I think you'd really like it. You're a smart kid, after all. You just need to learn the academics," he said happily.

"Yeah, I'll go to school," Lucius replied. If he was being honest, he was quite excited. He was excited to feel like a normal kid for once, even though he felt nervous at the same time.

"Great! So once you start, you'll go every day instead of working. And we'll just bring you in on weekends. How does that sound?"

"It sounds wonderful!" he said. Lucy felt ecstatic. Life was starting to finally seem normal. It might never be exact, but at least it could be close.

"I'm glad you feel that way because I have a surprise for you."

Turning to face his friend, Lucius gave him a puzzled look.

"Close your eyes."

He did, and he heard a loud thud on the counter in front of him. "Can I open them?"

"Yes," Adrik said, his smooth cat-like voice purring with excitement.

He opened and rewarded his friend with a big toothy smile. Before him on the counter was a backpack filled with notebooks and a case full of pencils. The backpack was a light-blue color, his favorite.

"Careful, Lucius. Your pearly whites are showing," Adrik said, giving him a smile.

Lucius flushed red and covered his mouth.

"Don't be embarrassed. They're very sharp, but they're beautiful teeth. Very white. Just be careful not to scare the other kids with them at school tomorrow."

Removing his hands, Lucius smiled again. "I'll only smile lips open at home."

"Smart," Adrik said, cleaning the dishes from dinner. "You should go to bed so you aren't tired for school tomorrow. I'll wake you up and drive you. Take a shower first, okay?"

"Okay," Lucius said, taking his backpack and putting it on. He felt the straps; it was nice. He walked to his room and set it down by his bed. Then he undressed and went to take a shower. In the week, Adrik had bought him four different outfits so when one was in the wash, he could wear another one. His friend was being so kind to him. Lucius thought, maybe he was just lonely. It was nice to have someone with him, to take care of him. Lucy swore to himself that if Adrik ever needed him, he would always be there.

Turning on the shower, he stepped inside. He liked his water warm, but not too hot. He scrubbed all over, his hair, his legs, and down by his privates. Looking down, he was filled with pride at the small amount of pubic hair that had started to grow. He scrubbed under his arms and found hair there too. Both patches of hair were white, just like on the top of his head.

After he finished scrubbing himself from head to toe, he got out of the shower and dried himself off. Then walked back to his bedroom, and put on some pajamas. Although, it was really just a big shirt. He went to go see Adrik, and thank him for everything.

The blond-haired man was sitting in the chair by the fireplace, nose deep in a book. As he turned the page and brushed his blond hair behind his ear, Lucius tapped his shoulder. Adrik turned to look at him and gave him his famous cat-like smile.

"I wanted to thank you for earlier, for getting me that backpack and the supplies and driving me to school and everything. I don't know what I could ever do to thank you."

His housemate smiled before resting his book on the table beside him. "Your thank-you is more than enough. You know, sometimes you remind me of myself when I was young," Adrik said.

"You've never spoken about when you were a kid," Lucius said, sitting on the couch.

"Well, it wasn't exactly a happy childhood. We grew up very poor, my family and I. A horrible sickness was sweeping our town. Typhus, it was called. It caused a high fever and rash. My father had been killed in the Second World War, and my mother and younger brother were killed by the disease. I had nowhere to go. But I found the Dixie Drug Cartel, and Mister Feliks took care of me. He gave me the chance I needed to turn things around and start a new life. I might have starved if he hadn't been so generous as to take me in. I guess when I saw you trudging through the snow that night, I thought of myself when I had nowhere to live. That's why I took you in."

Lucy felt like he and Adrik were more connected now than ever. He smiled as he brought his knees to his chest in the chair. "I never knew that about you. Thank you for sharing it with me."

He smiled. "So where did you come from? Before you came to live with me if you don't mind me asking. You mentioned you were human-trafficked to Russia, but what about before? You said you had a sister and you never met your dad. What about your mother?"

Lucius fidgeted uncomfortably. "I think she was forced to have us from my dad. She didn't ever really want us. We lived in a house in the woods, and she locked us in our room every day so we couldn't go outside. When we were maybe five or six, I'm not sure, she tried to starve us. She killed my sister, Eileen, and I was so angry I went downstairs and killed her. Then…" He paused. This was definitely the hardest part for him to accept. "I…I ate her," he said, resting his head on his knees. He was an adult. He had hair down there. He shouldn't cry, but he wanted to.

Adrik must have been able to tell. "Oh, that's a terrible thing for a kid to have to go through," he said, getting up to move over to him. "There, there, it's all right," he said, sitting beside him.

Lucius leaned into him and wrapped his arms around him tightly before letting himself cry. He remembered his strength and tried to loosen his grip, but Adrik just held him and stroked his hair. Lucy felt so relaxed, so comfortable.

After he finished crying, Adrik let go. "Would you like some water?"

Lucius nodded, and his friend got up, bringing him back a glass of water.

"Are there any foods you do like? Anything I can give you to make you feel better?"

"I ate a candy cane this week. It didn't make me sick, and I sort of liked it. It was very sweet. But I'm not really sure why." He sniffled.

"Maybe you can have other candies too. I don't have any candy canes, but I have butterscotch if you want to try some."

He nodded, and Adrik handed him a small yellow candy. He popped it in his mouth. It was sweet and earthy tasting. He liked it a lot, but he wasn't sure which he liked more.

"Any good?" Adrik asked.

Lucius nodded, wiping away his tears.

"You should head to bed," he said, helping him up. "It's very late now, and school starts early."

He nodded. "I'm sorry I cried on you so much. I meant to only come out here to thank you for your kindness."

"It's not a problem." He smiled, tucking him into bed. "You act like you're all grown up, but you have to remember, you're still a kid despite how you might want to believe otherwise. But I'm glad you feel comfortable enough around me to share things like this."

He nodded, giving him a small smile.

"Sleep tight, Lucius." Adrik smiled. "I'll see you tomorrow morning," he said before leaving the room, closing the door behind him.

Chapter 19

LUCIUS

FIRST-DAY TROUBLES

The next morning, Lucius woke up early. He felt so excited. He was going to school, to be around other kids! It was his only chance at a decently normal life. Getting dressed, he pulled up his high-waist black pants. Then he slipped on his white long-sleeved button-up shirt, taking extra time to make sure it looked smooth when tucked in. Looking at himself in the mirror, he couldn't help but think his school uniform looked very plain. But if it was what everyone wore, then he would wear it too.

Walking out, Adrik was still asleep, completely tucked under every blanket. Lucius had never woken up earlier than him before. He stared a few moments as his friend dozed in bed. Should he wake him? He was awful excited, and he didn't want to wait. But it seemed more considerate to let the man get his rest. After a long time, Lucius couldn't stand it any longer.

"Adrik," he whispered, walking into his bedroom. Adrik slept soundlessly.

Lucius let out a sigh, decided to let him sleep after all. He always knew when to wake up. Surely he would not oversleep today, on one of the most important days of Lucy's young life. Going to the kitchen, he decided to do something nice for his dear friend. He got out a pan and put it on the stove, turning the knob below. He heard the hiss, but he didn't see any fire. How did you start the fire? He had never seen Adrik do it. He was always asleep or in his room. That, or he just didn't pay that much attention.

Lucius looked around and spotted a box of matches. He knew what those were. As he grabbed them, he took one out. Maybe the fire just needed a little helping hand. He flicked a match and put it by the stove. With a sudden start, the match lit the fuse on the stove.

Lucius nearly jumped out of his new school clothes. He didn't expect the fire to start so quick! As he put the pan back on the stove, he went into the fridge and grabbed two eggs and two slices of bacon. He put the eggs in and started trying to scramble them. He had seen Adrik do this before, but they never stuck to the pan this bad. In the same pan next to the eggs, he laid down two slices of bacon and waited. As he continued to stir the eggs, he noticed they started to turn a strange brown color from the bacon grease. So he removed them to a plate. Upon closer inspection, he realized that the eggs weren't brown from just the grease but because he'd burnt them.

Lucius got out two spoons and started trying to scrape the burnt parts off. As he was doing so, he noticed that something smelled funny. Looking up, he saw smoke filling the ceiling! He turned around, moving the bacon from the stove, burnt black to a crisp.

Adrik came out of his bedroom. "Trying your hand at cooking?" he said with a light chuckle, coming over to turn off the stove. "Next time, I might start on low."

Lucius felt his face flush with embarrassment. "I was trying to do something nice to thank you, but now I think maybe it's best you cook another breakfast," he said, setting the pan on the cooler side of the stove, trying to avoid his friend's gaze.

"Nonsense. I'll eat your breakfast since you worked so hard to cook it for me," he said, sitting down at the counter. He looked down at the burnt bacon and eggs and cut himself a bite.

Lucius didn't want to watch as Adrik took a bite out of his eggs, chewed, and swallowed. "Well. It could certainly use some work.

If you want to learn, I could teach you. But it might not serve you many uses."

Lucius shrugged. "I think it needs more than just work, you don't have to spare my feelings."

"Nonsense. It's the thought that counts," he said, eating the rest of the breakfast without a complaint. "Are you ready to go?"

Lucius smiled and nodded, picking up his backpack.

"Then let's go," he said, walking to the car.

The whole ride over, Lucius could barely sit still. What sort of things were they going to teach him first? Would he learn how to read first? Or learn how to write? He heard that there were art classes in school; maybe he could become a painter like Misha. Or perhaps he could learn to build things. He couldn't stop his mind from racing.

Then Adrik broke through his thoughts. "Lucius, there's something I have to warn you about. The other kids, they've been going to school since they were five or six. They'll probably all be much further ahead of you. So you'll most likely end up in a younger class than your age. You'll definitely be the biggest kid there, but I talked to some of the teachers, and we set up something with the counselors. You'll be going to sit with them to focus on reading and writing, while the other kids work on other things. Is that okay?"

"Yes," he said. Lucius knew he would be needing the extra help. His mom was able to teach Eileen how to read, and she picked it up super fast. But he could never figure out how to get the words and letters to stop moving. Maybe his new teacher would show him.

Adrik pulled into the front of the school and slowed to a stop. "All right. This is the place."

Looking out the window, he suddenly didn't feel so sure. He wanted a normal life, but in so many ways, he was different. What if the other kids didn't like him, and he couldn't make any friends? He mentally slapped himself. What a bunch of silly childish fears.

Adrik handed him a piece of paper. "This has all your classes on it. Ask someone if you need help finding anything. Are you nervous?"

Lucius took the paper and shook his head. "I'm never nervous! It can't be harder than the other things I've done," he said, but that was a lie.

"Good attitude, kid." Adrik smiled.

Lucius got out of the car, pulling his backpack on. Walking in, he looked around. The school walls were a light-brown khaki color, and the floor was made of wood. Children were everywhere. Some were talking; others were sitting in classrooms, waiting for class to start. Lucius looked down at his piece of paper. He couldn't read what any of it said, but thankfully, each teacher had their name posted outside the door.

He walked into the teacher's classroom that matched the first name on his list. At the front of the room was a woman sitting behind a desk. She had on a pretty plain gray business-casual dress. It looked like it was made of thick wool. Her skin was a soft caramel color, and her head was covered in dark-brown curly hair, tied back. She was reading some papers on her desk though some reading glasses on the end of her nose. Lucius thought she looked awfully young to be a teacher, only in her late twenties, early thirties.

"Hi, um…" He hesitated. "Mrs.…uhh…"

"Mrs. Blum. Are you my new student? Lucius?"

He nodded.

"I didn't see a surname listed, Lucius. What is your last name?"

"Um…" Lucius thought for a long moment. He didn't know what his mother's surname was. "Kilesso," he said. It was Adrik's last name. Maybe it could be his too.

"Lucius Kilesso. Sit down. Class is starting soon."

Doing as he was told, he set his backpack on the floor beside him in the middle of the room, not wanting to stand out too much. As the other kids walked in, he tried not to seem conspicuous. He opened his journal and started doodling with his pencils and pens, thankful that Adrik had gotten him a few different colors.

A big burly kid sat down in the chair next to him, dropping all his stuff. "Nice bow, faggot. Your mommy give that to you?"

Lucius looked over at him. "Excuse me?"

"I said, 'Did your mommy give that to you?'"

"No, my sister did."

"Are you trying to be smart?"

"Zach, that's enough," Mrs. Blum said as the rest of the kids sat down.

Lucius felt a tap on his shoulder and turned to look at a girl covered in freckles with dirty-blonde, almost-brown hair.

"I'm sorry. Zach can be such a jerk. I really like your bow. I wish my brother wore the stuff I gave him. He just says it's too girly."

Lucius smiled. "Thanks. I love my sister. She's the best. I really miss her sometimes though because she had to stay with my mom in Germany," he said, making up a story on the spot.

The girl got a sad look on her face. "Well, maybe we can be friends. My name is Yana."

"My name is Lucius. I would love to be friends!"

"Maybe we can hang out or play during recess."

"I'd really like that!"

"Quiet, children!" Mrs. Blum said, writing the date on the board. January 15, 1963.

She waved Lucius to the front, and he happily complied. "This is Lucius. He's going to be in our class starting today. He will, however, be spending the first half of the day catching up on what he's missed earlier in the school year. Lucius, tell us about yourself."

He turned and looked at all his new classmates, suddenly feeling very nervous. His clothes felt too tight, and he could feel everyone's eyes focused on him.

"I...uh..." He hesitated, trying not to stutter and to speak in a clear, concise voice. He needed these kids to like him. This was almost as terrifying as being in the fighting ring. "My name is Lucius. I like blue. I live with my friend Adrik, and I love the ocean. And I love trees. I think they're nice and comforting, with how big they are and all the leaves."

"Thank you, Lucius. We are all very happy to meet you. Please grab a notebook from your backpack and a pencil. Ms. Ivanov is waiting for you outside."

"Yes, Mrs. Blum," Lucius said, grabbing what he needed out of his bag and heading out of the room. He saw a woman in a plain dark-blue dress. It reminded him of the night sky. She had red wavy hair, lots of freckles on her pale skin, and the most beautiful blue eyes.

"Are you Lucius?" she asked.

"Yes. Ms. Ivanov…?"

She smiled. "That's right. You are very smart, aren't you?"

Lucius let out a deep stressed sigh, trying to relax from his small taste of public speaking. "I sure hope so," he confessed, not feeling nearly so confident as he was last night.

"I'm sure you are. Let's go," she said, leading him down a hallway and into a small private room. It had only her desk and a small teaching table with some bookshelves and file cabinets.

"This is my room. I only do one on one teaching with kids. Once you are all caught up, you'll be able to join the other children full time! How's that sound?"

"Good. Thank you, ma'am."

Ms. Ivanov smiled big. "Now I need to know where you are academically. Do you know how to write at all?"

Suddenly, Lucius felt embarrassed as he shook his head no.

"Don't be embarrassed. That's okay. Your father met with the principle and me. This is your first time going to school, isn't it?"

Adrik? His father? He figured it made sense. He did just claim his last name earlier this morning, and it would raise a lot of questions if he were just some kid. He thought about it for a brief moment. He rather liked the idea of Adrik being his dad. He was kind to him, and he looked out for him. And besides, it was obvious that his real father didn't give a shit, or he would have at least shown up by now.

"This is my first time going to school, yeah," Lucius agreed.

"All right then, we're going to focus on learning letters first," she said, pulling out a big colorful sheet of paper.

Learning letters was fun! As he learned the letters for *A, B, C,* he recognized some of the symbols, but he couldn't exactly remember from where. He read on and just assumed he had seen them from one of Adrik's books or a sheet of paper.

When lunch came, Lucius walked back to the classroom. He put his notebook filled with letters and sounds back, and made his way down to the cafeteria. Being a little late, every kid was sitting at a table already. Lucius didn't want to get in line for food he'd have to pretend to eat, so he decided to look for Yana. Eventually, he spotted her smiling face as she waved him over.

Making his way across the room, he sat next to her with all the other little girls at the table.

"Yana, who's this?" the bronze-skinned girl next to her said.

"This is Lucius. He's new in my class. He's really nice!"

"Hi!" Lucius said, holding out his hand to give her a handshake. She stared at him. Feeling self-conscious, he pulled his hand back to his side.

Yana looked at him. "Alla can be a little hard to get to know, but she'll come around. Do you have any food?"

"I'm not hungry, but thank you."

"You'll be hungry after. Here, Mom packed me an apple, but I don't really like apples. Do you want it?"

"That's so nice, but really, I'm not hungry," he persisted, trying to do anything he could to convince Yana not to share her food with him.

"Suit yourself. So you lived in Germany, huh? I have always wanted to go to Germany. I hear they have a lot of pork there. What is your favorite food from your home country?"

"Uh, ah, um…" Lucius didn't know what to say. He couldn't say his favorite food from Germany was Katherine, although the thought was funny for about half a second before he felt bad for thinking it.

"I like pork and, um, I like the bread."

Yana gave him a weird look, clearly not getting the answer she expected. "What about the music? I've read all sorts of books about composers in Germany. Bach, Beethoven, Mozart? Well, Mozart is from Austria, but still close, right next to Germany. Do you like classical music?'

"Uhhhh, the music? Yeah, I like classical. I love it. With its… uhh…" He hesitated. "Booming and beat."

Yana gave him another odd look. Suddenly, he realized he might not be very good at improvising speech. Improvising during fighting? Hell, yeah! But talking? No. He was starting to feel very uncomfortable with the questions and with how little he knew about his home country.

"What about you? What are your favorite things about Russia?" he asked, desperately trying to get the subject off him.

Yana beamed. "Oh, don't think I don't love my home country. I do! We have ballet here, and Saint Basil's Cathedral, which I've never seen, but I want to! And we have borscht, which I don't like so much, but my father loves it. We also have piroshkis. Those are my favorite. Have you had one?"

Lucius nodded, lying. "I think Adrik made them once."

"Who's Adrik?"

"My dad," Lucius said, trying to keep up his lie.

Alla turned toward him. "You call your dad by his first name? That's really stupid."

"Alla, don't be rude!" Yana said. "It's not the weirdest thing. Maybe things are different in Germany."

Alla sneered and turned herself back to her lunch of carrots and a half-eaten sandwich. "Anyway, a piroshki is a bun that's filled up with meat, potatoes, cheese, and cabbage. It's really good! I'll bring one for you."

"Oh, no, no thank you," Lucius stuttered, trying not to sound ungrateful. "I just don't eat that much. I have a sensitive stomach."

"Oh, that would explain a lot. Do you care if I ask another question?"

Lucius shook his head, knowing if he refused her questions, he would start to look suspicious.

"Why is your hair so light? I've seen blonde hair almost as light as yours but never pure white before."

"My mother has hair like mine," he lied. "I don't know why it's so light. I do spend a lot of time in the sun, if that makes sense."

"Maybe that's it," Yana said, taking a bite out of her apple. After taking a bite, her face twisted a little in disgust.

Lucius breathed a quiet sigh of relief. *I better be careful*, he thought. *These lies are going to start building up, and then what will I do?*

After lunch ended, he headed back to class with the rest of the students. As he sat at his desk, all the other kids started pulling out their school books. He dug through his backpack, finding that Adrik had packed one for him too. He pulled it out and turned to Yana.

"Pssst! What page?"

"Thirty-six," Yana said, giving him a smile. "We're supposed to have that chapter read by the end of class."

"Lucius, Yana, this time is used for quiet reading. Then we will go over the material," Mrs. Blum barked, trying to do some papers at her desk.

He opened his book to page 36, thankful the book had lots of pictures. It had pictures of animals and all sorts of things. He turned to the cover to attempt to read it. "Science," it said. As he turned back to the page, he started carefully trying to sound out each word.

He held his finger to the page, desperately trying to get every word to hold still long enough for him to sound it out. Some of the words just refused to stay put, and it made him want to scream. How could everyone else read so quickly? It was like trying to catch a rabbit through a briar patch. He couldn't catch every letter, and every word was difficult. He sounded each one out, wondering if he was getting them right or if he just didn't know what they meant in the first place.

"All right, children, put down your books and pull out a piece of paper. Write down what you can remember of what you read," Mrs. Blum announced.

Oh no. Writing. He could barely read, and now he had to write? He grabbed the pencil in his left hand, trying to write some of the words he remembered. He looked at the inside of his hand as he wrote and saw the burn Boris had left on his first day on the ship. He wished he had been in school then. If he had, maybe he wouldn't feel so stupid and so far behind all the other kids. He turned around and peeked at Yana, who was writing at light speed. She had at least four paragraphs! Lucius didn't even have four words!

"Put down your pencils, children," Mrs. Blum said, walking to the front of the class. "Now, everyone, tell me three things you learned, and I will write them on the board. Try not to repeat any of the other students," she instructed, picking up a dusty piece of chalk. Every student seemed to have something unique and interesting for her to write.

Lucius couldn't hear what they were saying. He was panicking too much, trying to think of what he was going to say. He only had four words, and one of them was *science*. He stared at his paper and then at the board. Not that it made a difference. She was writing in cursive, which made it only more difficult to read. Finally, she called his name.

He stood up as all had done before him. "I learned…" He paused, looking at his chicken scratch handwriting, not remembering what he wrote and not being able to read it. "Science is neat."

The whole class went silent, staring at him before erupting in laughter. He felt his face turn beet red as he sat down and tried to cover his embarrassment with his hands.

"It's all right, Lucius. Try to stay more focused on the reading next time," Mrs. Blum said.

Yana tapped his shoulder. "I like science too," she whispered, giving him a reassuring smile.

At the end of the day, the two of them walked out of the school. Lucius could still feel his face burning from embarrassment. "Yana?"

She turned to look at him, pulling her kitty backpack higher up on her shoulders. "What's up?"

"I meant to thank you back there, for not laughing at me and for not saying I'm dumb," he said, feeling his eyes sting a little from the threat of tears.

Yana smiled. "I don't think you're dumb. I think you just are smart in other ways that don't involve school. My younger brother is like that too."

Lucius smiled, feeling a little better from her words. Walking to the front after the day was over, he saw Adrik in his blue GAZ M21, waiting for him. He ran to the car and opened the passenger seat, leaping in before slamming the door behind him.

"How was school?" Adrik asked, giving him a smile.

"Let's just go," Lucius said, not feeling in the mood for conversation.

The car drove off, and both sat in silence. Finally, Adrik was the first to speak. "I'm sorry your day was bad. Do you want to talk about it?"

Lucius crossed his arms, still not sure he felt up to talking. He could have beaten any one of those dinky kids in a fight. Then they wouldn't think he was so funny. But Yana had been nice to him. And Ms. Ivanov was trying to be patient.

"I got laughed at because I couldn't read. It's not my fault I never learned. All the other kids are so ahead of me! I knew they'd be further along, I'm not stupid. I just didn't know they would be this much further along. I made a fool of myself in front of the entire class! Got called a faggot because of my bow and got called weird by some girl I didn't even know named Alla. I couldn't eat lunch with all the kids. I wonder how long I'll be able to keep that 'I have an upset stomach' gag up. It was a disaster," he said, his eyes heating up with the tears falling down his cheeks. He quickly tried to wipe them away, but they were only replaced by new ones.

Adrik said nothing as he listened to Lucius rant and rave. When he had finally finished, he spoke. "Did you make any friends at least?"

"Well, I did make one."

"Good! What's their name?"

"Yana. She's really nice, and she's got dirty-blonde straight hair and a lot of freckles."

"She sounds very pretty."

"I guess so," he said. If he was being honest, Lucius didn't think much about her features being pretty. He more thought about how different she looked from his sister.

"Maybe you two will hit it off together and become a couple," Adrik joked.

"What? Ew! No, thanks."

"You said you thought she was pretty."

"I mean, yeah, I guess so, but not like that. I don't want to date her. We're friends! And she's like…" He didn't know what to say. He really didn't like the idea of dating Yana. "No, thanks."

Adrik smiled and laughed. "I'm just teasing you. You don't have to date her. I just like giving you a hard time."

Lucius felt his lips turn up in a smile. Adrik always seemed to make everything better somehow. When they got home, he went to his room to start on the homework. He pulled out his notebook and memorized the letters and sounds the best he could, saying them out loud over and over.

Dinner came and went, and Adrik went off to bed, suggesting Lucy do the same. As he lay in bed, he thought about the day that went by. Yana was so nice to him and so understanding when he wasn't like the other kids. Would he ever want to date her? He knew Adrik had only been joking, but Lucius really hadn't given it any thought until then. It made sense. Boys dated girls, didn't they? But he didn't really want to date a girl. He felt much more comfortable with the idea of dating a boy.

Chapter 20

LUCIUS

GOODBYE, SCHOOL

As Lucius's eyes grew heavy, he thought about what Ms. Ivanov had taught him, all those letters and symbols. Where had he seen some of them? He thought harder and closed his eyes, trying to remember. Then it dawned on him. He hopped out of bed, tripping over discarded clothes as he ran to the body mirror, ripping his pants off on the way. He stared at himself, then turned his hips toward the mirror. There it was, the brand. "BG," it said. He thought back to Boris. No doubt that was what the *B* stood for, but the *G* he had no idea.

Adrik opened the door sleepily. "What's with all the racket?" he said before staring down at Lucy's mark. "You were branded? Oh, honey, that must have hurt," he said, coming in to pet his hair.

"What's *branded* mean?" Lucius asked, feeling very stupid for not knowing.

"Branding is a procedure people usually do to livestock, like cows, in order to keep track of them or claim them as their property," he started before trying to take back his words. "But that doesn't mean you are property. You must have just been in a bad situation. Is this from your days in human trafficking? Do you want to talk about it?"

Lucius stared at him, then looked back to his hip in the mirror before pulling up his pants. "No, I don't," he said, not wanting to discuss such matters with Adrik right now.

Adrik gave him a small smile before patting his head again. "You're a tough kid, you know that? Just don't forget. I'm here to talk if you ever need me, okay?"

Lucius gave a little nod before giving him a hug and climbing back into bed. Livestock. Boris had branded him like he was livestock. The thought disgusted him. He had never given his mark much thought since he couldn't tell what it meant. He only assumed it was another punishment. He never imagined it would be a way to mark him as some sort of property. The thought made him sick to his stomach all over again. Remembering Boris, he could feel the pain on his hip, and he could feel the worms crawling inside him again from down below. He shivered, remembering the feeling of his fat, greasy hands touching him, holding him down, touching his backside, looking at him with those hungry, lust-filled eyes. He turned over to his side, wanting to throw up but finding himself unable to. Instead he shut his eyes tightly and tried to focus on sleep. But it never came. He didn't want to admit it, but he felt scared.

He sat up in bed and walked to his housemate's bedroom. After quietly knocking, he peeked in. Adrik was tucked in snugly like usual, sleeping very quietly. Lucius tried to tiptoe until he could crawl under the covers with his friend. He scooted over to him, laying his head on his chest.

"Did you have nightmares?" he heard Adrik mumble before pulling an arm out to pet through his hair.

"I just couldn't sleep," he admitted. "Can I sleep with you tonight? I promise it won't be every night."

He chuckled sleepily. "Yeah, you can sleep with me," he murmured.

Lucius stared off into space, not feeling afraid anymore now that he wasn't alone. The thoughts of Boris quickly vanished from his mind. Instead he thought about what had happened during the day. He really did like Yana as his friend had said, but he hoped she wouldn't get the wrong idea. He didn't feel interested in dating her.

As he snuggled up to the blond-haired man beside him, his thought process changed to a new topic.

He remembered what Miss Ivanov said earlier that day. Adrik? His father? The more he pondered on it, the more his friend really did seem a father figure to him. He took him in, tried to make him food, drove him to school. He did everything a father was supposed to do for their kid. But in another aspect, he wasn't his dad. He didn't know where his dad was or who he was. The thought bothered him a bit. If only things had been different. Eventually, as his figurative father's breathing slowed, Lucy found his eyes drifting closed for rest.

The next day went the same as before, except Adrik cooked his own breakfast.

"Will you be okay today?" he asked before he could get out of the car.

Lucy nodded before leaving. He went into Mrs. Blum's class. Ms. Ivanov was waiting for him.

"Miss Ivanov and I have decided that it would be best for you to spend all day with her. You will still have my lunch period, and once you have caught up, you will be free to rejoin our class. Does that sound all right, Mister Kilesso?"

Lucius nodded, sad he wouldn't get to see as much of Yana but happy he was being spared from embarrassment.

"Then please take your backpack to her classroom," Mrs. Blum said.

He did as he was told and followed Miss Ivanov.

"This will be fun. I'll help you learn reading in no time. Then things will be back to normal," she said, smiling, trying to make the best of the situation.

"Thanks for all the help," he responded, not knowing exactly what he was supposed to say.

When they got to the classroom, Lucius set his backpack in a cubby and sat at the student desk. His personal teacher seemed very impressed by all the work he did. When lunch came, he sat next to Yana again.

"I didn't see you in class. Did you go straight to Miss Ivanov's room?"

"Yeah, I'm going to be with her full time for a while, just till I'm more caught up."

Alla scoffed and rolled her eyes. Yana ignored her. "Well, maybe that's for the best. It's no fun going to school if you don't understand anything."

He nodded.

"Say, you didn't bring lunch again! Aren't you going to get hungry?"

"No, I really don't eat very much. And I have a sensitive stomach, remember?"

"If you insist," Yana said, sounding somewhat concerned.

After lunch, Lucius returned to the small classroom. He was really starting to feel confident about his letters. At the end of the week, they moved on to words and sentences.

"How do I get the words and letters to hold still?" he asked. "The other kids do it so well. Is there a trick to it?"

Miss Ivanov gave him a funny look. "Move around? What do you mean?"

"All my letters keep moving, so I can't read what the word says."

She thought for a moment before reaching into a drawer. "What's your favorite color, Lucius?"

"Blue?" he answered, wondering why the sudden question was so important.

"Then I have a present for you," she said, pulling out a little strip of see-through blue film. "Just place this over each sentence you read. It'll help the words to stop moving. I think what you have is called dyslexia."

"What's dyslexia?"

"It's exactly like you said. It's a condition where your brain tries to 'fix' the order of the letters, making it harder for you to read the words that are printed. But this should help," she said, handing him the blue strip.

Lucius placed the blue strip on the sentence he was trying to read. As he placed the film on, the letters magically moved back to their places. They still switched and shook every now and again, but it was a lot easier.

"The cat drank the milk, purring happily," Lucius read. *It's still hard, and it still sort of hurts my head. But I'll use this if I have to read,* he thought to himself.

"Wonderful! You're making leaps and bounds Mister Kilesso. We're going to practice reading and counting like this for another week. Then you'll learn numbers and basic math. You'll rejoin the other students after. How's that sound?"

"It sounds good, I'll learn fast!" he said with confidence.

The next several months went by with ease. He studied and went to school during the week and spent all weekend delivering medicines. Making money was nice, it made him feel capable and independent. Adrik set up a situation with Feliks where the company would provide people who couldn't pay their deals to Lucius so he could eat in secret. It was enough to keep him fed for the most part. As time went on, he continued his schooling career and was even able to join the other classes! He struggled behind due to not knowing the material, but at least he was learning. Every day he sat next Yana as she ate, but Alla still refused to speak to him. Six or so months went by like this, and the leaves started littering every tree. It had even started to get warm outside.

"Lucius, guess what," Yana said during lunch.

"What?"

"Me and my family, we're moving to America this weekend! I wanted to keep it a surprise, but I also didn't want to tell you because, well, I was worried you would be sad. I don't like goodbyes." She seemed upset. "That, and Mom and Dad told me to keep it a secret," she whispered.

Lucius was sad, but hearing her worry about it made him pretend not to be. "I'm happy for you! You always talk about wanting to travel. Now you'll get to! What are you looking forward to most?"

"Oh, I am definitely looking forward to learning to speak a new language! I know some English, but I want to learn American English. I know Russia and America are going through difficulties right now, but my grandma lives in America. That's why we're moving."

He nodded. He had picked up from the media and from those around him that America and Russia were not exactly friends at the moment, but for the most part, he tried to ignore it. It didn't seem to affect him in any way, so he saw no reason to give it any leverage.

"But it's going to be really fun!" Yana continued. "I can't wait to taste all the American food and make new friends! But I am going to miss you guys."

"I'll miss you too, Yana," Lucius replied.

"It's not like you can't write. You'll write me letters, won't you?" Alla questioned.

"Yes, of course! I'll write to you both!"

As the bell rang, all the students went back to their classrooms, and when the day ended, Lucius gave his friend a hug. Watching as she climbed into her parents' car, he wondered if he would ever see her again. America was an awfully long way. He seemed to only travel by accident. So unless she moved back, he thought it was unlikely he'd ever get to see her smile or hear her laugh ever again. The thought made him really sad. Even though it had only been a few months, he really liked hanging out with her.

Maybe he could hang out with his other friends at lunch from now on. But once he thought of it, he realized he didn't have any other friends. He could always hang out with Alla? No. She didn't like him; she thought he was weird. He could hang out with the boys? Except they all called him a faggot and liked to make fun of him. Lucius already learned basic reading, and now he could do addition, subtraction, basic multiplication, and division. So why stay? To learn more history? Science? Lucius didn't think he would ever need those things with the way his life was headed. He was working in a drug cartel, for crying out loud. Any science and mixing he could learn from his coworkers. Any history he could learn through stories told to him.

"What's wrong?" Adrik asked on the drive home, breaking him out of his thoughts. "You've been silent the whole car ride. Did something happen at school today?"

Lucius let out a big sigh. It was frustrating sometimes how easily Adrik could tell what he was thinking. "My friend Yana is moving away this weekend. I don't know if I'll be seeing her again."

"Oh, I'm sorry, buddy," Adrik said.

"I think I'm going to quit school then," he said, making up his mind.

"What? You've only been in school for half a year!"

"I know how to read. I know how to write. I know how to count and do math. What more do I really need?"

Adrik's face twisted. It was clear he didn't like this idea. "Lucius, you need to keep going to school. It's good for you!"

Lucius crossed his arms. "No, I don't. Besides, the reading makes my head hurt, and everyone knows I'm the stupidest kid in the class. Besides, what good does it do me to walk around and pretend to be human? I'm not, and who knows how much longer I'll be able to hide it? Kids are already suspicious that I don't eat. And if I do, I have to run to the bathroom immediately after lunch. Adrik, why bother?"

His friend opened and closed his mouth, and Lucius knew he had him. He did have excellent points. He just couldn't live around humans in such close quarters like this. He was bound to be discovered eventually.

"I just think it's important to learn more than the basics."

"I don't," he said stubbornly.

"Lucius, have you heard the term *knowledge is power*? It means the more you know, the safer and better prepared you are."

"Then why don't you teach me?" Lucius compromised. "I don't want to stay long enough to have no friends in class. The other kids are mean to me there, and I feel stupid whenever Mrs. Blum calls on me."

Adrik sat silent for a moment, eyes set on the road ahead as if he was mulling over what he had just heard. "Fine," he said reluctantly. "But I can't guarantee I'm a good teacher. I don't exactly have a ton of experience. Plus, we can only do it at night when I'm out of work."

Lucius smiled. "Thanks, Adrik," he said as they rode the rest of the way home in silence.

Chapter 21

LUCIUS

BACK TO BUSINESS

The next morning, Lucius got ready for work. The best part of not going to school was it gave him the ability to make more money, doing twice as much work. He got dressed in jeans and a jacket. It was almost summer now, so he didn't need to dress too thick. Lucius brushed out his hair before putting it in a bow. In the six or so months with Adrik, he had let it grow out quite a bit. He didn't need to wear his bow like a headband anymore and could wear it up in a ponytail. He liked it better this way. Even though his hair was long, he thought he might ask Adrik to try bangs on him soon. It would hide his eyes better. Then people couldn't tell when he was hungry.

After tying up his hair and getting dressed, he slipped on Boris's silver-buckled belt. The buckle was a pain to put on, but he always wore it anyway. He wanted to have something of Boris's so he would never forget what he had done to him. He might forgive him one day. He might even get over the trauma of their life together, but he never wanted to forget. In a strange way, he wanted to remember Boris the same way he wanted to remember his mother and his sister. Despite how he hated him, he had still been an important part of his life.

Lucy's big regret was that he had never taken anything from Oleg or Misha to remember them by. But this belt was enough to make him remember what had happened to them. In a way, it was almost comforting. Almost.

As he walked out of his bedroom, Adrik was already eating breakfast as usual. Then the car ride was peaceful. He liked the drive. It had been stressful at first, but now he felt it very relaxing. It allowed him to see new things in the ever-changing scenery around him. The bumps in the road were soothing, and the soft hum of the vehicle almost rocked him to sleep.

Maybe I'll get a car of my own one day. But a motorcycle would be better, he thought.

"So after we get finished with work, I want you to show me what you already know. Then maybe we can continue from there," his friend interrupted, clearly trying to plan the lessons for tonight.

"I learned how to read, and I can write. I can count and do basic math too."

"Do you know how to read in only Russian?"

"Yes," Lucius said, wondering if that was enough.

"Well then, I'll teach you in English. Russian is the native language here, but almost every country speaks English along with their native tongue. Do you know how to read any German from your home country?"

Lucius hesitated, suddenly feeling a little silly. "No."

"I can teach you, although I only know a little. It'll suppose it'll be a learning experience for both of us, right?"

Lucy nodded, feeling very thankful his friend was willing to learn a new skill just to teach him.

When they finally got to work, Adrik helped him out of the car and went to his office to start on the finances. Lucy went to Rupert as usual.

"Good morning. I have a new assignment for you." He sniffled. How was he still sick? It was summer time now?

"Are you ever going to get rid of your cold?"

"Oh, I did! Now I'm going through allergies," he said before pausing to blow his nose.

Lucius thought it seemed like a whole lot of overkill. They made a business in selling medicine. Didn't Rupert have the sense to take any? He had come to know that Rupert wasn't married and didn't have any children despite wanting them or not. Maybe if he wasn't so sniffly all the time, he could go out and meet women and at least try to marry one of them. But who was he to tell Rupert how to live his life?

"What am I delivering today?"

"Well, summers here, so first, I have you delivering allergy medicines to some poor families with children. Then you'll be making your first delivery to the richer parts of town. I'm going to need you to come back to me to pick up the drugs to sell since they're illegal and more punishable than just giving out allergy medications."

What sort of medicine did the rich need? They had the money to afford health care and brand drugs. Why did they need to go behind the government to get basic medicine they could afford to get legally? He decided it might be best not to ask questions. After picking up the shipment and address, he headed out. He always liked delivering to families the best. They were the most grateful. He headed into town. It was midday, and he wore a backpack filled with the shipment. As he was walking down the street, he spotted a police car parked in front of a house on his delivery sheet. Best to avoid them. He knew he might not get in trouble for carrying allergy medication, but still they would ask questions, and it would be difficult not to divert them back to the company. So before they could see him, he turned down a different street, deciding he would come back to that house later.

Going to his second stop, he knocked.

A tall man answered. "Hello?"

Lucius gave a light smile. "Hello, I'm from DDC. I have the things you asked for."

The man quickly ushered him inside. "Thank you. The police have been running through our neighborhood all week, trying to crack down on illegal drug use."

"Well, hide these somewhere safe," Lucius said, pulling out a small bag of pills.

"I will. Thank you," he replied, taking the bag and hiding it in a compartment under his sink.

This was always the way of it. Every customer paid in advance. It made for fewer complications, which meant fewer deaths. Unfortunately for Lucy, this meant less food as well. He didn't mind, though. He would rather go a long time without eating than have people die on his behalf.

After making all his other deliveries, he went back to house number one. The police were gone, so he walked up, knocking on the door. No one answered. He knocked harder. Still no answer. As he was turning around, he heard a shout from behind.

"Don't move, kid!"

Cautiously, he did as he was told. The police officer walked up to him carefully, opened up his backpack, and sifted through the bags of pills.

"Why do you have these?"

"They're for my mother," he lied, trying to throw him off the scent. "I live here."

He was met with a disbelieving glance. "All right, kid. We're just going to have to take you in for a minute for some questions, then you'll be on your way."

Lucius nodded and followed him around the corner to his car. As he was about to step inside, Lucy yanked away as fast as he could and kicked up against the car, shooting himself away from it.

"Hey! Stop!" the officer shouted, running after him.

He turned on heel and ran away from the house, turning a quick corner after corner. Lucy was fast, but his pursuer was as well. As Lucy's legs carried him faster, his strength made him able to take more powerful steps with longer strides despite being shorter.

When he turned his thirteenth corner, no longer able to hear the officer, he then took one strong jump onto a roof. Within a few moments, he heard his chaser huffing and puffing, trying to keep pace with him or at least find him. They had been running for several minutes; it was no surprise the adrenaline had worn off. Still, he continued to search.

Lucius stayed safe and silent lying on top of the roof, occasionally switching sides so as not to be seen for the better part of three hours. Several cops had come to the neighborhood to look for him but found nothing. Within another hour, they gave up and left. He finally felt safe enough to sit up on the roof, dumping the contents out of his backpack. He turned the bag inside out, returned the items, and zipped it up. He couldn't get the bag completely closed, but it would work for the time being.

Then he did the same with his sweatshirt. It was furry inside and would look a little weird, but at least he would be unrecognizable. Pulling the hood up to hide his hair, he climbed down. He walked slowly in the crowd of children coming home from school until he could take a turn back toward work.

"What did you do?" Rupert asked, less than happy. "All over the radio, the police are looking for you!"

"There was nothing I could do! I avoided them the best I could, but they snuck up on me!"

"You should have let them take you in. Then you could have gotten out unsuspiciously if you just lied, right?"

"I got nervous," he admitted, never having had a run-in with the police before.

He had seen them, but this was different. "Go talk to Feliks. He wants to see you," Rupert said, sitting back down and angrily digging himself back into his work.

Lucius rubbed the back of his head before going up to see the boss. He knocked on the door softly.

"Come in! I heard you ran from the police?" Feliks said, tapping a finger on his desk somewhat impatiently.

"I'm sorry, sir," Lucius replied, suddenly feeling very small. The man was old and wrinkled yet somehow still made him feel threatened despite his inability to walk.

Feliks let out a long sigh. "It's only your first time. I forgive you. However, you need to be more careful when you walk up to the doors. If you know the police are on the prowl or had just been to a house, maybe skip that house for the day. And never ever run from the police unless you absolutely have to, say, in the event you are carrying a really heavy illegal drug, not just allergy medication."

He nodded, thankful to be forgiven but still feeling very foolish for not thinking his actions all the way through.

"You will find that the people who go farthest in life think before they act. I had high hopes of making you the next leader after I'm gone. If you're going to become the next head of Dixie Drug Cartel, you'll need to be smarter."

"Me? The next leader? What about Adrik? Didn't you practically raise him? Why wouldn't you make him the next leader?"

"I offered it to him, but he turned me down. He doesn't feel comfortable being in charge of others. This job requires you to really play your pawns well or risk the lives and well-being of those in the company. And between you and me, Adrik is too kind for this job. He wants to help everyone. I'm afraid he would be so kind and giving he would give the company away. He might not at first, but his compassion always manages to get the best of him. It's why he took you in, it's why he is lying to me about you being a vampire, and it's why he's trying to give you everything you could ever desire."

Lucius' eyes widened. "But I didn't... How did you..."

"That's right. I know what you are. Do you think I lived in Russia my whole life? No. I've traveled to Germany, Scotland, and England—three places where vampires are far more than a myth. I'm not going to take action against you for it. The fault is not yours. However, your type leading the company would certainly work well. Being a vampire and all, I trust you should be able to dispose of any...problems much more easily than a human would. And you won't be afraid to make the hard decisions, hmm? Blood won't discourage you, so should the workers below not follow you, use threats or action. Yes?"

Lucius held his tongue, but he thought Feliks had him all wrong. He didn't want to threaten anyone, and he certainly didn't want to hurt them, especially people he was close with! But he knew that was a thought for another time. This was an opportunity, wasn't it? And if Lucius had learned anything, it was to seize information and opportunity.

Lucius pondered. He thought about Feliks and how he knew of his vampirism. He knew Adrik had mentioned needing the bodies to Feliks, but it seemed his boss was already aware. Lucius remembered where he came from. He knew about vampires in Germany, but England? Where was England? They had vampires too? Did they live in fear as Germany did? Or were things different there? And why was he only hearing about it now? He had too many questions, but he couldn't ask Feliks. It was not like he would know anyway. And what did he mean by his type? He felt a little insulted, but he knew it wasn't meant in a malicious way.

"I didn't expect you to give me so many compliments after I just messed up," Lucius confessed.

"Between you and me, I'm surprised it took you this long to make a mistake. You've got more skill in transporting than most newcomers. You've already almost surpassed all the others in the company."

"Thank you, sir."

"But don't think this means you're going to get off easy. You still aren't allowed to come in for work for at least three weeks. I don't want to raise any suspicions by having you around. But when you come back, I think we can arrange for you to start learning how to be a leader. How does that sound?"

Thinking on it, it would be a boring three weeks, having nothing to do and being forced to stay home, but with the promise of being a leader, it wouldn't be the end of the world.

"You have great reaction time and response. So I'm sure you are an excellent fighter should you need the skill. You do, however, need to learn more about business, finance, trading, and company policy. You need to know how to react when something goes wrong. And above all else, you need to learn how to care for your workers. A company is like a car. If everything works, it runs perfectly, but if not, it can cause disaster. Since you're here today, we'll start your training, then we'll continue it in a few weeks."

"Thank you, sir," Lucius said.

Feliks gave a curt nod. "Go back to Rupert. It's probably best you learn from the ground up."

"Yes, sir. Thank you, sir," he said before walking out. The new leader…how exciting! He promised himself he would try to be a just and honest leader. He wanted to do what was best for everybody in the company. It was like Feliks said. If things ran well, the company moved forward like a car.

He went down to Rupert, who was nose deep in work.

"I'm going to be promoted to head of the company after Feliks! Isn't that great?" Lucius exclaimed, unable to hide his excitement.

Rupert tensed and looked up. "You're being…" He paused like he couldn't believe his ears. "Promoted?"

"Yeah! Aren't you happy for me?"

"I've been working in this company for fifteen years, and I've only been promoted once to the job I have now! Unbelievable," he muttered. "Yes, and I suppose Feliks wants me to train you in my position first, right?"

"Right," he said, not having thought about how Rupert might feel being skipped over in the totem pole.

"Fine then. Come here," he said, pulling out a stack of five pages. "Read over those. Tell me what you think they are."

Pulling out the blue film bookmark from his pocket, he started reading the best he could. He read all sorts of numbers, words of medicine, times, dates and names. He could hardly understand the words on the paper before it dawned on him what he was looking at.

"These are expense reports saying the drugs sold, to whom, how much, and all that. Right?"

"Exactly. These go on file. I keep a copy in here for future sales and send a copy to Adrik so he can control the finances of the drugs we purchase and how much we sell them for." Handing the papers back, Rupert put them away, getting out a different stack of papers and handing them over.

"Take a look at these. It's every transporter's work ethic. How many transports they've done, the number of times they've been caught or questioned, whom they deal with, etc."

"Is this why you always want me to check in?"

"Mhm, you are just like any employee. You have your own report and record. This is mainly what I'm in charge of—keeping the smaller fish in line."

"What about drugs that come in?"

"Well, we have transporters and importers. Importers are under me as well, but they are in charge of bringing the medicine in, usually in big trucks of some sort. Adrik handles most of the finance and such for that. I just see the jobs through."

"Oh." Lucius felt amazed by how little he knew about all this. Just when he thought he knew most everything there was to know about the company.

"Not as easy as you thought, hmm? Well, wait till you get to Adrik. He has a whole new layer of difficulty surrounding his job," Rupert said with another sniffle.

On the drive home, Lucy wondered what being a financier for the company entailed. It seemed like Rupert handled everything. What was left for Adrik to do? And where did Feliks fall into the company? Was he really only the leader, working hard to make sure everyone gets along?

After dinner, Lucius was trying to study reading and spelling in his bedroom when he heard a knock on his door.

"Ready to start?" Adrik asked.

"Yes," he said, cleaning off his desk. "But first, I wanted to ask you for something. Since I'm a wanted criminal now, I should change my look. Can you give me bangs?"

"Bangs? I wouldn't say you're a wanted criminal, so you don't have to change your look if you really don't want to."

"No, I guess not. That was just an excuse. I really do want to change my hair."

Adrik laughed. "Sure, kid. You should have just said so! Come to the bathroom."

Lucius followed him, and Adrik pulled up a stool for him to sit on.

"Do you want bangs that go over your whole forehead? Or are you trying to play the edgy teenager card and put bangs over only one side of your face?"

Lucy thought for a moment. He never considered half bangs. He liked the idea, and it would make his hair especially unique.

"Half bangs!"

"Half bangs, it is," Adrik said, separating his hair.

He put a big chunk of hair in front of his eyes, and Lucius held it still while he tied the rest into a ponytail. After brushing the part a long time, adding some hair, putting some behind. He finally started cutting, brushing the hair out for him to see when he was finished.

"How's it look?"

"It looks amazing!" Lucius said, turning his head side to side. His new bangs barely went past his right eye, but his hair was so light he could see straight through it.

"Edgy enough for you?"

"Yes, perfect, very edgy." Lucius laughed.

"Good, but now it's late, and we need to sleep."

"Tomorrow we'll study?"

"Yes." Adrik smiled, patting his shoulder and heading to bed.

The next day after dinner, Adrik poked his head into Lucy's room as usual. "I hope you're excited to learn!"

"Yes! I'm ready! I've been going over what I know as a warm up all day."

"Great! So I decided we'll work on German first. Since you speak it already, it will be easiest to learn to translate."

Adrik opened a book he brought in and started the lesson. When the night ended, his teacher was struggling to keep his eyes open, but Lucy felt wide awake. He loved learning, but even more so, he loved feeling smart and useful. He never felt very smart in school, because everyone always said how behind he was. But learning his home language was not only comforting but exciting as well!

"All right, kid, I can't do it anymore. I'm off to bed. You can stay up as long as you want since you'll be home mostly alone for the next few weeks. Here's what I was going to start tomorrow," Adrik said, setting an English book on his desk. "Review and learn some on your own, and we'll start after work. Good night, Lucius." He exhaustedly dragged his feet to the room across the hall.

"Goodnight!" Lucius replied. He studied all night. He wanted to make as much progress as possible while he had the time to do so, and nighttime was always when he felt the best. He stayed up so late that he was still awake when Adrik climbed out of bed the next morning.

"Have you been up all night?" he asked.

"I was just having such a good time learning. I didn't want to go to sleep."

"Well, it's morning now, so you should probably get some rest so you aren't exhausted for our lesson tonight."

"All right," he agreed, stripping down and climbing into bed. Lucius found that learning wasn't half bad when he didn't have to worry about being better than his classmates. He remembered his mother and Eileen. As he pulled the covers up over himself, he thought about how he should have paid more attention to the lessons his mother had taught while he'd had a true best friend he could have learned them with. But the thought didn't last long. Lucius must have been more tired than he realized, because the second he lay down, he couldn't remember anything after.

Chapter 22

LUCIUS

LEARNING TO LEAD

The next three weeks went by quicker than he had expected. Adrik went to work every morning, and Lucius stayed up almost every night, studying German and English. He thought it was quite exciting, the thought of knowing how to speak in multiple countries. He understood now what Adrik meant when he said that knowledge was power.

When finally allowed to go back to work, he continued training with Rupert. "All right, kid, today's a big pick up day." He sniffled, handing him a piece of paper.

Lucius read over it. "So the shipment hasn't been paid yet?"

"No, imports work a little differently. We get the drugs and medicine, then we pay. The whole transaction is recorded on security cameras in case something happens. If an importer steals the money we give to pay for our product, we don't want people coming to us claiming we never paid."

Around noon, he was taken to the back, where a huge truck was waiting with a strange man standing next to it. Rupert opened up the truck's cargo hold, looking over the contents.

"Looks good, Lucius! Time to move stuff."

"Got it," he said, grabbing several boxes and bags of things to move into the warehouse.

After all was said and done, they paid with cash held in a small white sealed envelope, and the truck drove away.

"See? Easy enough. Now we just have to organize where things go and put them away inside."

Lucius did that too. He wanted to prove he was efficient in every job he was assigned. He was already ahead in the company, but sometimes you should do something extra, with the only reasoning being to stay ahead. After he organized and sorted everything, he was taught how to track drugs, ship them, collect payment, and track employee transports. He thought this all seemed like a lot of work. No wonder Rupert wanted a raise so badly. But that was up to Adrik and Feliks. Time went by like this for a year as Lucius learned how to work, with schooling on the side. Then one day, he was given a strange assignment.

"You need to learn about the more illegal transactions before you go to Adrik," Rupert said.

"What sort of transactions?"

"The harder drugs. Heroin, cocaine—those sorts of things. You need to go on another transport so you can know what to expect," he said, handing him the address. "It says on there what exactly you will be shipping and where to. But these people didn't pay in advance. They never do for these sorts of drugs. So collect first, deliver second. Got it?"

"Got it," Lucius said, looking over the paper.

"Now listen here, kid. This isn't like our other transactions. I mean it. These drugs are illegal. If the police catch you with these, they'll kill you on the spot and kill all of us next. So don't get caught! You understand? Or you'll put us all in danger."

Lucius felt his blood run cold, and he gave a serious nod.

"Now go. And be careful. Don't forget what I said, understand? And don't take any extra stops or talk to anyone not being sold to."

Lucius nodded and headed out the door. He felt so nervous now as he collected the ten grams of heroin. He needed to collect five thousand rubles for the transaction. Lucius only hoped it would go by smoothly.

Following the address, he wandered into the richer part of town. Knocking on the door, it was answered by a teenager with black hair that matched the huge bags under his eyes. He was wearing nothing but a tank top and pajama pants.

"You got the stuff?" he murmured, ushering him inside.

"Yes," he said, getting out his bag before remembering. "Five thousand rubles first."

"Yeah, yeah, I got it. Give me the drugs."

"No, money first," Lucius said stubbornly. He didn't want to take the risk of returning with nothing.

"Fine, fine," he said, reaching into his pocket and pulling out a huge wad of cash. Lucius took it and counted it over. One, two, three, four. "You're missing one thousand rubles."

The teenager scoffed. "Just give me the drugs, and I'll give you the last of it after!"

"No, do you think I'm an idiot?"

"Fine, fine!" he said, marching down a hallway. After a few minutes of rummaging, he came out with the money. "Here, take it. Now give me what I paid for!"

Lucius could tell he was getting impatient as he tossed the drugs toward him.

"Good. Get out."

He happily did as he was bid, not wanting to spend too much time here before returning to work.

"And how did it go?"

"It was...different than the other transactions."

"The rich aren't as nice, are they?" Rupert sniffled, wiping his nose on his sleeve.

"No, they're less thankful for the help."

"That's because harder drugs like that aren't needed so much as wanted. It's why we charge them more so the people who actually need medicine and are sick can buy it for cheaper."

Lucius nodded. After learning all about the rich and their fancy illegal drugs, he went to train in finance. He had never been inside

Adrik's office before. It was clean, just like his house, and it smelled strongly of bleach and floor cleaner. Everything had a spot, and everything was organized, unlike Rupert's, which had papers everywhere and dirty tissues stacked up in the wastebasket and covering the floor around it.

"So finally done learning the warehouse?"

Lucius nodded. "I'm ready to learn about money."

"Then you've come to the right place," he said, pulling up a chair next to his desk. "I handle every payment. Rupert delivers out all the money and payments I decide on and make. It's up to me to take the information he records, like the tracking of drugs, what's sold, and how much. Then I use it to predict how much we need to buy and stock for the upcoming transactions we make. I am also in charge of making sure every employee gets paid the right price for their time and sales in our company."

It sounded hard. How did Adrik make sure to keep track of all this information? What happened if his prediction was wrong and he bought too much or too little?

Adrik looked over at him and laughed. "You look shocked. Don't worry. It's not as hard as it seems. All the information I need is written in documents and put into proper files. That's why this is my job, not Rupert's. It takes a much more organized mind to do this sort of work," he said, patting his head. "Not to say that he isn't smart—he just has different skills. He's very good at managing people. That is something I cannot do."

Lucius smiled. "It's good you do this then."

"Well, you'll be able to do it soon too. Here." Adrik handed him a piece of paper. "Here's a list of every employee and how much money they brought in and how much they made."

Lucius looked over the papers. He was amazed by how much some people sold, and he thought they must be using their cars to deliver faster. But when he looked at the dates on a few of their paychecks, he noticed that during some months, even though no sales took place, they were still paid.

"Why would they be paid if they didn't make a sale?"

"Ahh, our most loyal workers get paid during the slow months as a reward for their continued loyalty. The longer you stay in our company, the better we'll treat you," Adrik said.

Lucius thought it was all very confusing, but after a full year and a half of working and watching Adrik work, things finally started to make sense. Fall was approaching soon, and he thought he was doing an excellent job moving forward in the company. Finally, it was time to train with Feliks.

"Close the door behind you," Feliks said the moment he stepped into his office. "You're learning at an alarming rate, Lucius. I'm quite proud."

Lucy could practically feel his head swelling with pride.

"But you're with me now. I won't let you become leader until you are at least twenty. Do you understand that? You're going to be training with me for seven years since you're only thirteen. It will be long and slow from here on out. Can you do it without getting discouraged about the pace?"

"Yes," Lucius said, very confident in his ability.

"Good. My job, and eventually your job, is all about leading the smaller fish of the company. What do you think makes a good leader, Lucius?"

Lucy thought for a moment before speaking. "A good leader is smart, brave, and knows how to command those around him."

"Is that all?"

"A good leader also demands respect."

"And how do you demand respect?" Feliks asked, watching him closely.

"Threats?" Lucas said.

"Yes, threats are one way, but threats don't do well if they aren't carried out. What else?"

Now Lucius wasn't sure. He shrugged.

"Appearance," Feliks said, moving his electric wheelchair out around his desk. "When you look at me, what do you see? Be honest."

"You have white hair and grayish eyes, and you need a wheelchair."

Feliks let out a laugh. "Yes, all those things are true, but look closer. How do I present myself?"

"You are wearing a clean expensive suit, your hair is styled, and you're shaved."

"Yes, exactly. These are all things that show power. The way I dress and present myself shows very clearly that I am the boss around here. I also have the biggest desk, the biggest office, and the most privacy in the company. Tomorrow I want you to dress for the job I have," Feliks said, wheeling up to him. "Can you do that?"

"Yes."

"Good, and get Adrik to help you with this," he said, reaching up and giving a soft tug on Lucy's soft patch of new facial hair.

Reaching up to his chin, he hadn't even noticed he started growing it. Sure, it was just in small patches, but still.

After returning home, Adrik went to cook, and Lucy headed to the bathroom. He knew he had to shave to impress Feliks. So grabbing the razor, he got his face wet and started on his own. He cut himself almost instantly—and jumped. Blood was softly running down his face. He could do this, couldn't he? He had seen Boris do this on the ship, but he had made it look so easy. After cutting himself several more times, he finally decided it was best to ask for help after all.

"Adrik?" he said, walking out into the living room where he had started reading.

"My goodness, do I wanna see the other guy?"

Lucius crossed his arms. "Ha ha, very funny. Can you teach me how to shave? Feliks says I need to start."

Adrik smiled. "Sure," he said, walking into the bathroom. He got two towels and soaked them in the sink filled with hot water. "Put this on your face."

Lucius did as he was told. The warmth was soothing, but it felt odd to have only one part of his body feel moist. His friend did the same as him and spoke muffled through the towel.

"Now we sit here for a few minutes. This will make our beautiful beards grow soft."

Lucius couldn't see it, but he could tell Adrik was giving him his usual cat-like smile under the towel. He appreciated Adrik trying to make a joke out of the awkward pains of puberty. It made him feel a lot better about having no idea what to do.

"Now remove the towel, and put shaving cream on the parts of your face you want to shave," he said, removing the towel and putting shaving cream in both of their hands.

Lucius looked in the mirror, attempting to do as Adrik did. When he looked over at his friend, he saw that his friend had shaving cream on his eyebrows. He couldn't help but laugh.

"I can't wait to see what you look like without eyebrows."

"Me either. I've been considering it for a long while now."

"Wait. Really?" Lucius was puzzled.

"No, not really. I'll wash it off after."

"Oh, good. I didn't want to say anything, but you'd look stupid without eyebrows."

"I think anyone would." Adrik laughed. "Next, grab your razor," he said, handing Lucy the nicer razor of the two he had. "Then shave with the grain of your facial hair, not against it. If you shave against it, you'll get really bad razor burn."

"Okay," he said, trying to do as he was told. It was difficult to tell which way his facial hair grew when it was covered in white puffy shaving cream. He had to wash off his razor frequently, which threw off his concentration and focus. The face wasn't so hard, but the neck was definitely tough.

"Finished? You did a good job, you only cut yourself maybe twice since we started! That's better than I did my first time. You'll get the hang of it. Now double-check your work."

Lucius looked in the mirror and turned his head side to side. He didn't have any more facial hair, but his skin was red and blotchy where he had shaved.

"Now rinse with cold water, and the red will go back to normal. Then put on this!" Adrik said, handing him a bottle of lotion as they both finished up.

"Thank you, Adrik. I don't know what I would do without you."

"I'm sure you'd manage, but I really did enjoy this experience with you."

"I enjoyed it with you too." Lucius smiled. "If you don't mind me asking, I'm a little confused. If you aren't really, well…I mean… have you ever had to shave your face?"

"Not exactly." He laughed. "But when I was younger, I used to practice all the time, pretending to be a boy. In reality, however, I've only ever had to shave my legs."

Lucius gave him a hug. "Even still, I really appreciate all you've done to help me. It means so much."

"Anytime, kid. Just keep practicing, and I promise you'll get better."

He smiled. "I'm tired, and I have to make a big decision about my clothes for tomorrow, so I think I'm going to go to bed, okay?"

"Smart man. Speaking of clothes, this weekend, we should get you some more. You've hit a growth spurt, and all your pants are starting to look a little short."

Lucius looked down at his pants. They hung down shorter than his ankles. "Okay, thank you. Adrik? I have a question. When will I learn how to drive?"

"When you're older for certain." He smiled at him, wiping off his eyebrows. "Why? Did you see a car you liked?"

"A long time ago, when I first got here, I saw a motorcycle. It was blue."

"Blue, hmm? Is that your favorite color?"

"Yeah, and I liked the bike because it looked fast. I like going fast. I want to buy one when I'm older. Then I'll ride it everywhere, and my hair will feel all flowy."

"Flowy, huh? Well, when you're older and you get one, I'll teach you to ride it."

"You know how?" Lucius said, not able to see the cat-like man balanced on a fast-moving bike.

"I was a teenager once, Lucius. I had a life before you." Adrik laughed.

"Oh, well, I mean, yes."

"When you're older." Adrik smiled, patting his head. "Now off to bed."

The next morning, he carefully looked through his closet. He didn't have any clothes that would fit him right, but he could make do with what he had. Despite how he had grown, he was still much shorter than the six-foot-three-inch-tall skinny Adrik. He doubted *professional* was keeping your pants rolled up all day. So instead he picked out his school uniform—black pants, a white shirt, and a black tie. But he added a gray vest on top and then a black suit coat on top of that. The shirt underneath was short-sleeved, and the suit coat did a good job hiding that fact. It would work until the weekend, which started tomorrow.

"Impressive. Your clothes look nice," Feliks complimented. "You can't tell at first glance, but you used your old uniform and turned it into something fancy. Very resourceful. I trust Adrik is taking you shopping this weekend?"

"Yes, he is, sir."

"Good, if there is one thing you can count on Adrik for, it's his fashion sense. The man knows clothes and etiquette. I respect that. Now onto bigger matters. Today, I want you to walk around and watch people. Just watch. Don't give any orders. Walk around like you are the boss of this place. See if you can make people respect you just with your walk. Try not to say anything."

"Yes, sir," Lucius said, exiting his office.

He started walking. How would Feliks walk if he could? He stood up tall and straightened his shoulders. He tried to remember how Boris walked. Everyone respected him, and everyone had a healthy level of fear for him. He didn't want to be like Boris, but he did think he was a good example of how to command respect.

Lucius took long, strong strides around the building. A few stopped to look at him, but most just went about their work. He felt proud that some noticed him at all. He walked by Rupert, who noticed him after a sneeze, then gave a curt nod before going back to his work. Respect. It felt nice. It felt *really* nice.

An hour later, he returned.

"How did it feel?"

"It felt great! I liked it a lot."

"Don't get too big of a head. That's every boss's number one mistake. It's important to appear in control, to appear collected and calm, but you need to make sure you don't get so bigheaded you can't see the big picture. If you get too cocky, an uprising could be starting right under your nose, and you'd be none the wiser due to your own arrogance. Don't be a fool."

Lucius nodded. He hadn't even considered that those respecting him might not even like him. He made a mental note to be careful of that when he was in charge.

"But how will I know if they don't like me?" he asked.

"Ahh, there's a trick." Feliks smiled. "You need someone on the inside, someone others don't know about who's on your side. I have Adrik and a warehouse worker named Grigory."

"Not Rupert? He really wants to be promoted."

"Yes, I'm sure he does. I like Rupert, but between you and me, he isn't the most trustworthy. It's why he's worked the same position for so long, while others have risen above him. He used to work for a different drug company, and he sold their secrets to us so we could take them down. Then he started working for us instead. If he was willing to do that to them, I can't trust he won't do the same to us someday. That's why Grigory keeps a very close eye on him. It's always important to know everything about a person before you trust someone, Lucius. Remember that. A mysterious person is an untrustworthy person."

He couldn't believe what he was hearing. He had no idea of Rupert's past employment. No wonder he hadn't gotten the promotion he kept moaning and groaning about. It seemed everyone had secrets. Lucius never thought that someone he had known for years could still keep some things hidden from him. It really showed that you never truly knew a person. Were there secrets Adrik kept from him too? Maybe. He didn't like to think about that.

The more he knew about Feliks, the more he was convinced how much he had to learn. He wanted to be a boss just as good someday, and as time went by, he learned more and more—how to act, how to conduct himself, how to conduct business affairs, how to dress, and most importantly, how to cover his tracks. But every lesson was important, and Feliks made that perfectly clear.

Training under Feliks was fun for the most part. Lucius got to sit in his office every day and listen to the important things Feliks felt he needed to know. Of course, there were boring days. But as the years went by, Lucius found the job easier and easier to understand. However, it seemed the more he understood, the more tired Feliks grew. His white hair had started to thin, and his wrinkles started to sag. As Lucius reached adulthood, he couldn't help but think that the once-intimidating man in the chair now looked like a mummy being prepared for a burial.

"You're eighteen now, Lucius, aren't you?" Feliks said to him one seemingly average day.

"Yes, sir."

"Good, you're a legal adult. I need you to do something for me. You know how to fight, correct?"

"Yes, sir, too well."

"Good, I need you to kill someone—the leader of a rival company. Can you do it?"

Lucius hadn't expected this. He knew people died from the hands of the company; it was how he got food. But he never expected it would be asked of him, though he should have known. After thinking about how far he'd come, he decided that he would do it if it was best for the business and for his people. Besides, what was one life?

"Yes. I can do it," he said, sounding more certain than he was feeling.

"Good, his name is Dagen. He's two towns away and is trying to sell the same drugs as us, for a fourth of the price. I've given him several warnings to stay away from our area and away from our regulars, but he just isn't getting the message. I've given him enough chances. Time for action. And with action, you have the possibility to prove yourself truly loyal to this company. Make sure you kill him with this," he said, handing him a knife with an engraved DDC on the side. "And leave it there so every other drug gang knows it was us."

"Thank you, sir. I will not let you down."

"I'm not finished. With this opportunity, I also have a gift for you."

"A gift?"

"Yes, follow me," Feliks said, wheeling out of the office and into the service elevator.

Once on the ground, he wheeled out behind the parking lot, where shipments usually came in. Sitting there was the last thing Lucius ever could have expected, something he had been wanting for a long time. But how did Feliks know? It was a shiny new ocean-blue Suzuki GT750 motorcycle. Did Adrik tell him about this? If so, he couldn't say he minded.

"Take it to Adrik. He'll teach you how to drive it. Make sure you know how to handle that thing before you take it to your assignment. Understand?"

"Yes, sir. Thank you, sir!"

Lucy spent the rest of his time ogling over the new bike, cleaning it, playing with the bolts and levers. At the end of the day, his friend came out to see him.

"Sweet wheels, kid."

"Feliks said I'm an adult now, not a kid."

"Oh well, excuse me," Adrik said, giving him a light punch in the arm.

Lucius could only laugh, moving his hair out of the way to get a better look at the controls. It was well down to his waist by now, even in a ponytail.

"Want to learn to drive it?"

"Yes! Will you teach me?"

"Absolutely. So first, you turn the key to the right."

Lucius did and jumped when it started.

"Good!" Adrik smiled.

As the evening went on, Lucius found that driving a motorcycle was harder than it looked. Front brake, back brake, throttle—it all seemed so complicated. But after stopping and starting and stopping and starting, he felt he had a decent hang of it by the time he finally managed to get home.

Lucius changed into more comfortable clothes and stayed up all night to practice, driving through the countryside for hours until he finally felt he had mastered the skill. Four hours before daybreak, Lucy went back and put Feliks's fancy knife in his pocket. He opened up the map, marking the address he needed to get to. He drove to the building of the other drug cartel. After parking a ways away and breaking a window; getting inside was easy. He immediately went to the boss's office. It was easy to tell which office that was, because it was huge just like Feliks's and had a nameplate that said "Dagen" in big fancy letters. Lucius slid into the coat closet to wait, standing for two hours at the least. It was excruciatingly boring, and he tried his best not to fall asleep. But he might have dozed off just one or two times before he heard the office door open and shut. He heard papers ruffling here and there before he cracked the door open for a peek.

A tall black-haired man stood over his desk, facing away from him, looking over papers. He was so close. Lucius knew if he were to step out of the closet, he would be heard. So instead he opened the door just a bit more, thankful the hinges were not creaky. Then he closed one eye, took aim, and threw the knife straight into the back of the man's chest.

With a gasp, he turned around and stared at Lucius before spitting up blood, falling to his knees and then the floor. A quiet success. Lucius piled up all the paperwork he had on his desk and anything else that seemed important before he opened the window and sneaked out. He drove back to Feliks for the report.

"Done," Lucius said with confidence, handing him the papers.

"Wonderful. Did he give you much of a fight?" Feliks asked, clearly impressed.

"He didn't give a fight at all. I hid in his closet and then threw the knife into his back."

"Oh really? I must say, your ability to kill is even more impressive than I could have imagined. And you got the paperwork containing his buyers and sellers! Way to go the extra mile. Well done."

Lucius did feel proud with Feliks praising him left and right. But a part of him felt bad. What made this man different than the little tied-up girl Boris had wanted him to fight? It was not like he gave

Dagen a chance to defend himself. He took him in the back before he could even know what was happening. He found himself wondering if Dagen had a family or people who would miss him now that he was dead. He tried not to show it, but a part of him regretted the decision. He didn't want to think about that, so instead, he shoved the guilt down in a tiny box where he kept all the other traumas he didn't wish to think of. It was better that way.

"You've finally proven yourself. Now I can really trust you with this company after I'm gone," Feliks said, editing Lucy's contract to be the next leader of the company and handing it over to him for a signature.

Lucius signed eagerly, and shortly after, before he was twenty unlike previously promised, Feliks passed away in his sleep due to heart failure. It happened suddenly. One day, he just didn't come to work—no call, no letter. When Adrik went to check on him in his home, he found his cold, lifeless body still in bed.

Adrik was near inconsolable all day. Lucius knew that Feliks had taken him in as a child. He should have known they were closer than they let on. He spent all day in bed, and Lucy wondered if he would react the same way if it was Adrik who passed. He imagined he would react similar since Adrik had played such an important part in his life thus far, practically raising him since he was ten years old.

The burial was long and sad. It was the middle of winter, so everyone went to the funeral. But very few went to the graveyard to see him into the ground. It was freezing. But Adrik stayed the whole time. During the speech, he talked about Feliks's wife that had died fifteen years earlier and about his connections to him. Lucius never knew Feliks had a wife at all. He never spoke of her, and he didn't keep a picture on his desk. He wondered how much of the man he never got to know. He had spent years training and learning under him like an apprentice. He thought that would be enough to know a person. But apparently not. It did make some sense. Feliks never spoke of his personal life with him or anyone else.

After the funeral ended, Lucy's leadership began. He walked into Feliks's old office, wondering if he could keep it as clean as his predecessor.

Chapter 23

LUCIUS

In Leading

He was the leader. Lucius knew what that meant. The time was now. All his training had led up to this point. Despite Feliks's death, the company ran forward. He only needed to make a first impression. This one speech could possibly shape how the company saw him for the rest of his days. He straightened his suit jacket, checked his hair in the mirror, and walked out in front of the company early that morning.

"I think we all knew Feliks's death was coming soon," he said, sounding purposefully cold. "He was in his late nineties, and no one lives forever. I have trained with all of you for this moment to become the next head of the company. If you have any questions or concerns, come to me about them. Other than that, keep up the good work. Don't think that just because I am new to the position, I will be taking it easy on the lot of you," he said sternly. He wanted to make sure everyone knew he demanded respect.

After his speech, he walked into his office. It still felt foreign. He would have to change a few things to make it more his. But before that, he had one more task he needed to do. He left to visit Adrik's office.

Adrik smiled tiredly from the past few days of mourning and turned to look at him, brushing his greying hair out of his face.

"You gave a good speech. You'll be a fine boss, Lucius."

Lucy closed the door behind him, locking it. "Please call me sir when we're at work, okay? I don't want anyone to think I am weak in any way," he said, giving his friend a nervous smile.

Adrik smiled back. "Understood, so what brings you to my office, sir?"

"We need to discuss living arrangements. With me being in charge now, I can't keep living with you. People will see me as someone who can't fend for myself if I keep mooching off what you have so generously been providing for me. You understand, right?"

Adrik gave a large sigh. "Yes, I understand. But I will be very lonely without you home."

Lucius laughed. "I think you have enough charisma to sustain the household on your own. If you get too lonely, just call me or maybe get a cat."

"Oh, ha ha! Get a cat? I don't like cats."

"Really? You know when I first met you, that was the first creature I compared you to. With your long strides, smooth movements and the purr-like way you talk."

"Ugh, really? I am offended." Adrik laughed. "But now that you mention it, I do see the similarities."

Lucius smiled. "So I'll be packing up tonight. Thank you for understanding," he said as he headed back to his office to start on the mountain of work Feliks had left behind him.

The job was easier than transporting that's for sure. As he sat at the desk and looked around the room, he pulled the expense reports out of his new desk drawer. Feliks had said to be careful of Rupert, he just wanted to make sure he memorized the way things were today. Just in case they 'mysteriously changed' next week.

He left a bit early. He had to find a new place to stay before he could move anywhere. He thought he should live in the richer part of town, just for the show. If Feliks had taught him anything, it was that appearance made all the difference. Looking at all the fancy houses made him feel very small. Adrik lived nearby, but even his house wasn't as fancy as the ones he was in the market for.

He finally found a house he liked. It was tall and white and had big pillars with a "for sale" sign out front. He didn't know what he would do with so much space but decided to use his savings to buy the house anyway. He was making more than enough to live in the house, plus extra. After talking to a realtor and signing the papers, Lucius moved his clothes out of Adrik's house and into the master bedroom closet in his own house. The house came fully furnished, so that took a lot of the work away.

After he was done, he sat on his new bed. He had no one to talk to and felt a little lonely. As he looked around at the gray walls and the gray plush carpet, he thought about how quiet it was. He felt like a boy locked in a cellar again, even though this time it was a big fancy house. But still, he didn't feel comfortable enough to leave and didn't feel brave enough to call Adrik and ask to move back after he had just spread his wings for himself. No, this was the way it had to be.

He went to the living room and sat on the couch. He looked around for the TV remote. Adrik never watched TV, but maybe it was enjoyable. It was certainly better than reading. Adrik had given him some of his books as a housewarming gift, but if Lucius was being honest with himself, sometimes reading was still too difficult to manage.

After finding the remote and turning it on, he was blasted with a too-cheeky, too-peppy host of a cooking show. Lucius hit the volume down button as fast as he could until he had finally gotten the sound to an acceptable volume. After flicking through the channels, he decided on a show called *Traveler's Club*. It wasn't very interesting, but it was definitely the best thing on.

The next morning, Lucius woke and found he had fallen asleep on the couch in his clothes. He looked at the time, thankful he hadn't overslept. After changing to a new suit and redoing his ponytail, Lucius rode his bike into work.

Things were going well. He tried his hardest to run the company exactly as Feliks had shown him how. But he had never thought about how lonely it would be at the top. Everyone was too nervous to talk to him. He had to constantly keep up appearances. Even Adrik had kept to himself more since he got promoted. A part of Lucius wanted to give the position away, but then he would look like a great fool. And who would take his place anyhow?

Day in and day out for a year, nothing had changed. They had even more customers and shipments now thanks to Lucy's work with Degan, which meant double the work and double the profit. Everyone was happy; at least he thought they were—everyone except him.

One sunny winter afternoon, he just couldn't take it. He needed to go for a walk. So riding his bike to a nearby town, he parked it and hopped off to walk along the street, kicking rocks like a bored little kid.

"Spare change?" an elderly old woman begged, holding out a shaky hand.

"Sure," he said, handing her a few spare coins in his pocket.

"Thank you, thank you! God bless," the woman said, bowing her head.

Seeing people on the street always made him sad. He remembered when he might have been in that position had he chosen to run from Boris sooner. He remembered a time when his life was hard. Why couldn't people just be kinder and more giving?

Suddenly, it dawned on him. *That's it! I can be much more giving now that I'm on the top.* But then he remembered Feliks's words about Adrik: "I'm afraid he would be so kind and giving, he would give the company away." Maybe it wasn't the best idea, after all. Giving away medicine? There was no business in that. But maybe there was another way.

Surely he could take these people in at least. I mean, no one was using the warehouse at night? It was just empty space. Or, it could be a roof over lots of people who need a dry safe place to sleep. The more Lucius thought about it, the more it seemed like a perfectly reasonable idea. Lucius spent the remaining part of his day handing out slips of paper with the address to the warehouse to homeless folk.

"You can stay here during nights, but you have to be out every day by sunrise."

Everyone was so thankful, and he finally felt he was actually doing something, actually making a difference. When night came and the employees left, he helped everyone set up sleeping bags and blankets, and then he headed home. No one needed to find out. And what if they did? A little act of charity never hurt anyone.

That was until it did. No less than a month after he started letting people sleep in the warehouse at night, things started going missing—medicine, drugs, keys, staplers, paper, Rupert's tissue boxes. Lucius couldn't help but laugh at Rupert's missing tissues, but the rest would be a serious issue.

He heard a knock at the door. "Come in!"

Adrik stepped in. "Sir, do you mind if I sit?"

"Not at all!" he said, noticing his friend's lack of his usual smile.

"Sir, we have a problem. I know you are just trying to do best by everyone, and letting people stay here at night is a very charitable thing to do. But they're stealing from us! Stealing our product! And now we have a new cartel threatening to take our customers on top of us losing money. We need to keep them out, sir. There just isn't any other way."

Lucius sat and listened before understanding his friend's concerns. "You're right, Adrik. I'm sorry."

"No need to apologize. You were just trying to do the right thing. I know that. But we need to fix this. The workers are already belittling you and saying you aren't really loyal to the company."

"I am loyal!" Lucius said, standing up.

"I know, sir. But Rupert has been spreading lies about you left and right."

"Rupert." *But between you and me, he isn't the most trustworthy,* he remembered Feliks saying.

He was furious. Rupert! Spreading lies and rumors! His sniffly sick infested ass thought he could climb the ladder just because Lucius was new to leading? He better not count on it!

"I see. Thank you, Adrik."

Adrik nodded and took the social cue to leave.

Leaning back in his chair, Lucius tried to control his fury, eyes flashing red every few moments. It was really time he learned to control that; it clearly wasn't the time. Now he had to figure out what to do about this problem.

He couldn't fire him. He knew too much about the company. Too much about Lucius. If he fired him, he might sell them out to a different cartel. He could send him off with a warning or a threat, but he didn't much care for threats and warnings. And what if his actions and threats made him disloyal? Was this really something he would be willing to risk?

After the day ended, he waited for Rupert to exit, knowing he would be last, cleaning up after his employees. When Rupert walked out, he grabbed his arm.

"Rupert, mind if we chat?"

Rupert sniffled before giving him a weary look. "Not at all, sir."

"Good. How is your work coming?" Lucius asked, locking up the building. No one would be sleeping inside from now on.

"Difficult as always. We have a lot of new hires this year. And with everything missing, I have to do reports on all of it."

"Mmm, I apologize for all the extra work," he said, trying to seem genuine as he walked toward the car.

"It's all right, sir."

"Well, are you fond of the new hires this year?"

"A few are useful. Most are just average. But we have some interesting ones, very pleasant to talk to."

"Mmm, yes. Talking is nice," he said, getting to Rupert's car.

Bending down to unlock his car, Lucius grabbed him by his neck and squeezed nearly lifting him off the ground. Rupert gasped, and clawed at his neck for air desperately. "Talking is nice. But I have to say. Sometimes, I think quiet is better. If I ever hear you talking about me again, There will be no second chances. I don't care if you were once my friend," he said, dropping him, then getting inches from his face as he coughed. "Understand?"

Rupert gave a sharp nod, then hastily got into his car and drove off.

Lucius watched him drive down the road until the taillights were gone. Then he walked to his own bike. Upon returning to his house, he went inside and cleaned himself off. His fury was gone, which left him with a clear mind once again. Was this what the job really was? Threatening his underlings into line? Strangling his subordinates? He hadn't imagined working in Feliks's position to be anything like this.

As the warm water ran over him, he washed his hair, wondering if Rupert would do as he was bid. Were his threats enough to throw him in line? Or would he only talk more quietly now? Only time would tell. Being the boss was harder than he could have imagined. It certainly had a way of taking all your friends. He might not have taken the job so happily if he had known that.

Chapter 24

LUCIUS

Trapped

As he drifted to sleep, Lucius dreamed himself sitting in a nice open field, surrounded by flowers. He was still a kid, and Eileen was still alive. As he picked the flowers and put them in a basket, Eileen sat, weaving flower crowns out of them. Things were so peaceful. It was sunny with very few clouds in the sky. It felt so free!

Then out of nowhere, a storm came rolling in. He looked around for his sister. It was going to rain. They needed to get inside! But she was gone. He was alone, and as he looked around, the flowers were dead. He grabbed his basket to run inside but dropped it. Those weren't flowers in the basket; they were eyes—the eyes of Misha, Oleg, Katherine, and Eileen. In that basket were the eyes of every victim of Lucius's violence.

He turned around to run. He had to get out of here! But as soon as he turned, he ran into steel metal bars. No! He turned again but was met with more of the same. He was in a cage! When he looked down at himself, he wasn't just in a cage. Now he was wearing a full tailored suit. Around his cage swarmed one hundred workers, all moving and counting and working through shipments. He saw Rupert walk by, then Adrik. He reached through the bars to his friend.

"Adrik! Help me out!"

Adrik only stood there, giving him a puzzled look. "What do you mean, sir?"

"Look around me! Adrik, I'm in a cage! Open it, please!" Lucius tried to bend the bars but found they were too strong even for him.

"I have to get back to work, sir. I thought you wanted to be here," he said, going back to his office.

As Lucius looked around in a panic, he saw that in his cage was his desk and file cabinets. He ran to the window and saw his bike outside. He desperately tried to break the glass, but nothing worked. He ran to the bathroom to grab some tweezers or a pin to use on the corner of the window. As he yanked open a drawer, he looked up at himself in the mirror. He wasn't an adult anymore, he was an old man!

His hair was the same shade of white, but his eyes were gray and old. His face covered in wrinkles, and his mouth sagged in an ugly frown. As he stared at himself, he reached up to touch his face and felt his old leathery skin. Then, before his eyes, his face transformed into Feliks's. Was this who he was becoming? Was this his fate! To become old and lonely his whole life and then die a meaningless death only to be replaced by the next? No! It could not be!

With a gasp, he sat bolt upright in his bed. What a horrid dream. Lucius got up and walked around his house, desperate to try to forget the horrible nightmare visions that had just plagued him moments ago. He went to the kitchen and ate a candy cane. Chewing up the hard candy, he had no one to talk to, no one to distract him.

It was enough. After his snack, he packed a bag with tomorrow's clothes and hopped onto his motorcycle, driving to Adrik's house. He didn't care that it was now one in the morning. When he got there, he knocked hard on the door until his friend answered, looking very tired.

"Lucius?"

"May I come in?"

"Why, of course," Adrik said, stepping aside as Lucius came through. "What brings you here so early?"

"I couldn't sleep. Do you mind if I spend the night here with you?"

Adrik smiled softly. "Being a leader not as easy as you thought?"

He shook his head and look to his feet, embarrassed.

"You don't need to be embarrassed. I couldn't do it myself. I left your room exactly how you left it."

"Thank you, Adrik. It's just for tonight," Lucius said.

He walked tiredly to his bed and flopped on top of it. The comfort of not being alone in the house caused him to fall asleep immediately. The next morning, as he walked into work, he caught the sound of his transporters' conversation and decided to listen from behind the stairs.

"I don't know why anyone would even try the stuff. It's supposed to be addictive as hell," the man facing away from him said.

"Supposedly, it mixes the chemicals in your brain to make you feel super happy and less hungry. That's why so many people lose weight when they use it."

"You must be awfully depressed to try heroin, though, don't you think? It would be easier to start with weed."

"Well, I think a lot of people do start with weed, but then when it doesn't do the trick, they move to the other. It's just a steady progression. That, and most other companies lace their marijuana with heroin to get them addicted without their knowledge."

"Really? I had no idea."

Rupert shouted at them to get back to work, and the men stopped their conversation and went back to counting medicines. Lucius went upstairs to his office and sat down in his new prison cell. Could drugs really have the power to make people happier? If that was the case, he wanted them. Ever since he had moved up to this position a little over a year ago, he felt more empty than he had in a long time.

At the day's end, he had reached a decision. When everyone left, he went down to transport and took out both kinds of drugs, in case marijuana wasn't enough. Entering his home, Lucius was excited to try it out. He changed into his night clothes, looking in the mirror, thinking how similar he looked to Adrik.

"I practically sleep in a suit nowadays," he said to no one.

Then he went to the couch, pulling out the joint he had taken. He would pay for it through Adrik tomorrow. He lit the end and took a deep puff in. After a few moments, he started to feel silly, like everything he saw had some twist practical joke involved. He sat on the couch and giggled, feeling like a complete moron. He thought of his actions the previous day. Of Rupert.

"Stupid fool. Does he think he can best me? Me? I could take him in a fight. I could take them *all* in a fight." He started to laugh, talking to the air as if it would respond. "Leading isn't as easy as fighting, though I wish it was! I wish I had never agreed to this stupid, prison-cell, lonely job! Now I have no friends, no one to talk to, and all these secrets I have to keep to myself. I hate it!"

When he said it aloud, he knew it must have been true. He felt so foolish for making such a poor decision, and the greater a fool he felt, the more his happy silly high turned dark, deep, and depressing. He felt like all his emotions were enhanced. He saw shadows where none existed and felt eyes upon him. He knew in the back of his mind that no one was there, but every now and again, he swore he could hear them. He covered his ears, but somehow the whispers were still there.

Monster. Stupid boy. Property. Vampire. Half-breed.

He tried to just sit, ride the wave of badness out until it was over. Then the squirming worms started. He felt it down below first. Then it felt like they were crawling up under his skin and through his chest and down his legs. He squirmed uncomfortably and curled up on the couch. Lucius shut his eyes tightly and tried to block it out. But when his eyes shut, he could see Boris, feel his hands holding onto his wrists, touching his back. He wanted to throw up. It had happened years ago. Why would he remember it now!

"Enough!" Lucius screamed to no one.

He grabbed a handful of the heroin as quickly as he could and smashed it into his face, inhaling deeply, willing to do anything to stop the voices, the memories, and the squirmy feeling. He held his hands to his ears tightly until it all vanished. He lay back against the couch. This feeling was a completely different experience. Now, nothing seemed funny, but nothing seemed frightening either. Everything seemed to have a happy haze around it. The lights seemed a little dimmer, and everything seemed to make him tired. As he lay back and closed his eyes, he suddenly understood why the boy he had sold this too so many years ago had been so desperate to have it. It was blissful.

The next morning or rather, afternoon, he woke. Looking at the clock, he saw how late it was and sat up. DDC had been in business for over five hours! He stood and changed into his fancy suit and tie then rode into the warehouse. As he walked up toward his office, Adrik gave him a funny look.

"Where have you been, sir?" he asked, voice filled with concern.

"I overslept on accident."

"You're eyes are a little red. What have you been up to?"

"As I said, I only overslept."

Adrik gave him a suspicious look, before continuing, "Rupert says someone came in and stole weed and heroin last night. But only enough for one. Do you know anything about that?"

"I'll take the losses out of my pay. The company won't have to suffer so don't worry about it."

"Lucius, what have you been up to?" Adrik whispered to him.

"I said nothing! I overslept!" he said, voice rising to a shout.

"Yes, sir. I'm sorry, sir," Adrik replied, giving a short bow before turning back to his papers.

Lucius knew it was a poor plan to tell Adrik what he was up to. There was a reason this stuff was illegal. It was hard on your body, horribly addictive, and everyone in town condemned the behavior. But at this point, he was willing to sacrifice all those things if it meant he would feel less lonely and depressed. He was tired of sitting by himself every night with only his own thoughts to occupy him. And he couldn't watch any more TV. It was just so boring that it only led to him turning into himself anyway.

After the day's end, Lucius told Rupert to keep the whole thing on the "down low" and just mark it out of his paycheck. Driving home, he decided to take the long way. If he drove around, maybe he would be less tempted to succumb to drugs again tonight. In order to keep from getting addicted, he knew he couldn't do them every day. He didn't want to end up one of those rich twerps who only looked for the next high, but moreover, he didn't want the drugs to ruin his brain for good.

However, he knew he was losing the battle. Two weeks later, he could hardly stand not to use it every day. When he wasn't using it, he was thinking about it. He didn't realize how much he was starting to need it until too late. But the high was fantastic. It didn't always put him to sleep, but it did always seem to make things "better." He never had to think of anything else. Never thinking of his mother, Eileen, his friends, Boris—none of it. It was all just a happy haze, which was fine by him.

It was funny when he really thought about it. He only took this job as the leader because he thought it would make him happy. But now, he spent all his free time looking for other ways to be happy. He never could have predicted that it would be so lonely at the top, and he regretted it. He missed living with Adrik. He missed just going on transport runs. He missed his friends down below that he didn't feel he could talk to now. After all, Feliks had made it very obvious that they need to fear and respect the top. That couldn't very well happen if he was acting all buddy-buddy with everyone.

Using drugs too often had made him grow numb to the problems in the company. Adrik was always coming to his office, telling him that the transporters below weren't happy with their pay, treatment, etc. But he hardly ever listened. It was at least two months since he had started using, and now every moment he wasn't was just a countdown timer until he could. Then Adrik told him something that he couldn't ignore.

"Rupert is trying to start an uprising, Lucius. I know you've been using heroin, but you need to stop! If you're unhappy or lonely, just come back and live with me! I'll do whatever I can to take care of you."

"Rupert is starting an uprising?" He looked over at his friend. "Why? I threatened to kill him the next time he did something like this," he said, feeling his fury rise.

"He says your only using the drug company to fuel you're own addictions. That you don't really care about the employees, money, or the company. Lucius, I'm begging you. You need to stop."

"I'll stop. I'll stop. Right after I kill Rupert."

Adrik balled his fists. "Kill Rupert? I agree he has his flaws, but that's not what's most important right now! Lucius, this is more than Rupert. This is you too! You need to quit!"

"Rupert has been talking behind my back this whole time! Feliks always said I shouldn't trust him. I won't let him be my downfall!" Lucius said, raising his voice in anger toward his friend.

Adrik sighed. "I would normally condemn murder, but if what you say is true, then maybe it's necessary. Just do what you need to do, and then quit this bad habit. Promise me you'll quit, okay? I'll help you if you need me. You know that, don't you?"

"Yes, Adrik. I promise. Thank you," Lucius said, losing interest in his friend's words.

As the day ended, he waited outside for Rupert as he had last time.

"Good evening," Lucius said as he exited the building.

Rupert jumped in surprise and leaped back, pulling out a pistol and aiming. "Don't come any closer, Lucius! I don't want any trouble!"

"What makes you think I want trouble?" he said, advancing forward.

"I know you know what I've been saying. I saw Adrik walk into your office this morning. He only goes in there lately if he's trying to rat me out! Little snitch!"

"Ahh, then I suppose you know why I'm here," he said, taking two more steps toward him.

"Stay back!" Rupert screamed, hand trembling. "You never deserved to be the leader, You don't have the balls!"

He tsked. "And you do? You've never killed anyone. It's obvious. Your hand is shaking like crazy just holding that gun," Lucius said, advancing even closer.

"I said stay back!" Rupert said, moving backward and taking a shot.

The bullet went through the side of Lucy's arm. He looked down at it and then up at his former friend. "Your aim is terrible." He laughed. "This shouldn't take long at all," he said, giving him a large toothy grin.

Rupert's face visibly paled, and he turned and ran for his car as fast as he could. Lucius chased after him, reaching his car just as he did. Rupert opened the door and Lucius slammed it closed.

"Oh, Rupert, don't you know it will be worse for you if you run?"

"I'll never disobey again! I promise! I'm sorry. I only had a lapse in judgment! Please! Forgive me!" he begged.

"Now, now, didn't I already give you a second chance? I don't give third chances. That would make me a fool."

Rupert yanked his pistol back up and aimed. "Just let me leave! Let me leave, and I promise you'll never see the likes of me again! I'll be gone, and I won't give you any more trouble!" he said, backing up from the threat in front of him.

"Oh, but see, you know too much. I know you sold out a different drug cartel to us way back when. Why wouldn't you do the same to me now?"

Rupert's eyes widened, and he took another shot. This one came at Lucy's face, but he tilted his head just in time for it to whiz past his ear.

"STAY BACK!" he screamed, clearly out of defenses for himself.

"No," Lucius said, grabbing onto the gun and yanking it out of his hand.

Rupert stood, frozen in his shoes, and watched as his gun clattered to the floor behind Lucius. His eyes were panicked as he looked up at his killer.

Looking down, Lucius thought about how pitiful the man looked. He looked like one of the slaves he had killed in the fighting ring when they knew they had been beaten, except he was different. When Lucius looked down at him, he not only saw fear and desperation but also guilt and regret. Maybe he was imagining it, though it didn't really matter.

Rupert turned to flee but was too slow. Lucius grabbed the back of his shirt before he could take more than two steps, and yanked him backward. With a harsh choking noise, Rupert fell to the ground and tried to crawl away.

"Please!" he screamed in between breathless sobs.

Lucius stared down at him. He couldn't help but think about how pitiful the man looked as he died. If he was going to die, he vowed never to do it in this cowardly, begging for his own life sort of way. It was time to end this. He grabbed Rupert's neck and heard him scream one last time before he turned his head swiftly to the side, killing him instantly.

He stared down at Rupert, feeling sorry for him. He was just a sniffly fool. Lucius had no desire to eat him, and with his recent drug activity, he didn't even feel hungry. So instead he hauled his body over his shoulder and carried his dead but still-warm body over to the entrance of the warehouse, dropping him there as an example.

Was this really who he was becoming? Had his life really reached such a low point, that he was willing to kill this man, that he used to be friends with? No, Rupert was the one starting the fight. He shouldn't have betrayed him as he did. Still, though Lucius didn't want to admit it, he did feel bad for his actions. As Lucy drove home, he thought about all the death on his hands. He had killed so many times in the past that he was starting to feel numb to the event of death. In reality, the real issue was that he couldn't believe his life had sunk so low. But there was no turning back now.

He was sure no one would be brave enough to start an uprising after this, but he still felt a feeling of unease deep in his gut. The next day, he took off and went to the hardware store. He wanted to make sure he had a backup plan in case things ever went south again. He wasn't about to let his enemies win at any cost. He did nothing to these people, so why did they suddenly want him gone? He supposed it was always easiest to hate those at the top.

After buying several fireworks and sticks of dynamite, he littered them in places unseen in his own place of business. Lucius didn't want the company to think he was doing anything suspicious. Besides, he wasn't even going to do anything unless the company tried to stab him in the back. He set the bombs at several different spots in the building. One by the door, one by his office, and several other spots where the drugs were kept. If things went south, Lucius wanted to make sure there was no chance anyone would be able to recover the business once he was gone. A part of him felt guilty, putting so many lives at risk. But he wanted revenge. If they were going to screw him, he wanted to make sure they got screwed worse. Now, the ball was in their court.

The next day, the employees had moved Rupert away from the building. He wasn't sure where he went but found he didn't care. Adrik said nothing to him, and everyone seemed more afraid to look at and talk to him than normal. Everything seemed safe, and Lucius found it even more difficult to stay clean. Then one morning he went in and found all his employees, short of Adrik, in an uprising against him. Everyone was blocking the front and back entrance, holding guns, and when he pulled in, they all pointed the barrels at him.

Chapter 25

RAELA

THE LONG JOURNEY

Raela packed her bag, not looking forward to the trip ahead of her. She was going to miss her children. Alise was just entering her pre-teens, and Nathaniel was turning five this year. She didn't want to go on some "family mission" when her kids were at such important stages in their lives. Who knew when she would be back?

"Are you ready?" came a familiar voice behind her.

"I think so," Raela replied, turning around to look at her father.

"Good, it's time you brought Lucius home. I thought their mother would have had the sense to kill the stupid brats when they were born, but apparently, she wasn't even smart enough for that," Egon said with venom in his voice.

"Father, what a horrible thing to say."

"Well, it's true. Now he's out in the world, making vampires a public spectacle. I will not have it! Bring him as soon as you can. If he resists, come back, and I'll send you with more people. Do whatever it takes, Raela."

"Yes, Father," she replied, latching the last buckle on her shoulder bag.

Egon gave an affirmative nod then walked off. Raela really didn't want to do this, but only a fool would openly disobey the head of the family. So she waited until night, cloaked in black, and left the safety of her castle in the mountains.

She hadn't known much about her half brother. She knew he had super strength, which was a rare quality in the family. Vampires were always blessed with one of three abilities: super speed, which was most commonly found in their family, a power Raela possessed; magic ability, which was not quite so common; and super strength.

Her father sometimes said she was smart, so maybe that was why she had been sent to fetch her brother. She could trick him into coming home, but more likely, this would be a chance to prove her loyalty. Raela had been known to empathize with humans in the past. Surely he was only trying to test her. It was the perfect mission, and should she fail? Well, she was only a daughter. Losing a son would be a much greater loss.

This was going to be a difficult trip, Raela had no doubt. She could only travel by night, as the sun was deadly to her. During the day, she had to find a cold dark place to sleep. Not to mention, she couldn't be seen. Maybe Lucius could get away with being in public, but Raela's glowing red eyes were a dead giveaway that she wasn't human.

Thankfully, the trip into Russia only took a few weeks due to her speed, spending every night running and managing to find a cave just before the sun came up. The problem now was finding her brother and leading him away safely. Egon had mentioned him fighting in rings, and he mentioned selling human medications in a drug empire. But he didn't mention how many workers she would have to avoid. As she started down the road to the Dixie Drug Cartel as it was called, she hoped there were only fifty people to worry about. Any more than fifty and the fight would be a struggle. And that wasn't even considering if her brother would be on her side. Raela gave a big sigh. Maybe this would be harder than she imagined. Raela looked up to the moon. The air was so much colder here in Russia. Raela supposed if she were to run away from the family, this would be as good a place as any.

When the drug cartel finally came into view, she heard gunshots. Raela ducked behind the side of a house, waiting and watching. More gunshots and lots of screaming. This had vampire activity all over it. From what she had heard from her father, Lucius seemed to attract trouble wherever he went. If that was true, then he must be down there now. But was it safe to go get him? Maybe it was best to wait until this whole thing was done with. If the people killed him, then her mission would be over, and she wouldn't have to worry anymore.

Just as Raela was starting to think it was over, the building erupted into a huge explosion, and a blur of white hair whizzed by on a blue bike. It must be him! Who else could it be? After he drove off, she followed him, reaching a house far too big for one person. She knocked on the door, and it flew open. There he was, glaring at her, pointing a gun in her face. Lucius's eyes widened before his hand lowered, staring at her in shock.

"Eileen?"

Raela only stared at him. He looked just like their father, except his eyes were very blue and much more bloodshot, as though he hadn't slept in years. She was not very well versed in Russian, but she could understand a little. "My name is Raela. Are you okay?" she said, feeling silly in her poor attempt at the foreign language.

He had several wounds, some in his arms, a few in his legs, and one on his side. When she said her name, his eyes hardened again as he pointed the gun back toward her, changing tongues to German. He must have been able to tell from her accent.

"Who are you? What do you want?"

"I'm your sister. Our father told me to come and bring you home. He didn't know you were still alive, and he wants to welcome you into the family!" Raela said, trying to sound happy. She felt bad lying to him, but she had to follow orders.

"I've never met my father. Why would he suddenly want me to come home now?"

"He sees what a success you've made for yourself here, and he wants you to come home and help our family's empire."

Lucius just stared at her, clearly unsure of what to think, before stepping aside. "Come in."

Raela walked into the house and looked around. It was shockingly clean like he had hardly used anything in here. There were a few blankets out, but aside from that, it was mostly clear of dirt.

"It's a lovely place. Did you buy it? Or build it yourself?"

"I bought it. So where is the rest of my family? Did they only send you?"

"Yes," Raela said, sensing the discomfort and mistrust in his voice.

"I see. This is all very sudden, and I've had a long and eventful day. Let me think on it a night. You may stay here if you wish to, but I need to bandage my wounds and rest," Lucius said, walking to the bathroom as though he didn't care.

Raela could tell he didn't intend to come with her. Why would he? He has lived life as an outcast. Why would he suddenly trust a stranger when he had been conditioned his whole life not to? She knew she had to take drastic measures, even if she herself wasn't thrilled by the idea. But Egon had said himself; she had to do whatever it took.

When he came out, covered in bandages and Band-Aids, Raela was lying naked on the couch, giving him her best seductive stare.

"Whoa, hey, what are you doing?" Lucius said, averting his eyes. "Put some clothes on!"

"I thought this might convince you," she replied, turning her body so her breasts naturally created a stunning appeal of cleavage.

"You said you were my sister!" he said, avoiding looking at her body at any cost.

"Yes? And? Don't you know anything about vampires?"

"I mean not much!"

"Vampires only sleep with their own family. We have to keep the bloodline pure, or else we'll lose our power and become ugly and horrible. So everyone says anyway."

"Gross! Raela, I don't want to sleep with you!" he said, turning to face away from her as his cheeks burned with redness.

"Why not? You're my brother, aren't you?"

"Well, yeah, but…"

"Then, of course, you want to. Then you can come back home," Raela said, rising off the couch and sliding her arms around him.

"I can assure you, I really don't. I'm only attracted to men," Lucius blurted out, squirming away from her pillow-like breasts pressed into his back.

She paused then let go of him. "Oh, I never knew."

"Obviously not. I haven't told anyone."

Raela felt very foolish, putting on her clothes as quick as she could. "I guess it's a relief. I didn't really want to sleep with you either."

"I thought you said vampires only slept with their own family?"

"We do, but that doesn't mean I want to sleep with a family member I just met. Besides, I already have two children. I don't feel the need for a third."

He nodded, turning back to look at her once she was fully dressed.

"Although I would keep this 'attracted to men' business to myself, if I were you. I don't know if Father knows yet, but seeing as having sex with your own gender doesn't create offspring, it's not usually an acceptable thing for our family."

"Noted," Lucius said with a big tired sigh. "I'm going to bed. I'll see you tomorrow, yeah?"

"Yes. I will see you tomorrow." Raela nodded, going back to lie on the couch. Lucius went to his bedroom, and she was very careful to listen, making sure he wasn't going to attempt anything, but he was so quiet. She suspected he was listening to her as well. When the next morning came, Lucius shook her awake. She was lying under a thick blanket with the curtains closed to block out any sunlight.

"Raela, wake up," Lucius said insistently.

"It's daytime. I can't go out in the day. I'll burn up."

He gave her a puzzled look. "Wait. Really? You'll die if you go out in the sun?"

"Mhm, most vampires are extremely sensitive to sunlight and fire."

"That seems inconvenient," he said, going back to his bedroom until the sun went down.

Raela was amazed. He really didn't know anything about vampires, did he? As she peeked into his bedroom, she saw him shove a handful of white powder up his nose before passing back out on the bed, where he lay. Raela gave a big sigh. This was the threat her father was so concerned about? He didn't seem like anything special to her.

As the day passed, Raela was the first to wake at night. She walked into her half brother's bedroom, finding him asleep on top of the covers, dressed in jeans and a leather jacket.

"Wake up," Raela said, giving him a soft push.

He didn't move.

"Wake up!" she said, pushing him harder.

"Ugh, I'm awake, I'm awake," Lucius said in a groggy voice before sitting up.

"Are you coming home?"

He only stared blankly at her before giving a long tired sigh. "Sure, I've got nowhere else to go now anyway," he said, sounding a little angry but mostly depressed.

After a short pack, Raela was shocked at how much Lucy didn't try to bring. All he packed with him was a few pairs of pants, a few shirts, and some powder stuff she didn't recognize. Then he walked out and climbed on his bike.

"We have to make a quick stop before we go. I have to visit my friend Adrik and give him my new address so we can write to each other. What will the new address be?"

"Lucius, you should know I can't tell you that. If a human finds out, what's to stop them from coming to our castle? Plus, no delivery man will be able to deliver the letter. All our mail is delivered by trained hawks."

"Well, isn't there a place he can send it that I can go to?"

Raela thought for a moment. "You can send it to your mother's old house. I know the address for that."

"That works," he said, helping her onto the back of his motorcycle, and driving to a similar looking smaller house.

As Lucius knocked, Raela darted to the side of the house. She didn't care how close Lucius and this friend of his were. If she was seen, it would surely raise questions. She didn't want to be noticed, for fear of her own safety. Lucius gave her a puzzled look before a tall gray-haired man answered the door.

"Lucius! There you are. What have you done to our company? Those people, did they all die in the explosion? Everyone is looking for you!"

"I've been at my house, hiding in plain sight." He laughed. "They surely thought I ran, and well, now I really am leaving."

Adrik looked at him with panicked eyes. "You can stay with me if you want to, Lucius. I can hide you somewhere in my house until this all blows over. Or I can buy some hair dye, and we can change your look completely."

Lucius laughed. "Aw, are you going to miss me?"

The man named Adrik crossed his arms. "Of course, I'm going to miss you! What a silly thing to ask! I raised you like my own kid. I want you to stay here with me," he said with sadness in his voice.

Lucius leaned in to hug his friend. "I promise to write, and I'll be back to visit very soon as soon as all this blows over."

Adrik let out a long sigh. "I guess this is goodbye then, hmm?"

"Well, in a way. But I brought you something so you won't have to look for a new job," he said, pulling out a huge wad of cash. "The rest I enlisted in your bank account. I stole that information from your office. I hope you don't mind."

Adrik chuckled. "I'm not at all surprised. You're too generous, Lucius, but thank you. I hope my retirement will be easier than my life at work."

"I'm sure it will be. Now you can read all you want! Oh, and here's my new address. If you want to write back to me sometimes, I would appreciate it," Lucius said.

"Thank you," Adrik said with a smile, as he took the piece of paper.

"I should be thanking you for all you've done for me. I'll come and visit very soon, all right? I promise." Lucius said as he gave him a big hug.

Adrik nodded. "I wish you well, Lucius."

Lucius gave a nod and a smile before Adrik closed the door.

Her brother let out a long tired sigh before climbing back onto his bike. Raela climbed on behind him. She could tell he was sad, though she didn't know why. These humans, they were all less than them. Didn't he know it was a weakness to show sympathy? They were his food, and if Egon knew he held empathy for them, he was sure to disapprove. Lucius started the bike, and they set off. The bike wasn't as fast as she was, but being so tired from the trip here, she was more than happy to sit back and relax on the way home.

"You'll have to tell me where to go. I don't exactly remember how to get to Germany since I came here by boat. Our family is in Germany, isn't it?"

"Yes," Raela said. "I'll show you. It's easy. But I can't ride during the day so we'll have to find a place to sleep when the sun comes up."

"Oh, that should be easy. I'm sure there are lots of motels."

"Are you crazy? I can't let people see me! It's obvious I'm a vampire. Look at my eyes. They're glowing!"

"All right, all right, geez. I'll get the motel, and you'll stay out of sight till I can get you inside. How about that?"

"I guess...I guess that would be fine, as long as I'm not seen."

"Good. It's settled then," he said.

As the sky started to get lighter, Lucius pulled into a motel parking lot. "Just stay here," he said, parking and walking inside. In a few minutes, he came out with a key.

"Everything went smoothly? It's all taken care of?"

"Yeah, let's go," he said, walking up to a room and unlocking the door.

Raela was thankful that there were two beds. She walked over to one and lay down. It was very soft and comfy. She watched her half brother set his bag down beside her and pull out the powder from his bag.

"What is that?"

"None of your business," he replied very shortly. Raela decided it was best to let the subject go, and she watched him take a deep inhale of a small handful of it. In about fifteen minutes, he was completely passed out on the bed beside her.

The whole trip back to Germany seemed to last forever. As they finally reached the woods, she rushed her half brother along, eager to see her children again. "This way," she said, leading Lucius to the cliff side on the mountain. "It's right in here."

He watched as she dug under a rock by a large beech tree to find a small key. Once she had it, she felt along the steep edge of the cliff side. She looked for several minutes until she found a small moss-covered plate that she moved aside and unlocked, revealing a door.

"Right this way," Raela said, leading him through.

Chapter 26

LUCIUS

ENTERING THE CASTLE OF MURDERERS

Lucius was either making the smartest decision or the dumbest one. He followed his sister through the door into their family castle. He had no reason to trust Raela, but it was obvious he couldn't stay in Russia. With his old life ending there, he might as well see where he came from. He had always wondered anyways.

As they walked through the entryway, Lucius saw some of the most elegant side tables and sculptures he had ever seen. Raela was so used to it. She hardly noticed the fine decor of the family castle. In the family dining room were several different elegant tables and about twenty dining chairs, maybe more. From the ceiling hung beautiful glass chandeliers, a few holding candles for a nice soothing dim light. Lucius couldn't help but compare the chandeliers to the one in Adrik's dining room.

"Wow, it's so beautiful!" he exclaimed, looking around with childlike wonder.

"I guess it is, isn't it? Wait here, and our father will be here to see you shortly," she said.

"All right," he said suspiciously before looking around at the sculptures.

Raela walked to her father's bedchambers. "Father? I'm back. Lucius is waiting in the dining room for you."

Egon looked up from the book he was reading. "Wonderful, you have done well. Now go and see your children. Their insufferable whining has caused us all to suffer. You baby them too much, but if it will get them to be quiet for once, then I will allow it for now."

"Thank you, Father," she said, giving a short bow before turning and running to their bedrooms.

As Lucius waited in the dining hall, he couldn't believe how extravagant everything was. As he walked around, he examined the oil paintings on the walls above the hearth. They were paintings of men and women. All of them looked stone serious, as though they had never smiled in their lives. Everyone had white hair and red eyes, just like his half sister. In the center of all the paintings, directly above the fireplace, was the largest portrait of a man. His eyes were cold, angry, and somewhat sad. No matter where he seemed to go in the large dining hall, his eyes followed him. It wasn't long before he felt completely creeped out. Not to mention, they looked exactly alike.

"Lucius, I presume?" came a voice behind him.

Lucius turned around. "Yes, that's me. Are you…uhh?" He hesitated. It sounded weird to say aloud. "My father?"

"Yes."

"Wow, you look exactly like me! I'd swear we were twins if you didn't have those wrinkles," Lucius said, laughing to himself.

Egon rolled his eyes. "I didn't bring you here for small talk and appearance comparisons. I brought you here because I have the means to accept you into the family. I need you to prove yourself first, however," Egon said, walking to the fireplace and staring in. He was slightly taller than his son and had much paler skin. He wore a fancy suit and a flowing black cape with a purple interior. Lucius thought that seemed very stereotypical, as if he bought all his clothes from a Halloween store.

"How so?" he asked suspiciously.

"Well, see that is the trouble. I am not yet sure. I need you to follow me until I can figure that out," he said, turning and walking out of the room.

"All right," Lucius said, following Egon. "Can you tell me more about my mother?"

"Another time," he said, walking down a long flight of stairs that led to a stone hallway with cells and metal-barred cages behind a large steel door.

Looking around, Lucius suddenly felt uncomfortable. Most of the cages were empty, but Egon pressed on, leading him to a cell at the very back of the hall with two wrist chains. Egon turned and gave his son a cold stare before looking into the cell.

Lucy knew it was for him and felt the sudden urge to run. Did he come all this way to get locked in a cell? This wasn't what Raela told him. But the longer he stared into the cage, the less panicked he felt. It was just a cage. He'd escaped cages before, and he could do it again. If he could maybe get some more information out of Egon about his mother, then he could escape later, and it would all be worth it, wouldn't it?

"I'm not going in there," Lucius blurted.

"We can't let you join our family without first finding if your intentions in our empire are pure. I have no intention of letting you walk among us until I have a clearer understanding of who exactly you are as a person. Until then, you will be staying here," Egon persisted.

Lucius let out a long annoyed sigh. "Fine, but I'm not going in until you tell me about my mother."

Egon rolled his eyes. "Your mother was a servant here. She started as a basic slave used for draining blood for our meals but proved herself to be very useful, and she moved up to helping us shave, cleaning our rooms, and the basics."

Lucius stepped into the cell. "Well, how did she leave? We lived in the woods when we were born."

Egon walked in and latched the cuffs to his ankles. Lucius followed the chain with his eyes and saw that it hooked into two spots on the ceiling.

"I set her free when she got pregnant," he said, walking out and shutting the cell behind him.

"Aren't vampires not supposed to breed with humans?"

"Well, that is why I never came to visit and why she was set free in the first place."

"Hmm, well, Mom hated me and my sister," Lucius said, crossing his arms and planning his escape in his head.

"Oh, I have no doubt. You look just like me, and she had enough hatred for me to last one thousand years," Egon said, pulling a lever on the side of the wall outside the cell.

Suddenly, Lucy's feet were swooped out from under him, and he was dangling by his ankles. "Hey! Ow!" he said, having hit his head on the floor on the way up.

Egon stared in at him. "We'll come back once we decide what to do with you," he said, then turned and walked back to the main floor.

Lucius had to admit his father was more clever than he had originally thought. Hanging by his ankles, he no longer had the ability to reach the bars and bend them open nor grab his chains and yank them off. As he looked around him, he found very few resources he could use to his aid. It was dark, and it was quiet. As he hung, Lucius felt the panic set in.

Chapter 27

BEN

THE STRANGE NEIGHBOR

Yesterday, things were normal. Ben woke up alone, spent his day alone, and went to sleep alone. It was all so boring. But he was used to entertaining himself by now. He would scratch things on the walls of his room or daydream about things outside. The only time he got to see others was during their two meal times a day. He always loved the company and trying to understand what the other people were doing in their cells with their families. He wished he was fortunate enough to have a family of his own, but it just wasn't a reality. Ben was born with one leg, so he wasn't allowed to recreate with his equals, if he should even call them that much. But they were always nice to him, and he had never any reason for resenting them besides his own jealousy.

Life was simple in Lovhart Manor. They made the rules. They picked the meals given. They chose who had children with whom. It took all thinking out of life. You never had to wonder if you'd find your soul mate, because it was decided for you. What would your children grow up to be? Food for vampires, just like everyone else.

Some of the slaves liked this life, the ones who didn't remember having any family in the outside world. Ben understood to some degree. Leaving this place, what would he do? Sitting in a cell all day and night didn't give you many talents to use in the outside world. But he'd be lying if he said he didn't often fantasize about escaping anyway.

On top of it all, Ben was deaf. He often felt very thankful his mother was from the outside. She was able to teach him sign language and teach his friends and family sign language too. He feared if it wasn't for her, he'd have absolutely no one to talk to. Not that it mattered now. He was sitting alone in a cell, blocked from all the others. He felt so alone here. Sometimes he couldn't help but wonder, what was the purpose of living anyway? Why were the vampires above even bothering with him? He was surely a waste on their resources to feed, and they refused to use him for meals. So what was the point? But ever since he was a teenager, Ben started noticing that the vampires seemed to be saving him for something, some plan he wasn't allowed to know about. He tried not to question it, but it was difficult. He was just so tired of being lonely. It was hard not to let his thoughts drift to darker things.

Then one day, Benjamin woke from inside his cell. He gave a big stretch and rubbed his eyes till he was able to wake up. Turning his head to crack his neck, he was surprised to see a white-haired man in the cell across from him, dangling from his ankles. He pushed himself up and walked over to the edge of his cell, banging on the bars.

The white-haired man across from him was asleep but woke when he heard the noise. He had the most beautiful blue eyes. When he started to talk, Ben didn't know what he was saying.

"I can't hear you. I'm deaf," Benjamin signed.

Lucius only stared at him, puzzled, before speaking again. When Ben didn't respond, he just stared at him, unsure of what to say.

"I can't understand you. I'm sorry," he signed, sitting back down on his bed and brushing through his curly short black hair with his fingers.

The man stared back at him before his eyes lit up with understanding. He looked around like he didn't know what to say or do.

Finally, he stared back at Ben and gave a small wave. Ben couldn't help but wave back and laugh.

Ben knew it was all for not, but despite that, the man across from him never quit trying to play an awkward game of charades with his new roommate. After a few days of bad communication, the mistress of the castle came down to speak to his neighbor. He could tell she felt horrible shame when visiting and his cellmate was furious. He watched as the man across from him crossed his arms, clearly doing his best to shut her out. He asked her for something, and she shook her head. This only caused him to pout even more. Lady Raela was quiet before speaking again. She must have said something interesting because he looked over at her, suddenly interested. They talked a bit more, then the mistress left.

The next two days were spent with very little conversation between the two. Ben wanted to talk, but it was difficult with such a language barrier. However, in the two days, he had noticed strange changes in the man across from him. He started sweating a lot and looked like he was horribly ill with fever. On top of that, he was constantly shaking. It was hard not to feel concern for him. Lady Raela then returned and gave the man a book; he seemed more than happy to have it as he grabbed it away from her. They spoke some, and she left once more.

Lucius opened the book and read inside for several moments before setting it on the floor above him. Ben was amazed all the blood running to his head hadn't killed him but assumed it had something to do with not being human. After all, he had never seen a human that young with white hair before. Only vampires had that trait. Although he did seem very sick, vampires didn't have normal blood and organs. Hanging upside down like that for so long would naturally kill any human, but humans also couldn't heal from stab wounds in less than a few hours. Maybe hanging upside down really was hard on him, but his spasms, illness, and other symptoms seemed something completely different than what you would experience just from hanging upside down. Perhaps his body just happened to heal him as fast as the shift in position hurt him, and the illness was something else entirely.

The man waved his hands at Ben to get his attention and signed with very sloppy sign language.

"My name is Lucius."

He smiled and signed back. "My name is Ben."

Lucius laughed. Ben couldn't help his eyes immediately shifting to Lucy's mouth as it opened. The laugh gave him an uncomfortable view of the sharp teeth inside. He tried not to let it bother him. It was obvious he wasn't "one of them" or else he wouldn't be down here. He must have been a part of the royal family; he looked just like them. But his eyes were blue, and he was trapped in a cell.

Lucius picked up his book a moment, eyes scanning the pages quickly before setting it down.

"It's nice to meet you, Ben."

"It's nice to meet you too," Ben replied. "Are you sick?"

Lucius flipped through his book, then looked back up to his new friend, and shook his head no. He started to spell out with his fingers. "H-E-R-O-I-N W-I-T-H-D-R-A-W-L-S."

Ben was unfamiliar with the term *heroin*, but he knew what *withdrawal* was. So he could put together the situation his new friend was in. The rest of the day was spent with very limited conversation, though Ben had to give him credit. Lucius was learning sign language at an alarming pace. By the end of the week, he would have no doubt mastered most of the book Lady Raela had given him. It would be a relief to have someone to talk to; he couldn't remember the last time he had someone in the cell across from him, let alone someone who knew or was willing to learn sign language.

Lots of practice and many days later, Lucius had learned most of the basic sign language skills. After that, the talking never stopped.

"How long have you lived here?" he asked.

"In this cell? I've lived here since I was a young adult. In my twenties, I think."

"How old are you now?"

"It's hard to say since I never see the sun and I have very little information about the passage of time. However, I think I am around the age of thirty."

"Wow, almost a decade! How did you not die of boredom and loneliness? Who did you live with before you were in this cell?"

"Before I lived in this particular cell I shared one with my mother. But now that I live alone. I take this time to think. I've had a few other cellmates across from me, so it wasn't all bad, though now I think I've been alone for at least a year."

"I think I would have gone mad," Lucius signed, giving a big exaggerated sigh.

Ben laughed. "Well, Lady Raela is in the habits of giving gifts to those of us she pities," he said, crawling over to the corner of his cell and moving a stone, revealing a small compartment containing some objects he had collected over time. He pulled out a red rubber ball, dusted it off with his dark-skinned hands, and bounced it against the wall and back to him, showing how he spent most of his time.

Lucius held out a hand, and Benjamin bounced the ball over to him. He caught it, turning it in his hands a few times to give it an inspection.

He laughed before signing, "Watch this."

Ben looked over at him and watched his new friend make a silly pose as if he was standing against a building, bouncing the ball against the ceiling of his cage. It didn't look exact, but it almost looked as though he was standing upright, bouncing the ball against the ground, except he was upside down. Ben couldn't help but laugh as Lucius threw it back to him. Ben caught the ball and put it back into his compartment. He rummaged around a moment and pulled out a Rubik's cube. It was mostly finished. He spun the sides around a few times as his friend watched. In less than a few moments, it was solved, and Lucius held his hands out.

Ben threw the toy over to him and watched as he scrambled it up again before giving it a shot for himself. It took Lucius only fifteen minutes, but Ben didn't mind watching as he tried to unscramble the puzzle. He had to admit, he was impressed by how quickly he had been able to figure it out. He solved it much faster than Ben had on his first try. The hardest part was not helping, letting Lucius solve it for himself.

He tossed back the finished cube, and Ben put it back. "So why are you down here anyway?"

"The head of the house is my father, but my mother was human. Raela came to get me from Russia one day, saying my dad wanted me to join the family. But it looks like that was a lie. I don't know why he wanted me locked up."

"Maybe he saw you as a threat. Egon has always been overly superstitious of people coming to take the throne from him. It's why you don't see vampires from other countries in his castle. I'm surprised out of everyone in your family, he hasn't turned into a nachzehrer."

Lucius looked puzzled. "A nachzehrer? What's a nachzehrer?"

Ben tilted his head. "A nachzehrer is a vampire who eats their own family out of jealousy, though the rest of their family is normally human. It's said that anyone who falls under the nachzehrer shadow or hears them ringing a church bell dies. My mom used to tell me about it, but in reality, I think it's only a silly German myth. I mean Lady Raela has cast a shadow on me, and I'm fine, right? My mother says that Germany has all kinds of crazy vampire myths and theories. I'm honestly surprised you've never heard one. Didn't your mother ever explain any of these things to you? Surely the town you lived in tried hunting vampires, what with people missing all the time."

Lucius nodded. "They did, but my mom didn't talk about it with us."

"Us?" Ben asked.

"My sister, Eileen, was born with me, but she died when she was just a child."

"Oh, I'm sorry."

"Don't be sorry. Nothing can be done about it now. But let's not talk about that, okay? Tell me about these vampires from other countries."

Ben nodded. "I don't know much, but I know there is a vampire colony in England and a few traveling communities around Scotland."

He thought for a long time before giving a small nod. "Yes, I think I've heard of vampires in England, but I didn't know about Scotland."

Ben laughed. "Of course, that's only if you believe in them. I know that a lot of people in the world, despite the obvious evidence, still don't believe in vampires, although I understand. It's hard not to give vampires credit. They do a good job keeping themselves hidden. Maybe someday if our colony gets discovered, we'll all be freed."

Lucius stared at him for a long time before signing. "How do you know all this? And why are you telling me?"

Ben shrugged. "These are the only things I can think of to talk about since nothing else of any importance happens in my life. I have friends I see during meal times, but they live very similar lives in cages and have nothing to talk about either. Really, the most interesting thing to happen is when Lady Raela comes to visit me to tell me about her struggles on the main floor. I think she's just lonely, with no one to talk to in her own family. I usually get all my information through her or my mother."

Lucius crossed his arms. "Lady Raela? Really? I don't see any reason to like Raela. But if she's nice to you, well, I don't know... How did you get here anyway?"

"I was born here, but my mother was taken from the nearby town one night. She was taken as a little girl, and she used to talk about it all the time before she passed away."

"Oh, I'm sorry," Lucius said, suddenly looking guilty, as though he had hurt his friend's feelings by asking about things in the past.

"You don't need to be sorry. It's not your fault. She used to talk about her friends in town and her mother, who owned a general goods store, and her younger sister, Gelda, I think her name was."

Lucius nodded. "Did you have any siblings?"

"No, I'm an only child. My mother married someone who was born here, well, not married but conceived me with someone born here. The royals are really specific about who is allowed to mate with whom. They have it all planned out to try to make the best-tasting blood. My mother said that's what she heard King Egon say once during a cleaning shift."

Lucius nodded. "It sounds awful to be trapped here all the time. Does my family ever take you from your cell for feeding?"

"They bring me out of my cage on occasion to feed me with the others. It's how I try and keep track of the days."

"That's not what I meant, Ben," he said grimly. Ben never thought he'd see a vampire look ashamed, but it was clear that was what Lucius was feeling.

"No," he said, hiding his things away under the stone slab. "No, they don't eat off me because I was born missing a leg. They don't understand it, so they don't think my blood is 'clean' enough for their consumption."

Lucius frowned. "That's horrible. I mean, it's not horrible that they don't eat you. I'm glad about that! But it's horrible that they see you as different. You have thoughts and feelings too. I hope the other humans in the castle can see that at least."

Ben gave a soft chuckle. "You don't have to pretend like I'm not deformed, Lucius. I know what I am, and it's fine. Honestly? It hardly bothers me at all. None of the other slaves treat me any different. But they don't understand me and I can't hear them so, I guess I wouldn't know. But even if they did, I have my own friends in the castle I eat meals with, and I'm happy to never get fed off. Being deformed has its perks," Ben said with a smile.

"I'm glad you're not bothered by it," Lucius signed. "I wish I could be that sure of my differences. I really admire your resolve, but I do have one question. This is going to sound very mean, and I definitely don't mean it that way, but why do they bother keeping you alive? If they don't eat off you, that is."

Ben gave a small laugh. "It's not mean. It's only true. I've wondered that myself. It would be so much easier to just kill me like they have so many others. Then they wouldn't have to waste the food to keep me alive."

Lucius crossed his arms. "Maybe they're keeping you alive for the same reason they're keeping me alive. They think you'll be useful later."

"Maybe, but if anything, I think it's probably just because Lady Raela likes me. We aren't friends per se, but she does come down to talk to me every now and again. So I wouldn't say we're enemies. I think my separation from the other people makes me easier to talk to, since I'm often desperate for company, so desperate, that I don't shun her for killing humans."

Lucius nodded. "I guess that would make sense. Do you hate vampires then?"

Ben hesitated. "I don't know if *hate* is the right word. I hate some vampires, but Lady Raela is very kind to me. I think a part of her wants to escape from her own family, but she has two children, who are also both very kind, from what I've heard of them. She doesn't like her father or her younger brother Azazel, and I can't say I adore them either."

"Why doesn't she like them? Raela made it seem like all vampires of the same family are so close they have sex with each other or something."

"Well, it's true that vampires in this colony have children with those in the same family, but from my understanding, Raela doesn't like having children without a loving relationship as the foundation."

"Doesn't her family love her?"

"Well, yes, but having children is seen as more of a task than a pleasure here. And the women always have to take care of them afterward, because the Lovharts are still stuck in medieval ages. They don't make a habit of going out and learning about the human world unless they have to. And they certainly don't accept human customs."

Lucius looked a little surprised. "It sounds awful, and she's just expected to spread her legs whenever a family member tells her to?"

"Not just any family member. Only for Azazel, but that's basically the summary, yes. I think it makes her feel very alone more often than not."

"Yeah, I know what that's like," Lucius signed, looking away a little.

"Being lonely?"

"Yeah, being lonely. It's funny. This isn't my first time being in a cage. Hell, it isn't even my second time. How pathetic is that?"

"It's not pathetic. How did you end up in a cage before?"

"Well, I accidentally gave myself into slavery. When my sister passed away, my mother and I had a…falling out, and I ran away from home. I joined the first new party I could find, and it didn't work out well for me. Before I knew it, I was being shipped out to Russia. Then I was placed in fighting matches for people to bet money on."

"That sounds awful. What was your mother's name? Did she come from inside the castle?"

"Yeah, that's what my dad said. He said she moved up to a cleaning slave. Her name was Katherine."

"My mother knew a woman named Katherine. Egon was romantically involved with her, but then one day she just vanished. We never found out what happened."

"Egon said he took her to the nearby town. He must not have wanted us around. After all, like you and Raela both said, vampires only sleep with other vampires."

"That's probably it," Ben agreed.

Lucius shrugged as he hung from his ankles, looking uncomfortable with the topic at hand.

"Doesn't hanging like that hurt?" Ben asked curiously.

He looked at his ankles, then back at his friend. "It hurts, but it's by far not the worst pain I've ever experienced. I do wish I was wearing thicker socks so the metal didn't bite as bad."

Ben laughed. "You must have a very high pain tolerance."

"Yeah, I guess I do," he said, giving him a big smile that he felt well comfortable with by now. "So how many people do they kill on average?" Lucius continued.

"It depends on how many they have to spare. They usually have men fight to the death for entertainment, and then they eat whoever loses. They don't have women fight, because they like to use them to have more babies, to acquire more 'livestock' as they would put it. But you don't need more than a few men to get a herd of women pregnant."

Lucius looked amazed. "This place is more horrible than I could have ever imagined. It's just like the fighting rings."

Ben gave him a puzzled look. "It can't be worse than here, can it? I always thought the world outside would be a lovely place."

"The world isn't that much better of a place outside, Ben. People are fighting wars every day, and no one really cares about each other," he said, crossing his arms.

Ben didn't know what to say. He had no idea what the world was like outside. He had always wanted to escape, just to know what freedom really felt like. But if it was really that bad, maybe staying here was best after all. And if he was going to stay here, at least he had a kind, intelligent, very handsome roommate across the hall to talk to.

Chapter 28

RAELA

THE HALFLING

Raela sat in her living quarters, brushing her daughter's hair. Alise had such pretty white hair, as they all did, but Alise's hair seems thicker than normal, and softer. Her ten-year-old daughter was sitting patiently, enjoying the feeling of the brush. Nathaniel, her five-year-old son, was happily playing with some toys scattered across the floor.

"Mother, why did you bring that other man here? Is he a part of the family?" Alise asked.

"Sort of. He's my half brother. His name is Lucius, but don't talk about him outside of this room, okay?"

Alise nodded. "Why did Grandpa want you to bring him here?"

"I don't know, sweetheart. I think Grandpa just wants to protect us. If Lucius was out in the world, showing everyone what a vampire was and what a vampire could do, then they could easily trace him back to us if he revealed he was from Germany."

Alise thought for a moment. "I guess it's better that he's here then."

"Well, I think since we brought him back, he should at least be allowed to talk to us! It's so boring here! I want to hear his stories

254

about the outside world. I want to see the outside world," Nathaniel said, pouting.

Raela smiled. "But it's safe here, and you want to be safe, don't you?"

"Not if it means I'm bored out of my brains," Nathaniel muttered.

Putting the brush down, Raela looked at her stubborn son. "Well, you have to stay here. If you were to go outside, the sun would burn you up in an instant."

"How do you know? You've never gone out in the sun. All you have are rumors."

"I just know. And besides, is it really something you're willing to risk?"

"Lucius can go outside. What makes it so I can't?"

"Lucius is a half breed," Raela said, trying not to get angry with her son's open defiance. "His blood is impure. It's filthy. He can go outside because he isn't one of us. He isn't really a vampire at all. He's a half-human monster."

She heard a knock at the door, which interrupted their conversation. Answering, she saw her youngest brother, Palas. "Hello, Palas," Raela said, smiling. Palas and her had always been close, closer than the rest of the family at least.

He gave a short nod. "Raela, how are you doing this evening?"

"I am well, and yourself?" she answered. By the seriousness in his tone, Raela could tell this wasn't a visit for fun.

"I am also doing well. Father has requested the three of us come to see him in his study at once."

"A meeting with all three of his children? Goodness! Is something wrong?" she asked, suddenly feeling a little frightened.

"I don't know. He wouldn't say, but I know he didn't include any other family members, like his own siblings, or any of their children. He told me the meeting was to be kept secret. With that knowledge in mind, I think it has something to do with Lucius."

"Lucius," Raela said, suddenly feeling a bit angry again. "I'll be right there."

Without another word, Palas turned and left. Lucius. Everything kept coming back to Lucius. She was really starting to hate him despite him having done nothing to her. Why did he have to be here at all? Why hadn't Father just sent out a few family members to kill him and be done with it? It certainly would make her life a lot easier. Then, she could simply stay at home with her children, and there would be no problems. But this man, her new half-breed brother was posing to be a bigger problem than she anticipated. She could only imagine what this meeting would entail.

Turning toward her children and leading them back to their own rooms, Raela dressed herself in a white dress with pearls around the base and neckline. It was a dress her father got for her on her birthday. He had always told her how beautiful she looked in it. Vampires only slept with their own family. She remembered she had said that to him. Maybe that was revealing too much. Either way, this dress was sure to catch her father's eye, and perhaps it would even make him less angry with her, if he was at all. She couldn't be sure, but Egon's wrath was something to behold. It wasn't a risk she was willing to take.

She fanned her hair out around her shoulders and went down to her father's study as instructed. Waiting inside were her two brothers Azazel and Palas. Azazel, the shortest of the three of them and the second youngest, was wearing a black and purple suit, clearly doing his best to mimic his dad. It made sense. He was to become the new head of family someday.

Palas was wearing slightly nicer clothes than usual—black dress pants with shined leather shoes, a dark-green vest and black tie on top. His hair, however, was unusually brushed back into a ponytail. He was clearly trying to make some effort to look nice, even if it was a small one.

Raela felt a little embarrassed being the last one to enter. Egon was already sitting behind his desk, wearing his black and purple suit, with a cape to match. He looked up, as though he had been waiting centuries for his last child to arrive. Raela felt herself sweating as she walked quietly across the shiny wood floor and stood next to her brother Azazel so they were ordered eldest to youngest.

"I have called you all here this evening to discuss some important events with you," Egon started. "Raela, excellent job retrieving the halfling." His eyes skimmed up and down her body, gazing at the beautiful dress she had picked out as planned. "You retrieved him in a remarkable time. I expected it to take you two more weeks at least."

"Thank you, Father," Raela said, giving him a small curtsy.

"However, I know you have a certain kindness in your heart for the livestock we keep here. You feel pity for them, which is fine as long as it doesn't get too out of hand. What is that slave's name? Ben?"

"Yes, sir. He lives down in cell section—"

"I know where it lives!" Egon interrupted. "You are to stop talking to it immediately! I have different needs in mind for him, and it doesn't involve your foolish pity. I have warned you about getting overly friendly with humans, but this is your last chance before I start giving you real punishment for your actions. Understand? So stay away from him. He lives too close to the half breed. I have plans in mind for both of them, and those plans do not involve you."

Raela bowed her head, avoiding his gaze. "Yes, sir, of course, sir," she said in a low tone.

Egon let out a short grunt. "Good. Palas? I have a new important mission for you."

Palas snapped back to attention as though he hadn't been listening. "Yes, Father?"

"You are my youngest son. I am not likely to have any more children, and while you need to learn to keep your feet on the ground, maybe a mission like this might help you gain that ability."

Azazel smirked over at his brother. "Ditz."

Palas's face turned red with embarrassment, and he looked to his feet, trying to sink into his tall lanky frame, clearly wanting to be anywhere else other than here.

"Azazel, do not tease your brother. He only recently reached adulthood and still has much to learn," Egon said sternly.

"What's my mission?" Palas asked, curiosity peaking again.

"Lucius made vampires known in Russia—not well-known, but enough so that our rivaling colony in Britain is sure to be sending over several troops to investigate. I need you to take one other woman from our family and start a colony in Russia before the English colony can make the first move. I have no doubt they mean to expand their group by taking the 'other vampires' back with them. However, they are not aware that the only 'other vampire' was the measly half breed creature Raela brought back with her."

"What if their family tries to attack us? To be rid of us before we can colonize? I'm not a good fighter like you and Azazel. I don't know if I will be able to fend them off."

Egon let out a short laugh. "It is unlikely that you will have to. The leader of the English colony is soft-hearted and stupid. Claudius is unwilling to risk any life for the greater good. If he finds you in Russia, already starting a colony, he'll most likely pack up his things and head back home like a dog with his tail between his legs. You're lucky our family killed his father, or you'd have a bigger obstacle to face." Egon laughed again.

Palas let out a visible sigh of relief. Raela had to admit, it was odd to hear her father talk about the leader of the British colony. He rarely ever spoke of such things around others, especially women. Everyone in the family knew that politics were a man's business, usually only discussed by the head. It just wasn't a woman's place to know such things. Raela had always resented that ideology, but it was one she had to live with. However, all this new information was exciting and new to her! She couldn't believe the English colony did things so differently. What else was different about their colony? She couldn't be sure, and she wasn't about to ask, lest he remembered she was there and commanded her to leave the room.

"Azazel," Egon continued.

He straightened himself up, trying to seem taller than he was. "Yes, Father," he said with confidence.

"I am putting you in charge of the halfling from now on. You will be in charge of keeping an eye on him, any change in his cell or behavior, and I want you to tell me immediately. And don't let him know you're watching."

Azazel looked put off. "Why me? He's just a filthy half breed, not a vampire, not a human, not anything more than a pest! Why would you put me in charge of something so unimportant?"

Egon stared at his son and watched as he slowly retracted into himself, feeling foolish for his small outburst. "It is I who decides whether or not he is of any importance, Azazel. We must get him to our side of the family. But he needs to prove his loyalty first. No task is too small for attention to detail. Your time with me and the position I am giving to you has made you cocky. If your head grows too much more in size, then it will burst at first opportunity once you take my place. I won't have someone so foolish be the head of our family empire."

Azazel looked down and gave a soft bow. "Yes, sir. I am very sorry."

Egon nodded. "Good, you ought to be sorry. All of you are dismissed. I will speak with you individually from now on about your special tasks and orders."

At once, all three of them left the room. Palas seemed to have grown two inches since he entered, and Azazel shrunk three. Not that Azazel could afford to lose any height. He was already the shortest of all of them and larger around in comparison.

"I was so scared I would be in trouble!" Raela burst out.

Palas gave a big relieved sigh. "Me too! Father hardly ever wants to see me unless it's to tell me to quit being such a slack."

Raela laughed, but Azazel looked more serious than ever. "You two should not be laughing right now. If you were in trouble, Raela, I'm more than sure you deserved it. And, Palas, you really should shape up. If you're going to be the leader of a new colony, you can't be such a pushover."

Palas only rolled his eyes, walking off nonchalantly. "Okay, Dad, whatever you say."

Azazel huffed, crossing his arms. "I have better things to do than argue with that stupid man-child. I'm the next head of the family! He should treat me with more respect!" he muttered to himself, marching back to his own quarters.

Raela rolled her eyes. It was not unusual for her brothers to get in petty arguments like this. It seemed like they were always fighting. When were they going to grow up from their own problems and get along? It was hard to believe after twenty or so years they could still be so childish. She wished she were a boy. Then she could be the head of the family, being the eldest. She could wear the gold-and-ruby earring her father wore and make everybody proud by solving all their problems much more quickly than Egon or Azazel ever could. The first thing she would do as a leader was knock her brothers' heads together and tell them to quit arguing. They were family, weren't they? They shouldn't fight like that.

Raela walked gracefully back to her room. Family. What did that word really mean to her? Her brothers were family, of course. Her father was family. Her children, cousins, mingled family members that were both siblings *and* cousins on her mother's side were all family—or rather her aunt's side. Raela sat down on the stairs, trying to count back to who was related to whom and how.

Being a vampire, sometimes family lines were difficult to track, though it hardly mattered. All that mattered was who the eldest was in "the family." The head of the family and his children. His "wife" was always his eldest sister, which prevented Raela from being with Palas as she had wished. Azazel's son, her son, Nathaniel, was the next important family member after Azazel himself. It hardly mattered whom his daughters were. Alise would only be as useful as how many children she could create for her brother. Just like herself. It was the sons that inherited everything. Sometimes, this made her so angry she could scream, but that wasn't very ladylike. If anything else, Raela had to be ladylike. Sometimes it was all she had—simple traditions and daily mundane tasks.

But what about Lucius? Was he family? He was related to her, sure. He was her father's bastard child. Technically, they were all bastards. Vampire's didn't marry. It was a bit funny to think about—a dark, evil vampire walking into a church for a marriage ceremony. Raela laughed to herself a bit before thinking that their tradition not to marry was sometimes the reason the family lines were so difficult to track unless you were the heir. The heir to the family was always required to have only one mate—their eldest sister. In turn, the sister was only allowed to be with him. But Lucius, he seemed to break all laws. Not only was he an unplanned child of the leader to the family, but his mother was a human.

Why had her father decided to go against tradition, to have sexual intercourse outside of his duty? Having sex with another vampire family member was one thing. But this was beyond forbidden. To mingle with tainted blood. Raela carried the last name Lovhart, just as her entire family had forever. It was the family name. For any Lovhart to get involved with another vampire community was absolutely foreign, *especially* a vampire who was partially human, like those dirty traveler vampires who moved from home to home, trying to make everywhere and anywhere suitable for living. Everyone knew those traveler vampires had human blood in their veins at some point in time, whether through their parents or some other distant relative. Most of them died off quickly because they were either found and burned or got themselves killed in some other gruesome way. Either way, vampires with dirty blood never lived as long as pure-blooded vampires, nor were they as healthy. That should go without saying.

But to mate with a human? That was beyond disgusting, completely unthinkable! Egon should have had her take Lucius back to Germany and introduce him to the other lower breeds. Then at least he would belong before inevitably getting killed. But he did not belong here. He was an outcast in his cell, and if he wasn't aware of that by now, he was a fool. Things would have been handled differently if Raela was the next leader of the family empire; that was for sure.

Lost in her thoughts, Raela's eyes drifted down to the design of the rug of the stairs. It had the most intricate pattern. Everything inside the castle was beautiful; it was meant to be. They are a beautiful family with beautiful family members and beautiful treasures hidden in every surface, even caked into the walls. All the chandeliers were gold and diamond, and all the floors mahogany, but as Raela stared at the rug, she considered something she hadn't before.

All the lines in the rug were tangled together in beautiful designs, swirling in and out of each other in an intricate dance. Except for every time the lines almost reached the edge, they darted back in toward the middle, turning over the opposing line. Every time they darted away from the edge they also left a little cube made of line, standing all by itself. It looked so sad on its own. Raela felt like that cube.

She often felt alone in the family. She was the only vampire who felt even a slight bit of remorse or pity for the slaves below, who were destined to die and feed them all. She was the only one who refused to watch the slave brawls. She still ate them afterward, of course. She had to if she wanted to live, but she took no pleasure in it. Palas always tried his best to comfort her and sympathize with her. But she could tell he didn't really see what she saw or feel what she felt. He was only trying to be kind. Still she was grateful for that much at least.

She looked down at the small little cubed line, wondering if Lucius felt the same. She couldn't imagine what it must have been like to grow up, not even knowing what you really were. He must have felt so alone, knowing everyone was normal, but he was different. How horrible it would be to live among your own food, to grow attached to them, to care for them, to want to *be* them, only to eat them when you got too hungry.

Raela closed her eyes, trying to imagine it. To imagine eating one of her own family members, one she liked. She thought about eating Palas. She opened her eyes and shook her head. It was too much to handle. How had her foolish little half brother managed to survive so long? How had he been able to live with himself? Raela felt more pity than she had in a long time, and despite being told not to, she found herself marching down the stairs toward his cell.

Chapter 29

AZAZEL

IF THINGS WERE DIFFERENT

Work, work, work. Everything was always work around here, especially for the next head of the family. Sometimes, Azazel wished he could have been born as his younger brother, Palas. He might be lazy and insufferable, but at least he didn't have all this work. And he didn't have a reputation to uphold. All Palas did was slack, and yet he still got to start his own colony, only furthering his distance from the family where he can goof off even more. Azazel turned to glance at his brother.

At least I get the privilege of inheriting an already built empire instead of having to start one from scratch, he thought.

As the family meeting ended, Azazel followed his brother and sister out the door.

"I was so scared I would be in trouble!" Raela burst out once they had left.

Palas gave a big relieved sigh. "Me too! Father hardly ever wants to see me unless it's to tell me to quit being such a slack."

Raela laughed, but Azazel looked more serious than ever. "You two should not be laughing right now. If you were in trouble, Raela, I'm more than sure you deserved it. And, Palas, you really should shape up. If you're going to be the leader of a new colony, you can't be such a pushover."

Palas only rolled his eyes, walking off nonchalantly. "Okay, Dad, whatever you say."

Azazel huffed, feeling his face burn at his brother's mockery. *I have better things to do than argue with that stupid man-child. I'm the next head of the family! He should treat me with more respect!* he said to himself, marching back to his own quarters.

Angrily arriving in his own rooms, he pushed over the desk. How dare Palas disrespect him like this, and how dare their father yell at him in front of his siblings! How were they ever going to respect him if they always saw him in such a weak state? But he probably should learn to grow up a little. As he stared down at the array of clutter now lying on the floor beside his toppled desk, he immediately regretted his decision. He couldn't let anyone see this mess and know that he had thrown such a foolish temper tantrum. Azazel turned his desk back upright before bending down to pick up the paper and quills he had so foolishly knocked over. Perhaps it was seeing Raela and Palas so easily talk to each other that had really set him off. It was just a reminder of another thing Palas had that he could never obtain.

Raela had always been more fond of Palas despite her refusal to admit it. She always laughed around him, smiled around him, and joked with him whenever they met. Azazel felt his mood drop, as it occurred to him that he had never once made her laugh despite his best efforts. She might be forced to bear his children, but he could never force her love.

That fact stung more when he was younger. When Azazel would fawn endlessly over her and do anything he could for a spare moment of her attention, Father said it was disgraceful to throw himself down at the feet of a woman instead of demanding her respect. But as he tried to demand, she only distanced herself further. Azazel sat back on the floor, remembering how much he loved her, and he supposed if she would have loved him, they could have raised the children together happily. But she didn't, and now with every passing day and every glance she gave to their foolish younger brother, Azazel only resented her more.

But despite everything, Azazel still remained faithful. He could have any woman in the castle, but still he couldn't bring himself to cheat. Azazel thought that if he could admit that, deep down some part of him must still care.

But he often wondered if Egon had ever cared about anyone. He was brutally strict with his children and seemed to think of nothing but business. Azazel sometimes felt like he would never truly live up to his name. As he put the remaining quills on his desk, his face burned with shame as he remembered his father's words to him the previous day.

"You lack discipline and courage and you fail to see the big picture in our family matters. If you're going to be the next head of our family, you need to stop putting yourself first. Individual names mean nothing in the grand scheme of our future," Egon had said far too often.

Those words stung just as much now as when they had first been spoken years ago. Azazel sat at his chair, wondering if perhaps Father was so strict with him because he had to live up to more than his brother and sister, but it still frustrated him how easy Palas had it compared to his own burdens. Azazel knew that Raela loved their brother for his kindness and empathy, while he had been forced to abandon those traits, which were seen as a weakness in the family. Raela had always sympathized with those weaker than herself. Whether or not Palas was truly empathetic and kind or just acting to manipulate their sister would always remain a mystery to him.

To top it all off, now there was Lucius. Azazel was horrified that Egon never even mentioned this little mistake of his, although he couldn't say he was surprised. Egon only cared about his outward appearance, and everyone knew it. That was why he sent Raela to go and retrieve him. She was only a woman, and her opinions didn't matter nearly as much as any man, no matter how noble her birth. And if she died on the journey, she had already provided the family with an upcoming heir and a partner to please him.

But why would Egon make such a monumental mistake in the first place? To mate with a human and create such a half-breed monster is not only beyond unthinkably disgusting, but it was a complete betrayal of the family lineage. After pondering the issue a few more moments, Azazel decided the best way to answer the question of why was to ask Egon himself.

Knocking on the door, he waited for the cue to enter. "Come in!" Egon shouted, and Azazel did as he was told.

"Father, I've come to ask you a question, if it pleases you."

Egon looked up from his paperwork and carefully set the quill back into its inkpot. "What is it?"

"Well, I hope I'm not intruding, but since I am the next heir to the family, I think it is important for me to know why Lucius was brought here or rather how he was made in the first place."

Egon stared at him long and hard before letting out a tired sigh. "I was a very different man when he was conceived, Azazel. You have to understand, it was before your time."

"I just want to know why. You of all people know that humans are filthy. You've said so yourself more times than I can count, so why would you ever…procreate with one?"

"I was young and stupid. I was bored with vampire women, who all looked the same, and I wanted to try the forbidden. I think everyone to some degree wants to try what we can never have. Well, I was no different. His mother had dark hair where we have white. She was thicker where we are skinny. She was the complete and total opposite in shape and appearance, in every way one could be. That, and she was easily susceptible to fear and control, so I never had to worry about her exposing my secret."

"But then she got pregnant," Azazel finished for him. "So why didn't you just kill her then and there? Or put her in the fighting pits? It would have been a much more simple and immediate solution."

"I realize all that now, but when I heard talk among the slaves that her period hasn't arrived, I panicked. I took her out into the woods, made her swear not to tell, and assumed she would be out of my life forever. If she had any sense, she would have killed the brats before they even took their first breath, but it seems she wasn't even smart enough to do that."

Azazel huffed. "You can't count on humans for anything, Father. They have a foolish amount of empathy and are horrible at making tough decisions in life. You honestly thought she would have the gall to kill her own children?"

Egon stood up from his desk, staring hard at his eldest son. "Watch yourself, Azazel. Just because I made a mistake does not mean I will have my actions questioned, even by you."

Azazel bowed his head, forgetting his place was always something he was guilty of. "I'm sorry, sir."

"You are forgiven," Egon said before sitting down and letting out an exasperated sigh. "You know why I have to be so hard on you, don't you, Azazel? If you're going to be leader someday, you need to have discipline as strong as steel."

"Yes, sir, I know."

"Good, I just want you to be smarter than me when you become the head of our household."

"Father? I'm not questioning your reasons, but I am curious. Wouldn't it be safer for our family if we just let Lucius become one of us? We don't have to let him reproduce. He can just live among us to use if we need him."

"Lucius is a year older than you, Azazel. If we invite him into the family, do you think he'd be strong enough to challenge you? He's already shown an immense amount of bravery on top of surviving in the human world. I wouldn't be surprised if one day he started wondering why he wasn't the heir instead of you."

Azazel felt his already white skin pale even further. "You really think he would do that? To question my authority?"

"I am almost certain he would."

Chapter 30

LUCIUS

WHAT I AM

Hanging from the ceiling, Lucius was fast asleep. When Ben wasn't awake, there wasn't much to do anymore. He had already memorized the sign language book Raela had given him, and he didn't want to get so bored that he would start picking apart his jacket sleeves. He had already solved the Rubik's cube over one hundred times since he'd gotten here about two months ago. He wished Raela had given him his heroin as he requested, but if he couldn't get high to distract himself, he was glad he had learned sign language to talk to his new friend instead.

"Lucius."

He heard his name being called, but he turned his head away, trying to sleep.

"Lucius!"

He opened his eyes. "Raela? What are you doing down here."

She looked around, then back to her half brother. "I'm not supposed to be here." She whispered. "But, I was thinking, I'm really sorry I brought you here. I should have told you from the beginning, that our father didn't intend to let you live with us as a part of the family."

He just stared at her. "Yeah, you should have."

He felt like more than a fool. His mother didn't want him, and his father never even attempted to make an appearance in his life when he needed him. Why would he suddenly show now? It was all so obvious, but he was so desperate for a family, he was willing to ignore the clues.

She looked down for a moment before speaking again. "You need to listen to me. I don't know what Egon is planning, but I can't imagine it's good for you. I'm forbidden from coming down here because he doesn't want me to interfere."

"So why are you here then, if he told you not to? Aren't you just his little lackey, doing as you're told?"

Raela sighed. "You're mad at me. I get that. But I'm really trying to help you now. Can't you see that?"

Lucius crossed his arms and scowled. "You should consider yourself lucky I'm chained up."

Raela reached through the bars and handed Lucius another book. "Whether you're angry at me or not, I've done some thinking. I brought you this book. It's a vampire's anatomy book. Most of us read this when we're young so we know what to look out for should humans come hunting us."

Lucius scoffed. "You guys act like humans only ever think of you. You aren't nearly as important in the real world as you might think, Raela. Maybe it's time you all get over yourself."

"I'm trying to help you!" she said a bit louder than she intended. "Can't you see that? By reading this book, you'll know what you need to do should my father or anyone else in this family try to attack you. And you'll learn more about yourself. Can't you be at least a little grateful?"

Lucius opened the book and read a little before letting out a reluctant sigh. "I guess. I mean, I wasn't in your situation when you brought me here. I might hate you for doing so, but…at least you're trying to help now. Thanks."

She nodded. "I have to go. If I'm caught down here, I'll get in horrible trouble. Stay safe, okay?"

"You too."

Without another word, Raela turned and ran back up the stairs to the castle above. Lucius opened his new book and started reading all about what he was and about his family. His eyes immediately caught the term *half breed*, a creature born of a vampire (pure-blooded or not) and a human. He remembered Boris calling him such a name once upon a time. Even all these years later, the words still sounded filthy to his ears, like he was less somehow.

As he read, several parts of his life seemed to suddenly make sense. Silver hurt him, as it hurt all vampires, monsters, werewolves, and demons. Apparently, it held significant Christian value, which was why it was so dangerous. Over three centuries ago, there was a horrible monster plague threatening humanity. So to rise to power, the Roman Catholic Church cursed the monsters with the silver weakness. That way, not only would it make the monsters weak, but it would also draw humans toward the church. Lucius thought that was very sneaky of them. But he supposed that was how most people were—sneaky to a fault. He did learn, however, that contrary to public belief, silver could never kill a vampire, only injure and weaken one. But it could be used to kill werewolves.

There were only three ways to kill a vampire: with a wooden stake, sunlight, and fire. Sunlight would never be a problem for him because it seemed that being only half a vampire made him immune to the deadly rays. He had never tested being stabbed with a stake, but he wasn't about to question it. He remembered his hand in Boris's coals and knew that fire must be an effective way to end his existence as well.

The more he read, the more he understood why humans would fear them. They drank human blood and were nearly impossible to catch or kill. Lucius flipped to a page about healing. He figured his family must heal at an alarming rate, considering how fast he was able to. He read on and discovered that it depended on the wound. Burns healed slow, but stab wounds, gun wounds, infection all healed overnight at the longest. Burns usually took two to three days.

When Boris had burned him, it healed completely in about five, maybe six days. Bullet wounds, he knew, healed in three. When his fingers had been broken or ripped off in the fighting rings, he grew them back in two weeks. However, the book said broken bones and missing limbs should be fixed in five to six days. It seemed to him that however fast a vampire healed, he took twice as long, but that was still way faster than any human could recover.

As he read on, he heard a light tapping on the cage bars across from him. He looked up and saw that Ben was awake. Carefully setting down his book, he started signing.

"How did you sleep? Raela came to visit while you were out, but said it will most likely be her last time. Something about her family not letting her down here."

Ben got a puzzled look that merged into concern. "I hope she's all right."

"Well, she seemed all right when she visited. I just don't understand. If she hates it here so much, why does she bother staying?" Lucius asked.

"I guess she doesn't feel she has anywhere else to go."

Immediately, he felt foolish. He had been trapped before. In Boris's cellar, he had been able to escape the whole time, yet he hadn't for fear that it was worse on the other side of the bars. Raela must feel the same way. Lucius briefly remembered Feliks mentioning another colony in England. But was that just another myth? Besides, even if there was another place to go, a colony in England, who was to say it was any better than the one here? He suddenly felt very bad for his sister. He was so mean to her, yet in a way, they were both in cages.

"Are you all right?" Ben signed.

"Yes, I'm fine. I was just thinking. Raela really is unhappy, isn't she?"

"Yes, she is. I always hoped when I was younger that she would end up hating it here so much that she would run away. I thought maybe she would take me with her."

"Did you have a crush on her?"

"Well, I mean Raela is the beautiful mistress of the castle. She's the woman highest in power. I wouldn't say I was in love with her. I was a little too young for that, but I did fancy the idea of being with her. She's kind, and she shows sympathy to those below her. She isn't like the rest of the family."

Lucius nodded. "I haven't met many other family members. I've met her and my father. But my father acted very cold toward me."

"From what Raela has told me, he's very cold to everyone. Creating a bigger family is only a part of a business to him. The bigger the family, the more dangerous they are as a group."

As Ben signed to him, Lucius was formulating a plan as best he could in his head. Trying to think of any way to escape. "How many are there?"

"How many? I don't know. At least 100. Maybe 150. It's an old family. Vampires live much longer than people. I know that much. But they don't get pregnant nearly as easy as humans. And the further you are from the top of the family, the fewer children you are allowed to have," he said, looking across the cell at the book Lucius had gotten. "Can I see that book? Maybe I can figure it out."

"Sure," he said, sliding the book over to him.

Ben pulled it through the bars and opened it up. After reading a few moments, he started signing again, "Here it is. Apparently, vampires only have about two or three kids on average in their whole lives. It's difficult for them to stay pregnant because their body doesn't create enough nutrients to sustain a child, which is why they feed on not only human blood but human meat during pregnancy."

Lucius thought that sounded terrible. Drinking the blood of a person was bad enough, he couldn't imagine having to voluntarily chew and swallow one.

Ben continued reading, "Even if a vampire mother does everything right, however, there is still a 90 percent chance the pregnancy will be lost due to the common vampire practice of inbreeding."

"What does it say about having half breeds?"

Ben turned a few pages forward in the book. "Half breeds are also rare, but not for the same reasons. If a vampire is being born from a human, it is likely to eat her from the inside before she can ever give birth. A human being born from a vampire is likely to get absorbed by the hungry mother before it has the chance to develop. It says the most common type of vampire is one that is turned by a pureblood. Turned vampires can go out in the sunlight and are able to hide and blend into society with little backlash," Ben read before looking up and signing. "I've never even heard of turned vampires! I guess purebloods like your family are rarer. That must be why they think themselves so superior."

"Turned vampires?" Lucius quipped. "We can turn humans into vampires?"

He turned through the pages. "Apparently so. It says here you have to bite the human, drink their blood, then feed them some of your own blood to complete the transformation."

"How long does it take?" Lucius asked curiously.

"Well, it says the turning takes about three days. But the most important thing is to make sure your victim isn't dead before you turn them," he signed as he read. "If the victim is dead before they drink the blood of the host, then the heart won't be able to pump the new blood through their system. Furthermore, the fastest way to turn a human is…" Ben continued, but Lucius's mind drifted to thinking about other things.

He remembered back to his own mother. To his twin sister, Eileen. So was it a miracle the two of them existed at all? As he thought about Eileen, he wondered what had graced his mother with such bad luck as to have not only have one vampire child but two.

Chapter 31

AZAZEL

THE SNITCH

As Azazel left the cells, he marched into his room, slamming the door shut furiously. How could she? After Father specifically told her not to visit that filthy halfling! It made him so mad that he could tear the whole room apart. And on top of it all, he heard Palas gossiping to their cousins his plans to take Raela with him to Russia. Had everyone in the family suddenly turned craven all at once? It was enough to make him scream. Raela was the mother of his children. She belonged to him! She knew that! Palas knew that! It was well past time they accepted it. Azazel left his room, angrily marching up toward his father's study.

Stupid Palas! Always slacking, always showing off! This was surely just another one of his tricks! One last blow to his older brother. He could just picture Palas saying, "Look what I can do. I can take Raela with me, and then you'll have nothing! I can do anything I want, and I'll get away with it." It made Azazel sick with fury. And if Palas succeeded, he wasn't even sure Egon would send someone after Raela. Everyone knew Palas was Egon's favorite. Maybe he would just let them leave, and then Azazel would have no one.

No. Azazel was sure that Egon would let Palas get away with it. Azazel never asked, but he knew deep down that his father had always wished Palas had been born first instead of him. Palas looked more like their dad, and according to Egon, he was very smart. Egon had never told Azazel that he was intelligent of any kind. Egon never told Azazel anything positive. He only ever explained what he expected him to do and then how disappointed he was in him when it wasn't done to the impossible standard he had expected.

Palas might have looked like their father, but Azazel was the oldest. He was the next in line! He was just as respected as his father. At least that was what his mother used to tell him. Azazel always loved his mother. She was nothing like Egon. She was kind, honest, and always cared for everyone. Even when Azazel was being an absolute brat, she was always patient. She always loved him, and she never asked anything too outrageous. As Azazel passed a picture of his mother, he looked up at her. She was shorter and chubbier, just like he was. She also had his downward-slanting eyes as though she was very tired. When was the last time he visited his mom? It hadn't been recent, even though she was only three floors below him. Had it been a year? Two years? He really had been busy following his father's every demand. And Egon didn't like it when he went to speak to the women of their family. He thought it was a sign of weakness. But in times like this, with Azazel hopping mad, he thought maybe it was best to have his mother with him. His mother always knew what to say to calm him down. She was like Raela in that way, but he couldn't talk to Raela about this. Raela would only deny it!

How could she do this to him? Raela knew how important it was that the next head of their household was viewed as a strong capable leader. How foolish he would look if he couldn't even keep his sister-wife by his side! How stupid he would seem if he turned a blind eye while she ran away with the youngest brother? They had children together! Was she going to leave them just for a lazy slob like Palas? It was unthinkable! Azazel couldn't take care of their children. He was too busy trying to meet their father's demands and run an empire! Perhaps Raela would take the kids with her, but then who would take his place when he decided to retire? Azazel needed them to stay here! And if Raela thought she was going to leave this house with his children, she had another thing coming.

When he reached his father's chambers, Azazel briefly wondered if he was overreacting. Was this really worth an outburst? As he stood outside his father's living quarters, he remembered the strict command Egon had given him: "Keep an eye on the halfling." Azazel was to tell him if there were any changes. Well, Raela going to visit him was the biggest change of all! She was directly disobeying their father! She was foolishly messing with plans that she was strictly forbidden from. Surely Egon would not be disappointed in him if Azazel presented him with this very alarming news. Perhaps he would even get praised for once. Azazel straightened his clothes and did his best to calm himself before giving a short confident knock.

"Come in!" Egon shouted from inside.

Azazel opened the door and stepped inside. He didn't realize the mistake he was about to make.

Chapter 32

BEN

I JUST CAN'T

Days of reading the book, and Ben was still able to learn new things and piece together more truths about his captors upstairs. Lucius, however, seemed to have grown bored of reading a long time ago. Whenever Ben would sign new information to him, he could tell Lucy was only half watching him and half thinking inside his own head.

Lucius was always more interested in his escape plan. He had built several different methods to escape the castle, but he could never figure out how to escape his shackles first. In the beginning, he was going to swing himself forward to grab the bars, then use them to rip himself from the shackles around his ankles. But after an hour of swinging, he found his cell was too big for him to reach the bars. It seemed Egon had already thought of that escape idea.

The next plan was to sit up from his chains and grab his own ankles. But Lucy didn't realize that he couldn't touch his toes. So he tried to bend his legs and grab his chains to break them. But once he got there, he was rewarded with an electric zap. Egon must have taken every precaution. Ben had to admire Lucius's inability to quit because he kept coming up with new crazy schemes to escape his shackles. But when none of them worked, instead of giving up, he just thought of a new plan.

At mealtime, Ben was supposed to ask the other slaves if they knew any secret passages that could be of use to their "master plan." As he was dragged by his arm to a darkly lit room, he thought about how with his new friend in the cell across from him; mealtime wasn't as exciting as it used to be. The meals used to be the highlight of his day, but now he found he just couldn't wait to get back to Lucius. As he was dragged into the room, bowls of food surrounded the floor. Ben crawled next to his dear red headed friend, Marie.

Marie smiled over at him before signing, "How's your boyfriend?"

Ben felt his face redden. "He's not my boyfriend. I don't think he'd be interested in someone like me."

Marie lightly punched his shoulder before turning back to her bowl of gruel. "You can never be too sure, you know."

Ben let out a small nervous laugh. "I guess that's true. But I'm telling you, he wouldn't be interested. He's nobility. Granted he's the lowest on the totem pole, but he still has status. Why would he choose to be with a caged slave?"

"He's caged too, dummy."

Ben gave a flustered little laugh before turning into his bowl of food. This was maybe the third time Marie had pestered Ben about Lucius. Ben knew she was only trying to look out for his best interest. But with Marie constantly pestering him like this, he thought maybe it would have been better if he had never told her whom he was interested in.

But wasn't it always this way? They confessed to each other who their latest crush was. Not that it mattered, boy or girl, they didn't get to choose who they were with. That sort of thing was decided by their vampire neighbors. But still, it was fun to dream. Dreaming of a normal life was the closest they would ever get to having one. So when Ben shared his attraction to Lucius, Marie got as excited as ever, asking question after question.

Ben could hardly explain exactly why his heart felt light around his vampire roommate despite Marie's constant questioning. Perhaps Ben felt a longing for danger. He had also loved Lucius's sister when he was young. Perhaps Lucius was just another outlet for his desire to take risks. But deep down, Ben knew that wasn't true.

What he had loved about Raela as a child was her kindness. He loved that she thought of the humans lower than her instead of only her family and empire. He loved that even though she had to eat them; at least she cared. She never wanted the humans to suffer. That alone made her kinder than anyone else in her family.

Lucius shared that same sort of kindness. He never spoke down to Ben as if he was less. He never called Ben names or any sort of derogatory term. In fact, Ben would say Lucius was overly conscious not to offend him. It was a nice change of pace if he was being honest. Ben was so used to vampires and people glancing at him and saying nothing or making some sort of comment he couldn't understand to those around him. Having Lucius overly include him in his thoughts and opinions and take special care to never hurt his feelings was a relief.

He treats me like a human, Ben thought. *And he isn't even human himself.* Perhaps Ben was only over-romanticizing things due to his own loneliness. But then again, he wasn't in love with Marie this way. Marie was different. Marie was his best friend, and he had known her all his life. Lucius was his friend too. But he was also more somehow. Lucius looked at him differently, not in a hungry sort of way like his relatives, but in a caring sort of way. Perhaps it was his looks that sparked Ben's feelings, though Ben still felt confident Lucius only saw him as a friend. But knowing that Lucius cared about him at all still filled his heart with joy.

As time went on from their first day together, Ben stopped minding Lucius's teeth. He stopped caring about what he was. Lucius was his friend. And though Ben might want more than that, he would understand if Lucius didn't feel the same. He was just thankful to know him. If he could accept that, why couldn't Marie? Was it really that important for him to be with someone? He could be happy alone. He had always been alone. It felt selfish to wish for anything more despite Marie's pressuring.

"If you like him so much, you should tell him. You never know…he might feel the same," Marie said, giving him a light punch on the arm.

Ben let out a small sigh. "Never mind. Let's drop it, okay? I had something more important to ask you."

"Such as what?" Marie signed.

"Lucius is trying to formulate a grand escape. I've been asked to ask you if there are any secret passages you might know of. You're a cleaner. Surely you've seen something suspicious. Maybe a secret tunnel you haven't explored. Anything would be useful at this point."

"Hmmm, secret tunnel, eh? No, I haven't seen anything like that, but I have heard of it. They say, back when Egon was younger, he used to sneak to the cell of a cleaning slave. I don't remember what her name was, but he had tunnels in the walls behind the fireplaces. Then one day, out of nowhere, she just disappeared."

"Behind the fireplaces? Which ones? Do all of them have a secret passage?"

"I don't know, Ben. That's all the information I have," Marie signed, finishing the last of her supper. "I'll try to look into it if I can, but I wouldn't get your hopes up."

"Thank you, Marie. Please be careful. I don't want you to face punishment on my behalf."

"I'm always careful," she signed with a laugh.

Returning into his cell, Ben watched as his friend hastily pretended he wasn't just attempting another escape, until his family members left them alone once more.

"What are you trying now?" Ben questioned.

Lucius signed, "I think if I can just tangle my belt around the cell bars. I can yank myself close enough to bend them open or rip myself from the ankle restraints."

Ben let out a sigh, finding it difficult to share his enthusiasm for escape. He had been trapped in a cell all his life, so it was different for him. But Lucius knew what freedom felt like, so he could hardly blame him for wanting it back.

"My friend Adrik would have known exactly what to do in this situation," he said, crossing his arms in an attempt to think of a new way out.

"Adrik was the man who took care of you, right?" Ben said, trying to remember the names Lucius had mentioned, and filling in the blanks.

"Yeah, and he always knew what to do. Whenever I was unsure, Adrik always had the answer for me. Even when I refused to ask, he always tried to lead me to the correct solution, though I didn't always listen."

Ben smiled, thinking that Adrik sounded an awful lot like his own father. "He sounds like he's very important to you."

"He is, and as soon as I break free, I'm going back over to him to forget any of this ever happened."

"Aren't there still drug lords and police looking for you in Russia?" Ben said, trying to remember their earlier conversations.

"Well...yes. Maybe. But I never said I was planning to stay there. I thought maybe Adrik could just come with me and I could take care of him in his old age somewhere else."

"How do you know Adrik is going to want to go with you?" Ben said, wondering how Lucy always seemed so sure things were going to just "work out."

"Why wouldn't he? He's been my friend for most of my life. I can't imagine he'd want to stay alone in Russia."

"I wouldn't be so sure," Ben insisted. "People can be afraid of what's unfamiliar."

Lucius paused and looked over at his friend. "You're talking about yourself now, aren't you?"

Ben looked down at his hands. "I can see it in your eyes, Lucius. You want to rescue me when you escape. But I can't let you do that. I know I'll be a burden the whole time, and honestly, I'm scared. These cells, these bars—this is the only life I've ever known. I'm in my thirties now. I don't know how well I would do adapting to a new world as an adult."

Lucius gave a big smile, and Ben knew he hadn't convinced him. "Don't be foolish, Benjamin. As if I wouldn't be there to help you the entire time."

Ben felt his face flush before his embarrassment turned to frustration. "But that's not what I want! You shouldn't have to help me. You should be able to go out and live your own life! I don't want to be the person holding you back from being happy."

Lucius gave him a puzzled look. "You wouldn't be holding me back, Ben. I promise. I'm not going to leave you behind."

Chapter 33

RAELA

I CAN'T LEAVE MY CHILDREN

It had been at least a month since she brought the book to her half brother. Everything seemed to go back to normal. Azazel was as dutiful as ever to their father, her children continued with their studies, and the other family members lounged around, reading, watching slave fights, and eating as always. Palas was packing as she knocked on his door.

"Almost done?" she said, giving him a soft smile.

He latched the last buckle onto his suitcase. "Yep, traveling light. I'm sure I'll collect a lot of things in my travels. Besides, Russia is huge! Lots of space, lots of places to hide, and lots of food. I'll be fine. Though I wanted to talk to you about something. I get to take one female family member with me," Palas started, talking quieter all of a sudden. "I know you hate it here. Come with me! We can build a vampire society for the better in Russia. Our father won't be able to bother us."

Raela let out a sigh. She was a bit worried he would ask her to join him. He should know better. "I'd love to, but I can't. Palas, I have children here. I can't just abandon them."

"Well, they can come too! It'll just have to be a few years. After a few years, then we'll come back and bring them to our new colony. It'll be perfect, Raela. I know Nathaniel hates it here, just like you. Think of how much fun he'd have in a new place. New places to explore and new things to see—he'd never be bored ever again!"

"Palas, Nathaniel isn't your son. He's the son of our brother. I can't take him. He's going to be the leader someday. Egon and Azazel would never let him go," Raela said, looking down to her feet.

"Alise then. We'll move Alise, and Nathaniel can be the leader back here," he said, reaching forward to take her into his arms.

"Palas, I can't leave my children!" she said, pushing him back. She instantly regretted it when she saw how hurt her brother looked. "Besides, you know Father will never let me leave. I may be a woman, but I'm still his only daughter! If I leave, Azazel won't have a mate for more children should he decide to want another. If Egon had more than one daughter, maybe I could go with you, and Azazel could have someone else. But it just isn't that way. He'll surely make you take a cousin. You should know that by now!"

He looked taken aback by her words. "Father and Azazel don't value you the way I do, Raela. I am sure I can convince him with just a little effort," he said proudly.

She looked down at her feet. "You won't. And even if you could, I'd still have to abandon my children. I won't do it. I can't do it. Palas, I'm sorry."

Letting out a huff, he turned away from her. "Fine then. I'll bring someone else," Palas said, picking up his suitcase and walking to the door of his room.

She turned and walked off toward her own room. Stupid brother, shouldn't he know better by now? He had lived in the castle all his life, as they all had. He should know the rules and what Egon would allow them to do. Raela wanted to scream that she wanted to go with him. If only she hadn't had children yet, everything would be fixed. Then they might actually stand a chance. But the thought of not having her children was another sorrowful thought. She loved them more than anything. The thought of losing them was enough to shatter her heart.

As she sat down on her bed and pulled out a book to read, she thought of her childhood with Palas and what it would be like when he left. Palas had always been her favorite brother. He was kind, caring, funny, and he never hit her or did anything against her wishes. He was a bit lazier than most and very untamed in his mannerisms, but at least he wasn't cruel like Azazel was.

When Palas was a child, he always tried to snuggle into her, telling her all about his day and what he was doing. He loved to read, and he always wanted to share with her the new information he was learning. Even when she was mean to him, he always came back later to ask her what was wrong. Palas knew that Raela never wanted to be mean; she just got upset sometimes. He was always so understanding. And if he couldn't understand, he at least listened.

When Azazel was a child, he would throw himself down at her feet, desperate for any kind of attention. Raela felt so bad sometimes that she gave him her love just to make him happy. But when she didn't give him exactly what he wanted, no matter what, he threw the biggest temper tantrums, kicking and screaming and biting and doing anything he could to hurt her or get his way. And their mother hardly stopped him. Raela didn't think he meant to be this way. Azazel just never thought before he acted. It was his biggest flaw by far, and everyone knew it. Azazel was impulsive, selfish, and cowardly to those who stood up to him. Then again, maybe that was why he felt such affection for her. He knew she was supposed to be his by birthright, and the only person more cowardly than Azazel was herself.

Raela would never say it to Azazel, but she loved Palas so much more than him. They were siblings, so vampiric customs required them to make children together. But Palas was more than that. She often found herself wondering if this was what true love felt like. She always felt happy when he was around, she spent more time with him than any other in the family, and even though her children were not his, she often pretended that they were. The thought of losing him, of losing her love and perhaps the only family member she could classify as a friend caused her a great deal of pain.

A week later, Palas visited her once more. "All right, I'm leaving now. I'm taking Emilia with me instead."

"I'm sure she'll love the adventure," Raela said, trying to sound happy for her brother.

He shuffled his feet and looked to the ground before speaking again. "Raela, are you sure you won't come with me? I would really love to have you by my side. I know it'll be hard, not having your children with you, but we can bring Alise over eventually at least. Then maybe we can have our own children. Wouldn't that be nice? No more Father to tell us what to do. Azazel won't ever be able to touch you again. Just you and me," he said, coming toward her.

Raela submitted as he wrapped his arms around her. She wanted to go with him. She loved her brother more than anyone. If she had to have any more children, she would want them to be his. But she had children here, and she couldn't leave them, even if it was for only a few years. It was a few years she would never get back, and she would probably never see Nathaniel again.

"I can't," she said reluctantly. "I want to, but I can't." She turned her face away.

Palas froze like he wasn't sure what to say. "I understand," he mumbled, turning toward the door. Before he left, he looked at her one last time. "Raela? You know I love you, don't you? I've always loved you."

She stared at him, unsure of what to say. She had always dreamed Palas loved her, but he had never said it out loud before. "I know" was all she could think to say back. It sounded so selfish, so wrong. She should say she loved him too, but in doing so, he would only get more persistent in bringing her along.

The hurt in his eyes was immeasurable and almost enough to make her truly admit her feelings. But the thought of her young son made her hold her tongue. "I'll be sure to write to you," Palas said coldly as he turned and walked out of the room toward the door of the castle. Everything was set for him to leave, and that night, he made his departure toward Russia with his bag and Emilia. Raela watched as they left, wishing it was her by his side.

Chapter 34

LUCIUS

I LOVE YOU

It had been almost five months since he had been strapped into this cell. Benjamin went out once a day to eat with the other slaves, but Lucius remained, growing hungrier and hungrier. Over the past five months, he had grown so close to his friend across the hall. And though he didn't want to admit it, he was starting to feel they were more than friends. They shared deep conversations almost every day, revealing intimate details about themselves. Lucius felt that Ben knew him better than anyone ever had, including Adrik.

Adrik was his friend and a good fatherly figure to him, but there were some things you just didn't say to your dad. Benjamin was different. He never judged him, and he always listened when Lucius shared his terrors with him. Ben had shared details about his life as well.

His mother was supposedly a gifted singer, but he always felt bad never being able to hear the beauty of her voice. His father absolutely loved to dance, and every night his mother and father would dance together in their cell. Ben's most treasured object was a ring his mother had received from his father. Ben's father had inherited the ring from his great grandmother, who was from the world outside. It was golden, with a large spike in the top of it, covered with beautiful intricate designs and patterns. Lucius thought it might have been the most beautiful piece of jewelry he had ever seen. It looked so old but seemed to be polished regularly, on clothing and rags if nothing else.

"How was dinner?" Lucius signed when Ben was placed back in his cell.

"The same as always. All mixed together into a strange sort of soup."

Lucius laughed. "At least you're getting fed."

Suddenly, Ben looked concerned, like it hadn't occurred to him. "When was the last time you ate, Lucius?"

He gave a big shrug. "I ate three months before I was taken into this cell. So I say it must have been, about eight months ago now."

Ben suddenly looked afraid. "Lucius, if you don't eat soon, you're going to break out and eat the nearest thing you can sink your teeth into."

He gave a big sigh. "I'll fight it. I am sure I can fight it long enough to get a meal that isn't you if that's what you're worried about."

"I didn't say that," he said, looking away.

"You didn't have to. I know what I am. I know I'm a human killing monster."

"No, Lucius, I didn't say that. I didn't mean that."

"You might not have meant it, but that doesn't mean you didn't think it. It's all right. I completely understand."

"I don't think you're a monster," he started. "I have never thought you were a monster. You're so kind to me, and you have feelings and feel regret, pity, and sorrow. A monster wouldn't be able to feel those things."

Lucius just stared at him. He couldn't believe Ben was able to say something so kind about him. He had always tried to be kind in life, but death had a strange way of following him. It was something he had always resented. Sometimes he thought it would be better if he was the one who died. Then the tragedies that followed him might die alongside him. He couldn't tell Ben that; it might hurt his feelings after he was trying so hard to make him feel better.

"Thank you. That's a really kind thing to say," he signed. "No one has ever said anything like that to me before."

Ben gave him his best smile and crawled over to the bars of his own cage. "Catch," he signed before tossing him a small shiny object.

Lucius caught it and examined it more closely. It was his mother's ring. He looked up in confusion.

"I want you to have it, for when you finally escape."

Lucius felt his mouth drape open. "No, I can't take this."

"I want you to have it," Ben insisted. "I know you're probably going to get out of here someday, and I want you to take it with you when you leave."

He looked down at the ring then looked back at his friend and tossed it back. "When I leave, I'll bring you with me. I told you that! You're my best friend. I won't leave without you."

Ben picked his ring up from off the floor. "I don't want to burden you, Lucius. I can't run. You're faster and stronger than me, and you know about the world above. I don't. I think it would be better if I stay."

"Didn't you say you always wished Raela would take you out of here? Why not me? Why can't I take you away?"

"I was young then. I didn't see how irrational and impossible the idea was. Of course, a part of me still wants to leave. Why wouldn't I? But it's just not realistic."

Lucius felt anger rising up inside him. Why was Ben always fighting him like this? Didn't he deserve freedom as much as anyone? Lucius couldn't stand the thought of being free if he knew his very best friend was still trapped down underneath a mansion of murderers. He crossed his arms tightly before giving a big huff. His hands felt clammy, and his brow began to sweat. He knew he had to tell Ben the truth if he was going to convince him to leave with him, but the thought still made him nervous.

"Ben, I love you. I love you more than a friend. I won't leave you here. I swear my life on it. Please stop turning me down. I want to save you!" Lucius said, trying to seem brave as he confessed his feelings.

Ben only stared at him, a look of shock written all over his face. And Lucius felt even more nervous.

"I know you think you're going to be a burden on me, because of your hearing and your disability. But I love both those things about you! I love how even through everything. You stand tall. I love how excited you get about learning new information. And I love how trusting you are. Even though I'm related to the family that has tortured you since birth, you see past that. You understand that I'm not like them. You see me for me. When I take you away, I'll find somewhere nice for us to live, somewhere peaceful. We can move somewhere nice, like America! I had a friend in Russia who said America was one of the best places in the world. We can go together, and we can live together and read books together, and…I don't know—just be together!" Lucius said. He knew he was running out of things to say but felt so nervous he couldn't stop himself from rambling. "It'll be perfect. We'll never have to see another vampire for the rest of our days, and I'll get you all the delicious food you could want! No more of this mixed-in soup that I know you hate—"

"I love you too, Lucius," Ben signed, cutting him off. "You're too sweet, you know that? I really hope everything you're saying can really be true one day." He looked sad at just the thought of it.

"It will, Ben. It will, I promise."

Chapter 35

RAELA

NO MORE FIGHTING

It had been almost seven months since she had brought Lucius to the cells and five months since she last visited them. She hoped she was safe, but it was hard to know. Egon was famous for withholding punishment until he thought you least expected it. So she tried her best to never let her guard down for even a moment.

Palas had been gone for quite some time now. Raela missed him more than she expected she would. But she still had her children, and for that, she was thankful. Aside from them, however, she felt very lonely. Sewing and knitting with the other women in the colony just wasn't the same. It provided some comfort and company, of course. But she couldn't be herself the way she could around her youngest brother.

As she carefully tried to knit a sweater for her son, she found herself getting stuck on the sleeves. She was never any good at knitting. Her mother looked over at her work before giving her a small sigh. Raela thought that after making about a hundred sweaters and knitting her whole life, she would at least be decent at it. But she never felt very good with small intricate tasks involving her hands.

Then everyone heard a knock at the door and turned to see Azazel.

"Raela, our father wants to see you," he said seriously.

Raela gently set down her project. "Can you take this to my room if I'm not back in time?" she asked her mother.

"Of course, we'll be done soon, so I'll bring it over in a few minutes."

Raela nodded and got up to follow her brother. "May I change into something more decent?"

Azazel looked her up and down. "No, you look fine as you are," he said, turning and leading her to Egon's study.

She looked down at herself and thought of how horrid she looked for the meeting. She was wearing nothing but a long wool dress to keep her covered, but because it was so close to bedtime, she wore little else. He opened the door and led her inside. Egon was sitting behind his desk, facing the door as always.

Raela walked in and gave a small curtsy. "You asked for me, Father?"

Egon stared at her silently. "What specific instruction did I give you several months ago?" he said calmly.

"You said not to visit Ben anymore, and I haven't," she lied. Maybe he wasn't aware.

Azazel looked over at her dreadfully, and Egon continued, "That isn't what your brother has told me. I gave him specific instructions to keep a close eye on the activity in that particular block of cells."

She bowed her head softly, fearing the rage she knew to come from this. "I am sorry, Father. I promise I haven't visited since."

Egon stood up and slapped her hard across the face. "You should have thought about your actions before. Your apology means nothing to me now. Azazel, leave us."

"Yes, sir," he said before dutifully leaving the room.

Raela stood where she was and avoided eye contact at all cost.

"On top of openly disobeying my direct order, you supplied that filthy halfling with books and knowledge! Where did he get the book on vampires, Raela? I know it was you that gave it to him!"

She bowed her head lower. "I should have thought before I acted, Father. I'm so—"

She was cut off by a hard punch into her stomach. She tried not to cough. "I did not give you permission to speak!" Egon screamed, pulling her up by her neck and backhanding her again.

Raela shut her eyes and withheld the tears threatening to fall. She felt as her father's grip tightened around her neck but said nothing. She could not die of strangulation. She knew that, but the thought of not breathing still frightened her horribly.

"I have been too lenient on you for too long. I let you have your silly wishes and hopes, let you take pity on the slaves. I thought it would teach you kindness toward your own children when you had them. I should have never been so forgiving of your treacherous habits. I thought perhaps you would grow out of it, as I did, but you are now many years past the age I stopped associating with slaves. Your excuse is gone!" he said, throwing her to the ground. "And even if I took pity on them, I would have never disobeyed a direct order. But now it's quite clear whom you truly care about more."

Raela hastily tried to climb back to her feet but was quickly slammed into his desk. She felt him hold her down with a hand on her back and another hand pinning an arm behind her. She stared ahead, fearing what would come next. She felt his hand leave her back and start traveling up her wool dress. It would be better if she ignored it. This was meant to be a punishment, so she tried to stop and pretend this was Palas on top of her. But Palas would never be this rough. Palas would never force her like this.

When the deed was done, he pulled her dress down and yanked her away from his desk back to the floor by her hair. "Maybe now you'll remember what happens to those who disobey the head of our family. Don't let this happen again, Raela, or maybe next time I'll have Azazel join me."

Raela sat up and stared at him. He wouldn't really shame her that deeply as to have more than one person take her at a time, would he? No. Deep down, she knew the kind of cruelty Egon was capable of. She knew he would. She was only a woman after all. All that mattered to him was that she stay in her place. He sat back down in his desk chair and called for Azazel, who appeared in the room at record speed.

"Drag your disobedient sister back to her room, through the most crowded part of the castle. Take no back hallways," he said, turning back to the papers on his desk.

Azazel walked over to her, helping her up and taking her hand before Egon stopped him. "Not so fast. This is meant to be shameful. This is a punishment. Drag her by her hair."

Azazel looked down at his sister and then back at his father before doing as he was instructed. Raela knew this was meant to be humiliating for her. Her face burned with embarrassment as she was dragged through the women and children's quarters. She was supposed to be an example, but her hair was hurting as Azazel pulled her and dragged her across the floor when she tripped over her own feet. Finally arriving at her room, he opened the door and tossed her inside.

Raela lay on the floor, turning away from her brother. For a long time, he said nothing, but she didn't hear him leaving either. She just wanted him to go away! *Don't look at me! I know I look horribly pitiful*, Raela thought to herself.

Finally, after several long minutes, he spoke. "I'm sorry, Raela. I didn't know he would do that," he said softly. "I didn't mean to get you hurt like this."

His sister stayed quiet, not looking up from the floor.

Azazel paused, trying to think of something else to say. But unable to do so, he gently shut the door.

Raela lay on the cold wood floor for several more moments before getting up and stumbling to her bed. She crawled into it, not bothering to clean herself up. She had never felt so used. At least when she and Azazel had reproduced, he made every effort to make her happy. This was different. This was forced. All she wanted now was to lie down and cry. She felt such horrible shame. She wanted to run inside of herself and die. She knew she was only supposed to reproduce for her brother. She had no other worth. It was shameful. But however shameful it was, it couldn't be worse than this. No.

Being openly dragged before the whole family with semen still running down her legs was definitely worse.

She thought of Palas. She should have gone with him as he wanted. She should have known better than to think she could hide anything from Azazel and her father. Just how big a fool was she? After an hour of crying, she dragged herself to the tub and cleaned the stickiness from between her legs. She decided then that it was truly over. No more visiting slaves, no more feeling pity. From this moment forward, she was going to be the perfect little stone-hearted daughter her father had always wanted her to be. Kindness had no place in this family. It was past time she learned that lesson.

Chapter 36

BEN

A FIREPLACE ESCAPE

As Ben was sat next to Marie, he picked up his bowl of food. "Any new information?"

"Yes!" the girl signed enthusiastically. "Behind the fireplaces! There is a tunnel leading into the outside world through Egon's fireplace, and it looks like Raela's fireplace used to have a tunnel as well. But they walled it off. I bet with a bit of pushing, Lucius could break the bricks, and you two could escape through there."

"Why not just escape through Egon's fireplace? It seems easier since his is already open."

Marie gave a dreadful chuckle. "You can certainly try, but I rarely see him leave his office, if ever."

"Oh…then I suppose that won't work," Ben signed as he glanced over at his captors, four lower-ranked vampire men who were dutifully standing guard at the door.

Ben gave a small chuckle before signing to Marie. "I know I must have mentioned this before, but thank God none of the vampires bothered learning sign language."

Marie let out a laugh. "None except Raela. Sometimes I feel like you're the only one I can talk to because of that. Anyone else I speak to has the possibility of our…unwanted watchers listening in. But enough about that. I want to know the juicy stuff! Are you and Lucius dating yet?"

Ben felt his face redden. "No, we're not dating. At least, I don't think. He told me that he loves me, but I think that is a horrible mistake."

"How could it be a mistake? That sounds like a great thing! Maybe if you two escape, you can be together for real."

"I don't think that's a good idea. I'd just be a burden to sneak out. He can run, lift, and hide better than I can. I'd have to be carried the entire time. If Lucius had any sense, he'd leave without me," Ben said, feeling a great sadness come over him.

Ben didn't want Lucius to leave. Well, that wasn't quite true. Ben wanted Lucius to leave if it would make him happy. He wanted Lucius to be happy. But Ben didn't want to be alone again. Just the thought of losing someone he cared so deeply about felt like a strike to his heart. But that was selfish, wasn't it? If Lucius wanted to leave, he should help him. And if Lucius was smart, he wouldn't bring along a cripple he'd have to lug around the whole time.

Marie stared at him as if she was reading his thoughts. She let out a long sigh. "Being in solitude for so long sure has given you an awful case of depression, Benjamin. You're much too hard on yourself. I think Lucius should be able to make the sensible decision of whether he wants to bring you or not on his own. And if he does, then don't you dare pass that opportunity up, Ben. Don't you dare! There are too many people here who would love to be given that chance, so don't you waste yours."

Ben sat and thought for a minute. Marie did make an excellent point. As he looked around, he couldn't help but think that any one of the other humans would die to be in his shoes. Well, shoe. Any one of them would die to escape, and here he was with the opportunity. Yet he was turning it down. He was turning it down! Why?

He looked down into his food. Lucius wanted to escape with him. Lucius wanted to escape with him because he loves him. Ben had always dreamed that someone would return his feelings. And here he was, with his wish coming true! So why the hell was he turning him away! Was he being a fool?

Maybe he should trust his friend. After all, Lucius definitely had more life experience than he did. Maybe Marie was right. Perhaps it was only his own self-loathing and pity that was convincing him not to travel with Lucius. Or maybe it was his fear of the unknown outside his cell. Ben was so used to being a burden; he dared to dream that for once, someone might have thought of him as a blessing. And if life was deeming him worthy enough for a chance to escape, was it really right of him to turn it away?

Ben loved Lucius. He really did. And for the first time in his life, someone returned his feelings. Lucius took the time to learn sign language, to learn about his history and his family. Of course, Lucius would take the time to sneak him out of this horrible place. He had already invested so much emotional support in him about his life and his struggles. Ben thought it was selfish to go along with him. To drag him down. But perhaps Ben was being selfish by denying Lucius future emotional support. Ben was being selfish by forcing Lucius to leave him behind. Well, not anymore. The next time Lucius offered to escape with him, Ben would tell him what he really wanted!

Chapter 37

AZAZEL

WHAT HAVE I DONE?

Azazel sat at his desk, thinking what a fool he was. How stupid was he? To act so hastily on a jealous whim. He should never have gone to see his father. He should have just kept his mouth shut. But how was he to know what Egon would do to his sister? He thought his father would just rough her up a little. He never imagined that he would punish her in such a cruel way. She was his daughter, wasn't she? Yet he treated her like he didn't give a damn about her well-being or state of mind.

After the event, Raela stopped leaving her room except to eat and visit their children. Whenever Azazel tried to confront her about what happened, to apologize for his actions, she stared right past him. When she did speak to him, it was just "Yes, Azazel," "Thank you, Azazel," "I'm sorry, Azazel," which hurt almost more than her staying completely silent. With his jealous rage gone and the recent events having unfolded, he wanted nothing more than to go back in time and slap himself for his idiocy. If Raela disliked him before, it was clear she hated him now. That, or she just didn't feel anything. It seemed as of late that nothing could make her smile—not him, not their family, not even her children, who were clearly growing more and more concerned for their distant mother.

Egon, however, seemed delighted that Raela had finally given up. He never had to worry about her speaking out against the slave fights. Her obedience was a relief to him, but it made Azazel worry. He had somewhat liked Raela's prideful defiance. She didn't use it often against their father, but she always had a bit of spark in her when he wasn't around. But now it seems that spark was gone, and Azazel couldn't feel worse about it. He found that seeing her without her spunk was so painful that he was avoiding her unintentionally.

Azazel didn't understand. How could Egon do such a thing? To his own daughter no less. Raela was supposed to be his, wasn't she? Azazel would have never raped her in such a brutal manner. She was forced to conceive with him, but that didn't mean he didn't at least try to make her happy. But now all of Raela's happiness was gone, and it was all his fault. He wanted to apologize; if only he could gather the courage to talk to her. But when she stared at him with those dead eyes, he said his apology, and she had no reaction. She had no reaction at all, as if all feeling in her had vanished overnight.

Azazel wanted to scream. He couldn't imagine how horrible she must feel. He couldn't imagine the horror of what their father had done to her. It was no wonder she hated him. And he didn't blame her. After what she had to go through, he deserved her hatred.

Azazel was surprised he didn't feel jealous. He didn't envy his father at all for what he got to do to his sister. No. Azazel didn't want to treat her that way. Azazel never wanted to force her, not like that. Never like that. He wanted her to love him. It was different than what Egon had done.

Egon probably didn't realize it, but what he did to Raela also affected himself. It made Azazel look like a great fool to the rest of the family. Not only that, but they saw him drag her back to her quarters on his command. It seemed no matter where he went now, all the women of his family looked at him as though he were a monster. This wasn't what he wanted. He only wanted to teach Raela and Palas a lesson. He only wanted to make sure she wouldn't leave.

No, he didn't want this at all. How could his father betray him like this? He was supposed to be passing the empire off to him some-day. He should be looking out for Azazel's best interest. Azazel failed to see how this could possibly be in his interest. All it succeeded in doing was making Raela and every other woman in their colony hate him.

He wanted to apologize to his sister, to make her truly under-stand how sorry he was. He never should have said anything to their father. Raela wouldn't leave her children, and with Palas gone, Azazel might have had the chance to jump in to comfort her. Azazel could have made her love him, if he hadn't been such a fool.

But there was hardly a thing he could do about it now. He couldn't revolt. Who would follow him? He couldn't leave. Where would he go? And if he tried to take Raela with him, to rescue her from this horrible place, what of their kids together? As Azazel walked into his bedroom and shut the door behind him, he started his bath. Staring down into the water, he saw his reflection. He really had grown large, living such a pampered life. No, he could never survive out in the world beyond the castle. He was pampered and short and weak. A coward beyond reason. It was no wonder Raela loved Palas. Palas was smart and tall and brave. Palas was tall, slim, and kind. Palas was everything that Azazel had always wished he was. Palas might have been lazy, but at least he wasn't a brute. At least he wasn't a fool.

Chapter 38

LUCIUS

THE PAINS OF LOVE

Nine months since he had been chained, a year since he had eaten—it was unbearable. He wasn't growing anymore, so he didn't need the nutrients as bad as when he was a child. But the feeling of starvation was the same. His stomach growled, and every day, he had to fight his eyes turning red and losing control. Although it wouldn't matter if he did, he didn't have any way of escape. But he could see that every time his eyes turned red, Ben was growing more and more frightened of him, even if he denied it.

"I need you to distract me." Lucius signed one day, doing everything and anything he could to control himself.

Ben thought quickly. "What's your favorite color! And why?"

"Blue. It's the color of the ocean, and of my twin sister's eyes. I love the way the ocean feels. It's so cold and refreshing. I love the freedom it makes me feel, and the open skies are so relieving. It's so open and reminds me of how big the world is," he babbled, trying to keep his mind off his stomach. "Yours?"

"My favorite color is green. It's the color of grass and plants. It makes me think anything can grow in even the darkest dampest places, even in a castle when all the odds are against you and you're held in a cage. What is the happiest moment of your life?"

"When my friend Adrik told me it was okay to be weak. I had been so hurt and torn up inside for so long, to have someone accept me despite that, made me feel so happy. He is the closest thing I'll ever have to a real father. What about you?" he said, trying to keep the conversation quick so he could distract himself. Ben caught on to this.

"The happiest moment in my life was when I met you. You finally provided me with comfort and companionship unlike I had ever known before. I'm so glad you're here, Lucius. Please, keep trying to hold yourself back. I know it's hard."

Lucius paused. His happiest moment was meeting him? Was he really that important to Ben? The thought was enough to bring him to tears. He had never considered himself important to anyone before. The moment his eyes dampened, his hunger took control again, and his eyes turned red. He shut them and punched himself as hard as he could in the stomach. *Don't lose control!* When he opened his eyes, he saw one of his family members, he wasn't sure which, taking Ben from his cage.

Ben glanced at him briefly before signing "I'll be back after I eat."

Lucius nodded and remained, having no other choice. He shut his eyes tightly and tried to focus on his self-control. Then the same relative came back to visit him.

"My, my, aren't you something?" he said, looking him up and down.

"Which one are you?" he said bitterly.

"My name is Azazel."

"So you're my half brother then?"

"I would never associate myself as being related to a monster like you. But technically speaking, I suppose I am," he scoffed, rolling his eyes like it was obvious that Lucius should feel ashamed.

"Did you only come to mock me? Or was there a greater reason you decided to show your fat face."

Azazel reddened with anger. "How dare you speak to me like that! I am to be the head of the family! You're just some chained-up half breed. You have no right to insult me like this!" he shouted, clearly more than sensitive about his shorter larger frame.

"Oh, I'm sorry. Did I hit a weak spot? I give you credit. You may be a pureblood, but at least I'm not the same height as a woman." Lucius knew that would hurt. From what he had gathered, women held very little respect here. So being compared to one must sting harder than any other insult.

His brother's face turned so red he looked like a cherry tomato. He let out a few angry huffs before turning and straightening himself up. "There is a reason I am down here. Father has asked to see you," he said, pulling the lever, letting Lucius down from the ceiling and opening the bars of his cage. "He requests you down that hall. Take three lefts then a right and through the doors," he instructed. "He'll feed you once you get there. I imagine you're hungry."

Lucius felt his stomach gurgle but tried to ignore it. "You're not coming with me?" he asked, rather appalled he was being left to his own travels.

"No, I have other places to be, unfortunately. I trust you can find your own way," Azazel said, walking in the opposite direction.

Lucius's stomach made itself known once more, and he felt his eyes turn red. *No. No, I have to resist it. I have to resist*, he thought. Turning toward the hall, he carefully followed the instructions given to him. Three lefts, one right. This whole setup screamed trap. But he was so hungry. The promise of food was enough to convince him to keep moving.

He walked down to the end of the hall and opened the door. The sudden light was blinding to him, even if it was only a little. He was so used to sitting in the darkness; even the dim candlelight was almost too much for him to handle.

As Lucius looked around, he wondered where he was. The walls were so high, and the ground was made of stone, just like his cell. All around him, above the walls, were his white-haired relatives, staring down at him like he was a part of some show. He felt lower than everyone else. The whole room was in the shape of a circle, and his

mind flashed back to the fighting pits he had been forced to participate in. No. No, this couldn't be. That part of his life was behind him.
Never again. He would never participate in something so horrible!

His eyes flashed red, and his stomach growled. He stumbled
blindly toward the smell of food. Blood, he could smell blood. He
was so hungry. He wanted to eat! In a rage of hunger, he looked up
and started toward the delectable smell. When he saw who it was
coming from, he snapped out of it. In the center of the pit, tied with
his hands behind his back, was Ben with a huge gash in his forehead,
blood running down the side of his face.

Lucius gasped and covered his nose, plugging it before any
more of the smell could reach him. Ben looked up at him in fear,
and Lucius turned his face toward the wall, shutting his eyes tightly.
What was going on? Why was his family doing this? Azazel had lied
to him. He should have expected nothing less. Ben had told him how
cruel his brother could be to Raela, and she was a pureblood! Lucius
was less than a monster to him, why wouldn't he lie.

A thought occurred to him. Was this really all Azazel? Or was
he just a puppet in this? No, Azazel said he was to be the head of
their house, but he wasn't yet. This was Egon's work. He was no
true father to him. A true father wouldn't torture their son like this.
Lucius should have never come here. He should have never entered
this castle, never grown feelings for Ben, and never walked through
the doors into this feeding arena. Lucius held his breath the best he
could, but when he felt a horrible sharp pain in the side of his shoulder, he let out a gasp, and his hands flew from his nose toward the
pain. He yanked an arrow out of his arm and looked up at his family.
There, he saw Raela holding a bow, slinging another arrow into position. Her eyes looked different than when he saw her a few months
ago. They seemed grayer somehow, reminding him of a porcelain
doll who had been broken.

He felt his eyes shift to red again, and his stomach growled. He
went to cover his nose, but another arrow hit him through his hand.
More blood, and suddenly, it was over. The whole world turned red,
and he could do nothing to stop himself as he sprinted toward his
companion. He tried and failed to hold himself back before he could

grab onto him. Ben tried to turn and crawl away, but Lucius caught him.

No! Stop it! You love him! Lucius thought to himself. *Don't do what you did to your mother! Haven't you learned anything!* He wanted to scream at himself, but he couldn't. It was almost like he was viewing the whole event through a third lens. He couldn't do a thing as he felt and watched his teeth sink into his treasured friend. He tasted so good. He tried to stop drinking before he killed him completely, but no matter how much he tried, he failed.

When he finally drained every drop of blood from the shorter male, he yanked his mouth off him. Ben's eyes were growing gray. As he closed his eyes, he rested a hand on his arm and squeezed with his last remaining energy. Lucius scooped up his hand and held it close, tears flowing down his cheeks. What had he done? What had they made him do! He tried to remember back to the book Ben read with him. He tried to remember how to make a vampire. Surely it wasn't too late. He dug his nails into the skin of his thumb and shoved it inside Ben's mouth. He had to drink some of his blood. He had to! He couldn't let this be the end for him!

They were going to escape. They were going to live together! Lucius couldn't stand the thought of all their dreams fading so quickly. "Wake up! Wake up!" he wanted to scream. This had to be a nightmare. He stared into his pale-gray dead eyes. *Wake up. Wake up!* He couldn't force Ben to swallow the blood in his mouth, and after about thirty seconds, he decided it must have been too late. He heard the applause of his family around him and knew if he waited any longer, his father would command Raela to shoot him and they'd both be dead. *It's probably too late*, he thought to himself, trying to sound convincing. He squeezed Ben's hand tighter and tried to withhold his tears. But it was far too late for that. The best he could do now was try to calm himself. He felt a poke in his palm and opened his hand.

Ben was wearing his mother's ring! He remembered how desperately he wanted the ring to make it to the outside world and how much it meant to him. As sneakily as he could, Lucius slipped it off his finger and put it on. It was unlikely anyone would notice. It wasn't as though Egon paid him any attention when he brought him here. He was still wearing all his old clothes, and he hadn't showered since his arrival.

Lost in his own thoughts of death and despair, he hardly noticed the relatives coming toward him until they yanked Ben's cold, limp body out of his arms.

"Wait! You can't take him!" he shouted before looking up and seeing his father's judging eyes.

"He's only a human," a woman said, yanking Ben harder out of his arms. He heard an audible snap as one of his friend's arms broke. Lucius winced, closing his eyes.

Move forward! There's no reason to stand and idle in the past. Focus on what's in front of you. He wiped his eyes and turned to look up at his father, who stared coldly down at him. Egon leaned over to Raela, saying a few words. She listened, then gave a short nod. After everyone had left Lucius in the pit, Raela came over to him.

"Father says you've done well. You've truly proven yourself as a member of this family. Well done—" She was cut off.

Lucius grabbed her by the neck and lifted her to his face. "Why are you here? What does that horrible bastard have to say to me? How dare you show your face after you played such a large role in his death! How could you? I'll never forgive you for this, I swear it!" he said, throwing her away from him.

Raela stumbled and fell. Lucius backed away from her and faced the wall, trying to regain his composure and not take his rage out on his sister.

She sat up on her elbows and rubbed the back of her head, feeling a bump starting to form. "Father wants to see you," she said in a quiet voice. "You don't have to forgive me, but I was told to deliver you that message. That's all."

Lucius turned and scowled at her. "Why should I see him? I want you to let me out of this horrible castle, out of this horrid, inhumane place."

Raela climbed to her feet and noticed the tear in her fancy event gown. It wasn't her favorite anyway. "You should know I can't do that. Do you think I have that kind of power? Lucius, use your damn head. Ben was my friend too. You think I wanted to see him dead?"

Lucius sneered and crossed his arms, looking at the floor. "Why does he want to see me?"

"He wants to congratulate you, and welcome you into the family. He said you have earned your first assignment as a part of the Lovhart Empire."

This only infuriated him more, but he didn't want to show it. How dare he ask something of him immediately after such a huge loss in his life! Egon must have known he and Ben were in love. He must have manipulated the whole scene. Why else would he put him in a cell across from him? Why else starve him? So when faced with the opportunity, he would have no choice but to react on pure monstrous instinct. Why was Egon so cruel! Lucius had done nothing to him! Now he didn't even have the decency to give Ben a proper burial or let Lucius have the privacy of some time alone to cry and mourn over his death.

Though, hasn't it always been this way? When Misha and Oleg passed, he wasn't given any time to mourn over them either. He just had to get over it, right then and there. Move forward, just take one more step, and you'd survive. One more step, one more fight, one more body in the pile, one more day feeling stupid in school, one more drug sale, one more day without food. Why must it always be one more? Couldn't he just be left alone to his own happiness? Life must truly hate him if it was willing to torture him this much. It wasn't fair.

He heard Oleg's voice in his head. *Life isn't fair, kid. You should be thankful it isn't you.*

Lucius turned and looked at Raela, who was holding her hands tight to her stomach in discomfort. "Why couldn't I turn him? Ben and I had read that book cover to cover, multiple times! Was it just too late?"

Raela looked up, pity written all over her face. "Half breeds can't always turn humans into vampires. Sometimes they're just too human themselves," she muttered, looking back toward her feet.

Lucius stared at her, feeling more than dead inside. "Oh" was all he could bring himself to say. Had Ben read him that from the book Raela gave him? He should have paid more attention. He had to get out of here. He wasn't sure where he would go, but the thought of staying was worse. It was like being trapped in a little cottage in the forest all over again, but this time, it was a mountain and escape wouldn't be as easy as running out the door away from all your problems. Lucius always seemed to move from cage to cage, except he knew there was no way he could kill his way out of this situation. They were vampires like him. His strength was no match to whatever speed, magic, or strength they had. He could probably match one in a fight, but everyone in the castle? That wasn't a risk he was willing to take.

"Where do they keep the dead humans?" he blurted.

"Anyone we're done with, we put in the old abandoned cells. They're so rusted out they aren't capable of holding anyone in anymore. It's below the castle. We take them down there and dust out the remains once every few years. That's probably where he'll be taken if that's what you're wondering."

"All right. Take me to our father. I'm ready to see him."

Raela gave a small nod and turned, leading him through the long hallways. As he walked through, it occurred to him just what a fancy life his family led. Everything was perfectly clean, almost sickeningly so. Everything had gold trim or fancy lace on its edges, which was only further proof that his family had lived here for a long time. Did they take or acquire all these things? It must have taken decades.

Following Raela, they turned a corner toward Egon's office. Lucius spotted a young red-haired woman on her hands and knees, scrubbing a section of floor. Unlike Ben, she wasn't dressed in sack rags. She wore a plain gray dress with no sleeves and a belt made of rope around her waist. He remembered his father talking about how his mother was a cleaning slave and wondered if this used to be her life. He made a mental note to seek her out later for questions.

Chapter 39

LUCIUS

TALKING TO DAD

Raela opened the door to his office and stepped aside. Lucius walked in, and she closed the door again behind him. Egon was in his desk chair, staring at him. He felt uncomfortable with his inability to decipher his father's emotions based on his facial expression.

"You asked for me?" Lucius said, trying to sound respectful despite his anger.

"Yes, you did a good job in the pits today. I am very proud that you would pick our family over some useless slave boy. Well done."

Lucius bit his tongue. He wanted to defend Ben, but now was not the time. "Thank you," he said through clenched teeth.

"I understand you are upset, but the pain will lessen in time. Meanwhile, I have your first assignment. This will prove that you are truly loyal to us, should you comply," he said, taking a letter from his desk. "Your brother Palas—"

"My half brother," Lucius interrupted.

Egon put down the letter and stared at him for several moments before speaking again. "Lucius, I know you are new to our family, so you don't quite yet understand the rules. But do not interrupt me again, understand? If you are going to be a part of this family, you have to abandon the part of you that is human. Palas will be your full brother."

Lucius put his hands into his pockets. "Yes, sir."

"Take your hands out of your pockets. Stand up straight. I will not have you looking like some measly slacker."

He did as he was told. "Yes, sir."

"Good. Now as I was saying, your younger brother Palas has been working hard in Russia to start a new colony. He left a few months ago and sent us a letter recently saying that the colony in England made no attempt to settle in Russia once they found him there, as I predicted. However, now I need someone to scope out what they are up to. Azazel is too important, Raela is too disloyal, but you have done nothing as of yet to make me think you would betray me. I am trusting you now. Am I making a mistake?"

"No," Lucius lied.

"Good, and better yet, you can travel during the day. So I expect you to leave immediately. Find Claudius. He's the leader of the main colony in England. Find out what he is like, what he is up to, and if he has any plans. Then report back to me. Are we clear?"

"Yes, sir. Thank you for this opportunity, sir," he said, giving a small bow.

"You are welcome. I expect you to leave by tomorrow night at the latest," Egon said, turning back to his work. Lucius took his cue to leave.

Raela was waiting outside the door for him. "What did he say? What was your mission?"

"Wouldn't you like to know?"

Raela sighed. "I brought you something," she said, holding out some rolled bandages.

He took them, wrapping up his hand. "Thank you," he muttered.

"Will you please tell me what your mission is?"

He remained silent for a moment before considering. Raela was likely to be his only friend here. Azazel was obviously too cruel to ever treat him like a brother, and he was willing to believe the rest of the family felt similarly.

"He wants me to 'scope out the situation' in England," Lucius said reluctantly.

Raela led him down the hallway. "Well, that should be easy at least," she replied. She led him to a room and opened the door. Inside was a bed, a bathroom, and lots of fancy furniture that looked like it could have belonged in a study. "This will be your room from now on."

Lucius looked around. It was much too fancy for his tastes. It reminded him a bit of his bedroom in his big fancy house in Russia, but everything here was outdated and looked like it belonged in a Victorian mansion. The whole room had too much red and too much black. The carpet was red, the bed sheets were red, the walls were red with black trim, the ceiling was black, the doors and all the furniture was black. Lucius thought it seemed very cliché for a vampire's bedroom.

"Uh, thanks," he said, turning toward her.

Raela nodded and took out a bundle of gauze. "Let me help dress your wounds."

"No, thank you," Lucius said, turning his back toward her.

Raela approached him, trying to undress him to get a better look at his wounds. "I insist. It's the least I can—"

"I said no!" Lucius shouted before pushing her off. Her head bumped the floor as she fell, and for a split second, he felt bad. But remembering Ben, he turned his back on her. "You can leave now," Lucius said coldly before taking the gauze.

She nodded and turned to leave, closing the door behind her. Taking off his leather jacket, he started wrapping the gauze around his shoulder the best he could. As he wrapped it up, he tried not to wince at the movement. It wouldn't matter. In a few days, it would be healed anyway. The gauze got stuck on his finger, and he pulled his hand away. It was Ben's ring. He untangled the gauze off the golden decorated spike and twisted it around his finger. He looked around the room, feeling very alone. This wasn't his family. They didn't really want him. His father might say otherwise, but he was lying. Lucius felt like such a fool. He left his real father figure back in Russia to come to this place, where he wasn't welcome.

Everything about this room was so neat. When he looked down at himself, trying to bandage the rest of his shoulder, he stopped and realized he wasn't coated in only his blood. Some of it was Ben's as well. His blood, Ben's blood…did it matter? Sometimes he felt like he was always covered in blood. He walked to the bathtub and tried to scrub himself clean, not that it did much good. He still felt disgusting on the inside. He scrubbed harder till his skin was red and blistering. After he started bleeding from the sponge on his arms, he finally realized it was the deed that made him feel this way, not the dirt on his skin.

He sat in the bath and brought his knees to his chest. *Don't cry. You're not a kid anymore! He's dead. Just get over it. What, did you think you'd escape, then live happily ever after? Grow up. There's no happily ever after for you. Monsters never get the happy ending. It's past time you knew that. So don't cry! You've known all along it wouldn't work!*

Despite his best efforts, he felt tears slipping down his cheeks. He tried to wipe them away, only for them to be replaced just as quickly. Finally giving up, he wrapped his arms around himself, succumbing to the sadness. It all happened so quickly. Just this morning, he and Ben had been talking about their future. It was impossible to believe only hours later he would be dead and Lucius would be sitting in this room all alone.

After another half an hour, he got up, dried off, and headed to the bedroom. He stared down at the fancy bed, feeling too unwelcome to even peel back the covers. Instead he took a blanket off a chair and lay on top, using that instead. The next few hours went by with very little sleep. In the night, he sat up to the sound of his door creaking open. It was the young red-haired girl.

"Oh! I'm…I'm sorry, master," she stammered, giving a little bow. "I was not informed you would be staying in this room. Please forgive me." She turned to leave.

Lucius bolted out of bed and grabbed her arm. The short woman flinched away from him. "P-please don't hurt me, sir! I promise I won't make such a foolish mistake again!"

"I'm not going to hurt you. What's your name?" he said, leading her back into the room as gently as he could.

"M-Marie. Please, I would feel so grateful if you would let me return to my work," she said in a soft voice, eyeing the door as he closed it.

"You don't need to be afraid of me. I said I wouldn't hurt you. Can you keep a secret, Marie?"

"If you wish me to, master," she said quietly, her eyes falling to the floor.

"Stop being afraid, Marie. I'm not the biggest fan of my family either."

"Oh no, master, that's not true. I love your family. I…I'm so grateful they have given me the opportunity to serve them. It is such an honor," she said, giving another bow.

"You don't need to lie. It's all right. Have you ever heard of a woman named Katherine? She was a cleaning servant just like you— quite a while back, I imagine."

"I…I have heard of her, but we aren't supposed to speak of the other servants. Please, let me go back to work," she said, trying to move toward the door.

He blocked her. "I won't tell anyone what you say, I promise. She's my mother, I need to know what you know."

Marie looked around before glancing back down at the floor. Lucius thought it was such a shame; she had such beautiful green eyes. They looked just like Misha's had. "Katherine, with the dark black curly hair? Blue eyes?" Marie said, finally looking up at him.

"Yes, yes, that one. Did you know anything about her?" he said, eager to know more about the life his mother never spoke of.

"I…I didn't know her myself. I hadn't been born yet. But my mother knew her well. They were cleaners together. I…I shouldn't say anything more," she stammered, looking back to the ground.

"Marie, please," he pleaded. "It's important. I won't tell anyone what you said to me."

She gave another glance at the door, then up to him. "Rumor among the cleaners is, Master Egon got her pregnant. Lady Raela was only a little girl at the time, and Master Azazel hadn't been born yet. We all thought he would just arrange a quick and sneaky death for her. My mother says that Katherine lived every day in horrible fear of her fate. Everything pointed toward her death—her situation, the father, the fact that she was given a private cell with no witnesses. We all assumed she would be dead before she could start showing, but no one was ever called to clean up her body. She suddenly just…" Marie looked around before whispering, "Vanished. Overnight." She looked to the door once more and then again at the floor.

"Why did my father get her pregnant. Do you know?"

She shook her head. "Master Egon was much younger then. My mother says she thought he was bored with women who all looked the same. Katherine looked the exact opposite of any of the royal family—dark curly hair instead of white straight, blue eyes instead of red. She thinks maybe Egon only wanted change, and maybe it felt good to dominate another person, to hold your power over them while you did whatever you wished. Katherine always told my mother how much she hated Egon. She hated his smell, his touch, and he was always violent with her."

Lucius couldn't imagine what it must be like to live here as a slave all your life. He felt so horrible for his mother. She had suffered her whole life in this dreadful place, only to be thrown out blind into the world. Then before she could enjoy her new freedom, she had two children forced on her. It was no wonder she tried to abandon them. Lucius thought for a moment. As much as he hated to use this girl, she was likely the only person in the castle to give him helpful information. He needed to seize this opportunity while it lay in front of him.

"Raela. You know her, I'm sure."

"Yes, sir," she said, trying to avoid direct eye contact.

"You've heard of what happened to Ben, one of the slaves, didn't you?"

Marie hesitated and looked deeply saddened very suddenly. "Yes…master."

"Why do you think Raela shot me. I wouldn't have killed him if I wasn't so starved."

"I know, sir. Ben and I, we were very close friends. He spoke very highly of you. But I shouldn't say anything else."

Lucius paused. Ben hardly spoke of this girl unless it was to discuss their escape plans. It never occurred to him that Ben's Marie might be this Marie. But that hardly mattered now.

"Why did Raela participate in his death? I thought they were somewhat close?"

"Lady Raela received a horrible punishment just a few days prior to the event. Master Egon was furious when he found out she was still sneaking down to see you, rumor tells. And because of that, he punished her. I'm not sure exactly what he did, but the other cleaners that cleaned her room say that he...raped her."

"I see," Lucius said, suddenly feeling more pity toward his elder sister. "Thank you, Marie. I've heard all I need to," he said, stepping aside from the door.

The woman rushed to the door and opened it. "I am so sorry to have bothered you, sir," she said, turning around to give one last bow and then leaving and closing the door behind her.

It all made more sense now. It wasn't Raela that shot him; it was Egon. Raela was just following orders, and who could blame her after the punishment she faced after her last disobedient act? No, Lucius couldn't blame her for this. She was just as much a victim in this house as he was. He gave a small sigh before crawling back in bed.

Chapter 40

LUCIUS

LEAVING THE CASTLE

Packing was easy the next morning. There was nothing he owned here. Despite that, he took the blanket off the bed that he had used and carried it under his arm down to the lowest cell in the castle. He opened up the doors that were filled with the rusted cells, and the smell hit him like a ton of bricks. It was horrid! He covered his nose and closed the door. He couldn't believe they would put Ben in such a filthy, horrible place. After bracing himself once more, he opened the door and ran inside, peering over the melting and rotting dead bodies sprawled before him. Finally, under the newer corpse of a woman, he spotted Ben's hand. Lucius yanked the woman off him and scooped him up into the blanket, ran out, and slammed the doors shut.

He tightly wrapped him in the blanket and carried him out of the castle. It was daytime, so everyone was asleep. He passed Raela and watched as she stopped, opening her mouth like she was meant to speak. She looked exhausted, as if she had been waiting all night to talk to him, but the glare he gave her was enough to silence her. She looked down at her feet and walked back to her room. It might not be all her fault, but Lucius didn't feel quite ready to speak to her.

After exiting the castle, he felt relieved to see that his bike was undisturbed. It had been overrun by grass, but after clearing all the plant life, it was still in decent condition. He tried to start it. Nothing. He looked it over again, then gave it a second shot. It worked! He cradled Ben in his lap and drove to the town's cemetery. Even if no one else knew him, he didn't want his lover to have to rest in an unmarked grave. He deserved better. Carrying him to the nearest funeral service, he wasn't quite sure what to do or how to do it. He didn't need a whole big thing. Lucius couldn't afford it, and no one would show up anyway. So all he bought was a headstone and a spot of land.

Ben only had his first name, since slaves weren't allowed to have much else. "Benjamin, you were kind and caring and taken too soon. May you rest peacefully. You will be missed." He wanted to have so much more written on the stone but decided it was best to keep things short and sweet. After paying the funeral home with the money he had kept for himself since his drug cartel days, he oversaw the burial of his dearest friend.

After standing at the grave for several hours, he turned back toward his bike and saw an older dark-skinned woman staring at him. She walked over to him and looked him up and down.

"Can I help you?" Lucius said, feeling a bit uncomfortable being approached and analyzed by a stranger.

"Are you Katherine's son?" she asked.

"Um. Maybe I am. Who are you?" he said, starting to feel really creeped out.

"My name is Gelda. I'm sorry if this is sudden. When you ran away from the cottage, you bumped into me first, remember?"

He thought back, trying to remember the event. It was so long ago, and everything had happened so fast then. He found it difficult.

"I think I remember. I don't know," he said, shoving his hands into his pockets.

"It's all right. Your mother and I were friends. I thought we were close until she died, but I suppose there were a lot of things she was hiding from me. She's buried right over here," she said, leading him to another gravestone. "Today's her death anniversary, you know. I assume that's why you're here, isn't it?"

"No, I had no idea," he admitted. He had tried so hard to block the event that he struggled to remember a lot of it.

"I wanted to apologize to you for all those years ago. I sent a search party after you but realized I was wrong too late. If you don't mind me asking, where did you go?"

"Oh, I, um, I got on a boat to Russia. I guess it was a shipment boat."

"Oh well, I'm glad you're safe at least," Gelda said, smiling sweetly.

"Um, thanks. Say, what did you know about my mom? I'm sort of asking everyone and anyone for answers."

"Oh, well, I thought I knew her very well. But thinking back, I don't think I knew much about her at all. One day she just suddenly moved into that cottage on the forest path. I offered her a job at my store, and we became friends almost instantly. She was already pregnant with you when I met her."

"What about my sister? What happened to her when I left?"

"Oh, the other little girl? I'm sorry. She didn't make it."

"No, I know that. Where is her body? Did she get buried with Mom?"

"I thought it would be best, yes. We buried them together in the same coffin."

Lucius looked down at Katherine's grave, staring at the headstone. "She would have hated that, my mom. She could hardly stand to be around us. I know she wished us dead on more than one occasion," he said, looking away from the grave, suddenly finding it a little painful.

"Did you kill her?" Gelda blurted out.

Lucius's head shot up, and he stared at her. "Why the hell would you ask me that? What a horribly rude thing to say to me!"

"No, no, I won't fault you if you did. I just…I guess I'm trying to get a better understanding of what happened," she said, trying to take her foot out of her mouth.

Lucius stared at her for a long time before answering. "Yes, I did. I didn't mean to! It's just…I was so hungry. It was an accident," he answered, gaze falling to his feet. He felt like a child right then, answering for something he had done years ago.

"It's all right. I always wondered if she was mistreating you. She avoided all my questions, and I thought maybe she was just a private woman, but deep down, I knew it was more than that."

He didn't know what to say. Gelda was being so nice to him. Her name sounded so familiar. Suddenly, he remembered where he had heard it. "Did you have an older sister by chance?"

"I did, but I don't remember her. She ran away before I was even three. Why do you ask?"

"I don't think she ran away. I was in the vampire castle until just recently."

"So it is real? Where is it? The whole town has been looking for it for, well, centuries! I thought it was just a legend until I met Katherine."

"I can't tell you where it is. I...I don't want you to look for it. There's no way you could take them down on your own. It's just not realistic."

Gelda paused, looking down at Katherine's grave. "I see. Why did you ask about my sister?"

"I think she got kidnapped by my family. She's gone now. I'm sorry. But I knew her son very well. We were going to run away together, but..." Lucius looked for words. He didn't want to admit that he was the cause of Ben's death. "But my family killed him first. His name was Benjamin," he said, pointing to his grave.

Gelda glanced over at the grave, then at him. "What did you say your name was?"

"I didn't. It's Lucius."

"Oh, well. I'm very sorry, Lucius. It sounds like your life has been very hard and filled with a lot of pain."

"I really don't need your pity, but thank you anyway, Gelda. You seem like a really nice person."

She smiled and gave him a nod. The next several minutes were spent staring down at the gravestones before she started talking again.

"Well, it certainly was nice to meet you, Lucius. You don't look hardly anything like your mother, you know, except your eyes. But I have to say, you are quite handsome now! Such defined cheekbones and such a strong-looking face."

"Thank you. That's nice of you to say, but I really should go. It was nice to meet you," he said, not feeling in the mood for small talk.

"Maybe we can meet again someday," she said with a big happy smile. "I think we have the potential to be friends."

"Um. Yeah, maybe," he replied, not feeling so sure.

Before he headed to England, he just wanted to check one more thing. As he drove, he wondered just how private a person his mother was. It seemed very odd to be discovering so much about her all through the eyes of others. What were the odds of meeting Gelda? And even more so, what were the odds of her being Benjamin's aunt? It really was a small town they lived in, making it all the easier for tragedy to continuously strike with no media coverage. It was like the town was cut off from the rest of the world. He had to give his family credit. They really knew how to work the system.

Reaching the house where he and his mother had lived together, he checked the mailbox. He remembered Raela giving him this address for Adrik so they could keep in contact. The box was packed to the brim with letters. As he pulled them out, he started reading them by date. Every letter was sent about two weeks apart. He wasn't surprised. Adrik loved reading. Why wouldn't he love writing too? As he read the first letter, he was happy to hear that his father figure was doing well. People were still looking for him in Russia, but Adrik had stayed out of the mix, keeping him very safe.

The next letter spoke of his day-to-day activities and what new books he was reading. A lot of the letters said things like that. After about three letters, Adrik expressed his concerns that Lucius had not written back to him yet. Four more letters later, and Adrik was sick.

He spoke of what a horribly cold winter it was and how concerned he was that he hadn't heard anything from him. He still spoke of his books, but his handwriting was a bit more sloppy. He mentioned briefly that he had picked up a terrible cough, and Lucius laughed a little as Adrik compared himself to Rupert.

But upon reading his fifth letter, he no longer felt like laughing. Adrik wrote how desperate he was to hear from him. He said how horribly afraid he was that he was standing on his last legs. He wasn't getting better as he had previously hoped he would, and no amount of medicine was doing the trick. He begged Lucius to come back to Russia, saying how no one was looking for him anymore and he would be safe. He seemed very desperate, and Lucius hastily looked for another letter from his friend. But it was no use, the rest of the mail was only ads and promotions for business. He read the date of the last letter and found that it was written roughly three to four months ago. Lucius knew what that meant for his dear friend.

Shoving the letters in his jacket pocket, Lucius wanted to scream. Why was this happening to him all so suddenly? He felt like to cry, but no tears came. The events in play were all happening so quickly that he found himself very numb to every new blow. He couldn't believe his friend was dead. Just a year ago, he had seemed perfectly healthy. Maybe his hair had gotten gray, and he had some wrinkles. But now, he was just gone? He didn't have anyone to blame; sickness was what killed him. At least with Ben, he could blame his father, but Adrik had been killed by the circumstances of life.

Lucius had somehow never imagined Adrik would die while he was away. He wasn't even gone that long. It didn't seem fair! He couldn't even be there when he needed him most. He could have cared for him, nursed him back to health. He could have been there in his final moments. He shut his eyes tightly. Life wasn't fair. But there was nothing he could do about it after the fact. It was done, and Adrik had surely been buried by now, and if not, well, there was no chance he would make it back in time for the funeral.

Lucius climbed onto his bike. Maybe he should visit anyway. As he stared down at the letters in his hand, he remembered how happy he and Adrik had been as a family, like father and son almost. Adrik was dead. His family was gone. But as he stuffed the letters into his jacket pocket, he remembered Raela. Raela still had a family very much alive that she needed to care for. Raela was a mother to two children. Lucius wanted to visit Adrik's grave to remember everything he had done for him. But there were more important things in the present. Adrik would have to wait.

Lucius rode to the nearest car shop to get his bike all fixed up. After it was in suitable condition again, he drove it to England, only stopping to fill up on gas. It was a surprisingly short distance, with the exception of a boat trip. Getting there took less than twenty-four hours. And once he arrived, he felt exhausted. He needed to figure out a plan. Where would another vampire colony even be? It wouldn't be in the city; that's for certain. Egon said it was in England; that was a start. But England itself was huge! Surely it would be in somewhere not heavily populated, Lucius thought. So going into the country fields was his best bet for now. As he walked through the country, he couldn't help noticing how beautiful it was. It had amazing grassy plains, forests, and gorgeous lakes. It was raining, but Lucius could tell the clouds might clear soon. The colony couldn't be out in the open sun, so it must be hidden by trees. Maybe traveling to the small nearby town would give him more insight.

The nearby village was small, with several shops selling bread and other assorted foods. He couldn't help but be reminded of the small town he encountered before boarding Boris's ship. As he walked around, he listened to countless conversations, trying to find out any information he could use. But it was no use. All anyone wanted to do was talk about their day-to-day chores and duties. Lucius rented a motel room every night, exhausted and irritated by how little information he was able to find.

After many weeks, Lucius was about to move on. As he packed up what little things he had, he did one last perusal of the town.

"Bread for sale! Freshly baked every day!"

"Fresh fish! Caught just this week at half price!"

"Jewelry! Fine jewelry for the ladies! Make your wife happy with this fine jewelry!"

Everything was as usual. At least that's how it seemed. The young women fawned over the jewelry, while the mothers and housewives bought fresh food for their homes. Lucius was about to give up. Then he felt a tap on his shoulder. A slightly taller than average, slim woman with red hair stood before him. She had bright green eyes and sharp teeth when she smiled at him.

Chapter 41

LUCIUS

In the Underground

What was he supposed to say to her? He felt his mind draw a blank as he dumbly whispered. "Are you a vampire?" he asked in German.

She nodded and laughed, responding back in German. "So are you. It's nice to finally see you again. Maybe we shouldn't talk here." She looked around. "Come with me," she said, grabbing his hand and leading him into the forest.

He followed her dumbfounded. Again? Where had he met this woman before? Why was everyone coming back into his life all of a sudden? Her red hair did spark some memory, but who was she?

"Uhhhh… I'm sorry, who are you?"

"My name is Lidewij. I'm not surprised you don't remember me. We met in the cargo hold of a ship, remember?"

"Oh! You're the, uh, the girl! With the brother, Edward! Did you find him again? I'm sorry I couldn't save you…"

"His name is Edgar." Lidewij laughed. "And yes, I did. I wouldn't worry about it. Things worked out in the end, I suppose. But how are you? I can't believe how different you look. Your white hair is so long now! It has to be down to your knees at least, and you still have the same red bow. Why don't you get your hair cut? I know a very nice hair stylist."

"I guess I could," Lucius said, noticing how long his hair had grown while locked up. "But I think I sort of like this length. I mean, it's harder to hide the color, but it looks very elegant. Wouldn't you agree?"

Lidewij laughed. "I mean, I guess… But if you want elegant things, why don't you just buy them?"

"Oh, I don't have the money for that, and I don't want to have to keep track of whatever I buy. No, my long fancy hair is definitely enough."

"If you say so."

"You look different too. You've grown a lot taller. And your hair grew, but not as long as mine."

"Thank you, I like to keep my hair down to my midback. That way, it's easy to manage and doesn't get in the way when I'm working or eating."

"Speaking of eating, I had no idea you were a vampire! How did you live in the bottom of the ship so long?"

"A little blonde girl kept giving me some of her blood. I don't remember what her name was. We didn't speak the same language. Did she happen to make it out?"

"No, I found her again in the fighting pits of Russia when I was a child. I seriously doubt she lived past that year," he said with a sigh.

"Oh," she said, looking down a moment. "Well, that's awfully sad to hear."

"I've learned that sometimes life is just like that. You'll never be able to save everyone in every situation. It is what it is."

"I suppose. But that doesn't mean it isn't still very unfortunate."

"No, that's true, but I'd rather not think about it. So instead, I have a question for you."

"Hmm?" She tilted her head to the side, reminding Lucius of a puppy.

He looked around and took her to an alley where nobody could overhear. "The vampire colony in England, do you know where it is?"

"Oh yes! I live there. It's very nice."

"Can you take me?"

"Yes! I would love to!" she said, taking his hand and giving it a squeeze.

Lucius stared down at his hand before gently pulling it away. "Uh. Wouldn't it be faster to ride there on my bike?"

"Oh! What a pleasant idea!" she said, climbing onto his bike with him.

Lucius started up the engine and felt her wrap her arms around him. He turned to glance at her, and she gave him a sweet, innocent smile. He couldn't be sure, but it felt like she was purposefully trying to press her chest up against his back. Driving off, he followed the directions Lidewij gave to him. It led them into a deep forest.

"We have to walk from here," she said, and Lucius shut off his motorcycle. Picking up the bike, he lifted it over his shoulder and started carrying it where she led.

"Wow, you are very strong," she said as she glanced him up and down.

"Well, it has its advantages. I'm not willing to leave my bike again. I just got it all fixed up, and I don't know how long I'll be in the colony for."

"I'm sure King Claudius won't have a problem with you bringing it." Lidewij smiled, climbing over a large series of rocks.

"Claudius, is that his name? Tell me about this 'king.' Is he nice?"

"Oh, he is very kind! He belongs to a family of purebloods but ended the practice of incest. His sister refused to have intercourse with him, and on her wishes, he ended the tradition. Then they decided to open up the colony to vampires of all kinds! Half breeds, mixed blood, turned vampires—we're all welcome there, and it's wonderful!"

He thought how different this man seemed from his father. Egon would surely have a fit should they follow the same practices in Germany. "What about slaves? Does he hold pens and breeding grounds of humans to feed on?"

"Oh no. He assigns vampires that are less sensitive to sunlight to work in our own blood donation building. That's what I was doing when I ran into you!" she said, smiling at him.

"Oh. Do the humans know what the blood is going to?"

"Well, no, of course, not. But even if they are donating to vampires without realizing it, I still think it's safer for them than having to die by our bite."

Lucius felt intrigued. It must be really nice in this colony. If things were really as nice as they seemed, he might move here, abandoning his own family. But was it right to leave all the slaves alone in the castle? And what of his sister Raela? She was still stuck over there. He still felt angry at her, but he was really trying to forgive her. He knew she never wanted this, never wanted to hurt him or Ben. But they were both in bad situations. Maybe if this colony wasn't so bad, he could move her and her children here. Then at least she would be away from Egon.

Slipping behind some rocks, she moved some bushes to the side. At the base of a tree, she lifted a rock off a wooden cellar door. It looked old and abandoned. Lucius opened the door and peered down inside. It had at least a hundred stairs leading deep into the earth. He couldn't even see where it ended. The whole situation screamed trap, but if he had come this far, what was the point of turning back now? Taking a few steps down the stairs, Lidewij followed, moving the rock to fall on the door when she closed it. As she closed the door, they both heard a loud thud.

"The rock isn't actually that heavy. It just serves as a good way to hide the entrance."

Lucius looked around, letting his eyes adjust to the darkness. Once they did, he continued down the steps. He felt like he had been walking for the better part of an hour when he finally reached the bottom. Panting, he set his motorcycle down.

"So. Many. Stairs!"

Lidewij smiled and let out a laugh. "It's to deter any humans that might find this place. No one would want to bother. That, and it gives us lots of space below the ground."

Lucius followed her down the hall until they reached a big beautiful opening to a large fire lit cavern. Inside, were rows and rows of little houses and shops. Unlike his families colony, this place had more than one building. The inside of the Lovhart colony was just one giant hidden castle. Nothing like this.

He walked around the dark town square. In the center was a large burning fire, but getting closer, he didn't see any wood keeping it alive.

"King Claudius isn't fast or strong, but he's a very skilled user of magic. That's how the fire stays lit."

"Huh, that must come in handy," he said, looking toward the back of the town, where a huge exotic mansion stood. It looked like what Lucius imagined a castle was supposed to look like from the outside, with large arches and beautiful rose windows. The entire building was made of stone, like the rest of the houses. He immediately made his way to the castle before noticing the guard standing full armor.

"Uh. Hello, sir?" he said in the best English he could speak, not quite sure how else to address them. He wasn't amazing at speaking English, but Adrik had taught him enough to hold a conversation during their studies together.

"You are from the German castle. It's obvious by your hair. State your business," came a surprisingly high voice for the very tall knight.

"Oh, um. My name is Lucius. I'm just here to talk."

The knight took off their helmet, revealing the face of a beautiful woman with shoulder-length black hair and red eyes. "Very well, I will lead you to my brother."

Lucius set down his bike and followed. Her brother? Was this the sister that decided she didn't want to continue incest? As he walked through the inside of the castle, Lucius couldn't help but notice it was even bigger than it looked. The walls were all different colors, depending on the room, and some had carpet, while others had wood flooring.

"You must be his sister then! What's your name?"

"You may call me Sir Adeline," she said, turning up the stairs. Every room had a chandelier, just like the castle in Germany. But they were made of brass here, not gold.

"You're awful serious, aren't you?" he joked, pausing a moment to look at a painting of her and two other young men he could only assume were her brothers.

She stopped in her tracks, turning to stare at him. "Forgive my seriousness, but I do not know a thing about you. If you prove yourself trustworthy, then in time maybe we can joke. But not right now," she said, going back to the stairs.

"Understood," Lucius said as he continued following her up the stairs until they reached a hallway. At the end of the hall was a large study. Adeline led him in, then stood at the door.

Walking inside, a tall man with dark lush black hair running down to the middle of his back was trying to write something at his desk. Upon hearing Lucius enter the room, he turned and stood up and walked over to greet him. Claudius grabbed Lucius's hand and shook it. Lucius was so startled he just let it hang like a limp noodle.

"I see my sister Adeline brought a guest! Though I must say, I'm surprised to see a vampire from the German colony. Welcome! What brings you here today," he said in a chipper voice.

"Oh, um...uh, my father, Egon, wanted me to, um, c-come meet you!" Lucius stammered, feeling like a fool. He was caught very off guard by this sudden kindness from the man he had previously perceived to be just another power-hungry vampiric monster. Lidewij really hadn't exaggerated about his open hospitality. "How did you know I was from Germany?"

"Your hair. White hair is a specific German vampire trait. I could be wrong, but you also have quite the German accent to match. So is Egon finally deciding on merging our colonies? We have been enemies for so long. It would be nice if we could finally become friends. What is your name?" Claudius said, seeming ever as chipper as a child making a new friend.

"It's Lucius," he said, feeling a bit unnerved by how observant and friendly Claudius seemed to be. He felt certain he was hiding something. No one could be this kind outright, could they? "I don't think my father is interested in connecting with the colony here. I think he mostly just wants to gain intel on what's happening."

Claudius gave a disappointed sigh. "That really is too bad. If that's the case, then…well, I hate to be rude, but I will have to ask you to leave. Egon has never been known to take kindly to his enemies, and I don't want you bringing back any info that could put us in jeopardy. I can't have the safety of my people compromised. I hope you understand. Adeline will escort you out," he said, giving a nod to his sister, who grabbed his arm.

"Well, wait a moment! Hold on. Lidewij told me this colony accepts all sorts of vampires. Is that true? And you don't keep slaves?" he said, trying to yank his arm free from Adeline, but finding her grip much too strong.

"Yes, both those things are true. Why do you ask?"

"Why are you so kind to humans and people who are different but Egon is not?"

"I'm not going to tell you that if you're going to report to your father."

"I'm not. I swear. I just said that's what he *wants* me to do. But believe me, it's just horrible there, and I was hoping to move to someplace safer and nicer as soon as possible. I just wanted to know if this is a safe enough place to transfer myself."

Claudius gave him a suspicious look. "And why should I believe you, Lucius? No offense, but I just met you."

"My mother was human. She conceived me with my father, and he disappeared from my life until suddenly he decided he needed me about a year and a half ago. Then he locked me in the cells of the castle, killed my companion, and demanded I complete this trial to become 'one of the family.' I am not taking orders from that bastard! I just wanted to let you know his plans."

"How can I trust you? How do I know this isn't just some story you made up to cover your own tracks? Sure, your eyes are blue, but aside from that, you look exactly like your father."

"I came here in broad daylight. Is that proof enough? If not, do you have any sugar? I can eat sugar, like candy canes and butterscotch. Anything super sweet with very little other flavor."

"All right, Lucius, all right. I believe you. Why are you so desperate to know about this place? If you can stay in broad sunlight, surely there are other places you could live."

"That's true, but my sister could never live out in the world. Her name is Raela, and she's currently still trapped in Germany. She's stuck over there, getting raped and abused for only speaking out of turn. If I don't find a new place for her and her children to move, then I'll be forced to leave her there. This is the only place I can think of that's far enough from the outside world and our father for her to be safe."

"Hmm, I see. She must be very sensitive to sunlight then?"

"Yes, she's a pureblood," Lucius confessed.

"Well, I would like you to spend some time here first. But if all is as you have said and you are trustworthy and her situation is truly dire, then I would say bring her over as soon as you can."

"Thanks, Claudius. I just want to know some things about this place first. I'll spend a few days, even weeks here so you can keep an eye on me. But I would like to ask you some questions."

"All right, I will comply," Claudius said, taking a seat in a chair by the bookshelf. He motioned for Lucius to join him.

Lucius complied. "Let's start with my earlier question. Why are you so kind to humans and people who are different but Egon is not?"

"Well, I'm a different person than your father, Lucius. My parents were just as strict about bloodlines and purity. However, they didn't keep the family as large as your father. So when Egon's parents sent men over to kill our empire. My sister, brother, and I all hid. Then being the eldest, I vowed to break the tradition of keeping humans as slaves and decided I would provide a safe place for all vampires to live. Not only purebloods. It doesn't seem fair that some should be deemed worthy based on their parents, does it? Besides, we're all safer if we stick together in groups. Wouldn't you agree?"

"Yeah! It sounds great if I'm being honest. It sounds kind of too good to be true," he said, shoving his hands into his pockets.

"Well, I assure you it isn't. Besides, keeping a colony like this not only protects us but also keeps humans more in the dark about our existence. If we never hurt them or interfere with their lives, then they never bother looking for us."

"How do we get food if we don't kill humans?"

"Simple! Humans run blood donation centers all across the world. We just happen to own one, except it isn't a real blood donation center. None of the blood given to us goes to hospitals of any kind. Instead we use it to feed. I think if the humans knew we were doing this to protect them, they wouldn't object. However, I'd rather not make our presence known. I hope you can understand that. The more humans know about us, the more dangerous of a life we lead. I think your father has yet to figure that out. I wouldn't be surprised if it got him killed one day."

"I'm going to kill him myself. At least, I hope to."

"A lot of regrets can come with that sort of talk, Lucius. Killing a family member is different than killing for food, I assure you."

"No, I'm aware. I can do it. Don't worry. Any moral turmoil or regrets I can handle on my own. What's important at the moment, though, is getting Raela out of there."

"I completely understand. Adeline will lead you to one of our vacant houses. How many kids does she have?"

"Um. I think she has two?"

"Then we will find you a house with four bedrooms, one for each of you," Claudius said, standing up and straightening his fancy suit. "Adeline? I believe we have a house that would fit his needs, wouldn't we?"

"Yes, on the east side, by Lidewij's house. We just built that new living area. I believe one of the houses over in that section should fit the bill perfectly."

"Wonderful! In that case, Lucius Lovhart, you are always welcome to speak to me whenever you please. My sister will escort you to your new house for the time being."

Adeline turned to leave, and Lucius followed. He couldn't help but think that Claudius seemed very kind and too trusting. It was clear that he had lived a much nicer, gentler life than he had. He wondered just how young he was. Perhaps he was just acting trusting to make others let their guard down around him. If that was the case, it was a very clever ploy. However, if things were really as good as they seemed, Lucius had no intention of causing any ill will here.

Adeline led him to a larger sized stone house with two floors. "Will this suit you?"

"Yes, I think it will. Thank you," he said, giving her a smile before setting his bike outside by the door.

Adeline gave an affirmative nod before turning and marching off like a stone soldier.

Lucius looked up at his new house. He turned and saw Lidewij staring at him through her window next door. When she noticed he had spotted her, she looked away and pretended to clean. She was starting to really creep him out. Nevertheless, he opened up the door and saw that it was already furnished. The furniture had this very old fancy look while obviously being newly made. This house must have been sitting reserved for any new visitors. When looking around, Lucius couldn't help but wonder just how many "move-in ready" houses were just waiting down here.

The floor was covered in dark-gray carpeting, and the walls were all a dark shade of green to match the old Victorian feel. He snatched the house key off the coffee table and put it into his pocket. Walking up the stairs, he immediately claimed the master bedroom as his own. Taking out Adrik's letters, he put them in the nightstand by his bed.

Adrik. He still couldn't believe his best friend was gone. If only he had been there for him. All he had now was his memory and these letters. It was too much. It was just too much! Everyone he loved seemed to be dying around him. But then again, weren't they always? This wasn't really anything new. It was just another body to add to the pile. Suddenly, the sadness of his friends passing hit him like a ton of bricks. Lucius crawled under the covers of his bed, and let himself feel the sadness of losing his fatherly figure so far away.

Chapter 42

LUCIUS

THE GIRLFRIEND

As he started to drift to sleep, he awoke to an insistent knocking at his door.

Walking down, he opened up and saw Lidewij.

"Hi! Do you need help moving in?"

He tried to regain his senses but was still seeing foggy from having just woken up. "Uhh. Yeah, I was just doing that," he said, trying to rub the sleep away from his eyes.

"Oh, it looks like you were asleep. I didn't wake you, did I?"

"No, no, it's fine," Lucius said, waving away her apologies. "What can I help you with, Lidewij?"

"I have a new job for you, if you're interested. Adeline told me to offer a few jobs to you, in case you were willing to work."

"Yeah, I'm willing," Lucius said, shaking off the last of his sleepiness. He looked down at her. She was wearing a short red dress, that pushed her boobs up, maximizing the cleavage her small breasts were capable of.

"Oh, uh. Nice dress, Lidewij. Do you have a date later?"

"You like it? I am so glad." She gave a little turn. "I was hoping we could spend the day together. We could go to the firepit, maybe go down to the pond and swim. It would be fun!"

"Yeah, sure, if you want to. Anyway, what were you saying about jobs?"

"Right! Right. Jobs first. Adeline says we are always looking for builders. Since you're so strong, I think it would be a perfect job for you!" she said, giving a perhaps too intentional bounce.

"Sounds easy enough. Take me to the houses that need building."

"Follow me!" Lidewij said, grabbing his hand and leading him farther into the underground. A huge empty space was surrounding another firepit. There were no buildings here. The whole place seemed very empty compared to everywhere else. There was no one walking around and no torches, candles, or lights aside from the firepit in the middle. The only thing taking up any space was lots of rubble and stones. It was like this new area had just been dug out. "You can turn this whole place into a living area or a place for business," Lidewij said enthusiastically. "We always need new homes since refugee vampires are always looking for a safe place to live."

"Yeah, yeah, this could work," he said, feeling happy to be a part of something nice. He was doing good for others, like DDC. But this time, there was no sneaking around and no killing and illegal activity. No. Just building homes and helping the community. "I'll have to pick up some books on working with stone, but after that, I'll get right to it."

"Perfect! Until then, can we spend the day together?"

"Huh? Oh, yeah, sure!" Lucius had to admit, he was much more focused on the new project than he was on spending the day with Lidewij, but perhaps this could lead to a friendship, which didn't seem like it could be a bad thing. For a few hours, they walked around and talked.

"So after you freed the slaves under the cargo ship, what did you do then?" Lidewij asked.

"Well, I fought some illegal slave fights. But after I escaped, I joined a drug company called DDC. We sold some illegal drugs, but we also sold a lot of pharmaceutical drugs for half the price to low-income houses."

"Sounds like a good deed."

"Well, I always thought it was. But the police didn't seem to agree." Lucius laughed. "But I met one of my very best friends there. Adrik, he was like a father to me. He always looked out for my best interest and had my back when I needed him. But the cold of Russia this year killed him. He got sick, and I guess he just never got better," Lucius said, trying to control his emotions.

"I'm sorry. It sounds like he was a good man."

"He was, and I would go back to visit his grave. But honestly, I don't see the point. It's not like I can talk to him when I'm at the cemetery. And besides, I should focus on new things that actually matter, like gaining the trust of Claudius so I can bring my sister Raela and her kids here. I want to protect her from our family. I know they're horribly mean to her, and I think she'll be happier here."

"Is she pureblooded?"

"Well, yes, but even for purebloods, my family's castle can be an awful place. I bet she'll love living here, though. I don't know how she would react to having so much freedom." Lucius said with a laugh. "What about you? After you found Edgar, where did the two of you go?"

"We ran for a long time, staying at different houses during the day before leaving in the middle of the night. Finally, we arrived back in Germany. After that, we quickly discovered that the family of vampires we had been taken from had all disappeared. But then we heard of an accepting colony in England. It took a lot of searching, but we finally found the colony in England. We've been living here ever since."

"What does your brother do? I know you work in the blood donation center, but I haven't met Edgar yet."

"Oh, he's in charge of organizing the blood supply so that everyone gets equal rations. I don't want him to go out into the world of humans again. He's my little brother, and maybe I'm babying him, but I just want to keep him safe."

"Does he want to go back into the human world?"

"If he does, he's never mentioned it. He seems perfectly happy here."

"Well, if he ever does mention it, maybe you should let him go out—make his own decisions, you know? Otherwise, he'll only come to resent you."

"Maybe. It's just… Can I tell you a secret?"

"Of course."

"Well, Edgar has never killed anyone before. He might be the only vampire in the world who has no blood stains on his hands. Sure, he's dealt with dead bodies and blood donations. But he's never taken a life. He's so gentle. I don't think he'd have it in him. If he went out and something happened, I don't think he would fight back. And if he got hurt, I could never forgive myself."

"You're worrying too much. He's an adult, isn't he? I'm sure if something happened, he'd do what needs to be done."

"Maybe you're right. He is an adult. I shouldn't treat him like a child. But he'll always be my little brother."

"Of course, he will. I don't know. I suppose you don't have to worry about it since he doesn't seem to have any interest in going out anyway."

"No, I suppose not. Maybe someday you can meet him. But I warn you, Edgar is really into his work. I think working gives him satisfaction. It's like knowing you're useful for something or knowing that you're needed. So he might not want to take too much time away from that."

"I'm sure it'll be fine, Lidewij. I'll meet him later when we both have the time."

"Great." She smiled. "Hey! Look! We're to the pond already! Let's swim!"

Lucius followed her to the pond. It was so dark inside since there was no sun to help him see the bottom. Lidewij stripped down to her underwear and waded in before turning to look at him. Her hair was so pretty as it fell down her back and touched the tip of the water. It was such an unusually bright shade of reddish orange.

"Well, are you coming?" Lidewij said, giving him a happy smile.

"I suppose," Lucius said, undressing down to his boxers. He folding his clothes neatly by some rocks before wading into the water. "It's cold!"

"You're a vampire! The cold doesn't hurt you, silly. You'll get used to it," she replied, splashing her way over to him.

He walked in deeper, trying to get away. "Don't splash me. I'm not used to it yet."

"Oh please, you big baby." Lidewij laughed as she splashed a huge wave over toward him.

"C-c-cold! Stop it!" Lucius said, adjusting slower than she had.

"All right, all right," she said, walking over to him.

"Thank you."

With a sudden jump, she threw herself at him. In surprise, Lucius fell back away from her, into the water all at once. After he came up, he saw her standing beside him, laughing.

"That's not funny!"

"You should see your face!"

Lucius crossed his arms and pouted, moving his half bangs to the side.

"Oh, don't be mad at me," she said, giving him a big hug and pressing her chest to his. "I'll keep you warm, all right?"

"Uh, thanks, but I think I've adjusted to the cold by now," he said, gently pushing her off him.

"Oh, well, that's good!" Lidewij said, diving into the water.

What was with her? She was acting so strange. Lucius supposed that they were friends now, but only friends. Could she really have a crush on him so soon? How often had she thought about him before they finally met again? Or was it really just that Lidewij was lonely? This all seemed so sudden. But he supposed love could start suddenly. Ben and his love had started suddenly. But it had ended suddenly too.

After a few hours of swimming, Lucius felt ready to get out. It was nice feeling clean after having not taken a shower since he had arrived. His new "friend" climbed out with him and started using a towel to dry herself off.

"You know what?" she said. "Let's go by the firepit in our neighborhood. It's nice and private there since no one really lives in that section yet."

"Uh, private? Lidewij, listen, I like you, but I think you're—"

"I'll show you! It'll be fun!" she interrupted, scooping up his clothes and taking his hand, leading him to the pit.

Lidewij sat down and put her hands up. "It's a nice way to dry off. Sit with me, will you?"

"Um. Yeah, okay, I guess," he said hesitantly, sitting down and enjoying the warmth.

Taking off all her clothes, she stretched out. As he looked over, she gave him a sweet smile.

"So, uh, why are you naked?"

"I wanted my body to get dry before I got dressed again."

"No, no, I get that. I mean like…" He hesitated, not really quite sure how to word it. "Never mind," he said, never finding the words.

Lidewij laughed before grabbing his arm and nuzzling into him.

"Listen, I know you're flirting with me and stuff. And you're very pretty. It's nothing against you. I don't think I'm right for you. I mean, we didn't really meet that long ago, and—"

"You're breaking up with me before we even had the chance to get started? Come on, you don't really know if you don't like me yet, Lucius. You're not one of those family breeders, are you?"

"Well, no, but I—"

"Come on, just give me a chance! We have so much in common. We can both go out in the sun. We were both victims of the slave trade. We both have special people we care about and want to look out for. Just give us a chance, will you?"

"Lidewij, I'm gay. So maybe it's best we don't really, uh, do this. Whatever it is."

Her face turned completely red, and she let go of him. "Oh, I didn't know! I'm sorry!" she said, turning away. Obviously, she was a little bit hurt.

"You're a nice girl and all. It's just…I don't understand why you would want to be with me. We just met again after all this time. And you make good points we do have a lot in common, but it's just not going to work out."

"I just…I thought it would be a good thing. Everyone here is a traveling vampire. But most of them came with a small group, you know? Edgar and I, we didn't. And since you didn't either, I thought maybe we could understand each other."

"Yeah, I guess that makes sense, but I'm still gay. I'm sure you'll find someone who will really love you and understand you, but maybe we should just stay friends," he said, trying to ease the tense situation.

"Yeah, maybe so. Uh, I have to go," she replied, scooping up her clothes and going to her house. "I'll see you later?"

"Yeah, I'll see you later."

She nodded, closing the door to her house. Lucius felt a little bad. He knew he must have hurt her feelings. But it was better to tell her he wasn't interested now than let this go on and build her hopes up. After spending another hour by the fire, he decided to go in and get dressed again.

Chapter 43

LUCIUS

RETRIEVING RAELA

After spending two weeks walking around the city and clearing the rubble all to one side of the new building site. Lucius left the underground only a few times to buy books on how to build proper houses. He couldn't have imagined it would be as hard as it would be. He had certainly bit off more than he could chew, but maybe with help from the others in the colony, it would be fine. Finally feeling he had a place he belonged, Lucius decided to make another trip to Claudius before he left. Adeline was standing by his side as he stood and stared into the main town fire. He looked very peaceful and very lost in thought.

Lucius cleared his throat. "Ahem. Claudius? I need to have a word with you, if that's all right," Lucius said, walking up to him, a bit fearful of disturbing his thinking.

"Oh, of course! Don't mind me. I was just thinking about our community. I was thinking of planning a sort of celebration soon since the human holiday Christmas is coming up in a month or so. I know we have no reason to celebrate such a silly holiday, but I think it might be fun. And with so many newcomers, it's a good way to bring people in a community together, wouldn't you agree?"

"You're right, and speaking of people from this community, I need to learn more about them. Well, not them specifically, but I need to learn if vampires really do shrivel up if they touch sunlight. I plan on bringing my sister here. Do you remember? But if she can't go out during the day, that might prove difficult."

Claudius gave a long sigh. "I'm afraid if she's pure blooded, it might be a hassle. We have the unfortunate disadvantage of being extremely weak to light. You're correct. We don't burn up immediately—that's just a myth. But being out for more than an hour will cause severe damage. It's because some of the first vampires were 'damned creatures' and cursed by priests. It's the same reason we're weak to silver. But so much time has gone by since those days. We've slowly been able to withstand it more and more. If everyone stopped inbreeding with their cursed pureblood siblings, I'm positive one day the gene might die off. But of course, old habits die hard, I believe the humans say."

Lucius nodded, happy to learn all this new information. "Is there any way we could avoid the sunlight while still being out in it?"

"Simple. Cover up. You aren't like to see me wearing it here, but if and when I do go out into the human world above, I wear a very fashionable cloak to cover myself from the sun. I still feel drained, but I don't die. So it does its purpose as designed."

"Perfect! Thank you, Claudius. I really appreciate all your help," he said, happy to shake his hand this time around.

"The pleasure is mine."

Lucius thought it was well time he returned to his father. He had been away quite a while, and he worried if he was gone too much longer, Egon would start to get suspicious. If anything, he had to seem loyal.

A boat ride and a day's drive later, he walked to his father's office as instructed. "Lucius, it's nice to see you've made it back safely."

"Thank you. What problem do we have with the colony in England?"

"They're our rival colony."

"No, no, I get that, but why?"

Egon let out a long sigh. "Claudius is naive and foolish. He thinks just because he's king, he can let everyone and anyone into his colony for free food and living. There is no way we as a species can fight the misfit vampires and humans if we keep letting them in through our front door!"

"Well, I suppose. I heard you killed Claudius's parents when you were younger. Or your parents did. Why?"

"That is none of your concern. Do not overstep your boundaries, Lucius."

"I have the right to know, or else I'm not telling you anything I learned."

Egon gave him a look filled with anger before releasing the information. "My father and Claudius's father had some serious disagreements. They were fighting for overlapping territory and who could claim it. You have to understand, this was all a very long time ago. In the end, through perseverance and lots of fighting, my father won. So that is that."

"Oh. It's really that simple, huh?"

"Sometimes the biggest wars are caused by the simplest things. Now what did you learn from Claudius?"

"Well, I learned that they are expanding every day and that a lot of their defense is held by women."

Egon let out a laugh. "Of course, he would have women fighters. What a stupid fool. This is perfect then. I need you to do something. It shouldn't be too hard for you. My plan is to kill Claudius, both for a message and because he and I do not see eye to eye. Can you do this?"

"Yes. I can," he said confidently.

"Perfect. Is there anything you need to take with you from our estate? Or perhaps anyone to help fight alongside you?"

"I need to bring Raela. I think she would be a proper distraction for Claudius. Then I can kill him and his sister very secretly, and we'll leave before anyone notices."

Egon gave him a big sinister smile. "Very good idea. Go and get her then."

Turning, he walked down the long hallway to his sister's room. On his way, he spotted Marie again and motioned her to follow. He quickly changed directions and headed to his own room instead, closing them both in once inside.

"Marie! How are you doing?" he asked. "I was planning on coming to check up on you since I came back from England. Are they treating you all right?" he said, trying to show his compassion, fearing that his family had somehow found out about their previous meeting.

She looked up at him, then started to cry in choked, gasping sobs. Lucius stared at her, confused, until she opened up her mouth and showed him her missing tongue.

He stood and stared at her in shock. Why was he surprised? He knew his family was cruel. But to cut off this girl's tongue just for speaking to him? Of course, why wouldn't they? She was only a slave to them after all, nothing more than a piece of meat at their disposal. And she had disobeyed. The only thing that gave her any value were her beautiful looks and her blood supply. He gave her another hug, letting her cry into him until she felt well enough to gently push him away. Then without another word, she bolted from the room to continue cleaning before she was caught a second time and had another body part removed.

Lucius stood a moment, thinking about how delicate the balance of his family's empire was. So delicate, they couldn't even let one slave girl get away with talking to him. The thought only disgusted him. Making him that much more eager to leave. He made his way back toward Raela and came in before knocking. She was half dressed, and hastily covered herself. "Lucius! What are you..."

"Shh!" he said, closing the door behind him and locking it. "I am on a mission to kill the leader of the England colony, and you're coming with me. I need you to distract them while I get the job done. Egon has ordered it."

"He has? But my children. How long is this going to take?"

Lucius leaned in and whispered, "Your children are coming too. Have them ready, darkly dressed, and hidden by morning. You as well. We're going at first dawn, when everyone is asleep."

"What? My children? Coming on an assassination project? No!"

Looking around, Lucius dragged her into her closet. "Do you trust me, Raela?"

Her face contorted in confusion before she confessed. "I don't know."

"Well, figure it out. I have the means to get you all out of here to live a better life if you'll let me. We aren't really going to kill anyone. Claudius in England has a house all set up for you and your children to move to."

"I'm not sure. I want a better life, but what about the light? We'll shrivel up and die! I might be able to get out, but they'll never be able to escape with me."

"Not necessarily. Claudius told me, that if you wear dark hooded clothes, as long as the sunlight doesn't touch you, you'll be fine. I only need to smuggle you to my mother's old cabin until dark, then, when everyone is waking up, we'll go before they know you're gone."

"Lucius, we can't. We'll never get away with it! What would make living in England any different anyway?"

"Raela, I know you're scared, but you need to listen to me. Things *are* different there. I saw it. Claudius's own sister is a guard and knight, appointed by Claudius himself. You'll be happy there. Your kids will be happy there. Then you can be with someone you actually like, and Azazel and Egon will have to leave you alone. You just have to be brave, and trust me."

"Palas offered to let me leave with him too. But I turned him down because there is no way Azazel and Egon would let me leave with my children. How is this any different? I might be leaving with my kids this time, but what guarantees we'll succeed? Egon will surely come to retrieve us. And then I'll be in more trouble than ever."

"You and I both know that Egon isn't brave enough to leave his precious castle. And besides, I'm not Palas. Palas, I'm sure, planned on keeping contact with the family after he took you. When I remove you and your children from this horrible place, we will never have contact or have to deal with them ever again. Your children will be safer there. You'll be safer there. You can start a new life, completely free of Egon."

Raela stared at him, hands clenched to her chest. After several silent minutes of thinking, she felt confident enough to reply. "Okay. We'll be ready by dawn in my room, dressed in all black with large hoods."

"Perfect."

When the time came, Raela took the hands of her two children and led them beside her half brother.

"Momma where are we going?" Alise whispered.

"Shh, I'll tell you later," Raela said in a stern voice. "Don't speak."

They sneaked around the corner, then cautiously walked through the dining room toward the door. Raela was terrified Azazel would pop around any corner to reclaim his children. At the sign of first light as the doors opened, Alise let out a terrified scream, but Raela clamped her hand down over her mouth.

"Neither of you make a sound, and keep yourself completely covered," she said, pulling her sleeves down over her gloves.

Both children looked fearfully at their mother before nodding. Lucius carefully led them to Katherine's cottage. It was a mess inside, covered in dust and rubble, but it would suffice for a hiding spot. At least for now. Lucius grabbed a blanket off his mother's bed and spread it over the three of them, protecting them all from the sun until dusk. Then he returned to the castle to fetch his motorcycle.

As dusk arrived, he yanked the blankets back from his family. Raela was holding her two children, and she opened her eyes first, looking around.

Nathaniel spoke up, feeling not so brave as he usually did. "Mommy, I'm scared. I don't want to explore anymore," he said, hugging her close.

Raela patted his head softly. "Don't be silly. This is going to be fun. It's going to be like an adventure! Won't that be fun?"

He looked at Lucius, then back to his mother and sister. "I don't know."

"Of course, it will be fun," his mother said, standing up and sounding very brave for her children. "Lucius is going to take us somewhere safe. It'll be wonderful there, lots of interesting and unique people. You'll get to play with all sorts of other kids who aren't even related to you." She gave them a happy smile.

"People who aren't related to us? We'll get to play with them?" Alise asked, following her mother and Lucius outside to the bike.

"Yes! But we have to get there first," Raela said, looking at Lucius's bike with concern. "There's no way we'll all be able to fit," she said worriedly.

Lucius helped Nathaniel on in front of him and Alise on the back, wrapping her arms around his body. "I have a solution for that. You said you were born with the gift of speed, didn't you? You ran all the way to Russia, so just run beside us, and we'll rest somewhere in the morning."

Why hadn't she thought of that? Raela lived with her incredible speed all her life, yet it was her half brother who was able to come up with a useful plan on how to use it. If she wasn't impressed already, this was enough to make her so. She ran beside her children and brother all night and then took a boat the next day. That was definitely the hardest part. They had to hide in large suitcases and trust Lucius to carry them across the boat and into England the next day.

When Raela had her case opened, she looked around in the dark of night and saw the beautiful open sky. Her children were rubbing their eyes, having just woken up from their trip inside a suitcase.

"Come on, not much farther," Lucius persisted, climbing onto his bike and helping the children on with him. It was clear he planned on leaving the suitcases where they were. They had served their purpose.

Raela nodded and stretched her cramped legs. The suitcase she had been in seemed so small, and it hurt to walk, let alone run, but she persisted. After running for another hour, everyone safely arrived in the forest. Her half brother led them into the woods, behind a bush, and through a hidden cellar door.

"It's so dark in here, Momma. I'm scared!" Nathaniel said, clinging to her leg.

"We just don't have candles, darling. It's okay," Raela said, calming her young son.

"What about Father? Is he going to find us here?" Alise asked.

"No, and if we live here from now on, we'll never see him again," Raela said with certainty.

Alise looked relieved, but Nathaniel seemed conflicted. Neither of them saw Azazel often, but he was definitely kinder to Nathaniel than he was to his daughter. Alise was always trying to get his attention, but Azazel pushed her aside, demanding that Raela train some manners into their daughter.

Nathaniel clung to his mother's leg tightly until they reached the steps at the bottom of the stairs. From there, Lucius took them to his new house.

Alise was the first to speak, looking up at the house. "It's so cute! Look at its cute little windows!" she said, running inside.

Raela followed her, carrying Nathaniel. "It looks lovely. Thank you, Lucius, I appreciate this more than I could ever say."

"You're welcome. The master bedroom is mine. Anything else is up for grabs." Nathaniel's eyes widened as he squirmed from his mother's arms, eager to find the best room before his sister had the chance. Raela gave a small giggle as he ran in, nearly running into the couch.

Before she could follow, Lucius stopped her. "So I need to make a suggestion to you. Here, you'll have lots of ability to do things to help the community. You should see if Adeline can train you to be a guard. Your archery skills are amazing," he said, the last part with a slight bit of bitterness in his voice.

Raela looked at the floor before she looked back up at him again. "Lucius, I'm so sorry. I know you really loved him."

He gave a big sigh. "I forgive you. I know it wasn't really your choice. Make it up to me. Join the guard, all right?"

Raela smiled and gave a small nod. "I will," she said, giving him a tight hug. "You're such a good brother. I'm so happy we met."

Lucius hugged her back. "So am I. Now get comfortable. I have to go talk to Claudius."

Raela nodded and let go of him, walking into the house.

Chapter 44

LUCIUS

THE PLAN

Adeline was standing in front of the firepit alone for once, staring in. She seemed very peaceful. Lucius felt bad disturbing her private time but did so anyway.

"The fire is pretty, isn't it?" he said, walking up to stand next to her.

"It is. My brother's magic ability has always been amazing to me. Having magic, even for vampires, is a very rare trait. I've always wished I had it."

"Aren't you strong? That's a trait just as useful." Lucius said, feeling proud of his brute strength.

"Well, it may be useful, but it isn't exactly ladylike. I could never use it in cooking or use it to do quick needlework or be a fast sewer or anything of the sort."

"Is that why you decided to train in fighting instead?"

Adeline looked over at him, giving him a proud smile. It was the first time he had ever seen her look happy. "Not only did I train in fighting, I dare say I became quite good at it, much to my mother's dismay, if she could see me now," she said, letting out a loud unla-dylike laugh.

He smiled. "I wanted to talk to you about fighting. I asked my sister to join the city guard with you. I imagine you could use the help, but in reality, I need her to make some friends. Would you mind helping her out?"

Adeline stared at him. "I don't believe we honestly have that much work to do in the city guard. It's not like the city needs much guarding. No one has ever found our hideaway, except for other vampires. If she needs a friend, however, I'd be happy to let her join. I'm sure with a bit of training, she'll be a very skilled fighter!" she said, laughing again.

"I'm relieved to hear you say that," Lucius said, turning to go into the castle. "And do me one more favor?" he shouted to her as he walked.

"Hmm?"

"Don't go easy on her!" Now it was Lucy's turn to laugh.

Walking into Claudius's castle, he heard the soft sound of the piano from a different room and followed the noise. At the bench, Claudius was playing while reading a piece of music. When he entered the room, he stopped to look over at him.

"Ah, Lucius. Did you bring your sister and her children successfully?"

"Yes, it went much easier than I expected, actually. I half expected my brother Azazel to catch up to us and drag her back or at least notice his children missing, but that's not why I'm here today."

"Right to the point then. What's on your mind?" he said, getting off the piano bench to sit in a chair by the several dozens of bookshelves.

"My father has ordered me to kill you. I just thought I would get that out of the way," he said, sitting across from the man dressed clad in black.

"Should I be worried?" Claudius said in a jokingly egotistical tone.

"No, actually, I had quite the opposite idea. I've been thinking about it for a while. Maybe it's time there wasn't a German colony. What do you think?"

"I didn't think I would be hearing these words from you," he said, looking shocked and leaning back in his chair. "I suppose your family's village does pose some very distinct problems. I have heard rumors from some of the low born vampires that moved into our little underground city that they keep human slaves in Germany and openly reject any half breeds, lowborns, or anyone that doesn't belong to their family."

"All those things are completely true," Lucius confirmed. "And because of those things and a few others that I don't wish to mention, I think the best thing we could do is to put an end to their rule."

"Do *you* wish to rule in your father's place?" Claudius said, reaching over to take a book in hand.

"Not particularly. I think one colony is enough. Anyone who wants to step in and take ownership of the castle is welcome to, I suppose."

"What happens in Germany is none of our business, Lucius. I would never normally suggest this route. But if they ordered you to kill me first, then I suppose perhaps it is time to take action before they send another more loyal family member. I do, however, have some concerns about you being involved. Are you sure you want to do this, Lucius? They're your family. I completely understand if you'd like me to send someone else."

"No, I want to do this myself."

"I know you're a determined man, Lucius, but I have to say I would normally advise against this. I have no doubt in my mind that you are strong enough to deal with the after-effects of what will happen. But I don't want you to have to shoulder the burden of what will become of your family. I honestly think it would be better if you weren't involved," Claudius insisted.

"I appreciate your concern for my well-being. But I promise you, I won't have any regrets. I can't explain it, Claudius, but some-how, I feel like I was meant to do this. This family, they've never acted like my family. From the moment my mother was pregnant, she was cast out in hopes that I wouldn't even survive. Every moment since then has been a struggle, and every interaction with them has been horrid. I feel like I need to do this—if not for me, then for my mom and my twin sister, who wasn't able to live through what I did."

"Were you close with your mother and sister?"

"I was close to my sister, but my mother never really wanted me. When I was just a kid, I always blamed her for it. I hated her for not loving me as her own child. But now, as an adult, I can sort of see it a bit more through her eyes, now that I've met her captors. Living with my family must have been torture, and to top it off, she had two vampire children forced on her. I've met my dad. I know I look exactly like him. I can't imagine having to raise a son that looks exactly like my abuser. If I were her, I would have struggled to love me too. And between us, it's not like I made it easy for her," Lucius said, giving a small awkward chuckle.

Claudius stared at him a long time before giving a tired sigh. "If you're really certain about this, then I can't stop you. But I would advise you to think about this at least a day or so."

"Again, I appreciate your concern. But I don't need to think. I need to act."

"If you're certain then. I will help you come up with a plan to see this through. But it's your family, so how do you want to go about this?"

"I want to bring some powerful fighters with me. I know I'll never be able to take all of them down. There are at least fifty to one hundred, and I don't have the advantage of being physically stronger than all of them."

"All right. Who would you like to bring to help you?"

"Well, I'm completely convinced your sister is an amazing fighter, and Lidewij adds an element of speed that I think we really need. I'm sure the three of us could take them down if we're sneaky. I don't want to take any more than that. I want to risk as few of us as we possibly can."

"Not Adeline. She will stay with me, but I would suggest taking Holly. Have you met her? She is a very kind woman with magic ability, not quite as strong as mine, but she would still be useful. Not to mention she's a turned vampire and is able to travel by day."

"Holly? All right. I'll go talk to her then Lidewij, and we'll head out as soon as we can. What does she look like?"

"She has blond hair and light hazel eyes," Claudius said. "She is very short and extremely sweet. I have been training her in magic for some time now, and I think she's finally ready to put that magic to use."

"Perfect! I'll go find her," he said, smiling.

"Wait," Claudius said, grabbing his arm to halt him.

"What's wrong?"

"You need a backup plan in case things go south. You need a sure way back to England."

"Can't we just run back? It's worked well so far."

"You could, but I would feel better if you found a way back that hid you from the humans and vampires alike. I don't want to lose any of my citizens."

"Fair enough. I'll think of an escape plan in case we need it, all right?"

"Thank you," Claudius said, sitting down to read a new book.

"No problem," Lucius replied before walking out of the castle.

Walking around town, he finally spotted a woman who looked just like Holly, according to Claudius's descriptions. She was hunched over in front of her house, growing some sort of odd plant.

"Why are you trying to grow plants? You know they won't grow without sunlight," Lucius said, leaning over her to watch her dig dirt for a plant resting in a small pot beside her.

She gave a small laugh before looking up at him. "That's where you're wrong. This is a snake plant. It grows best with artificial light, and the fire should be plenty to keep it alive so long as I water it," she said, smiling at her own cleverness.

"Oh, I didn't know such a plant existed. That's really interesting actually. Did you do a study on plants?"

"Well, before I was a vampire, I was a gardener. But things change, you know?"

"Yeah, tell me about it. My names Lucius. Is your name Holly by chance?"

"That's my name! Don't wear it out," she said, giving his leg a light punch. "What can I help you with?"

"Claudius says you would be perfect to come on a mission with me. We're finally putting an end to the German vampire colony. Could I possibly convince you to come along?"

Holly's smile disappeared as her face flushed. "Really? Claudius said that about me? I don't know, Lucius. I don't think my magic is really well enough to do a siege on another colony. I mean, I'm okay, but I'm still in training!"

"I'm sure you'll do fine. We're going to be extremely sneaky about the whole thing. No one will know we're coming. Besides, Claudius told me your ready, so I'm sure you will be a great help! And if we succeed, there's fancy gold and jewelry involved," he said, lowering his voice a little to try to tempt her.

Holly laughed. "You think I care about gold? I'm wearing overalls and sitting in the dirt. No, gold is the least of my desires. I can promise you that."

"Well, then what do you desire?"

"Nothing you can give me. That's for sure." She smiled up at him from the dirt. "Meaning no offense."

"None taken. Isn't there anything I can do to convince you to come with us?"

"Um…just let me think about it, then I'll decide. I just need a moment to consider."

"Done, I'm going to go talk to Lidewij about coming too. Then I'll be back tomorrow when we leave."

Holly dug her hands back into the dirt to make the plant's hole a little wider. "And I will be here."

Lucius strode to his own house, thinking to check on his sister before he made his way next door. Adeline was already there, speaking to Raela just outside the house. As he approached, he only caught the last part of their conversation.

"It will be great fun to have a friend in guarding. Besides, it will give you something to do. And should anyone come to threaten your children, you will be properly prepared to defend them."

Raela looked very torn. "I don't know, I've never even held a knife, let alone swung a sword."

"Who said anything about knives and swords? I hear you are very skilled with a bow. We could use someone with that skill. First, we'll train on the bow and blocking. Then we can move onto close combat weapons. Someone with your speed will surely flourish in hand to hand combat," Adeline said, sounding prouder than ever.

Raela looked at her feet, then up at Adeline under her brow. "Well, women aren't allowed to learn to fight where I am from, but I suppose it could be fun."

"Yes! You will love to train. The release of stress you feel when winning a battle is an exhilarating rush I cannot even begin to describe. If you don't mind my asking, where did you learn to shoot arrows?"

"My brother Palas taught me in secret when we were children. When we were found out, my father beat him so bloody that he had to lay on his stomach for the better part of four days. He was always trying to break the rules for me," she said sorrowfully.

"Well, the way Lucius has described your bowmanship, he must have been very skilled even as a child! Let us start training tomorrow morning after you have had a day to get relaxed. I will meet you here."

Raela nodded, and Adeline marched off, seeming taller with pride. Lucius strode over to his sister, ruffling her hair.

"I think you'll really like it. Adeline seems like a really nice person, and besides, if you're going to live here, you should really make some, you know." Lucius paused, giving her a light punch on the shoulder. "Friends."

"Ha, ha." Raela laughed dully. "Is that supposed to be some sort of joke?" she said, giving him a small playful push, glad her brother was finally warming up to her.

"Well, you can be a bit rigid. And you tend to venture off in solitude from what I have gathered about you from Ben and watching you myself. I think it's time we changed that."

"You're probably right," she sighed. "Lucius? I meant to thank you for bringing me here. It really means a lot that you would help me, even after everything I did to you." She gazed down, feeling guilty once more.

"I know it wasn't really you who did those things. I'm not completely stupid," he said, giving a small awkward laugh. "You wouldn't have done all that stuff if you weren't forced to. It just doesn't add up, you know? Ben was your friend as much as he was my companion."

She gave a small nod and hugged her brother tightly, sniffling as she withheld tears.

"Hey now, don't get all mushy on me," Lucius said, trying to cheer her up. "You're going to train with Adeline to be a fighter. You gotta be tough to do that. Come on, I have to go," he said, giving her a tight reassuring hug.

Nodding, she gave a small smile. "I promise to be tough, as long as you promise not to get into any more trouble."

"Well, I can't promise anything that drastic," he replied, smirking at her as he walked next door. Raela rolled her eyes and walked inside to join her children.

Knocking on the door, he stood and waited for what felt like an eternity before Lidewij answered. She was wearing nothing but a towel around her body and hair, as though she had just finished a bath. Her face turned red, and she tried to cover herself when she saw him.

"You don't need to rush if you want to get dressed and talk in a few minutes," he said, sensing her unease.

"No, it's fine," she insisted. "What can I help you with?" She pulled her towel up a bit more.

"Quite a bit, actually. I have a very important task I would like to ask for your assistance in. And since we're friends, I trust you even more," he said, giving her a friendly smile.

"You consider us friends?" she asked, seeming shocked.

"Well, I mean, yeah. I said that at the firepit, remember? There's no reason we can't at least be friends, is there?"

She gave a happy smile. "No, I suppose not. What did you need?"

"I am going on a very important, self-assigned mission. I'm going to go and end the German vampire colony. They've caused too much harm, and it isn't right for them to remain after repeatedly proving themselves to be vicious untrustworthy monsters. If we don't put an end to them, Egon has the mind to kill Claudius."

"Really? I always took your father for a coward, hiding in his castle behind a mountain. At least Claudius goes into the human world from time to time. I have never seen a leader leaving the castle in your family. They always just send some lackey to do their work." She laughed, thinking her joke the funniest thing she'd ever heard.

"That description is fairly accurate," he said, giving a light chuckle. "Will you come with me?"

"Yes! Of course, yes, I get so bored here sometimes. And I've really had the taste for killing ever since my first man."

"Perfect, I'm so glad to hear that. Say, who was the first man you ever killed?"

"It was the man who was dragging me away from my brother at the docks. When we were both in chains. I killed him, then killed my brother's captor shortly after, and we ran away."

"That must have been a difficult feat, considering you were so young and small."

"The hardest part was the hiding. We're a lot faster, so it wasn't that difficult to escape."

"Ah, yeah, I've had similar struggles with hiding myself," he confessed.

Lidewij smiled. "I have to go dry off and get dressed. When are we going to leave?"

"Tomorrow morning. We have to get Holly to see if she will join us, then we'll be off."

"Oh, Holly! I like Holly. She's got quite an obsession with plants. But I need to get dressed and get some things ready. I'll see you tomorrow?"

"I'll see you tomorrow," Lucius said, smiling as Lidewij closed the door to finish with the aftermath of her bath.

Going back into his own house, he went up to his bedroom and thought about how he should go about doing this. He should have an archer with him, so he could bring Raela along for help. But involving Raela would be too unfair. This was her family; he could never ask her to do this. He wasn't even sure he wanted her to know. He thought maybe it was best to keep his activity a secret. Then he could tell her when it was done. After all, they were going to need to finish the family off either way for their own safety. But if Lucius knew anything about his sister, it was that she struggled to act in difficult situations and would much rather just sit and let things happen to her. It was hard to blame her, though. All her life, she had been taught that doing nothing was the appropriate response.

Lucius got up, thinking about what he needed to do to prepare. He decided to pay another visit to Claudius. Perhaps he had a map of his home. After all, Egon knew a strange amount about the England colony; maybe Claudius knew more than he was letting on as well. He knocked and went in, finding the man exactly where he had left him.

"Oh! You're back!" Claudius said with obvious surprise. "Need something else from me?"

"Uh, yeah do you happen to have a map of my family's estate? Even if it's a partial one?"

"Hmmm, let me see. My father might have had such a thing," he said, closing his book. He searched the bookshelves for several minutes before pulling out a smaller book, handing it to Lucius.

Opening it, Lucius found a folded map on the inside. "Wonderful! This should be enough! Do you mind if I borrow this?"

"By all means, help yourself," he said, going back to his chair.

Taking the map, he headed back to his house, scheming all night. The next morning, before Lidewij came to see him, he stopped by Holly's house. Knocking on the door, she opened the door wide before he could finish, wearing a backpack and some exercise gear.

"I've thought about it, and I've decided to come!" she said, marching out of her house in her tennis shoes. On her legs, she had two knives strapped to her exercise gear.

"Really? I was positive I would have to do more convincing," he said as she pushed past him.

"Well, you were going to, but I thought about it. Claudius is right. This will be good practice for my magic! So I'll come," she said confidently, her short stature seeming a few inches taller than usual.

"Perfect!" he said, feeling good about the mission so far. On his way back to the house, he spotted Lidewij running over toward them with loads of weapons falling off her. "Hey! Wait up!" she said. "I thought we were meeting at your house then going to get Holly."

"We were, but I woke up early, so I thought I would just go get her myself," Lucius said, smiling. "I don't want to waste any time."

"Well, now that we're all here, what's the plan?" she said, tying her short sword and knives to her waist a little better.

Lucius reached into his pocket and pulled out the book, revealing the huge map of his family's estate. "So the most important thing is that we go in undetected. Then we need to injure everyone in my family."

Lidewij gave him a funny look. "Injure? I thought we were going in to kill them. I'm not really looking to make enemies who will want to come back and hunt me later," she said, suddenly seeming unsure and a bit afraid.

"We are going to kill them, but we need to injure them first. Have you ever tried to kill a vampire, either of you?"

They both shook their heads.

"Well, you'd be amazed at how difficult it is. There are only two effective ways to do it—burning them alive or stabbing them in the heart with a wooden stake."

"Why don't we buy wood-tipped bullets and some guns?" Holly chimed in.

"Well, I considered that. But that would mean they could hear every shot. Guns make a lot of noise, which would alert them to where we are. It takes away the sneak factor, which we desperately need, given our numbers," he said, turning back to his map. "If we can injure them badly enough to immobilize them, then we can walk around and stab everyone after the situation is safer."

Lidewij looked at the map. "Yeah, that seems like a smart idea, because it looks like there is only one entrance to the castle," she said.

"Almost. There's one other secret exit," Lucius said, turning the page to the basement. "It's where the slaves' corpses are kept. My father took my mother through this exit, I imagine. I figure if we enter through here, then we can free the slaves first, they might even join us to fight."

"Well, I know how we can be sneaky after that," Holly said, trying to seem useful. "I can use my magic to make us invisible to your family, but not each other. Would that be helpful?"

Lucius stared over at her. "Yeah! That would be super helpful! Can you actually do that?"

She fidgeted a little. "I can, but only if it's the three of us. If all the humans try and fight with us, I won't be able to make us all invisible at the same time," she said, suddenly doubting her own ability and eating her words.

"No, no, the three of us will be plenty," he said, turning back to the map, suddenly feeling much more confident of their success. "Now, getting there will be tricky. Holly and I will take my bike. Lidewij, are you fast enough to follow? You said earlier that you had speed on your side."

She smirked. "You're looking at the fastest vampire of our time, and you have the nerve to ask if I can follow?"

Lucius laughed. "All right, take it easy, hotshot. Don't get cocky before we even get to the castle," he said, folding up the map. "Now, of course, there is going to be stuff we can't plan for. I figured we all stick together until everyone is wounded at least. Then we can branch out and kill individually from there. If we stick together mostly at first, it will decrease our chances of getting stuck in individual sticky situations. Sound like a good plan?"

Both of the girls nodded before he put the book back into his pocket. "We need to discuss one more thing before we leave. Claudius said he would be most comfortable if we had a proper escape plan. I insisted that we could travel back the way we came, but he seemed unsure. Do either of you have any ideas?"

Both of the girls looked at each other before Holly spoke up. "I guess I could bring my flower truck if we needed to escape in secret."

"Flower truck? What does that mean?"

"It's a refrigerated transport truck for the flower business I'm starting. I have a greenhouse in the city that I grow flowers in and sell to buyers. We can use the truck to escape in secret if running away doesn't work, and it's an excellent place to hide," Holly said.

"Wonderful! It sounds like a perfect plan. Then, Lidewij, you can ride in the back." Lucius said. "But we shouldn't waste any time." He helped Lidewij pack up her remaining weapons before leading the girls out of the colony.

Chapter 45

LUCIUS

THE JOURNEY AND THE BLOOD

After Holly cleared her truck of shipments, they set off to the road. The drive seemed to take forever, but perhaps it was just his nervousness that was making it last so long. Holly was very quiet as they drove through the country, and he couldn't help but think how fortunate that the two vampires he was traveling with were resistant to sunlight.

"You never told me what you desired, Holly," he said, trying to make conversation during one of their rest stops.

"No, I didn't. I guess it's a little uncomfortable to talk about," she said, stretching her limbs from sitting in one place so long.

"I won't pressure you then. You don't have to tell me. I completely understand," he responded, not wanting to make her uncomfortable.

"No, it's all right. I think my biggest desire would be to be human again. I was only turned a few years or so ago. But the vampire who turned me killed my parents," she said sadly.

"Oh, I didn't know. I'm sorry."

"It isn't your fault. But I thank you for listening."

"Hey, we're friends now. I'll always be here if you need me," he said with a smile before getting ready for the drive again.

When they finally arrived at the base of the mountain, Lucius led them around to the secret entrance. It was the middle of the day, so every Lovhart was sure to be asleep inside, making things much easier. Feeling along the side of the mountain, he finally found a slight indent beneath a patch of moss. It was a small handle, but when he tried to pull it, it wouldn't budge.

Lucius dug through his pockets. Key, Key, Key. He knew he had one! He used it to get Raela. As he finally pulled out the heart shaped key, he jammed it into a panel behind the door handle, and turned.

With one pull of the lever, the door latched open. When they entered, they were surrounded by cages and corpses. His stomach turned, and he covered his nose and led them to the next level. Both girls gagged at the smell until they were led away from it. On the second floor, they ran down the hallway to the cells. Holly used her magic to unlock every cage. It took them all of one hour to free everyone. Lucius then rounded everyone up to speak to them one last time.

"You're free now! We plan to get rid of the rest of the vampires. If you want to act with us, I cannot guarantee your life. I would much rather you all leave through the back exit. Some of you know the way already, and I urge you to take everyone with you."

Without another word, everyone started bolting toward the back entrance, much to his relief. He wasn't surprised none of them wanted to fight. Most of them were malnourished and had been fighting all their lives, even if it wasn't always a physical battle. It was better this way. It would be easier to stay hidden using Holly's magic.

Lucius pulled out the map and studied it for a few minutes before deciding to go to his family. Once they started killing and injuring, they'd have to act quickly. It would be better to know the layout as much as he could now before things entered high speed.

Lidewij read over his shoulder. "Where do the least amount of vampires live?"

"Well, that's the problem, I'm not really sure. I've only lived in the upper part of the castle for a few days."

"Well, where are the women? I know your family doesn't train or let women fight, so it might be easiest to take them out first."

Thinking on it, he wasn't sure how comfortable he was with killing women, but then again, he had before in the fighting rings, hadn't he? This shouldn't be any different. Ben had even said it himself. These women didn't feel any remorse or guilt. Raela was the only one who visited them in the dungeons and at least tried to make their lives a little better.

Folding up the map and putting it back into his pocket, he started walking up the steps to the main house. "I guess we'll find out, won't we?"

"Now both of you have to stay in my line of vision, or else I won't be able to keep you invisible. Okay? And be as quiet as you can. I might be able to keep us out of sight and silence our voices, but I can't silence our footsteps," Holly said as they reached the door.

"Okay," he replied, really wanting to get this over with. "And if you see my dad, don't hurt him. I want to be the one to end his life."

"Fair enough." Lidewij said, pulling out her short sword.

Opening the door, they walked into the castle. The girls' mouths opened in amazement as they stared at the beautiful chandeliers and the amazing portraits on the wall. Lucy walked forward, trying to stay on the task. But it seemed as though his partners had completely forgotten about their end goal.

"Hey, focus," he said.

Holly was the first to snap out of it. "Right! Sorry," she said, pulling Lidewij with her.

As they walked down the hallways, they reached a large lounge-like room with five doors connecting. Every door was closed shut. Walking to the first door, he tried the knob gently. Locked.

Lucius looked at his two friends. "I don't have a key to these rooms," he whispered.

"I think this is where Claudius thought I should come in," Holly said, holding her hand up to the door. With a small click, the door unlocked.

"How did you do that?" Lucius exclaimed.

"Magic. I can't unlock any door, but these locks are old and outdated."

"Thank you, Holly," Lucius said, opening the door.

Inside was a woman knitting. Upon seeing the door open, her eyes snapped to attention. "Who's there!" she said, getting up and looking around. "I'm warning you. If you hurt me, Egon will hear about it!" she said, sounding frightened. After a minute of silence, she walked to the door to close it.

Lucius stepped out of her way. Then Lidewij struck first, swiping her short sword up and through her neck. The woman made a choking noise and grabbed at her throat desperately before falling to the floor. Her eyes looked around, trying to find the perpetrator, before Lidewij came down with another strike to her neck. This one cut off her head completely, but still she was alive. Lucius thought it was best to stab her now, and he did so with a wooden stake before Lidewij could take another blow to a different limb.

"Lidewij! Can't you kill without being cruel?" Lucius said, feeling a bit angry at her level of violence in doing the deed.

She panted heavily, and Lucy couldn't help noticing the faint glow from her eyes. They were no longer green but a deep dark red with large black bags underneath. Her skin was a deathly gray, and her teeth even seemed to grow in length and sharpness. All her beauty was gone, and she suddenly really did look like a monster. A thought disturbed him. Did he look like this when he was lusting to kill? It would explain all the fearful looks people gave him when he was hungry. He couldn't believe he had looked like such a horror without any knowledge of it. When she took a step toward him, he instinctively stepped back, suddenly feeling a little afraid. No, she wouldn't hurt him; they were friends.

"Let's get a move on," she said in a raspy, monstrous tone. She sounded as though she hadn't spoken in years.

Even Holly looked frightened as they moved to the next room. She opened the door, and Lidewij jumped in before anyone could react, slicing the head off the woman asleep in bed. Holly sensed Lidewij's urge to kill faster and faster and decided to unlock every door at once. Their red-haired friend killed two more vampires in the lounge, and Lucius killed one. Then it was on to the next sector of sleeping quarters.

Every sleeping quarter for women was the same—a large lounging room with five doors attached. Most of them were asleep, but a few were knitting, reading, and even eating. Lucius found those eating the easiest to kill. It reminded him why he was doing this as the dead human corpse stared up at him from the floor. He couldn't help but wonder whom they had been before death.

After every woman section was done, they moved up to the next floor, where he thought the men would be. He pushed open the door to the lounge and found children's toys littered across the floor. His heart filled with dread, as Holly instinctively unlocked all the doors before she saw the toys. Lidewij ran in first, stepping over the toys and barging into a room.

Lucius ran toward her, but she was too fast for him.

"Lidewij! Stop!" he screamed.

Lidewij yanked one of the children out of their bed and held up her sword. Lucius grabbed her shoulder and yanked her back. "No! Not these ones. They're children!"

"I'm not taking any survivors, Lucius!" she screamed as the small boy under her quaked with fear.

Lucius glanced at the boy under his friend. He was so young. Only ten at the oldest. He found it difficult not to see himself as a child in those fearful eyes.

"We aren't killing any kids, Lidewij. We can take them back with us to the colony."

"So what? They can grow up resenting us and lead to our eventual demise? I'm not here to leave any living enemies that could come back to destroy me!"

"We can change them. They're young. We can still change who they become."

"We can't change them past this! We're on a mission to kill everyone, including their entire family. We'll have scarred them for life! People can't change and forgive something like that."

"Yes, they can! I forgave my mother, and she killed my twin sister when I was no more than six. People can forgive, Lidewij. We can't kill them!"

"You don't know that these kids are capable of forgiveness. Just because you forgave your enemies, doesn't mean they will."

Lucius yanked Lidewij off of the boy, and the child ran and hid under his bed. "They're just kids. We aren't killing them, and that's the last I want to hear of it."

"I'm not here to leave surviving enemies!"

"Then you shouldn't have come! You should know that any time you kill anyone, you make an enemy. This is my mission, and I call the shots. I don't care if you don't agree with me. We aren't killing children!"

Lidewij let out an angry huff before walking out of the room. Holly had relocked all the bedrooms. Lucius knew she was angry at him, but he couldn't condone the killing of children. It wasn't moral. Not that murder of any sort was moral, but killing children was different.

They walked ahead. "I think this whole floor is children, just like the whole floor below us was women. If I had to guess, I would imagine the whole castle is separated in order of importance. Slaves, women, children, then men must be on the top floor, with my father. Don't forget to leave him to me, Lidewij. If you kill him, I won't ever forgive you," he said, giving her a stern stare.

"He's all yours. I'm content to just kill the lackeys," she said, licking the blood off her sword.

Lucius felt a shiver up his spine as he watched her, thinking it was more than disgusting. Killing humans was horrible, but they had to for food. But killing and drinking the blood of their own kind? That was a new thing entirely that he had never even considered. But now wasn't the time to confront her about such matters. As they climbed up the stairs, they made their way to the first lounge area. Holly unlocked the door and let them both loose to do as they pleased. With a flash of red hair and a few sword swings, half the room was decapitated. Lucius gave a sharp twist of the neck to the remaining men, glad this was going fast. He enjoyed the feeling of avenging his mother, but at the same time, he just wanted to forget about this place.

Chapter 46

LUCIUS

AZAZEL AND EGON

They easily breezed through every quarter until they happened upon a room by the stairs that stood alone. He had an all-too-familiar idea about whom this room might belong to. Holly unlocked the door, and he pushed it open. Inside was Azazel, fast asleep. When they walked into his bedroom, he sat up.

"Who's there!" he shouted.

Lucius turned to Holly. "Drop the invisibility shield," he said before turning to his half brother once again.

Azazel stared at him before turning to look at Holly and Lidewij. "You brought guests!" he said, standing up. "How dare you! Bringing filthy mixed-blood vampires into our elegant home! Into my living quarters!" he said before staring at the blood covering their clothes.

"Hey, Azazel. I don't know or care enough about you to give you any sort of comfort. We're here to kill you," he said with a smile.

His half brother stared at him in disbelief.

"You're joking. That's not our family's blood, is it? You wouldn't!" Azazel said in disbelief.

He and Lucius stared at each other for several moments before Azazel realized he was wrong. He bolted to the door. Lidewij swung around and punched him in the face, knocking him to the ground before he could reach it.

Lucius stood over him and turned to speak to Holly. "All right, let's make this quick," he said, pulling out a wooden stake.

But before Lucius turned back to his half brother, Azazel was up racing toward the door again. Except for this time, he reached it.

"Lidewij! Stop him!" Lucius shouted.

Except Azazel was already halfway up to Egon's chambers. Lidewij bolted after him and grabbed his arm. Lucius ran after him as quickly as he could, finding Azazel kicking and biting at Lidewij's hands and arms as she tried to contain him.

"Let me go!" Azazel screamed, elbowing Lidewij hard in the stomach.

Lucius grabbed his neck just before Lidewij keeled over, groaning in pain.

"Now that wasn't very nice," Lucius said.

"Not very nice! You've killed everyone in the family! After we brought you here out of the goodness of our hearts and made you one of us!"

Lucius scoffed. "Yeah, after too many trials. A real family doesn't expect its members to kill their loved ones to prove their obedience."

"And what would you know of real family? You've moved from place to place since you were born! I doubt you've ever felt a shred of love or care for anyone, you filthy half breed!"

Lucius slapped him. "You know I hate it when people call me that. What does that even mean…half breed? Half human, half vampire. It sounds so made up, so derogatory."

Azazel struggled against Lucius's hand wrapped around his throat, trying to think of a way out of his current predicament. "If you let me go, I'll leave. I'll leave the house, and you can do whatever you want to the remaining family members. You'll never hear from me again. I swear it! Just let me go."

Lucius stared at him angrily. "And if I say no?"

Azazel stopped struggling. "Then…I deserve it."

Lucius stared harder. What was his half brother playing at, saying he deserved it? Was he just trying to trick him into letting him go? He glared into Azazel's eyes. And beyond the fear were depression, guilt, and loneliness. Lucius wondered where all these feelings came from. Perhaps Azazel didn't have it as easy as Lucius had liked to believe. What did he feel guilty for? Was it guilt for Raela? Azazel must be aware of what Egon had done to her. And if Azazel could feel guilt, then was it possible that he could feel compassion?

Lucius pondered a moment. Azazel had asked to be freed, and if he did decide to let him go, it was less blood on his hands and less to feel guilty about. Then again, if he let him go, who was to say he was telling the truth? Why wouldn't he come back? And would Lucius really have succeeded in ending his family empire if the next heir was allowed to walk free? What of Raela? How would Raela feel if she knew he killed everyone in the household but her forced husband was left alive? Not to mention that he was raised by Egon. Egon, the murderous self-absorbed rapist. What was Azazel really like if he was raised like a monster like that?

But Lucius couldn't kill him based on his parents. After all, if people only ended up like their parents, he would have ended up much more like his mother. And if there was one thing he knew for sure, Lucius was not his mother. No, he couldn't kill him because of Egon. But he could kill him for Raela.

"Where will you go?" Lucius questioned. "You've never been outside the castle. Where do you plan to hide?"

"Anywhere! I'll hide in Russia as you did. I'll go find Palas. I'll do whatever it takes to stay away from you and Raela if that's what you want."

Lucius dropped him. "Fine. Just get out of here," he said before Azazel dashed off.

"Are you sure that was smart?" Lidewij said, crossing her arms. "I told you I wasn't planning on leaving any survivors. First the children and now your half brother? Maybe you do have a soft spot for your family after all. I thought we were here to end your family line."

"That situation is my business. Just leave it be, and stick to the plan."

"Fine," Lidewij scoffed. "But don't expect me to approve."

"I don't," he said as the three of them walked up the long stairway to Egon's office.

"Well, here we are," Lidewij said. "Are you going to let him go too? He's the whole reason we're here, you know."

"Lidewij, stop. I know you're upset about my decisions, but this is my family, and it should be me who decides who gets to survive. No, I'm not letting him go."

She gave a small angry huff. "I'm going to clean up the mess and kill any chance survivors. Call me when you're finished," she said before stomping back down the stairs.

Lucius gave a tired sigh before looking to Holly. She looked torn, agreeing with his decision but understanding Lidewij's anger. "Go join Lidewij, I'll finish up here, and meet you down there," he said, turning toward the door.

"I won't be able to make you invisible if we get separated," Holly reminded him.

"I won't need it. Thank you," he said, giving her a soft smile.

"Be safe, okay?"

"You're worrying too much." He laughed. "I'll see you after I'm done, all right?"

"Okay," she said, trying to sound sure of herself, before leaving him alone. Lucius turned and strode toward the door, surprised to find it wasn't locked. Egon was resting inside, reading a book in the chair by his bed. When he heard him walk in, he looked up.

"Ah! I was wondering when you would finish the task. I assumed it would take longer for Raela to work up the courage to distract them," he said with a laugh, putting down the book. "She really is a coward, isn't she?"

"Don't talk about her that way," Lucius said. He had no intent to hide what he was about to do, but first, he wanted to talk to him as an equal, not as though Egon were a god amongst men like his father so desired to be.

"Excuse me?" he replied, standing up from where he was. "What did you just say? Don't get cocky just because I'm giving you some freedoms. You still take your orders from me."

Lucius locked the door behind him and strode over to his father. "Tell me about my mother. What did you do to her?" he said, trying to keep his voice calm.

"Your mother? That filthy cleaning slave? Why would you want to know about her?"

"Do you even remember her name?" he said, feeling more and more disgusted.

"No. And why would I? She was just some common human, nothing special, nothing interesting. She had soft hair—I will give her that much—and very beautiful breasts. But aside from those two traits, I wouldn't call her anything short of a disappointment. After all, she couldn't even silently clean herself out. Instead she let herself get pregnant."

Without thinking twice, Lucius swung his hand up and back-handed Egon as hard as he could, sending him backward, smashing through the bed and up against the stone wall, cracking it. The crack went up into the ceiling and caused the chandelier to swing and fall. Luckily, when it fell, the candles went out, except one by his bedside.

Egon tried to stand up, but his shoulder was broken where he had hit the wall, and his arm was badly twisted, bone poking through his skin. "You slapped me, filthy brat! I should have never let you out of that wretched cell!" he screamed, trying to regain his footing.

"You're right. You shouldn't have," he said, giving him a hard kick to the knee, hearing the crack of it breaking as well. "How many times did you rape her?"

"You think I kept track of that number? Stupid boy, I could do with her whatever I wanted. She was my personal cleaner. And she was only a filthy whore," he grunted stubbornly.

Grabbing his better arm, Lucius twisted it backward and kicked his body, yanking the entire arm out of its socket and ripping it off, before tossing it to the side. Egon let out a grunt, refusing to scream and submit himself to weakness.

"How many times! You can't imagine what it's like to be raped! The horrible pain and disgusting feeling afterward. And guess what, it doesn't ever go away! There isn't a single day that they don't think about it, feel it, remember it, and hate themselves for what happened.

There isn't a day I don't think about him! How could you even think of doing that to another person!" Lucius screamed, remembering the feeling of Boris and the wormy dirty feeling he felt after the event was done. The memory alone was enough to make him shiver. It made him angry at Boris all over again and angry at himself for not struggling when it happened. Luckily, he had the perfect outlet for that anger right in front of him.

"I killed them all, you know, even Azazel. The entire family, and the children," Lucius lied. He no longer felt remorse for lying or killing the family when he spoke to his father. Listening to his mother get called crude names had removed any sort of regret he might have felt.

Egon's eyes widened before he stared at him in disbelief. "No, you wouldn't! Azazel would never let you see it through!"

"Oh, you should have heard how your eldest son screamed when we got to him, begging for his life, crying like a baby. If I didn't know better, I could have sworn he even pissed himself," he fibbed, letting out a laugh. He felt so cruel, but he wanted to feel cruel right now.

His father just stared at him in shock. Lucius grabbed him by his neck, lifted him up, and pinned him to the wall. "What's the matter, Dad? Are you sad? Sad that your prized son is dead and that your empire is finally over?"

"Fuck you!" Egon shouted before spitting on him.

Lucy wiped it off his cheek. "Now, now, that's no way to talk to someone who currently holds your life in the palm of his hands. I want to get back to the subject at hand. What really happened after you got my mother pregnant? Did you just throw her out to fend for herself? Hoping one of us would be enough to end her life or the other way around? You're disgusting."

Lucius grabbed the shiny gold earring on the side of Egon's head and ripped it off, dropping his body to the floor to pick the parts of his ear off the shiny gold jewelry.

"What a pretty earring you have. I think I'll keep it," he said, cleaning it all the way off before jamming the point through his left ear.

"No! You've taken enough! You killed our empire. At least let the family heirloom die with us," Egon pleaded, attempting to stand and reach for it, but he winced when his broken shoulder gave an unsettling crack.

"Why should I? If you can name one thing you've done for me, I will consider giving it back." Lucius smiled, knowing it would be impossible.

Egon paused before speaking again. "I gave you your only true friend! Ben! You would have never met him if not for me."

"He was more than a friend to me! And you took him. You made me kill him! Try again. It's fun to watch you beg."

His eyes darted back and forth in a panic. "I gave you a place to stay! When your gang life in Russia was falling apart, I let you stay!"

"In the dungeons, where I was tied up by my ankles and starved. Almost. Keep going."

"I *gave* you your *life*! You wouldn't even exist if not for *me*!" Egon pleaded angrily, standing up the best he could. Lucius heard a few clicks from his knee and shoulder as he watched them heal partially back to normal.

"Except I never *asked you to*! Do you know how many times I wished you hadn't given me life? How many times I would have rather been dead? Of course, you don't. That's enough chances for you! I'm keeping the earring," he said, turning to grab the last wooden stake.

With his back turned, Egon took the opportunity presented to him. He jumped onto Lucius's back, grabbed him, and pushed him to the floor. Lucy felt a hand tighten around his, as his father tried to wrestle the stake out of his hand.

Pinned to his stomach, he tried to wrestle free of the mangled man on top of him. He felt his father try to hold him down with his weight. But in an attempt to reach the weapon in his hand, he put too much weight on his left side. Lucy smirked to himself. It was obvious his father had never fought a day in his life, or he would have pinned his right side while reaching for his left. In one swift movement, he rolled left with his father and on top of him.

"That was a good effort. Do you have that fighting spirit out of your system now?" Lucy laughed.

"Why are you so cruel!" Egon spat. "You're only out of your cell because of me. You have no right to kill me!"

"Oh, I think I can kill whomever I want. And I guess you could say I inherited my cruelty trait from you, my sweet father." He smiled.

Suddenly, he felt a knee to his back and fell forward. Egon pushed Lucy off him and bolted up. In a desperate attempt to escape, he ran to the door, unlocking it.

Lucius reached up in the split second Egon had to stop, and then he grabbed his ankle, yanking him backward. His feet shifted out from under him until he was flat faced on the floor. Lucy got back up to his feet and watched as his father tried to crawl pitifully out the exit.

"You clever bastard! I completely forgot how fast you are. Just like Raela. Is that a family trait? I mean, it couldn't be. I'm strong. But Eileen was fast, I believe. Maybe I'm just the odd man out," he said, stepping on his back leg, breaking it.

Egon let out a scream and struggled harder away from him. Lucius grabbed him by his bad leg and dragged him down the hallway, then down the stairs, letting his head bang on every step. Egon struggled against him, kicking him with his good leg, but it was no use. Lucy's grip was stronger.

As he dragged his father down the stairs and through the hall, he finally stopped at his old cell. Hooking Egon's ankles to the shackles, he pulled the lever.

"You're a monster! A filthy half breed!" Egon screamed, no longer thinking clear enough to shout anything other than petty insults. "You'll die for this! I swear on my life you'll suffer and die for this!"

"It doesn't matter if you swear on your life. Your life is mine now anyway," he said, his voice devoid of all emotions. Lucius handed his victim the wooden stake, staring into his eyes coldly. "I hope you enjoy solitude. If you're going to die, you'll have to do the deed yourself."

Egon's mouth gaped open before he looked up at his son fearfully. "No, no, if you're going to kill me, just kill me! Don't leave me here! Don't leave me here, you coward!"

Lucius smiled and closed the cage, enjoying Egon's final screams as he left him to his own demons. He deserved nothing less.

Chapter 47

LUCIUS

WHERE DO I GO NOW?

The whole endeavor left Lucy feeling exhausted but very satisfied. He finally felt as though he had gotten justice for Ben and justice for himself. He couldn't help but compare this feeling to how he felt when he strangled Boris to death—satisfying, relieving, nearly relaxing at the thought of this evil man being gone from the world. He could never hurt anyone ever again. There would be no more slaves, no more feedings, no more human fights for vampire entertainment. It was over.

Walking up the stairs, he found his friends Holly and Lidewij. They smiled and waved at him.

"It's finally over! We did it, and we stayed almost completely invisible the whole time!" Holly screamed enthusiastically, clearly proud of her work.

"Great job, Holly. You did amazing!" he said, giving her a hug.

Lidewij looked a little guilty, staring down at the floor. "Lucius, I'm sorry for how I acted earlier. I wasn't thinking clearly. I didn't want you to see my bloodlust like that."

He walked over and gave her a tight hug. "It's all right. I was never angry at you," he said, feeling her relief as she hugged him back.

Lucy looked around the house. It really was a shame they would leave so much behind, but then he remembered what he told Holly a few days prior. "So I guess you guys can go and take whatever you want from the house. I already got my souvenir," he said, gesturing to his earring.

Lidewij ran off first, happily looking through all the jewelry, while Holly just idled around, eyeing the pretty rugs and candelabras. Lucius let them do as they bid, and he walked to his sister's old room. There must be something here that she would want. It wasn't likely either of them would ever visit this place again, so he might as well grab anything worth keeping now. As he entered her room, he looked around; it was so clean. Sitting on the chair was a half-knitted sweater that was missing an armhole. It made Lucius laugh to know she was so bad at knitting. It was just like her to pretend to be good at something girly that she hated, only for appearance. He glanced around the room, finding a small book sitting on her fireplace mantle. He picked it up and opened it. Inside were amazing drawings and writings in cursive of her life. She couldn't knit, but man, could she draw! He flipped through the pages till he happened upon a drawing of him with several writings and words next to it. He couldn't read her handwriting but could see how accurately she drew him. In her picture, he looked sad—not the kind of sad that would make you cry but the kind that cut deep enough to turn into numbness.

He closed the book up and tucked it under his arm. She might like to keep this. It was her journal after all. Perhaps later she would want to look back on it to think about how this all started. On the bookshelf next to her bed was a family painting album. Opening it up, he noticed every painting had been painted in the same style as her book. They must have all been done by her. He decided on taking this as well, but nothing else.

As he walked from the room, he thought about how much he still didn't know about his sister. He knew she was kind and compassionate, but he had never guessed she would be a painter. He supposed when you spend every day with nothing to do, you would pick up a lot of hobbies. As he walked down to meet his partners in crime, he spotted Holly trying to calm down the kids.

"I'm normally really good with children, but I can't seem to calm them down," Holly said tiredly as she turned to Lucius. Lidewij was nowhere to be found.

"I guess we can't blame them. The best we can do is lead them to your truck safely. It'll be easier from there."

"You're right. I'll go get it ready out back," she said, dusting herself off as she stood up. "Do you think you can handle it here?"

"Yeah. Have you seen Lidewij?"

"She's trying to clear the um…meat to make it easier for the kids," she said, not wanting to startle the crying children any more than she had to.

"Ah, that makes sense," Lucius said. "Go get ready. I'll watch them till you get back."

"Got it."

As Lucy turned his attention to the crying child in front of him, he looked around. He hadn't realized how many children there really were in the house. Fifteen at least. He tried to console some of the kids, which was proving to be a more difficult task than he thought. The eldest child was a girl who was only maybe twelve. She had her arms crossed and refused to cry. It made Lucy wonder just how old his family considered an adult to be.

When Holly came back, she had each kid pack up whatever belongings they wanted to keep before blindfolding them and leading them to her vehicle. Lucius thought the blindfold seemed a little much, but as he led them to her truck, he noticed all the bloodstains they couldn't remove and thought maybe it was best they couldn't see after all.

As they led the kids into her truck, Holly tried to calm them, promising them things would be all right and that they were going to a nice place. When some of the kids realized they were leaving their home, they only cried harder, clinging to stuffed animals and other little personal belongings.

Lucius felt bad ripping them from their home, but after they were all loaded into the truck, he realized that it would be worse to leave them for dead. At least moving them to a new colony could teach them how to be good, if it wasn't too late. As the truck left, he climbed onto his bike.

"You two drive on without me," he said. "I have a few things I want to finish."

"Are you sure you'll be all right?" Holly asked. "I really don't mind waiting for you."

"No, that's all right. I'd rather you get those children to safety. I'll be fine, I promise."

Holly gave him a nod before driving off with Lidewij back to their homes.

Lucius looked around. The forest really was beautiful. It's a shame that it had to hide such horrible people killing monsters. As he looked at the door to the castle, he decided to leave it open. That way, if the humans from town went looking again, they could find the castle and put their fears and suspicion to rest forever.

Lucius revved his engine before taking off down the forest path. He had a feeling with all the humans being freed, he'd know exactly where Ben's old friend might be. Pulling up to his mother's cottage, he saw a familiar old woman and red-haired girl standing at the door. It was Gelda and Marie.

"You set them all free!" Gelda said, running to him and grabbing him into a tight hug.

"Oof!" he grunted, trying to hug her back. Then Marie grabbed him from the other side. "Yeah, I guess I did. Gelda? I have a big favor to ask of you. All these new people in town...some of them have never been outside the castle. Can you make sure everyone will be all right? I won't be able to stick around now that it's all gone. I need to get back home."

Gelda gave him a big smile before nodding. "I'm thinking of a new program to safely introduce them back into society. The rest of the townspeople are taking them in left and right, trying to help them take hold of their lives and build a better future. With all these people, it'll surely make our fishing town even stronger!" she said, feeling very confident.

"That's great!" he said, smiling, before looking over at Marie and regretfully saying, "I'm sorry for what my family did to you. I know I can't ever give you back your speech."

Marie only smiled before hugging Gelda's arm.

"She's going to be living with me," Gelda said, kissing her head. "She'll be like the daughter I never had, and I'm going to take great care of her."

Lucius smiled, watching them both together. Marie started happily signing to him.

"Keep Lady Raela safe if you can. Thank you for everything, Lucius. You can come and visit us whenever you want," she signed, giving him a big grin.

Lucius signed back. "Thank you. I will."

Marie let out a little choked laugh before giving him a tight hug. Lucius was stunned but hugged back anyway.

"I know you'll be fine. You're a good girl."

Kissing his cheek, Marie waved goodbye as he rode off on his bike. The journey took only a day, but Lucius was still the last to arrive back in England. By the time he got back, all the children had already been taken into new homes with new foster parents, and Raela had just finished her day of training.

"Is Adeline giving you a good fight?" Lucius asked with a smile.

Raela took off her armor and winced as she rubbed her bruised shoulders. "I would certainly say so, but I've gotten so much better! And now the other kids are all here? Lucius, how did you get them out without our father noticing?"

Lucius turned his left side to her, showing her the earring. "I'm sorry I didn't tell you why I was leaving so suddenly after dropping you off here," he started, looking down a bit. "But I couldn't let them continue to torture humans. I killed them—Egon and every other adult family member that lived there, except Azazel. But I made him promise never to bother either of us again."

Raela stopped taking her armor off, staring at him. Her eyes wide and filling with tears, she looked stunned. "You killed them? No. How can that be?"

Lucius nodded, shoving his hands deep into his pockets. "I'm sorry, Raela. But I brought you back some things from your room back home," he said, pulling out her books in an attempt to make things better.

She took the books into her hands and stared down at them.

"Please say something, Raela," Lucius pleaded, sensing her sadness. He was afraid it would turn to anger if unaddressed.

"I don't know what to say. I can't believe you actually went and did it," Raela said, refusing to look at her half brother. "I should have known when I saw all the children. But I just couldn't imagine something like this was really possible. I always thought the humans would kill us eventually. But it was you. I can't believe it was you."

"Raela, you of all people should know how awful they were. You should know why I couldn't let them continue to live and torture humans at leisure."

"I know what they did was wrong! I know! But they were still my family. I should never have helped you escape! I should have never gotten involved with you at all!"

"Raela, let's calm down. I know they hurt you. The cleaning slaves told me what happened. What sort of father rapes his own daughter? I know what that feels like. I know how awful that is. I was just trying to do the right thing! Please don't forget how horribly you were treated just because you're in a better place now."

"No, I know. I know they were horrible, and I'll never forget what he did. Egon was horrible. I'm not saying what he did was right. But even so, he was still my dad! I know they deserved it. But I wish you had come and told me what you were doing."

"Why? So you could stop me? Raela, I didn't tell you because I didn't want to burden you with the knowledge of what was being done. It had to happen. It had to! Do you honestly think that you knowing would have changed my actions?"

"No. I guess not."

"Exactly. All it would have done is made you feel guilty for not stopping me while it was happening. And it would have distracted you from your training with Adeline."

"What about the other women in the family? Egon was bad, but what about my mother and my cousins? You killed them, but you don't know…their minds could have been changed! They could have been spared!"

"Maybe so, but that wasn't a risk I was willing to take, Raela. I'm sorry. In a perfect world, everyone gets to live, everyone gets second chances. But this isn't a perfect world, and I didn't have the time to spare making sure every last adult in the building was capable of changing their ways. I spared the children at least. Doesn't that count for anything?"

Raela choked down a cry. "I guess that does stand for something," she said, feeling horrible pain at the thought of almost everyone she'd ever known being dead in a castle far away.

"I know you're upset. And I'm sorry. I don't regret what I did, but I'm sorry that I didn't take more time to consider your feelings. I truly thought you'd be much happier with this news. I was only thinking of the wrongdoings they've done to you. I didn't think of the good times you've shared with your family or your mother and cousins. I'm really sorry, Raela."

Raela looked up from the book in her hands. "I don't know if I can forgive you right now. But I know you really are sorry. I believe you. And I know that as much as I hate to admit it, you only did what you thought was right. Just give me some time to process all this, okay?"

"You can have as much time as you need."

Raela turned and started up the stairs before pausing and turning back to him. "Thank you for getting some of my things," she said. "I hope we can still be friends after this. I really want to forgive you, Lucius."

"I know. I promise I can wait however long it takes. And when you're ready, I'll be happy to resume our friendship right where it left off."

"Thank you," Raela mumbled. "I really appreciate it."

"Don't thank me. This is all my fault anyway. Just take the time that you need, and I'll be here."

Raela nodded before going to her room and shutting the door behind her.

Lucy gave a big sigh. Maybe he should have talked to her first. He knew she was going to be upset regardless. No, no, it was over now. And the more he thought about it, the surer Lucius was that he made the right decision.

And who knows? Maybe after some time, Raela can even feel safe and happy enough to contact Palas or maybe find a new person to be with in the colony, he thought.

As he looked out the window, he saw Nathaniel running and playing with another kid, and Alise in a circle of girls, all making beaded bracelets by the firepit. He was happy to see them adjusting so well. Walking to the couch, he sat down and stared into his own lit fireplace. It was so warm. It felt good to finally relax after all the stress.

After a few moments, Alise came in through the door. She hopped up on the couch and turned to her uncle.

"I made you something, if you want it," she said shyly.

"Oh really? What is it?" Lucius asked, turning to face her.

Alise held out a bracelet made with pretty beads and different colored threads.

"Wow! It looks lovely."

She giggled. "You don't have to act like it's some sort of treasure. I know it's just a bracelet, but I made it for you since you got my mother and me away from the castle. I'm going to be twelve this year. I wouldn't say I'm an adult, but I'm old enough to know what my fate would have been if I had continued to live there. But now that we live here, I can be with whomever I want, and I can make an identity for myself. Maybe I'll even join the knights with my mom and Adeline when I'm older. I just want you to know that I'm thankful," she said as she put the bracelet on him and grabbed him into a tight hug.

Lucius hugged her back. He never considered how his niece might feel. In his eyes up until this point, she was just "one of Raela's kids." But she had no real identity for herself. At least that was what Lucius had assumed. But it seemed even the most shy and quiet girls still had opinions and thoughts of their own. Lucius kissed the top of her head. He hoped that living here would help her come out of her shell and grow as a person. As he sat back into the couch, Alise laid her head on his lap and fell asleep.

Lucius looked around the room. Everything was so peaceful here. He couldn't help but wonder, *Could this be the life I was meant to have?* He could be a guardian to his niece and nephew alongside Raela, living happily in a house with them. He could be their new male role model, taking care of them and building new houses for the colony in England. It seemed like a simple life. An easy life.

As he drifted to sleep with Alise in his lap, he thought about the past few days. In his dreams, he was a child again. He looked around and saw a long beach by the ocean. The sand felt so soft, and the gentle wind was refreshing. Sitting down, he glanced at his sister sitting beside him.

"Eileen? Do you think I made the right choice? Killing our family?"

Eileen let out a big sigh before looking over at her brother. "Well, it's really impossible to say. I personally think you did, and Mother would probably be proud."

"You think?"

"I do. You killed her captors. You avenged her. I think she'd be very happy if she knew that."

Lucius stared at the sand underneath him. "I wish you were really here. I wish you could have met all the friends I made. You would have loved Misha and Oleg. Adrik was so kind. He would have wanted to take care of you, just like he cared for me."

"I might not have been able to meet them personally, but I saw them through you. They all seemed like nice people."

"I wonder if they'd be proud. Adrik and the others didn't have the same fiery temper that mom had. They might not like how stained in blood my life has been."

"I'm sure that's not true. Your friends would have seen that you did what you had to. And besides, you saved all those people trapped below the castle. Oleg and Misha freed slaves with you, didn't they? They would be proud that years later, you're still doing good deeds."

Lucy looked over at her and smiled. "Maybe you're right. Thanks, Eileen. Say, I know it's difficult to know for sure, but do you think Raela will ever be able to forgive me?"

"Of course I do, Lucy. She'll come around. It's just hard for her. You have every right to hate your family. They shunned you and didn't care about your well-being. And while maybe Egon didn't care about Raela, I bet there were others in the castle that did. She must have had some people that she was fond of. She did spend her whole life there after all."

"Maybe you're right. Do you think I made the wrong decision?"

"It was happening so fast, and in a situation like that, it's really not possible for everyone to come out happy. But I think you did the right thing."

Lucius looked over the ocean waves and picked up a shell next to him. He turned it over in his hands a few times, admiring the pink middle and white edges.

"Are you happy in the English colony?" Eileen asked.

"I guess? But that's a complicated question," he said.

"I'm not accusing you. I just want to know. I want you to be happy," she said, giving him a slight smile.

Lucius looked out over the sea, thinking. "I don't know. I want to be. I really do. But I'm not sure if I'm really safe here. I've felt safe before, and it was just an illusion of self-security. I don't want to play myself for a fool by making the same mistakes. I just have this horrible urge to run away if I get too comfortable, you know? But I don't want to kill any more people. I don't want to run."

"You're not a fool for wanting to feel safe, Lucy. And you don't have to run. But are you happy?"

"I guess I am. It's really nice here, and I have a family in Raela and her children."

"Do you want to stay?"

"Honestly? I really do. I've just never had a place to live before that didn't require something of me. Will I really be able to make a life here?"

"I guess all you can do is try. What's the worst that can happen? If it goes wrong, you'll just leave and start new, like always. Just do your best, and I'm sure it will work out. Besides, now you're with other people like you. These vampires are good, and they can understand you. These vampires know what it's like to be different, but they chose to accept who they are anyway."

Lucy smiled over at her and gave her a hug. "You're right. Maybe this is a place where I can live without violence. I would love to have a place to just be myself. I've been so ashamed of everything I am. Maybe this place can allow me to feel differently. First, I want to visit Adrik's grave. I want to tell him how much he meant to me one last time. Then after that, I'll make a life here. I'll help Raela with her children. Things will be different this time."

About the Author

M. W. Upham has always daydreamed and lived in a fantasy world. Dreaming of action and adventure in everyday life, they have spent the last several years reading and writing thrilling and twisting stories that dip and dive at every turn. With an associate's degree from Grand Rapids Community College, they continue to learn more from school while working part-time as the lead server at a senior assisted living center.

When not writing, M. W. Upham spends time in their hometown of Rockford, Michigan, doing several different arts and crafts, baking, drawing, and playing with their guinea pigs and cats. M. W. Upham loves to go out with their younger sister and spend their time at art shows and museums. M. W. Upham is always looking for the next inspiration for a new writing topic.

CPSIA information can be obtained
at www.ICGtesting.com
Printed in the USA
FSHW010244110321
79321FS

9 781647 013776